MAFIA OBSESSION

L. STEELE

1

You are always new, the last of your kisses was ever the sweetest.
-John Keats

Jeanne

"Let me the F out of here." *Can't even let yourself say the f-word aloud when you've been kidnapped, eh?* Goddam politeness that's been drilled into me since childhood. To be honest, it's selective politeness. Ma was unequivocal that no occasion, no matter how frustrating, warrants saying that specific four-letter word aloud. But then, I doubt she was ever held against her will.

On the bright side, I haven't seen any more of my captor; not since he held something sweet-smelling to my face. Ether, I'm guessing. I was walking home from the bus stop in Palermo, and even though it was past ten p.m., there was still a smattering of people on the road—enough for me to feel safe. That was until someone darted out from behind a tele-phone booth—yep, they still have them in Italy— I'm fairly certain he was

wearing a mask. I seem to recall a black mask, a thick neck, large shoulders, and the man was overweight, and definitely not very tall. I tried to
yell, but whatever was in that handkerchief got into my blood stream with
just one inhalation. I blacked out and woke up here with a headache.

That was two days ago. At least, I think it's been two days because the
light pouring in from the skylight has shown me the passage of two nights.
Goddamn, I am not spending another day cooped up in here.

Food is delivered twice a day. There's a small, attached bathroom with
running water—no hot water, though—so I've managed to wash myself
the best I can; it also means I'm not dehydrated. But what I wouldn't give
for a proper shower. Also, I need to get out of here. If I don't, I'm going to
miss my first performance as the lead actress in *Beauty and the Beast*
opening in two days in Palermo.

I bang my fists against the door again. "Let me out, you... you...
Twerp." *Is that the best insult I can come up with? Who even uses twerp
anymore? I do, that's who.* I'm sure I heard Sister Mary use it once when she
didn't know I was eavesdropping on her conversation with a fellow nun at
the convent school where I was educated. An education, by the way, which
has not prepared me for the situation I currently find myself in. I hammer
on the door again. My wrists ache, and the edges of my palms protest. One
of my nails is chipped. Argh, I stare at it. Hate when that happens.

"Nails are the windows to your soul." That was the mantra my mother
lived by. We never had much money, but it didn't stop my ma from
making sure I always had well-manicured nails. No nail polish because...
nuns. But that hadn't stopped her from carting me off to the nail salon on
the least pretext. And when we didn't have money for the salon, we took
turns pampering each other. All of which seems so far away now, locked
up as I am in this room.

At least my captors didn't tie my arms or legs. I should be thankful for
that. And of course, there's a bed in the room, with a mattress that doesn't
smell too funky. On the other hand, there isn't much room in this space for
walking. And there's nothing else to do.

"Let me out of here... Please!" I wince. *Really? You had to add please at
the end?*

I bring my fist down on the door, when it's wrenched open and a man
is shoved in my direction. A big man. A big, tall man. So tall, I have to
crane my neck all the way back to try to make out his features. His bulk
collides with me. The scent of dark chocolate and coffee, laced with some
masculine scent that screams 'man,' fills my senses.

"Hey—" My voice is cut off when the man begins to slump into me. The full weight of his body pushes me down. My knees begin to give way. Whoever pushed him in here gives him another shove. Of course, I take the brunt of his weight, and both of us go tumbling down. I manage to wriggle out of his way in time to avoid being completely crushed. The door to the room is slammed shut.

"Come back!" I pull my arm out from under the behemoth, leap toward the door and hammer my fists on it. "Let me out of here. You can't do this. You can't keep me locked in here without any explanation. There are people looking for me, you nincompoops. What do you gain by keeping me in here? Let me out, and I promise, I won't go to the police when I get out of here." My voice cracks a little, and I pause. There's no one out there listening to me. Whoever shoved the man in here is gone—

Oh, wait. They shoved someone else in here... In my already tiny room. I turn to find the monster of a guy still hasn't moved. Not good; this is not good. I step over his feet and walk over to stand near his face. His cheek is pushed into the floor. I prod his massive shoulder with the tip of my boot. He doesn't move. Doesn't even stir.

"Hey, mister," my voice echoes in the space. "Hey!" I prod him with a little more force. Same response. Is he breathing? Yes, I can hear it now. I sink down on one knee and touch his shoulder. When there's no movement, I touch his hair. It's soft, springy. I run my fingers through the thick strands, and a weird heat trickles up my spine. *Umm, no, it's just hair.* So what if it seems to belong to a head attached to a particularly impressive torso. The man's black jacket clings to his shoulders, stretches across a broad back that tapers down to a narrow waist. His shirt—his black, silk, button-down shirt— has been pulled up, due to the fall, and a narrow strip of skin is visible above the waistband of his dark pants. I reach for the strip of skin, then pull back. *Eh, stop it. What are you doing, touching this guy without his permission, anyway?*

I turn my attention back to his head. Thick, dark hair that's long enough to brush the collar of his jacket. Unruly enough to have fallen over his forehead. The hair at the back of his head is matted with blood. I wince. Did they hit him? They must have, which is probably why he's unconscious. I drag my gaze back to his face, take in his thick eyelashes, strong nose, the square jaw with a stubble that I want to rub my fingers against... High cheekbones, the hollows under them lending definition to his features. My breath catches in my chest. Whoever he is, he's gorgeous. I would have called him a fallen angel, except his dark beauty is more reminiscent of the devil. He has the kind of good looks that wouldn't be out of place on the big screen. He could be the star of the next Godfather, if anyone ever decides to reboot the movie franchise; though admittedly, it would take someone with a lot of courage to touch cinematic history. I reach for the strand of hair that's fallen over his forehead and push it back. That's when his eyelids snap open.

Bright blue eyes. Like the sky at the peak of summer. Like water from freshly melted snow. Like freshly-laundered white which is so intense, you'd be forgiven for mistaking it for blue. He reaches out a hand. I scream, scramble back, but he locks his fingers around my ankle and pulls me closer.

"Let me go," I yell.

His grasp tightens. I reach over and try to pry his fingers off, but he doesn't let go. He continues to stare at my face like he's unable to tear his gaze away.

My heart slams into my rib cage. My blood thumps so loudly in my ears, I think I'm going to faint. "Please," I gulp, "please let me go." A tear squeezes out from the corner of my eye. It slides down my cheek and plops on his face.

His forehead furrows and he releases his grip on my leg. I scoot back as he raises his arm in my direction.

"Angel," he whispers, "don't cry." Oh, my god, that voice. Gravelly and sinful and everything wicked ever created. Definitely the devil in disguise. A fire ignites deep inside of me. It zips up my spine, down the length of my arms. I reach out to touch him, when his eyelids flutter down again, and his arm falls by his side.

The tension drains out of my shoulders. I stay there panting for a few seconds, then lower my hand and ease away from him until my back connects with the wall.

I take in his face, eyes now closed again, the way his dark eyelashes sweep down until the tips seem to sweep his cheekbones. That patrician nose I noticed earlier, the thick upper lip, the pouty lower one, the square jaw of his that hints at the power coiled under his skin. Even unconscious, the man exudes a raw power that thrums around him, that draws my attention, a presence that seems to suck all of the oxygen in the room, leaving me lightheaded.

I hope he didn't hurt himself when he fell. I hope the blood on the back of his head is superficial. Was he drugged, like me? Is that why he's out cold? It would have taken more than one man to overpower him, more like a crowd of them to take him down, given his size. Did he resist them as they hauled him here? Did he fight before they finally managed to overwhelm him?

And why is he dressed so formally? Was he at a wedding or a party or… Does he always dress like this? It wouldn't surprise me if he does. The look suits him. Not that formal clothes can disguise the brute he is. In those few moments when he stared at me with those disconcerting blue eyes, it was clear that nothing can cage this man for long.

I watch him for a few more seconds, but he doesn't stir. Guess I'll have to leave him on the floor. No way am I going to be able to move him. And after the last time I touched him, when he snapped his eyes open so suddenly… Well, let's just say, I'm not going to risk that again. I guess I could cover him up with a sheet, at least.

I rise to my feet, then shuffle alongside the wall, clinging to it as I make my way around him. When I reach the bed, I pull the cover from it, then walk over and drape it over him. I step back until the backs of my knees hit the bed, then sit down on it. I watch him for a few more seconds, until a yawn surprises me. Tiredness drags at the edge of my conscious mind. I lay down facing him, back to the wall, and bring my knees up to my chest. I fold my arms over them, and watch the back of his head until I fall asleep.

The next time I open my eyes, it's to meet that piercing blue gaze of his. No… Not completely blue. There are specks of grey, almost black, around his pupils. I part my lips to scream, and he clamps his palm across my mouth. I raise my hand, and he grabs my wrist and wrenches it over my head. My heart pounds in my ribcage, and my pulse-rate goes through the roof. Fear twists my guts, and my breath locks in my chest. What is he doing? Why is he trying to restrain me? If he thinks I'm going to give up without a fight, he doesn't know who he's dealing with. I bring my knee up, intent on kicking him, when he drops onto the bed, on top of me.

2

Luca

The hell are you doing? She's scared out of her mind, and instead of calming her down, I climb onto the bed, between her legs, and lean my weight on top of her. Not because I want to scare her, but because I can't afford to be kneed by her or hit by her flailing arms. It's the only reason I have my hand over her mouth and am trying to hold her down without hurting her.

"*Stai calmo*," I growl.

Her gaze widens, and I realize she may not understand me.

"Stay quiet," I snap.

She begins to writhe under me, trying to get away, but it only brings her in closer contact with the hardness between my thighs. She instantly freezes, her eyes growing even bigger. Color smears her cheeks. She begins to wriggle with even more ferocity. She bites down on my fingers, which I've clamped over her mouth, and goddamn, but I feel the pinch all the way to the tip of my cock. The blood rushes to my groin, and the column in my pants grows even thicker. Which, in turn, seems to inject a fresh dose of terror through her veins because now, she begins to fight me in earnest. She lashes out with her free hand and catches me in the face. I grunt.

The wound at the back of my head throbs. Pain slices through my head, and for a second, I see stars. She arches back and her thick curly hair spirals back from her face. Medusa. She's Medusa, sent to tempt me, then turn me into stone. Mission accomplished, on both counts. My head spins. A weird sensation coils in my chest. A current of electricity charges through me and I rear back.

She takes advantage of my lapse, manages to work one of her legs free and kicks me in the thigh. It doesn't really hurt me, but I've had enough.

"Stop fighting me, you little hellcat; they have cameras on us."

She continues to thrash around, then grows still, as if my words have suddenly sunken in.

I nod, then jerk my chin toward the ceiling. She follows my gaze toward the light unit in the ceiling.

"It looks like a light fixture doesn't it?"

She nods.

"Look closely," I prompt.

She squints at it for a second, another... then understanding flits across her features. She whips her gaze back to my face, a question in her eyes.

"Yeah, that's a hidden camera." I nod.

Her entire body stiffens then goes slack. I remove my hand from her mouth.

She swallows, "You mean, for all these days, they were..." Her voice trails off as realization sinks in. She pales. "They were—"

"Watching you. And now they're watching us. I wager they have microphones on us, as well."

Her throat moves as she swallows. The tension that pours off of her body seems to intensify. Her shoulders hunch, and every muscle in her body seems to coil with nervousness. Her chest rises and falls. Her shirt is snug and stretched across her tits. Nice juicy round tits that would fit nicely into the palms of my hands.

Heat sluices through my veins. Goddamn, her nipples are so hard their outline is visible through the fabric. The band around my chest tightens. I only realize I've leaned in closer to her when a jolt runs through her body. I raise my gaze to her face to find her pupils are almost fully dilated. The black has expanded until only a circle of gold, her irises, is visible around them.

"I'll remove my hand from your mouth, if you promise you won't scream," I caution.

She stills for a second, then nods.

Goddam, I don't trust her. Bet she's going to scream as soon as I take my hand off her mouth. And how long am I going to stay in this position, trying to keep her quiet, while the proximity to her body, the sweet scent of her, the softness of her skin, the warmth of her core—all of it ensures that my pants are getting tighter by the moment?

Cazzo! I remove my hand from her face, and instantly, she screams. So I do the only thing I can in these circumstances; I close my mouth over hers. Her entire body freezes. I absorb the sound, draw it into me as I thrust my tongue in between her lips, and kiss her soundly.

She stays still for a beat, then another. Then, she bites down on my lower lip, and *cazzo*, my cock jerks in my pants. I tilt my head, deepen the kiss, and she pushes her breasts up into my chest. She juts out her chin, relaxes her jaw, and I slide my tongue in deeper. The taste of her is sweet and complex, with a bite, the scent of her like crushed rose petals, the feel of her curves so soft, so lush, so goddamn sumptuous. My head spins. She writhes under me, and the hard column in my pants nestles into her core. My balls tighten. A hot sensation fills my chest, and my ribcage hurts. I squeeze her chin to hold her face where I want it as I swipe my tongue across her teeth, as I drink from her, and suck on her tongue, and my entire body goes on alert.

The hair on the back of my neck rises, and the muscles of my shoulders coil. I tear my mouth from hers and stare into her flushed face. Into those tawny eyes with pupils so blown, I swear I can see myself reflected in the blackness.

She stares back, the surprise I feel reflected in her features. Then, she raises her hand—and to be honest, I see what's coming, but I do nothing to avoid it—and her palm connects with my cheek. My head jolts back, and yet, I can't take my gaze off of her. Something electric crackles in the air between us, coils itself around my chest, and squeezes until I can't breathe. Can't think. Can't do anything but gape at her.

"Get off of me," she snarls.

"Only if you promise to listen," I shoot back.

"First, you get off me."

"First, *you* promise to listen."

"I'll do no such thing."

"In which case..." I place more of my weight on her and her gaze widens.

"You wouldn't." She scowls.

"Try me." I allow my lips to curve in a smirk. Using my weight to hold her captive while I try to make her... Listen to me? It's a dick move, but fuck that. We're in trouble, and the only way out is if I get her to follow my directions.

Her face pales a little, then her lips firm. "Fine," she says in a low voice.

"I didn't hear you," I drawl.

"A-hole," she murmurs under her breath.

"Heard that, and it's alphahole to you."

She opens and shuts her mouth. "You have an inflated opinion about yourself, don't you?"

"Not the only thing that's inflated, Angel."

"Don't call me that."

"I'll call you anything I want." I allow my grin to widen.

Her scowl deepens. "You… you… Dickwaffle!"

I blink, then can't stop the chuckle that rolls up my throat. I laugh so hard, my whole body shakes, and as a result, she shakes under me. "That's a creative insult, I'll give you that."

"I'm just getting started," she shoots back.

"You and I are going to have fun; I can feel it," I tease her.

"Get off of me." She slaps my shoulder, and the vibrations shudder through my brain. The back of my head begins to throb in earnest. I touch the space and my fingers come away wet.

"Is that blood?" She stares at it, then at my face. "Does it hurt?"

"Are you concerned?" I narrow my gaze on her.

"Of course not. But since we are, clearly, having a conversation, can you please get off me now?"

"We are, aren't we?" I roll off of her, and once on my feet, extend my arm to her. "Luca Sovrano."

She sits up, then pushes off the bed and stands facing me.

"What the hell did you think you were doing earlier?" She scowls.

"Trying to distract you so you wouldn't scream and make those guys come in here again."

She pales a little, and her gaze flicks to the door. "Did they take you, as well? I mean, obviously, they did take you... But how did they overpower you? You seem—"

"Strong? Virile? Sexy?"

She darts me an annoyed look. "Does everything always have to be about you?"

"Not always… but mostly." I wiggle my fingers. "At least shake my hand, will you?"

"If you think I want to be your friend after what you did earlier, you are sadly mistaken."

"Considering we've already exchanged saliva, a handshake doesn't seem that far-fetched."

She throws up her hands. "You're gross."

"And you're cute when you are angry."

"Eh?" She opens and shuts her mouth. "Who are you again?"

"Luca Sovrano, part of the Sovrano Seven."

"What are you, some kind of underground Mafia gang?"

"How'd you guess?"

"You're joking, right?" She begins to laugh, but she must notice the look on my face, for her lips firm. "You're *not* joking."

"Not at all," I confirm.

"Oh for F's sake." She takes a step back, as if she's just realized the predicament she's in. *Too late, baby. I've already set my sights on you, and I'm not letting go that easily.*

"So, you're part of a Mafia outfit?"

"I *am* the Mafia." I widen my stance. "And you're trapped with me in this cell."

3

Jeanne

"No shit." A shiver of unease runs down my spine but I push it away. Yeah, so, he's part of the Mafia. Big deal. We are in Italy, after all; it stands to reason that they're everywhere. Except... "Hold on a second. If you *are* the Mafia, as you claim, what are you doing on this side of the door?"

He folds his arms across his chest. "Clearly, my enemies have gotten to me. Which brings me to the question, who are you?"

I tilt my head. Do I want to tell him my name? Somehow, by not telling him who I am, I've managed to maintain some semblance of control over the proceedings. Once I tell him my name, I'll be much more vulnerable to him. Not like my situation isn't precarious already, trapped in here with him, but if I withhold my name, won't it give me somewhat of an advantage over him, at least?

He surveys my features and seems to guess my line of thought, for he holds up his hands. "Look, I admit, we may have gotten off to a rocky start—"

"Is that what you call climbing all over me and molesting me?"

"Didn't see you fight me off too hard, Angel."

Anger flushes my skin. My cheeks heat. "You took me by surprise, is all," I grumble. "Also, don't call me Angel."

"You enjoyed that kiss, admit it. And you still haven't told me your name."

"I did no such thing, and p.s., no way am I going to tell you my name." I tip up my chin, then clamber onto the bed. I flatten my back against the wall and as far away from him as possible.

"Look, I don't need to force myself on you, okay? There are enough women lining up to sleep with me."

"Hmph, you really do have an inflated opinion about yourself, don't you?"

"It's all true." He raises a shoulder. "The problem is, I couldn't stop myself, because we have an audience."

"Excuse me?" I blink as I try to follow what he's trying to say. "I really don't understand."

He blows out a breath. Then, to my relief, takes a step back. Not that it helps much, considering his bulk seems to take up most of the space in the room.

He drags his fingers through his hair then winces. *"Cazzo!"* He swears in what I assume is the 'F' word in Italian. Somehow, it sounds better than the English version. *Cazzo,* I roll the word around my tongue. *Cazzo.*

"What did you say?"

"Nothing." I scowl at him.

He purses his lips, then seems to come to a decision. "Remember the camera?"

I glance up at the small device hidden in the ceiling, and the hair on my forearms rises. "That's not creepy at all," I murmur.

"Well, I have this fetish."

I whip my head in his direction.

"Excuse me?"

"Now, don't jump to conclusions." His chest rises and falls. "It's just, I like being on display."

I blink. "You mean, like being watched?"

"Exhibitionism. It's my kink."

A pulse thuds to life low in my belly. *No, no, no. I will not be turned on by this talk of kink and fetishes and such.* "So, you're trying to say that—"

"Being on camera makes me horny."

I gape. Seriously, my mouth falls open, and I know I'm staring at him like he just told me he's from another planet—which he might be, because I've never in my life heard something so... kinky.

"So, if someone is watching you... it makes you want to put on a performance?"

He rolls his neck. "Although, that's not the only reason I kissed you. As I mentioned earlier, you were surprised, and I didn't want you to scream and get their attention."

"I... I honestly don't know what to say."

"How about we call a truce? If we need to stay in here together, we can't exactly keep fighting."

"I don't see why not." I bring my knees up to my chest. "And if you think coming clean about your perversions is supposed to be reassuring—"

"It's not. I was merely being open, so you'd begin to understand me."

"I don't want to understand you."

"Afraid, given the proximity of our situation, we may not have much choice but to get to know each other very well."

I lower my chin and try to read the subtext of what he's saying. A-hole that he is, he takes in the expression on my face—which I'm sure must be a mix of horror and fear—and he bursts out laughing, "Relax, Angel, I'm not coming on to you again; not unless you ask me to."

"Which I do not." I raise my hands. "Let's be very clear. I don't want anything to do with you. You stay on that side—" I stab my finger toward the opposite corner of the cell "—and I'll stay here."

"Now, that's not fair, is it? You get the bed and I get the floor."

"Well, I was here first." And this is an insane conversation. We're both trapped in here, and rather than discussing how to get out of here, we're squabbling like a couple of children. But this man... He's too big, too broad, too handsome, too confident of himself. Something about him just rubs me the wrong way. He's just too over-the-top. Too much. There's too much of him for this small space. And he smells too good. Goddamn it. For that alone, I should hate him. No one has the right to look so good. I mean, just being in his presence gives me an eyegasm.

"I have a better idea; why don't we share the bed?"

"What? No!" I straighten my spine. "I already gave you the cover earlier, didn't I? So why don't you take that and retreat to your corner of the room."

He glances around, then walks over and snatches up the cover. When he straightens, he sways a little. "*Cazzo!*" He squeezes his eyes shut. "Those *stronzi* sure did get to me."

"How did you get to be here anyway? Do you know who knocked you out?"

He stabs his finger over his shoulder in the direction of the camera.

Of course. I firm my lips. He walks over, places the cover on the bed, then stalks in the direction of the bathroom. He steps in, and I hear him moving around. Then he pops his head through the doorway. "Come 'ere."

"Eh?" I scowl in his direction. "You're joking, right?"

"There are no cameras here," he says in a low voice. "It's safer if we speak in here."

"I don't have anything to say to you."

"Are you sure?" He glances about the room again, then lowers his voice to a hush, "Don't you want to find a way out of here?"

"Not if it means being with you." Well, of course I want to get out of here, but no way am I going to admit that to him.

He leans a shoulder against the door, then narrows his gaze on me. "Come here, Angel." The low hum of his voice lights up my nerve-endings.

I hold his gaze for a beat, another, then shove my legs over the side of the bed. I straighten and walk toward him, not missing the flash of victory in his eyes. "I'm only coming to you because there isn't a camera in there."

He shuts the door behind me, and instantly, it feels like we're locked in a bubble. This space is so tiny, it's like the bathroom on an aircraft. There's barely enough space for the commode and the sink. Add his bulk, and there's no way to stand in there without touching some part of him. I flatten myself against the wall and try to hold in my breath.

A chuckle rumbles up his chest. "Now this is cozy, isn't it?"

"Save it," I snarl. "What is it you wanted to say to me?"

He turns on the tap over the sink, and the sound of running water fills the space. "Just to make doubly sure they can't hear us," he explains, then leans in closer until his chest almost touches mine. "I have an idea on how we can get out of here."

"Do I even want to hear this?" *Umm, yes, I do, but nope, not going to admit it to this egomaniac.*

"Do you have a choice?" he retorts.

I snap my jaw together and stare at him.

His grin widens. "So clearly, we've been put in the same cell together because they wanted us to meet."

"Or maybe they didn't have enough space?" I speculate.

"It's possible, but I'd say it's more likely they wanted to see how we would interact."

"You mean, like an experiment or something?" I hunch my shoulders. "This just keeps getting creepier and creepier."

"Maybe they thought we wouldn't get along?" He purses his lips. "More likely, they knew about my tendencies and wanted to see what would happen if they locked us in together. Although, there's one more possibility..."

"What's that?"

"They had you locked in here with the woman and her kids we came to save."

"We? Who's 'we'?

"Me and my brothers."

"More of the Mafia Seven?"

"The Sovrano Seven," he corrects me.

"So, you came to save these people?"

"They're the family of the man who attacked one of my brothers and his wife," he replies.

"Now, I'm really confused. Why would you save the family of someone who attacked your family?" I scowl.

"Because he was forced to do it, and he agreed to help us track down Freddie—that's the guy who's holding us, incidentally."

"Okay, so you and your brothers offered to help him and his family in return for—"

"Him giving us information on Freddie's whereabouts."

"So, you came to look for this man's family and ended up being taken yourself?"

"We underestimated Freddie. Two of my brothers and I went into the house where Freddie was holding this guy's family. We managed to get them out, but Freddie's men came after us. My brothers left with the family. I stayed behind to hold them back. I thought we had succeeded, too. Then, I was ambushed. The next thing I know, I'm being thrown into this cell with you."

"But why did he take me?" I bite the inside of my cheek. "I have nothing to do with the Mafia. I'm an actress and a jazz dancer, and I'm only in Palermo to perform an interpretation of *Beauty and The Beast*. I was on my way back from dance rehearsal when someone kidnapped me. I woke up in this room, two days ago... At least, I think it was two days."

"And you haven't seen anyone?"

"No one but you."

"Hmm." He rubs his jaw. "It makes no sense."

"You're telling me." I shuffle my feet. "Can we go back into the room now?"

He tilts his head, then nods. "Go on, I'm going to wash up quickly, and then I'll be there." I head out of the bathroom, but instead of clambering onto the bed, I begin to pace the room. This entire situation is so bizarre. Why am I here? Why did they bring him here? Why have they locked us together? What do they want to do with us? And damn it, why am I so attracted to my fellow prisoner?

That's when the door opens and a man walks in.

4

Jeanne

A scream spills from my lips. I scramble back until I hit the wall. "Who…
who are you?" I gasp out at the stranger who stands inside the door.

"Freddie Nielsen, at your service." He tips an imaginary hat, then grins
at me. His accent is British. He's of medium height, slightly overweight,
but muscular, with a bald head and a round face. His thick neck and the
shape of his biceps that stretch his jacket indicate he's stronger than he
seems. He's wearing black pants and a button-down shirt. What is it with
these men? It's like they don't go anywhere unless they're dressed
formally.

The door behind me is wrenched open before Luca bursts into the
room. "What the fuck, what happen—?" He spots Freddie and his features
harden. He draws himself up to his full height—which means he towers
over Freddie.

"Freddie—fucking—Nielsen." He rushes toward the stranger, who
pulls out his gun and fires.

I scream. Luca halts mid-stride. My heart crashes into my chest and
adrenaline laces my blood. I whip my head in Luca's direction to find he
has his hands raised. He's still standing; he's not hurt. Clearly, the bullet

missed him. The breath whooshes out of me. His features harden as he glares at the other guy.

"Next time, the bullet will be in your chest." Freddie smirks.

"Next time, I'll get to you first," Luca snaps.

Hands still raised, he sidles over to stand between us, so he cuts off Freddie from my line of sight. Huh? Is he protecting me? That full-of-himself jerkface is trying to shield me?

"The fuck do you want with us?" Luca lowers his chin to his chest.

"Ah, there's already an 'us' here, is there?" Freddie's grin widens. "I knew the two of you would hit it off."

"The fuck you talking about, *stronzo*?" Luca's shoulders flex, tension pours off of his body. I peek around and spot Freddie's face. His attention is focused on Luca.

"How predictable you Sovranos are, eh? A pretty face crosses your path, and you're instantly captivated. Not only that, but you become all protective toward them. Nothing like your father. Guess your Nonna did a good job bringing you guys up, eh?"

Every muscle in Luca's body seems to coil. "Don't talk about my Nonna, you *fetente*."

"What a tragic way to go." Freddie shakes his head. "I'm sorry for your loss, by the way."

"You... You were behind the shooting at her place that took her out?" Luca's shoulders seem to grow even bigger. The biceps that stretch his T-shirt sleeves bulge further.

Freddie laughs. "You have to admit, it was a smart move to shift the blame to Fabio." *Who's Fabio? Who's Freddie referring to? And is he responsible for the death of Luca's grandmother?*

"You *pezzo di merda*! I'm going to kill you," Luca growls.

Freddie chuckles. "You can try. But it would be a pity to hurt you, considering my plans for the two of you."

"The fuck you talking about?" Luca snaps.

Freddie glances past him and rakes his gaze down my body. I try to shrink back against the wall, then stop. If I show him I'm afraid, that's only going to encourage him. I straighten my shoulders and meet his gaze.

He blinks, then waves his gun in my direction. "The two of you are going to provide me with many hours of entertainment."

"You're fucking boring, you know that?" Luca drawls.

Freddie firms his lips. "Don't forget I have a gun."

"If you wanted to use it, you would've already." I tip up my chin. "Since you haven't, I have to assume you don't mean to hurt me, you—"

Freddie shoots. The sound ricochets around the room. I scream and clap my hands over my ears. Bits of plaster float down from the wall where I assume the bullet has embedded itself.

"That should show you how serious I am," Freddie murmurs.

"What do you want?" Luca snarls.

"To make you suffer. Your father made my life miserable," Freddie retorts.

"You do realize I had nothing to do with the actions of my *testa di cazzo padre*?" Luca asks in a low voice.

"The sins of the father will be revisited upon the son… In this case, you."

"Okay, now I'm confused. What did my father do to you, anyway?" Luca widens his stance. "Weren't the two of you partners?"

"The crime of the century was my idea, and he took credit for it."

There's silence for a beat, then another. Finally, Luca asks, "You're referring to the kidnapping of the Seven in the UK?"

"An idea I came up with. An idea that your father appropriated and took credit for. Thanks to that, the *Cosa Nostra* was, once again, taken seriously by organized crime syndicates around the world. It was my idea. Mine!" Freddie slaps his chest with his palm. "And your bastard father walked away with all the glory."

Luca's shoulders rise and fall. "So, you're pissed about it. It's understandable. But that's the kind of snake my father was. You should have known that, getting into an agreement with him. He wasn't exactly known for his honesty and straightforwardness."

"And then, you deprived me of the satisfaction of killing him," Freddie scoffs.

"Yeah, sorry about that." He raises a shoulder. "My brother, Michael, beat you to it."

"And now, you're going to pay the price for it." His eyes gleam.

"O-kaaay. So, that's me. What's the deal with her? Why is she here?" Luca stabs his thumb over his shoulder.

"I needed to get you a companion for what I have in mind." Freddie's lips curve.

"Your problem is with my father. I have nothing to do with it, but she…" He nods in my direction. "She has even less to do with it than I do."

"On the contrary, the scene I have set needs a female to accompany you. It so happens, this one fits the bill for the woman I need, so…" He glances past Luca, and his gaze intensifies. "She'll do very nicely for what's coming."

My skin crawls with revulsion and my stomach churns. I feel like I'm going to throw up, but manage to swallow down the bile that boils up.

"What the fuck are you talking about?" Luca's voice is tinged with anger. He takes a step forward and Freddie raises his gun again.

"Don't take another step forward."

Luca stops.

"Enough with the posturing. Why don't you come out and say what the hell you have in mind?" he snaps.

"Don't tell me you haven't guessed, considering..." Freddie jerks his chin in the direction of the camera in the ceiling.

"You're a fucking voyeur, you *figlio di puttana*," Luca growls.

"So are you." Freddie laughs.

Luca freezes. Anger seems to roll off his body in waves. The tension in the room ratchets up. My nerve endings are so stretched, I'm sure I'm going to faint any second.

"The fuck you talking about?" Luca asks in a voice so normal, I know it's not good. No, no, no. He's going to do something that he and I are both going to regret. He's going to lose his temper... and get himself shot, after which, that asshole, Freddie, is going to shoot me, or something worse.

I sidle toward Luca, hiding behind his bulk as much as possible.

"I'm talking about the fact that you like to fuck your women while being watched by an audience."

Luca raises a shoulder. "So? I've never denied that. My life is an open secret. But her? She doesn't have anything to do with it. You should let her go."

"Hmm, you might have a point there." Freddie tilts his head.

I hold my breath. Is he going to let me go? Is he?

"But you know what? Nah. Where would the fun in that be? Not after the lengths I've gone to get the both of you here to a place so secluded, no one will hear you, no matter how much noise you make."

Fear knots my stomach. What is this mad man up to? What is he going to make us do?

"As for your phone... I know you had a tracker in it. It's been used to divert your brothers in another direction entirely, while we brought you here."

"You moved me from the house where you found me?" Luca says in a hard voice. There's a dangerous edge to his tone that makes me wince. He has his fingers curled so tightly, his knuckles are white. So, does this mean they took him from another place and brought him here? My head spins, trying to make all of the connections.

"Exactly." Freddie nods his head. "The last thing you probably remember is us finding you in the house where you tracked my men."

"I fought you off," Luca says hotly. "You motherfuckers drugged me."

"Just a whiff of chloroform. Admittedly, you put up a good fight. You did take down one of my men; managed to wound another. But four to one is too many, even for a man your size. You were out like a light; and then we brought you here."

"Why don't you fight me face-to-face, you *stronzo*, and then we'll see who wins." Luca takes a step forward. He throws up his fists, and Freddie raises his gun. That's when I close the distance to Luca and grab his arm.

"Don't," I whisper-scream. "If you antagonize him, he's going to shoot you."

Luca growls deep in his chest. The sound is so rough, so abrasive, that a hot sensation swirls in my underbelly. My pussy clenches, my thighs quiver, and moisture beads the space between my legs. Damn, we're fighting for our lives, and all I can think of is how I want to throw myself at this guy, wrap myself around him, press my nose into his skin, and draw his scent into my lungs. I press my face into his back, and the hardness of his muscles is a shock to my system. What am I doing? I step back, putting space between us, but my touch must have distracted him enough that he lowers his arms to his sides.

He draws in a breath and seems to get control of his emotions. "What do you want from us?" he asks in a voice laced with steel. "And cut the crap, Freddie. Just tell me what that warped mind of yours has dreamed up."

Freddie chuckles. To my relief, he lowers his gun.

Some of the tension drains from my body. I step up next to Luca. "Yes, tell me why you brought me here. Also, whatever it is had better not take too long. I need to be back at Palermo for the premier showing of my musical in two days. I really can't afford to miss it."

"Afraid it's not that simple, because firstly, we're no longer in Italy."

"What? We're no longer in Italy! Then where are we?"

He shakes his head. "Can't go revealing that to you now, can I? Suffice to say, we're far enough from the mainland that you'll have a tough time getting back. Secondly, it's clear I chose well because the chemistry between the two of you should help the proceedings."

"Proceedings? What proceedings? You, motherfucker, better come clean or else..." Luca's voice trails away as Freddie once again glances at the camera, then at us.

A shiver rolls up my back and stiffens the hair on my nape. Luca must realize what the bastard is suggesting at the same time that I do, for his entire body tenses.

"No fucking way," he snaps.

"Oh, yes." Freddie laughs delightedly. "You're both performers." He directs his gaze at Luca. "Being in front of a camera fuels your kink. All I've done is provide the perfect setting for you to enact your favorite acts."

Luca leans forward on the balls of his feet. "Fuck you," he snarls.

"Not me. Her. And you'd better do it well, because the intensity of your performance decides how soon I'm going to let the two of you go free."

5

Luca

"He's joking, right?" Her voice reaches me from where she's been curled up on the bed for the past half an hour.

I stare through the skylight through which the sunlight pours into the room. It had been late evening when we'd walked into that house and tracked down the family we'd been searching for. Was that yesterday? It had to be. Surely, I couldn't have lost more than a day? It's hard to tell, though. But for the fact that I'm extremely hungry and feel like I've missed a few meals, I'd have no idea how much time has passed. My stomach grumbles and the sound seems too loud in the room.

"They'll bring us food before the sun goes down. At least, that's what they've done for the last two days. It doesn't taste too bad and it's freshly cooked, so they must have someone in the house."

I don't acknowledge her words.

After that announcement, Freddie backed out of the room and shut the door behind him. Of course, I wasn't able to stop myself from stalking to the door and testing it. It was locked; no surprise there. I turned to find her staring at me. Her amber eyes were huge in her face, her hair mussed up and falling about her shoulders. She seemed angry and confused, and I half expected her to throw a fit or have a breakdown. Instead, she marched toward the bed, threw herself down on it, then turned to face the wall. I walked over to the wall opposite the bed, then slid down to the floor. Which is where I stayed, until she asked me if Freddie had been joking.

"Afraid not," I finally admit.

"Eh?" She blinks rapidly.

"The answer to your earlier question." I jerk my chin in her direction. "He wouldn't have gone to the trouble of getting you and me here if all this were a farce. He's planned it out too well." I knock my knuckles against the wall. "This place is soundproof; so is the floor." I dig the heel of my shoe into the wood floor. "The place is temperature controlled. And then, of course, there's the camera."

She sits up and folds her legs underneath her. "Who is he? Why is he doing this?"

"As you must have gathered, he was my father's partner. And clearly, he's upset with what he perceives as my father's betrayal. My asshole of a father, who caused nothing but grief for me and my brothers." I balance my elbow on my knee and lean forward. "For whatever sick reason, he's determined to make me pay for what my father did to him."

"Why me, though? Why is he putting me through this?"

"Apparently, he needed a woman to fit the bill." I raise a shoulder. "You can't expect a sociopath to make sense. I suspect you were in the wrong place at the wrong time."

"So, that's it? I was unlucky? Is that it?" She firms her lips.

"Seems that way."

"And when you said you perform better when you're watched, what did you mean by that?"

I tilt my head. "Exactly what he said. I like to fuck in front of a crowd."

Color smears her cheeks. "So that's... That's your kink?"

"Why, I do believe that's the first time you've pronounced that word out loud."

She tips up her chin. "Don't be silly; I say it all the time." She glances away, then back at me.

"No, you don't." I smirk. "You have no idea what I'm talking about."

"Sure, I do. You like to have sex when you're being observed."

"And also, when I'm not," I drawl. "In fact, in your case, I'd happily fuck you either way."

"Oh, F off." She folds her arms across her chest. "I am not going to sleep with you, just so you're aware."

Isn't she cute? She can't even say the word 'fuck.' I struggle not to smirk. "Don't think you have much of a choice, considering..." I jerk my chin in the direction of the cameras. "He's watching."

"That's precisely why I can't." She scowls. "I am *not* sleeping with you, period."

"Is that a challenge?"

"A statement."

"Are you always this stubborn?"

"Only when I'm locked up in a room with an a-hole—"

"—Alphahole."

"—who thinks the world begins and ends with him."

"It does," I retort.

"Hello, open your eyes. We're trapped in this room and a pervert—"she glances with distaste at the camera and shudders "—is watching us, and he's made it very clear that he's not letting us leave until you and I... Uh, you and I—"

"Fuck?" I supply helpfully.

"Yeah, that." Her face seems to grow even rosier, if that's possible.

"I don't think I've ever met a woman who blushes so much," I state.

"I'm not blushing." She scoffs. "Who says I am blushing?"

"So, if you touch your cheeks, you won't find them warm?"

She shakes her head.

"Hmm, I think you're lying." I rise to my feet.

She squeaks. "Wh-what are you doing?"

"What does it look like?" I prowl toward her and she stares at me in horror.

"Keep to your side of the room, please," she says crisply.

I chuckle. "Nice professorial voice you have going there. Is that one of the roles you've played? Speaking of... Do you like role-play?" I close the distance to her. "That's one of my particular fantasies, actually."

"I-it is?" She gulps.

I nod. "To play teacher-student... Where I'm the professor, of course, and I fuck my student after I've turned her over my knee and spanked her for being impertinent to me." I reach the bed; she scrambles back into a corner.

"Anyone ever tell you you're romantic?" She huffs.

"Only all the time." I chuckle. "So, what do you say? You up for some horizontal action?"

"No, of course not," she snaps. "And don't think you're going to get any from me."

"Any what?" I can't stop my lips from quirking. She's so cute when she's all hot and bothered. And why do I find that attractive, anyway?

"Any…" She bites the inside of her cheek. "Oh, you know what."

"No, I don't." I tilt my head. "Why, my feisty little Angel, I do think you're embarrassed by the 's' word."

"No, I'm not," she protests.

"So, say it then."

"Sex." She throws up her hands. "Happy now? Don't expect to get any sex from me."

"Oh, but I am not going to get it. I am going to take it from you. But it's not sex."

"What?"

"I'm going to fuck you, Angel."

"No."

"Yes." I can't stop my grin from widening. "And when I do, you're not only going to welcome it… you're also going to ask for more."

"Keep dreaming," she scoffs.

"You do realize, until we do the deed, this bastard…" I nod my head toward the camera." He's not going to let us leave."

"You and he can take a flying leap. I'm not sleeping with you, and certainly not when that pervert is watching us."

"Hmm." I drag my finger across my lower lip. Truth be told, I'm not a big fan of that bastard Freddie watching us, either. It's not like I care if he watches me… But him watching her? A throb of anger pulses through my veins. Nope. No way am I going to let him get a glimpse of her in such a vulnerable position. But how am I going to stop it from happening?

"What was that 'hmm' for?" She grimaces. "I don't like the sound of it at all."

"Don't worry your pretty little head about it." I use the phrase, knowing it's going to piss her off, a-n-d bingo! She stiffens and her golden eyes blaze at me.

"Nice to know that you still think of women in such archaic terms."

"You mean to say you're not pretty? Or little? Or that you have a head of beautiful hair?"

She opens and shuts her mouth. "I think I'm going back to sleep. Wake me up when the food arrives." She lays back, then turns toward the wall.

I rake my gaze down the length of her spine, the way her torso narrows down to that waist I could span with my palms. The swell of her hips, those strong thighs with which she would hold me when I position myself between her legs, those slender ankles, those narrow feet, the heels of which she would dig into my back...

She wriggles around, trying to find a more comfortable position, then sighs. She adjusts her body again, before she turns on her back.

She stares up at the ceiling, eyes wide open.

"Can't sleep?" I ask.

She shakes her head, then blows out a breath again.

"Why don't we play a game?"

6

Jeanne

"A game." I shoot him a sideways glance. As if I am going to agree to anything he suggests.

"Don't look at me with such suspicion." He raises his hands. "An innocent game to pass the time is all I'm suggesting."

"Hmph," I scoff. "Nothing you say or do is innocent."

"Of course, it'll help us get to know each other; especially since we're going to be sleeping together."

"See!" I stab my thumb in his direction. "Knew it. There's not an innocent bone in your entire body."

"Can't refute that. I'm a Mafioso, remember? I lost my innocence—what there was of it, at any rate—a long time ago."

I wrap my arms about my waist. I don't want to play with him, do I? And the option is, what? Staring up at the ceiling?

"Come on, Angel, I'm hardly asking you to play strip poker."

"Wouldn't put it past you to weave the same conditions into whatever game you're suggesting."

"The thought had crossed my mind," he admits.

"Ha." I snort, then glance in his direction. "What did you have in mind?"

"Truth or Dare? Surely, that's an innocent enough game for you?"

"Not when you're the one I'm playing with." I turn over on my side. "I'll go first. Truth," I call out before he has the chance of saying anything. "When did you lose your virginity?"

"Hmm, let's see." He scratches his chin. "I lost my virginity at fourteen."

"Why am I not surprised?"

"To the wife of one of my clan members. She was fifteen years older than me."

"That's predictable. Cougar and boy toy," I scoff.

"My turn now. Truth." He leans forward. "Tell me something about yourself that you've never told anyone else."

I purse my lips. What can I tell him about myself without giving too much away?

"I, uh... I have a tattoo."

"A tattoo?" He tilts his head.

"It's in a place which you're never going to see." I tap my right hip.

"Now that's a challenge I'm not going to be able to resist."

"Get used to it because you're never going to be able to see it."

"What kind of a tattoo is it?"

"It's a line from my favorite book of poems."

"Which is?" He scowls.

"Wouldn't you like to find out?"

"You know I will, so why don't you save yourself the bother and tell me what it is?"

"What's the fun in that?" I retort.

"Didn't take you for a tease." He brings his knees up, then lowers his arms between them. With his hair drooping over his forehead, and that slightly disgruntled expression, not to mention the jacket and pants which still manage to be fairly uncreased, he's sex on a stick. Heat curls low in my belly, and a shiver runs down my back, but I ignore it.

"I'm not teasing you; simply stating a fact."

"We'll see." His grin widens. "The very fact that you don't want to show me your tattoo, after mentioning it, shows that you want to pique my curiosity. You want me to imagine you without your clothes, though you pretend you don't want to sleep with me."

"I want nothing of that nature." *Liar!* My cheeks flush, my nipples harden, a pulse flares to life between my legs, and I have to stop myself from squeezing my thighs together.

"Dare," I burst out. "I dare you to not say one suggestive thing for the next ten minutes."

He chuckles. "You've got it."

"You're not going to protest?"

"Why should I when I can do this?" He begins to peel off his jacket.

I stiffen. "What are you doing?"

He doesn't answer. He shrugs off his jacket, then starts on the buttons of his shirt.

"Hey!" I can't take my gaze off the strip of skin that he reveals as the lapels of his shirt part. He pushes down the sleeve of one arm, then the other, before he drops his shirt on top of the jacket. At least the floor's not dusty; it would be a pity to dirty those beautifully-cut clothes of his. And I'm only saying that to distract myself, for fact is, I can't take my gaze off of his chest. That incredible eight-, or is it ten-, pack chest, each pec demarcated. The valley between them leading down to his sculpted abs.

He rises to his feet, and my gaze follows. He raises his arms above his head, joins his fingers, then stretches long, deep, with such sensuous grace that my throat dries. He arches his body in a curve to one side, then the other. I rake my gaze down the column of his torso, the narrow waist, the hard slabs of muscle which are his belly, the waistband of his pants which dips low enough to hint at the trail of hair that disappears under it. My belly trembles, my thighs spasm, and moisture laces my core. I know I am gaping a little, but hot damn; this is like a real-life striptease by a particularly hot male model. And while I'm not unfamiliar with the male form, given I work in theatre and male actors take good care of their bodies, no one I have met so far is anywhere half as hot as this man—my cell mate, my fellow prisoner, the man I'm supposed to sleep with to get released from here. I gulp.

A sinking sensation blooms in the pit of my belly. I'm sure it's not lust. And I know it's not anticipation. It's certainly not me being so attracted to him that, despite the fact there may be someone watching us, I don't care anymore. With that kind of body... I'd do anything to feel his muscles on me. His weight holding me down. His lips on mine. His tongue in my mouth. His fingers inside my pussy... My core clenches. My toes curl. I turn over on my front and press my pelvis into the mattress.

He chuckles as he lowers his arms to his sides. Jerk! I'm sure he knows exactly what it's doing to me to watch his sexy body being unveiled in this fashion.

He winks, then turns and drops to the floor, so he's balanced on his palms and toes. Wait a minute? When did he take off his boots? I get a clear view of his back and gasp. What the—?

His entire back is one big tattoo.

The face in the center has soulful and piercing eyes, and the serpents that spring from the head are entwined with three sheaves of wheat painted the most brilliant yellow. Three legs bent at the knees radiate from the head.

The design is familiar, but I can't quite place it. It's a pattern that's haunting, macabre, primal, and somehow, seems perfect for this man I hardly know. It also doesn't quite hide the strokes of mottled skin which crisscross his back. One, two, three... I count ten of them that flow diagonally from shoulder to waist. The skin is puckered and scarred over, so it must have happened a while ago. When he was younger... When he was a boy, maybe? It must have been painful. How did he survive it?

There are more tattoos on his left arm. I spot a knife, a gun, a four-petaled flower, the scales of justice among the designs which run from wrist to shoulder.

On his other arm are scrawled the words:

Non Dimenticare Mai

"What does the writing on your arm mean?" I finally ask.

He pauses midway in a push up. "I don't want to talk about it."

He dips down, his chest parallel to the ground. His biceps bulge, and his shoulder muscles undulate as they take the weight of his massive body. He stays there for a few seconds, maybe longer, then pushes up so he's balanced on palms that are flat on the ground and on his toes.

"On the other hand..." He shoots me a sideways glance. "Hope you're keeping count." Then he flows into the next push-up. One, two, three. I start a count of a different kind... Truthfully, I do try to keep count, I promise. But the way the planes of his back contract, how his thigh muscles strain his pants as he stares forward with an intent expression, and sinks into each push-up is like a dance... And with those scars on his back... It's dangerous, and animalistic, and erotic, all at once...

Jesus, this is body porn. This is better than watching Elle Woods take down Warner Huntington III in *Legally Blonde*. OMG, did I just compare watching Luca work out to an event from *Legally Blonde*? That's a first because, thanks to my mom, Elle Woods is my all-time girl crush, and the fact that I could even think of both in the same vein means... Luca has made more of an impression on me than I would have given him credit for.

He continues to flow into the next push-up and the next and the next. A bead of sweat slides down his temple, and the tendons of his throat strain. The veins stand out on his arms, and his entire body seems to grow heavier, but he doesn't stop.

I sit up, swing my legs over the side of the bed, then pad toward him. He doesn't look my way, doesn't seem to notice when I pause in front of him. This way, I have a bird's eye view of how his shoulder blades come together when he presses down on his hands and lowers himself until his nose almost brushes the ground. Then he straightens and the planes relax, and his pants pull tight across his butt. A breath whooshes out of me. My breaths feel heavier, my stomach muscles feel lighter, and the space between my legs, definitely moist. My toes curl as I drag my gaze back up his torso to his face to find he's watching me with those piercing blue eyes.

I slide back a step as he pushes back and up to his feet.

"Enjoy the show?" His lips curl. Jeez, that smirk. It's mean, and cruel, and so hot. Why is it that the bad boy is always so much more appealing than the man you'd want to take home to meet your mother? Not to say my mother wouldn't appreciate the spectacle of a hot sex object of a man working out, either.

"It was okay." I toss my hair over my shoulder. "By the way, you barely made it to fifty."

"That's because you distracted me." He takes a step forward; I move back further. *Hey, stop that; hold your ground. Don't give in to this big bully.*

"You're not very good at keeping your focus if my mere presence causes you to get sidetracked," I sniff.

"Oh, you're causing me to get more than distracted... And that's the truth."

Instantly, I lower my gaze to his crotch, then wish I hadn't because the unmistakable bulge in his pants tells me exactly what impact I have on him.

He closes the distance between us. I watch him warily as he advances. He stops in front of me, then crosses his arms over his chest. He's so tall that I have to tilt all the way back to meet his gaze. The sole window high up in the ceiling is to his back. The rays of sun slanting in are blocked by his body.

"You... you don't scare me." I tip up my chin. "Truth."

"Lies, all lies." He scratches his bare chest, and I lower my gaze to those cut abs. My mouth salivates. This close, that dark chocolate and coffee scent of his intensifies. The heat from his body reaches out to me, and I lean forward before I catch myself. How am I going to resist him when I'm locked up in this room with him?

"I dare you to return to your side of the room and wear your shirt," I blurt out.

He smirks. "Where would the fun be in that now, eh?"

"I am *not* sleeping with you, okay?" I wrap my arms about my waist. "Why don't you play with yourself instead?"

"Hmm..." He gives me a considering glance. "Now that you mention it."

He reaches for his waistband and I jump up on the bed. "Stop! I didn't mean that literally. It was simply a figure of speech or something."

"You sure?" He pops the button of his waistband. "I'm happy to oblige."

"No, no, no." I turn around and face the wall. "Please, I was simply trying to get you to move back, that's all. I didn't mean it, I promise, okay?"

He laughs and the sound rolls across my skin. OMG, this is not good. Why can't I simply ignore the guy?

"Chicken," he murmurs in a low voice. I sense him moving away, so I risk a peek over my shoulder, and heave a sigh to find him walking over to the opposite side of the room. Once more, he sinks down to the ground and kicks his legs out in front. Only, he's still not wearing his shirt, so that wide expanse of his chest is bared to my perusal. I turn to face him and sit down on the bed cross-legged.

"So, truth. How many siblings do you have?" I ask.

"Seven. Six. No, seven." His forehead furrows.

"You don't know how many siblings you have?" I laugh.

"Xander died," he says simply.

"Oh, I'm sorry." I squeeze my eyes shut. Typical me—saying something stupid when I should have stayed quiet.

"He was killed by a bomb placed in his car. Luckily, Karma, my oldest brother Michael's wife, who was also in the car at the time, escaped. She lost the child she was carrying, though."

"Oh, no." I lock my fingers together in front of me.

"She's pregnant again." A small smile curves his lips. "Which means Michael will not leave her side. It's as if those two are on a perpetual honeymoon."

"That's so sweet."

"Too sweet, maybe." He bends one knee. "Between the two of them, then Christian and Aurora, Axel and Theresa, and Seb and Elsa, my brothers are falling like flies. They're all too busy bowing their heads in servitude to their wives."

"Servitude?" I scoff. "It's not servitude if you love your wife and want to take care of her and your child."

"Knew it. You're one of those suckers who believes in hearts and rainbows and Happily-Ever-Afters." He smirks.

"So?" I firm my lips. "It's normal to want to meet a man who thinks of you as the center of the universe. Something you wouldn't understand because the only person at the center of your universe is you."

"And don't you forget it." He stabs a finger in my direction. "Also, you're beginning to bore me." He yawns. "I think I might get some shut eye. It's a better use of my time than hearing you prattle on."

Jerk. I curl my fingers into fists. I really want to go over and slap his face, but if he were to retaliate, I'd be no match for his strength. Also, not sure if I touch him, I'd be able to stop at a slap. My fingers tingle. I'd want to run my fingers down his neck, down the valley that demarcates his pecs, to that flat stomach of his and down to— I glance away. Jeez, can't I even look at him without wondering how big he's going to be when I finally take him in my hands? I mean, that column in his pants can't lie, right?

I glance back at him to find him pulling on his shirt and his boots.

He must feel the question in my eyes for he glances up at me. "I prefer to be prepared for any eventuality. I suggest you do the same." He leans his head against the wall and closes his eyes, showing off the strong column of his throat. He has one arm balanced on his bent knee, but his body is relaxed. He's completely still. He can't be asleep already, can he?

I watch the rhythmic rise and fall of his chest. Rise and fall. We're hidden away from the world. It's likely no one knows we're here, and yet, I'm not as scared as I should be, because he's in here with me.

Is that crazy? Maybe. I should be more worried about the fact that there's someone spying on us. Someone who wants to watch us getting it on before he's going to let us go. Not that there's any guarantee he will, of course. For all we know, he may have been saying it only to test us. Not to mention, what if he records it? What if he's planning to blackmail us... Or sell it? Oh, my god. What if he keeps us here forever, forcing us to have sex so he can film it and sell it? No, no, no. I'm not going to think about that. People watching us have sex and getting turned on by it? I can't think about that. It's too embarrassing. None of it changes the fact that I'm not letting this man near me, and not because I don't find him attractive. Quite the opposite.

If he touches me once... If he runs his fingers over my breasts, down my stomach and between my legs, and if he rubs my clit... I'm going to explode. A shudder runs up my spine. I glance down to find my fingers between my legs. No, no, no, I can't be touching myself, and certainly not when I'm in the same room as him. Apparently, even being trapped here with a deviant watching us is not enough to deter me from fantasizing about my cellmate.

I swing my legs over the side of the bed and rise to my feet. I hesitate, then pull on my own shoes. Best to be prepared. I'm not doing it because he told me to but because it makes sense.

Making sure that he's still asleep, I walk over to the wall closest to the window, then I raise my arms over my head.

7

Luca

A thump vibrates through the floor and up the leg I have stretched out. I crack open my eyelids and find her poised on her toes on the other side of the room. She brings up her leg, circles it with her arm and holds it there for a minute… maybe two? Then, she flattens the foot she's balanced on, releases the other leg, and slides into a split. I kid you not, the woman slips into a split, and stays there for a few seconds. Fuck, is she flexible? The things I could do with that kind of agility. My cock lengthens. I watch as she places her palms on the ground, and pushes herself up to a standing position. She holds one arm out to the side, the other one in front of her, then pushes her right leg to the side, toes bent, before she twirls, all graceful and shit, on her toes, arms held up, again and again, until she reaches the wall and stops.

Next, she holds her arms out in a T-position, places her foot slightly tilted in front, leans her weight on it, kicks the other leg high up, places it down. Then she repeats the action alternating between legs. At least she's still wearing her shoes. That means she's taken my suggestion of being prepared for any eventuality seriously.

Her eyes are closed, she hums under her breath, and the muscles of her face relax as she comes to a standstill. She turns to face me. Hands on her hips, she takes a leap forward, arms shooting up into a V and another leap that brings her in front of me. That's when she opens her eyelids and meets my gaze. Her own widens. She loses her balance and stumbles forward. Before she can hit the ground, I lean toward her, hold out my arms, and snatch her up out of the air and into my lap.

"Let me go." She begins to struggle, but I hold her close. "Please," she whimpers.

"Not a chance." I rise to my feet, walk over to the bed, drop her down onto it, then cover her with my body.

She wriggles under me, then bucks her body—or tries to, at any rate. I lean more of my weight on her, and she huffs. She brings her hand up and her palm connects with my face once before I grab her wrist and twist it above her head. She raises her other arm; I do the same with that one.

"You've done it now." I peer into her features. "I'm going to have to punish you."

"What are you talking about?" she snarls. "You surprised me and I lost my balance."

"Or maybe you did it on purpose."

"I did not."

"Maybe you were dancing to get my attention?"

"I was dancing because I was tired of lying on the bed, you big oaf."

"Is that what you were doing?" I snicker.

Her face heats.

"I'm not going to let you get to me." She firms her lips. "I'm a good dancer, I'll have you know."

"Newsflash, baby, I've already gotten to you. And by the way, I noticed." I thrust my face into hers.

She stops struggling. "What are you going to do? If you think you can force yourself on me—"

"I've never had to force myself on anyone." I place my lips right over hers so we share breath. "I'm going to kiss you, okay?"

"Don't you dare—"

"Don't fight me. I'm trying to get his attention so we can find a way out of this goddamn space."

"Oh." Some of the tension seems to bleed out of her shoulders. "Why didn't you say so earlier?"

I brush my lips over hers. "I would have, if you'd let me speak." A slow pulse begins to thud at my temples. I press a kiss to the corner of her lips, and a warmth suffuses my chest. I lower my nose to her throat and draw in a deep breath. Her scent fills my lungs and my head spins. A pulse flares to life at my wrists, behind my eyes, even in my fucking balls. *Gesù Cristo*, I have never felt this… off-kilter before.

It has nothing to do with her, nothing to do with the softness of her body, the lush curves, the symmetry of her body as she danced, the rapturous expression on her features as she lost herself in her moves, the intelligence in her eyes as she tried to outwit me in our game of Truth or Dare. No, it's only because I can't stand to be cooped up in this cell for a minute longer. Damn the fact that I want her and the thought of being inside her— Hell, the blood drains to my groin at once.

"Umm." She wiggles her hips a little, then freezes when she brushes the column in my pants. "Thought you were going to try to find a way out?" she hisses at me.

I raise my gaze and stare into her features. "I am." *Or maybe I'm trying to find a way in.*

"This seems to indicate otherwise." She brushes against the hardness at my crotch again and a shiver runs down my back.

"What can I say? I'm a good actor." I allow my lips to curl.

"A likely story." Her flush deepens.

"I'm a man, and I'm between a woman's legs; it was bound to happen."

"What now? Do we stay like this until someone behind that camera notices us? And even if they do, doesn't mean they're going to set us free, you know?"

"We could fuck and take our chances—"

"No." She begins to struggle under me. "No bloody way."

"Hold on to your panties. That was only a suggestion. On the other hand—" I pause and tilt my head toward the door.

"Get off me, you jerk."

"Shh," I hold a finger to my lips as I bring my attention to the door. The unmistakable sound of someone unlocking it reaches me.

I roll off of her, then prowl over to the door and stand to the side. It swings open and someone enters with a tray of food in his hands. I grab his arm and yank him forward. The tray crashes to the floor. The man turns toward me, but I am already moving. I clap my palms on either side of his head and pull it down as I raise my knee. It connects with his nose. The sound of bones crunching fills the room. Blood blooms on his face, and I hurl him to the side before it can taint my pants.

He hits the floor, rolls over once, then staggers to his feet. I rush him, grab him around the waist, and push him through the door of the bathroom. He hits the wall on the far end and straightens, weaving a little. *Porca miseria.* I leap toward him and smash my head into his already broken nose. His body jerks, then he slumps. I step back as he hits the floor and stays there. Finally, fuck!

I pivot, race out of the bathroom, pausing only to shut the door. I glance up to find she's pulled on her jacket and holding out mine. I shrug into it, then follow her out of the room. I close the door to the cell and lock it. Of course, that *stronzo* Freddie is going to check the cameras and see the room's empty, but for whatever it's worth, maybe locking the door will buy us a little time?

I race past her and down the corridor, as a man steps onto the landing. I bend, kick his legs out from under him, and he falls headfirst down the steps and slides all the way to the ground floor, leaving a trail of blood. I jump down the stairs, two at a time, then turn to find her making her way around the blood splatter, a look of revulsion on her features.

Before she reaches the last step, I grab her by the waist, and place her down on the floor. Then pivot and run toward the main door, and straight into a room filled with men.

"*Cazzo.*" I skid to a stop and she slams into me from behind.

"What the hell," she protests, "can't you see where you are going, you —" Her voice fades as she takes in the bunch of guys who glance from me to her, then back at me. As one, they pull out their guns.

"Back to your room," one of them growls.

I hold up my arms. "Why don't you put away your guns and fight me? Or better still, give me a gun and we'll see who wins."

"I don't think so." One of the men walks toward me. I leap forward, grab his gun and aim it upward as he shoots. The bullet slams through the ceiling, and bits of plaster fall on us. I bring my booted foot down on his. He yells and his grasp on the gun slips. I tear it from his hands, turn the gun on him and shoot. Behind me, I sense her freeze as the man slumps.

"Stay behind me," I yell as I aim the gun and shoot and shoot and shoot. When I lower my gun, the room is silent. Five men lay fallen on the floor.

She steps around me when one of the men reaches for his gun. I throw myself on her, we hit the ground, and I manage to twist my body to avoid falling on her as I shoot him. The gun slips from his hand and he's dead before he hits the floor.

I jump up, lean down to help her up, but she's already on her feet. "I can take care of myself," she hisses as she reaches for the gun of one of the fallen men, then walks over to pick up a second gun.

"What are you doing?"

"Gathering the weapons to take with me, what does it look like?" she snarls.

I chuckle, then slide the gun I'm carrying into the small of my back, before I snatch up two more and head for the doorway, with her right behind me. I bypass the front door, heading for the kitchen, hoping the door beyond will lead to the garage.

I push open the door and the lights in the ceiling flicker on. A-n-d bingo. There are three cars, which I bypass as I head for the motorbike parked to the side. It's a Ducati, which will have to do. Personally, I prefer a Harley. Nothing like the classics.

"How did you know you'd find the garage here?" she asks.

"Lucky guess? Also, couldn't risk leaving by the front door in case there were more men waiting." Shouts, then footsteps sound behind us as I grab one of the helmets from the bike and smash it over my head, then snatch another and place it over hers.

"What are you doing?" Her scream is muffled.

I mount the bike, then jerk my chin at her. "Get on, Angel."

"Why can't we take one of the cars?"

"Because I prefer a bike."

"Jesus, can't you rein in your macho-ness and be sensible just once, you—"

I kickstart the bike, the sound of the engine echoes around the space.

"Get on," I shout so she can hear me over the engine.

She firms her lips as I slap the switch on the handle. The garage door begins to rise, revealing a row of men standing there, their guns aimed at us.

8

Jeanne

He's lost it. Clearly, he's lost it. Does he really think he can drive through the wall of men who have their guns pointed at us? Footsteps pound and I glance over my shoulder to find men pouring through the doorway we just came through.

Crap! My feet seem to move of their own accord, and I throw my leg over the bike behind him.

"Shoot at them." He jerks his head over his shoulder.

"Wait, what?"

"Just aim and shoot. You do know how to shoot, don't you?"

"I can try." I stab my tongue into my cheek, then pop the safety of the gun I'm holding in my right hand, as he raises his guns and fires. Bang, bang, bang. Bullets screech past my head. I scream, then huddle closer behind him. He careens to the right, then to the left, and I hold on with one hand, as I depress the trigger on the gun and keep it there. Oh, and I also squeeze my eyes shut. I know, I'm a wuss, but hey, while this is not my first time holding a gun, it's my first time aiming it at living men, and I honestly don't know if I want to see my bullets hit them. On the other hand, if I spend one more minute in that damn room, I'm going to lose it completely. So, between the two, yeah, I'll shoot. Besides, they're the ones who kidnapped me. That makes them the bad guys, right? I keep shooting until the empty clicks of the chambers reaches me.

"Hold on," he yells as the bike leaps forward. I tuck myself into his back, still holding the empty guns as he races out of the garage. We must pass the bodies he's shot down, but I still have my eyes closed, so I don't know. It's okay, it's not cowardly if you are protecting yourself against nightmares, right? He takes the next curve so fast, I almost slide off.

"*Cazzo,* hold on, will you?"

I crack my eyes open long enough to throw my arms around his waist. I'm still holding the empty guns, but I hold onto him the best I can as he guns the motor up the driveway and toward the steadily closing gates.

"Jesus, what are you—" He gathers speed and I squeeze my eyes shut again. He powers the bike up and we seem to fly forward and through the quickly-shrinking space between the gates and onto the road. I draw oxygen into my lungs, which burn. My throat hurts—did I scream? I think I remember screaming. My fingers cramp and the muscles in my arms protest. I loosen my hold on him, then scream again when the bike jumps forward. Twerp! I hold onto him as we hit the main road and he guns the motor again.

We travel that way for another ten minutes, then he swears, "*Cazzo,* we're being followed."

I can hear him clearly. That's when I realize the helmets are equipped with a two-way communication channel.

"I'd hoped we'd have a little more time, but we don't have a choice now." He turns so suddenly, the bike seems to scream in protest. I confess, I scream, too, and hold onto him.

"What are you doing? Have you lost it completely, you—"

He straightens, then zooms toward the oncoming car, which I recognize as one of the ones from the garage. Keeping one hand on the handlebar, he shoots at them. And he doesn't veer off of the road. He sets us on a collision course with the car. My heart slams into my rib cage. The pulse thunders at my wrists. I squeeze my eyes shut again and huddle behind him as he continues to shoot. Then I hear the sound of brakes squealing, and I'm accosted by the smell of burnt rubber.

I open my eyes in time to find the car sailing off the road and into the adjacent field. Only, there's another car coming at us. While I don't recall seeing it in the garage, he must, for he gives it the same treatment. I manage to keep my eyes open as he continues to fire. The windshield of the car cracks. The driver slumps forward and the car swerves off the side of the road and into the field on the other side. He slows down a little then—thank God—before he turns the bike around and comes to a standstill.

He clicks on the safeties of the guns, then reaches forward to open the carrier on the bike. He slides the guns in, then takes the empty gun from my hand and tosses it in, as well. He snaps it shut, kicks off the stand of the bike, then eases forward.

We travel at a normal speed, which is wise. At least this way, we'll attract less attention. Not that this man is able to walk into a room without everyone turning to look at him. It's the way he is—his presence, the way he can't help but absorb all of the oxygen in the space. He's also arrogant, has a big opinion of himself, and thinks he can overcome any challenge thrown at him. Which, to be fair, he just did.

"Do you think we got out of there too easily?" I burst out.

"What do you mean?"

"I mean, wouldn't Freddie have been more careful with how he got us food; wouldn't he have anticipated something like this happening? Shouldn't he have tied you up or something?"

"Then he wouldn't have been able to watch us fuck."

"Not that I would have let you... but yeah—" I purse my lips. "Still, I find it weird that we got out of there that easily."

"I wouldn't call shooting up two cars and a dozen men too easy."

"A dozen men?" I wince. "Do you think they're dead?"

"I know they're dead."

I push my forehead into his back. "I know they were bad men, but still, they may have had families, and children, and—"

"They knew the risk they were taking when they came into this business."

"So, do you and your brothers leave home every day, knowing you might not return?"

"We are... prepared. Several of my brothers are married now, and that complicates things. It's why Michael wants to try and turn the business legit, in as much as it's possible to minimize the risks."

"But once you're in this life, you can't really walk away, can you?"

"That's true," he agrees, "but it is possible to bring down the level of uncertainty you deal with every day."

"So, what happened earlier—the number of men you shot, the cars you wrecked—is that not a normal occurrence?"

"It's not abnormal." He blows out a breath. "Look, I was brought up in the Mafia. This is the life I know. Some of us trained to have a profession beyond it. Like my brother, Massimo is both a qualified finance professional and a

lawyer, Xander was an artist, Christian is also a lawyer, Seb is going to start up
a media business, and Adrian's investing his money in a chain of coffeeshops.
Michael, my older brother, knew he would become Don one day, while me?

"This is the life I know. The intricacies of this way of living... It runs in
my blood. There were no guarantees for me. I wasn't the oldest, yet something about this lifestyle suits me, you know. I never thought I'd become
the *Capo*. Then Seb gave up his title, and Michael made me *Capo* in his
place."

"So, do you feel all your efforts so far have been worth it?"

"You'd think," he says in a low voice. "You'd think, after everything I've
seen and done, I'd be ecstatic to finally be recognized for my efforts. But..."
He shakes his head. "Becoming a *Capo* didn't make a damn difference. It
didn't fill this empty space inside of me. It didn't feel like a big achieve-
ment. There was something anticlimactic about it, and *cazzo*! Why am I
telling you all this?"

He bends over the handlebar and the bike leaps forward.

"It's okay to share; it's not going to make you less of a man," I murmur.

He doesn't reply. We ride in silence for the next hour. I take in the
passing fields, the grey clouds in the sky that seem to hang so low. We
reach a roundabout with the signs pointing toward St. Ives—signs in
English—and that's when it strikes me. "We're in the UK?"

"In Cornwall, actually," he clarifies. "But you surmise correctly."

"Oh, my god, they brought us to the UK?"

"It would seem that way," he agrees.

"You don't seem surprised?"

"Probably because Freddie is from the UK. Though, why he'd bring us
here, to the back of beyond, I don't know. Could've saved us some time if
they'd decided to keep us in London, but no, they had to choose a place far
away from civilization."

"We're in Cornwall; that's not exactly uncivilized," I point out.

"It's not London," he retorts.

"Where did you grow up, anyway?" Not that I am curious or anything,
but if I am going to be stuck with him for a while longer, then it's best to
know more about him, right?

"I spent some of my early years in Palermo, and before you ask, yes,
Italy is excluded from the list of uncivilized places. It's the cradle of civilization, after all."

"I won't refute that, but to negate any other city is a bit narrow-minded,
don't you think," I scoff.

"My formative years were spent in LA, so that city's off the list, too," he declares.

Hmm, I went to drama school in LA, so we do have something in common, not that I am going to tell him that.

Instead, I snort, "Wow, so generous."

"I know, right?"

I raise my eyes skyward. "Were you born with such an inflated opinion about yourself, or did you become that way, or...? You know what, don't answer that."

"See, you are getting to know me so well."

"Now that I know we're in the UK, I think I can make my way to London on my own," I declare.

"With no cash? Not to mention, they're probably not far behind us."

I purse my lips. He has a point. I do need money, and some ID, and a cellphone, ideally.

"You don't have any money, either, so how do you reckon we're going to make it back?"

"Wait and see."

I hear the smirk in his voice. Jerk. He drives past the turn off for St. Ives and keeps going.

"Don't want to risk staying in town," he explains as he continues up the highway.

"Where are we going?" I should have asked the question earlier, but it's not every day that I'm shot at or shoot back, so guess I'm excused for the delayed reaction.

"You'll see," he replies.

"How do you know where to go? You seem to have a destination in mind."

"I do; it's a safe space."

"According to whom?"

He blows out a breath. "So many questions. Chill, enjoy the ride, will ya?"

"Don't talk down to me. I'm not one of your women who's going to shut up just because you tell her to."

"God forbid I'd ever think that." I can't see his face, but I can hear the smirk in his voice. "And it's one of the scenarios we drew up, if ever one of us were in such a situation in the UK."

"We, as in—"

"Me and my brothers."

"So, you expected that you'd find yourself in Cornwall and know where to go?" I shoot back.

"We have a few designated safe spots in each of the key countries where our rivals are located. UK is one of them. And yes, there is one such space not far from us. Now, can I focus on the driving without your honeyed tones filling my ears?"

What an ass. Don't know what he's complaining about. I do have a right to know where he's taking me, after all. Anyway, I shut up and watch the scenery zip by and it's quite spectacular, actually. On one side of the road are hills, and on the other, waves crash on a beach far below. Didn't I read somewhere that this area is called the English riviera? Now I know why.

We drive for another hour, then he pulls off the highway and into a service area. He parks the motorcycle and I jump off. I take off my helmet and draw in lungfuls of air. He takes the helmet from me, locks it to the bike, along with his, and I follow him into the small complex of shops. I head toward the restrooms when he taps my shoulder. "Make it quick. We need to be on our way."

I nod in his direction and keep going. He's right, of course. It's best not to linger in one area for too long, or we may be found out. But still, he could have asked me politely instead of ordering me, right? I take care of business, and when I walk out, I find he's paying for food at the Waitrose counter.

"Wait, you had money with you?" I draw abreast with him.

"I had some hidden away in an inner pocket of my jacket." He raises a shoulder. "Standard practice; we always carry extra money in a place where it's difficult to find."

"Standard Mafia protocol, you mean?"

He shoots me a sideways glance. "Is my background such a problem for you?"

"No." I shuffle my feet. "I mean, yes. You have to realize, I've led a normal life so far. Then I'm taken, and I find myself in a room alone, and then they throw you in with me and expect us to... you know..." I grip my fingers together in front of myself. "You have to admit, it's not a usual occurrence."

He surveys my features. "You've done exceedingly well, considering what you've been through. In fact, it's because you've been holding up so well that I forgot how bewildering everything must be for you."

I stare at him. "Are you actually empathizing with me?"

He frowns. "I did, didn't I?" He snatches up the paper bag with the items he's purchased, then turns and walks toward the exit.

I follow him as we head back out and toward the bike.

"How much longer are we going to ride?" I raise my arms and drop them toward my feet, stretching out. I hold the pose for a few seconds feeling every single muscle in my body separate. A groan escapes from my lips. I straighten to find him watching me with a strange expression on his features.

"What?" I scowl.

"You really are flexible, aren't you?"

"So?"

"Brings to mind possibilities, if you change your mind about letting me fuck you—"

"I won't, and even if I did, it would be me f'ing you."

"So, you did think about it?" His lips kick up and his eyes gleam. A gust of wind raises the hair on his forehead and my heart stutters. Whoa, what was that? I don't know this guy at all. He may be good looking— okay, he's bloody gorgeous to look at, has a body I'd do anything to get my hands on—but he's part of the Mafia, for heaven's sake. He and I have nothing in common. Also, he seems to think he can snap his fingers and I'll fall into his arms. And when that creep Freddie told us what he expected of us before he'd set us free, the man didn't blink an eyelid.

If I had encouraged him, he would have fucked me, too, not caring who was watching. He definitely did seem to get turned on by the idea. He's kinky and filthy... *and that's so hot.* No, it's not. I don't want to sleep with someone who gets off on the idea of being watched. I don't want to be ogled in my most intimate moments. And let's not forget, that weirdo Freddie might have even been planning to film us, and then what would have happened, eh?

"I wouldn't sleep with you if you were the last man on this planet."

"Oh?" He looks me up and down. "I do believe that's an *official* challenge."

9

Luca

"You don't expect us to share that, do you?" She narrows her gaze on the single bed in the room above the pub that I found. The place is far away from the nearest town, and so secluded that I'll be able to spot anyone coming from a mile off. Thank god the Brits liked their countryside pubs, many of which kept the tradition of hiring out rooms by the night to travelers.

I was able to pay for it with the money stashed in the lining of my jacket, which those *stronzii* had never found. An old Mafioso tradition which Michael had insisted on keeping alive. Thank fuck.

I shoot her a sideways glance. "Thought you'd have gotten used to the idea by now."

She scowls at me. "You're taking this joke too far. And just to remind you, we haven't spent a night together... so far."

"Easily rectifiable." I walk over to place the paper bag with the food supplies on the bed. Then I shove my jacket down my shoulders.

"What are you doing?" she squeaks as I shrug off my shirt and drape it with my jacket over the lone chair in the room, then reach for my pants.

"I don't know about you, but I need a shower." I toe off my boots and my socks, then shove my pants down, along with my boxers. I fold my pants, drape them over the arm of the chair, drop my boxers on the chair, then turn toward the bathroom.

She pivots around to glance the other way, but not before I notice the flush on her cheeks. Oh, she's attracted to me, all right; she's just going to keep fighting it. Fine by me. She's not the kind of girl I'd want to bed anyway. Too many hang-ups; too many romantic notions. She's probably the type who expects a man to put a ring on her finger if he sleeps with her twice.

Too bad, she has the most luscious body I've ever come across. Those curves bely the litheness with which she can stretch. And when she dances? *Gesù Cristo*, I can't look away. She is something special, no doubt about it. Too bad she rubs me the wrong way. Nope, she's too much work.

Oh, I'd fuck her, all right. Problem is, if I did, chances are, I wouldn't be content with doing it just once. And that'd only complicate matters. Also, she's exactly the kind of woman my Nonna would have encouraged me to be with. Which is exactly why I need to steer clear of any entanglements with her.

Ideally, I'll get her to London, then back to her troupe in Palermo— Shit, that'll only put her in danger again. There's nothing stopping Freddie from coming after her again, so unfortunately, I can't part ways with her yet. I need to make sure she's safe first, so for the moment, she's stuck with me, like it or not. I'm not going to change my ways. She'll have to put up with me; no choice.

I stalk into the bathroom and step under the shower. It's a tiny space, but at least the water is hot.

I reach for the soap and begin to wash myself, when a draft of air hits me. The door bangs shut and I turn to find her walking into the bathroom. Naked. Not a stitch of clothing on her body. And what a body she has.

I knew she was curvaceous, obviously, but Angel without clothes is... My favorite wet dream, come true... Firm breasts, tipped with plum-colored nipples that are erect, a narrow waist that flares into hips which are wide enough to tempt me to grip them when I position her just so as I breach her opening with my cock. As I squeeze those creamy thighs and mark them, before I bend her knee to the side and next to her chest and bury myself balls deep inside her heat.

I take in the flesh between her legs... Plump pussy lips that fold in toward her clit. She slides into the space in front of me and cuts off the flow of water. She raises her head as the water flows over her shoulders, down her back, and over the swell of her butt cheeks. The blood drains to my groin and my thigh muscles tighten. A pulse flares to life in my balls as

I take in the spectacle. I open my mouth to speak, but no words come out. I clear my throat.

"The fuck are you doing?" I growl.

"Trying to have a shower."

"You couldn't have waited until I was done?"

"You couldn't have asked if I wanted to shower first?" She huffs.

"Did you want to shower first?" I snap.

"I'm here, aren't I?" She flips her hair over her shoulder. The strands slap against my chest. That crushed rose-petal scent of her seems to amplify, thanks to the hot water.

"Can I have the soap please?" She holds out her hand.

I am about to place it in her palm, then change my mind. Instead, I lather up the bar and swipe the suds down her back. She stiffens.

"What are you doing?" She glances at me over her shoulder.

"Trying to help you have a shower." I smirk.

"That isn't why I came in here."

"You could've fooled me." I drag my soapy palm down the indentation of her waist, over the width of her hips, down her thigh. Her entire body trembles. Her shoulders rise and fall. I sink down to my knees and soap up her calves, the backs of her feet. Then tap the outside of her thigh.

"Turn around."

Her breath hitches.

"Now, Angel."

She pivots toward me and I tap her foot. She raises it, and I place it on my palm. The length of her foot is smaller than that of my hand. I soap between her toes, around her ankles, up the front of her legs, her knees, along the outsides of her thighs. A trembling grips her, but she stays steady.

I drag my fingers over the cursive writing inked onto her left hip.

Out of the ash

"I rise with my red hair,

And I eat men like air." I complete the rest of the stanza at the same time as her.

Silence descends for a beat, another. I glance up to find her watching me with a strange look on her face.

"Didn't think I could quote Sylvia Plath?" I twist my lips.

"No offense. I don't expect most people to recognize the words."

"I'm not most people."

She swallows. "I'm beginning to realize that."

"Why this specific poem?" I ask.

"People think the poem is about death because she wrote it in the months preceding her suicide. And it does touch on her previous attempts at trying to die by her own hand. But it's also about her resurrection and taking revenge on her enemies. It's that spirit I identify with. According to Plath, dying is an art. You have to keep at it until you perfect it. As an actress, I do the same. Each time I go on stage, I die a little and am reborn. And I'll keep doing it until I perfect it. Only, there is nothing like a perfect performance, for you're only as good as your last one."

Her words sink into my blood and head straight for my groin. My cock extends further. I don't think I've ever been so turned on as when she's speaking with such passion.

"You're not like most people, either, Angel."

A blush smears her cheeks.

I carefully place her foot down on the floor, before I grab her hand and place it on my head. "Hold on."

She grips my hair and tugs; a shiver zips down my spine. My dick lengthens further as she raises her other foot. I treat it similarly, and as I run my fingers up her inner thigh, a moan bleeds from her lips. I stop short of brushing against her clit, and her grasp on my hair tightens. I place her other foot down, then lather my palms before the soap slips from me. I grip the tops of her thighs, rise up slightly until my face is opposite her pussy. I slide my soapy fingers around to grip her ass cheeks and squeeze.

"Oh, god, Luca," she gasps.

A thrill coils in my chest. My name from her lips… It sounds different. It sounds right. It sounds… like something I need to avoid… In the future. Right now, though— I close the distance to her melting flesh and swipe my lips up her slit.

"Luca," she half-screams. "Please, you—"

I strum my lips across her pussy lips, then curl my tongue around her swollen clit. She moans as I stab my finger inside her soaking channel, even as I massage her ass cheeks and pull them apart. I continue to slurp on her cunt as I slide a finger inside her back hole, and that's when she goes rigid. She rises up to her tiptoes and I follow. And thrust my tongue inside her again and again. I curve my finger inside her as I pull out my tongue from her channel, only to latch onto her clit. I bite down and she cries out. Her back curves. She digs her fingers into my scalp, and that's when moisture bathes my tongue as she comes. I lap up her cum as I grab the soap and lather it again, then reach up to cup her breasts. I wash them with quick strokes and she bites her lips.

"Luca, stop. I can't think when you touch me."

"That's the idea." I glance up into her tawny eyes, pupils blown as she holds my gaze. She releases her grip on my hair, and I rise to my feet without breaking the connection. I peer into her face as I cup her breasts, then pinch her nipples.

She shudders. "This is not why I came in here."

"But you stayed."

"I did," she whispers.

"Do you want me to stop?"

She swallows.

"Do you?"

She nods.

I raise my hands and step back from her, then pop my head under the stream of water. I run my fingers through my hair to rinse the dried blood from the back of my head. The wound itself, though, seems to have started healing. I walk out of the shower and head for the door, grabbing a towel on the way. The door shuts behind me.

I dry myself, then fling the towel on the nightstand before I clamber into bed. *Cazzo.* What was that? It's not like I've never seen a naked woman before, but seeing her without her clothes completely floored me. It's like I lost my mind, overwhelmed by the sensations of lust, and something more… A need to take, to possess, to claim her. To make her orgasm so she knows just how much she affects me.

I'm not a selfish lover, but I've never put a woman's pleasure before my own desires. What is it about her that made me want to floor her with desire, to overwhelm her with endorphins so she couldn't think clearly anymore? So she'd be pliant in my arms as I took her and ravished her and showed her just how good it could be between us. So I could love her…

Che cazzo? I barely know her. I can't be falling for her so quickly, can I? Nah, it's just lust talking. The kind that overwhelms me every time I step into the room in Venom—the nightclub owned by me and my brothers— where I perform in front of a crowd. Where I bring women to pleasure as I get myself off. It's been a while since I did that. That's the only reason I wasn't able to hold back. That's why I felt overwhelmed. I just need to see her to safety; then I can be rid of her and return to my life. Yep, that's it. I pull the sheet up to my waist, then fling my arm behind my neck.

By the time she steps out of the bathroom with a towel wrapped around her tight little body, I have my eyes half-closed. I track her as she walks around to the other side of the bed and slides under the covers.

She keeps to her side, which, considering how narrow the mattress is, means she's almost falling off. Too bad it's best we keep distance between us.

That's when her stomach growls.

10

Jeanne

"Are you hungry?" He sits up and reaches for the bag filled with food on the nightstand and puts it on the bed between us.

Yeah, I am. If only it were for just the food. The way he made me come in there... It's mind-boggling. I swear, I saw stars at the edges of my vision. I still felt dizzy as I walked to the bed. I don't think I've come that hard ever before.

Oh, I've had a couple of boyfriends, but not one of them has gone down on me... Sad truth. And this man... This almost-stranger... He ate me out, and touched me all over, and did the kinds of things to me that I've only read about in books, and never experienced in real life. Look, it's not that my love life is vanilla... Okay, maybe it is a tad. But that's okay, right? I hadn't thought I was missing the kind of rough and raunchy sex I read about. I've always thought that, given how focused on my career I am, I'd never have the opportunity to meet someone who'd make my body sing the way this jerkhole did.

Why does he have to be part of the Mafia? And why does he have to be this cocky? This full-of-himself? Why couldn't he be someone more ordinary? But if he were, perhaps he wouldn't be this appealing... If he were a fellow dancer, or even someone with a nine-to-five job... Well, even then, if it were Luca, he'd own his life. He'd be in control. He'd be confident and persistent and wear that smirk that makes my panties melt.

Christ, this is embarrassing. I'm sitting next to him and I can't stop thinking of how he had his tongue inside my pussy, his finger inside my ass, how he'd washed me and massaged my butt cheeks and my breasts, and if I'd let him, he would've fucked me. I squeeze my eyes shut. *Don't go there; don't go there.* I clench my thighs together.

"You okay?"

I pop my eyelids open and meet those startlingly clear blue eyes of his. "No, actually, I'm mortified."

"Because of what happened in there?" He jerks his chin in the direction of the bathroom.

"Isn't that reason enough?"

"You walked in without your clothes on. What else did you think was going to happen?" He scoffs.

"Not that, for sure. And I only did it because you pissed me off. You could have let me have the bathroom first, you know."

"Remind me to piss you off more often." He chuckles.

Jerk, and if he thinks I'm going to risk taking off my clothes in front of him again, he's mistaken. Also, what was I thinking walking in there naked?

"You were trying to make me lose control, weren't you?" He peers into my features. "Were you trying to test my patience? Is that it? You wanted to know how it would feel to have my hands, my mouth, my tongue on you. Admit it."

"I'll admit no such thing." A blush steals up my skin. "All I know is that I was so pissed with you for ordering me around, I decided to take matters into my own hands." I knot my towel more securely around my breasts. "Speaking of, are you naked under the covers?" I glance at his towel on the table. "You *are* naked under the covers."

"Not going to wear those filthy clothes to bed." He pulls out a couple of packed sandwiches from the paper bag and offers them to me.

"You couldn't, at least, wear your towel?" I scowl as I accept one of the sandwiches from him.

"I am covered, aren't I?" He tears open the packaging of his sandwich and digs into it.

I peel open the covering of my own and begin to eat at a more sedate pace. The juiciness of the tomatoes, combined with the fresh slightly sour taste of the mozzarella cheese, and the tanginess of the pickles explodes on my palate. I glance down at the sandwich again. "These are pretty good."

"One thing about the British, they know how to make sandwiches, and how to package them." He takes another bite of his sandwich, finishing one half of it.

"I take it you're not a fan of the Brits?"

"Like their sense of humor, hate the weather, can't stand their food, but this—" he nods toward the second half of his sandwich that he holds in his hand"—is passable."

"At least we're not still stuck in that room." I shudder.

"Hey..." He tips his chin in my direction and looks directly into my eyes. "You're safe now."

"But for how long?" I lower my hand. "You said you thought they'd come after us. How long do you think we have? Are we even safe here? Maybe we should have kept going."

"We were both tired, and I'm still recovering from whatever it is they dosed me with. Can't believe I didn't even realize they were transporting me across countries." He shakes his head. "Still, there are worse places to be than the UK. We should have someone meeting us very soon."

"You called someone?" I lean forward. "While I was away, you managed to reach your brothers?"

His lips kick up. "Let's just say, reinforcements are on the way." He chomps his way through the second half of his sandwich, then dips his hand inside the paper bag and brings out another. He proceeds to tear off the wrapping and starts eating it. "They should be here later tonight, then we can figure out a way out of here."

I polish off my sandwich, then reach into the paper bag and bring out a pack of chips, or crisps, as they're called here in the UK. I tear open the pack and crunch my way through a few.

He finishes off his second sandwich and pulls out a bottle of beer. He twists open the cap and raises it to his mouth. The cords of his throat move as he swallows. How can someone's throat be this beautiful? He lowers the bottle and a drop runs down his chin. Before I can stop myself, I reach over and scoop it up. I bring my fingers to my mouth, and his blue eyes deepen to almost azure in color.

"You're living dangerously, Angel," he lowers his voice to a hush and my core trembles.

"I... I didn't mean that. I mean, I was only trying to help." *Gah, can't you do better?* I plop the open packet of chips into the bag. "Look, can we just forget I did that, and for that matter, what happened in the bathroom?"

"Can you?" He tilts his head.

I hold his gaze for a few beats, then glance away.

"Can you, Angel? Can you forget how it felt to have my tongue inside you, and my finger in your ass as you rode my mouth?"

"Oh, god." I squeeze my thighs together. "Stop already."

"That's what I thought." He places the paper bag on the side of the bed, along with his half-full bottle of beer. "It seems that *stronzo*, Freddie, was onto something when he decided to lock you and me up in a room." He turns to me. "It's why I have a proposition for you."

11

Luca

"Proposition? What do you mean?" She wriggles around, trying to make herself more comfortable on the bed. Her towel slips a little, revealing more of the curve of her tits. I watch, fascinated, as it stops just shy of revealing those ripe nipples of hers. Goddamn, if only I could get a taste. Why didn't I bend my head and sample them earlier when I had the opportunity? Oh, right, I had been too taken aback by how beautifully she had orgasmed under my ministrations, that's why.

"Luca?" She snaps her fingers. "My face is up here."

"Oh, I know darlin', just trying to decide whether I'll suck on your nipples or your clit the next time."

She inhales a sharp breath, and color smears her cheeks like blood dispersing in water. "There's not going to be a next time." She pulls the cover up over her shoulders, cutting off the sight of her gorgeous chest. Damn.

"You and I both know there will be, Angel."

"Stop calling me that, and whatever your proposition is, I refuse."

"Don't be so hasty." I lean back against the headboard. "You may find what I'm going to propose is the solution to all of your problems."

"My only problem is that I'm stuck in a room with you, again. The only thing that's changed is that there are no cameras in this space."

"Easily rectified." I reach under my pillow and pull out a phone, then open up the camera app and position it in her direction.

"What the hell?" She pounces toward it. I hold the phone up and out of her reach. "You bought a phone?" Her gaze widens. The cover slips a little, but her chest is still covered. Damn.

"At the service area, while you were freshening up," I explain, while keeping an eye peeled for a glimpse of her boob on the screen. Sneaky? Yea, a little—okay, a lot. Filthy? Maybe. But you can't blame me. She has the kind of gorgeous body that's made for being worshipped.

"That's how you called your brothers?" A furrow appears between her eyebrows. "You had a phone all this time?" She slaps her palms on her hips. "And don't you dare film me, Luca."

I lower the phone. "Oh, I'm not going to film the filthy things I can do to you; yet."

"Not ever," she huffs.

"It's still early in our relationship. Give it time, and you'll be asking for more than being filmed." I scratch my chest. "Also, this is how they're going to reach me. And now that they have my number, they'll be tracking us."

"Is that supposed to make me feel safe?"

"Being tracked by the Sovranos? You bet. Not even the FBI or the MI6 can do a better job of keeping us on their radar now."

"Fine, so you spoke to your brothers. They'll meet us later. Then we can bid each other goodbye."

"No." I yawn.

"What do you mean, no?" She stiffens.

"You're coming back to Palermo with me."

"I am returning to Palermo, but not with you."

"Yes, you are."

"Why would I do that?"

"You have no other way of getting out of the country, do you? No passport, no tickets, no money." I slide the phone back under my pillow. "Ergo, you need me, Angel."

She scowls. "So, you're going to take advantage of the fact that I'm at your mercy?"

"You bet." I fold my arms under my neck and close my eyes. "I'll be happy to loan you the money and make sure you get back to the theatre in time for the premiere of your musical, which is tomorrow."

There's silence for a few seconds, then she asks, "And what do you want in return?"

I crack one eyelid open. "How do you know I want something in return?"

"Don't you?"

"I do." I allow my lips to curve. "I want you to marry me."

She blinks. "Excuse me?"

"You heard me. Marry me, Angel. Just long enough to convince my brothers that you are my real wife and get them off my back."

She opens and shuts her mouth. "Let me get this straight. You want me to marry you, but not for real?"

"That is correct."

"Why in the world would I do that?"

"Because my Nonna passed away recently, but before she did, she made it clear that she expected Seb, Massimo, Adrian, and me to marry within a month of her leaving us."

"So, you want to make the spirit of your dead grandma happy by pretending to marry me?" She shakes her head in disbelief.

"Yes."

"I still don't understand. Your Nonna wanted all of you to marry within a month of her passing, so how will a fake marriage to me solve anything?"

"It will get my brothers off my back."

"What about your brothers? Did they keep their promises to your grandmother?"

"Seb did. He got married for real. Massimo is likely to settle for an arranged marriage with the Mafia princess of a rival clan, even though he's not happy about it. But I believe that's where he's headed. Adrian… Well… He's the quietest, but also the one who's most likely to pull a surprise. I wouldn't put it past him to find his balls and finally propose to Cass, our housekeeper, who he has a thing for. Which leaves me."

"You." She narrows her gaze on my face.

"The one and only." I grin. "You have to admit, I'm a hell of a catch. And I've decided to settle for you."

"You've decided to *settle* for me?" She lowers her chin to her chest.

"Exactly." I drum my fingers on my chest. "My brothers won't quit nagging me until I settle down, and I have no plans to do so. Also, you need to make it back in time to star in your play. I'll make sure that happens. All you have to do is pretend to be my wife."

"You do realize, even if you manage to fool your brothers, you can't hide the truth from your grandma, considering she's now a spirit?"

"My point exactly. She's a spirit; it doesn't make a difference to her either way."

"What the—" she splutters. "I can't believe you said that."

"It's true, right? And I don't mean for it to be disrespectful or anything, but she's popped it, so it doesn't make a difference to her. I mean, she's hardly going to know if I'm married for real or not."

"Of course she will." Angel throws up her arms. "She's probably up there right now, looking at us and shaking her head."

"She is?" I glance up. "All I see is the shoddily painted over ceiling with a large water stain."

"You know what I'm saying is true. You really shouldn't be trying to fool someone who's dead. And that it was her last desire to see you married... There's something sacred about it."

"It's why I'm making this effort, aren't I? I'm doing it to keep everyone happy, including myself."

"Especially yourself," she mutters.

"You bet. Only I can figure out what's right for me, and getting married is not one of those things."

"Hmph." She purses her lips. "So, you want me to pretend to be your wife."

I nod.

"So, no wedding ceremony or anything?"

I tilt my head. "Unfortunately, we may not have a choice in that. How else would they believe we're married?"

"Can't you tell them that we got married on the run or something?"

"You mean in the last twenty-four hours, during which time I was kidnapped, we were held by Freddie, then we escaped?"

"Hmm." She purses her lips. "Maybe we could elope or something and say we got married then."

"That could work, I suppose." I scratch my jaw.

"And it's not going to be permanent, right?"

I chortle. "In your dreams. I know I'm a catch, but if you think this marriage is anything other than a farce, think again."

"Hold onto your knickers," she scoffs. "First, only you would think you're a catch which, let me hasten to clarify, you are not. Secondly, the only reason I'm asking is because I want to make sure that you don't fall in love with me."

"Fall in love?" I chuckle, then burst into laughter. "Love? Did I hear you use the L word? You think I'm going to fall in love... with *you*?"

"Don't bust a gut. It has been known to happen. Men always fall for me, and then I have to walk away before it gets messy," she sniffs.

"How many men have you been with, anyway?" I frown.

"None of your business."

I narrow my gaze on her. "If you're going to be my wife, I deserve to know."

"Fake wife, and no, you don't. My past is my own. I am under no obligation to tell you more."

"Hmm." I scrutinize her features. "I'll get it out of you, one way or the other."

She firms her lips. "How long is this farce supposed to last?"

"Until my family's convinced our marriage is for real."

"Which is how long?"

"As long as it takes," I retort.

"Shouldn't we put an outer limit to the time?"

"Are you anxious to spend more time with me?"

"Oh my god!" She throws up her hands. "Your ego is unreal."

"Thank you." I smirk.

"That wasn't a compliment."

"I'll take it as one anyway."

"And the time limit?"

"No time limit."

She opens her mouth to speak and I hold up my hand. "This isn't a negotiation. Either we do this my way, or we don't do this at all. And you can figure out how to find your own way out of this country and back to your premiere in the next twenty-four hours.

She pales. Her entire body stiffens. Then, "Jerkwaffle," I hear as she mutters under her breath.

"What's that?" I drawl.

"Nothing." She covers her mouth and pretends to cough. "I was just clearing my throat, that's all."

My lips twitch and I swallow the chuckle that wells up. Can't remember the last time I was this entertained.

"So, what's your answer?" I roll my shoulders. "I'm running out of time, Angel. Yes or no?"

Her eyes flash and color smears her cheeks. She draws in a breath, then tips up her chin. "I'll do it, on one condition." A sly look comes into her eyes. "I want a real proposal."

12

Jeanne

Hello! What's that all about? What are you saying? You want him to propose? Where did that come from? This is a fake marriage. He doesn't want to marry you. He has no feelings for you. All of this is a ruse to pacify his brothers, so what's this business about having him propose to me? Is it some romantic notion that I can't get rid of? After all, this is the first time I'm getting married.

To be fair, I've never given the idea of marriage much thought. I've been too focused on my career. I hoped, at some point, I'd meet someone, and that person would fall for me as much as I'd be in love with him, and then we'd get married. And some part of me had been sure that when that happened, it would be for keeps. Instead, I've ended up with a Mafia guy who's proposing some harebrained scheme where we pretend to be joined in matrimony to fool his family. Something I'm not entirely comfortable with, to be honest. But if this is the only way for me to get back to Palermo in time for the premiere of my musical, then so be it. No reason why I can't milk the occasion, right?

"You want me to propose to you?" He pauses half-way to plopping a chip in his mouth.

"That's what I said." I snatch the chip from his fingers and crunch down on it. *Let's see you try to wriggle out of this one, buster.*

"As in, the kind of thing with a ring and stuff?"

"If we're going to get married, we need to make it look genuine so that your brothers buy it, so yeah, absolutely, that means having a ring and stuff."

He pales. The tendons of his throat move as he swallows. "You mean, I have to buy you a ring?"

I nod. "And you'll have to go down on your knee, and we'll have to make sure there's a photographer on hand to capture the moment so we can share it with your family as proof."

"No fucking way."

"Yes, f'ing way, *baby*." I reach for another chip, the last one in the packet, and bring it to my mouth, then pause. "Considering we are going to get married, here, you can have the last chip, as a show of good faith." I hold it out to him and he glances at it with suspicion.

"No thanks." He scowls at it as if he'd like to snatch it from my fingers and throw it on the ground, then jump on it.

"Come on, since we're now a couple, it's normal for us to show such acts of love to one another."

All remaining color drains from his face. "Wh-who said anything about *love*?" He says the last word as if it's a disease.

"It's normal. If we're going to convince your family that our marriage is not a sham, we'll have to pretend that we're in love, which means we'll have to indulge in romantic gestures."

"Romantic gestures?" He screws up his face. "What does that involve?"

"You know, like holding hands, gazing into each other's eyes, kissing on the cheek—"

"The only thing you're going to be holding is my cock in your hand; the only thing I'm going to gaze at is your pussy, to ensure you're suitably wet before penetration; the only thing you are going to kiss is—"

I hold up my hand. "I get the picture. And just so we're clear, none of what you just outlined is going to happen."

"And none of what you outlined is going to happen, either," he shoots back.

"Fine," I snap.

"Fine." He smirks. "Besides, you already came on my tongue, remember?"

My cheeks heat.

"I did stop before I fucked you," he points out.

I draw in a breath. "I meant to thank you for that."

"You can thank me for it by dispensing with this romantic nonsense you've come up with." He rolls his shoulders.

"*You* are going to thank *me* for it." I fold my arms across my chest. "You want to convince your family that you found yourself a wife, then we have to do this the right way."

"The only way I want to do it is with you bent over the bed, exposing your sweet little ass, so I can be the first to take it."

A-n-d Elle Woods was onto something when she declared all masturbatory emissions, where his sperm was clearly not seeking an egg, could be termed reckless abandonment. *You have no idea, Elle, no idea at all.*

"Is that all you think about?" I throw up my hands.

"You mean fucking? Do I have to answer that?" The look on his face is almost comical in its earnestness.

I blow out a breath. "We're going to have to work on your romantic manner, just so you know."

"Balls to romance."

"The balls come after the romance, actually." I snicker.

"Not when you prance in naked on a man you barely know in the shower," he points out.

I have the grace to blush. "I was pissed off, okay? The gentlemanly thing to do would have been to let me use the bathroom first."

"I am no gentleman." He scratches his chin. His fingernails rasp over the rough hair of his beard and the sound chafes my already sensitized nerve-endings. My nipples pebble, a pulse flares to life between my legs, and I'm ashamed to say, moisture laces my core. This is ridiculous. Am I so tuned into him that his every gesture draws a response from me? On the physical level; only on the physical level. The man is a complete asshole, and a criminal, to boot. No way am I going to get emotionally entangled with the likes of him.

"No kidding. You're so far from being a gentleman that if you said or did anything halfway chivalrous, I'd probably topple over dead."

"Don't do that. I'm going to need you alive and in good health, just until we get through this pretense."

"Gee, thanks." I crumple up the empty chip wrapper and throw it at him. He snatches it out of thin air, shoots it at the waste basket near the wall, and does he miss? Of course not.

"So, you're on for the wedding then?"

"The fake wedding, and only if you get me a ring," I retort.

"Done, but I have a condition of my own."

"Umm, do I want to hear it?" I scrutinize his features.

"Probably not." His eyes gleam. "But I'm going to tell it to you anyway."

"You're going to ask to consummate the marriage."

"How did you guess?" He has the gall to look surprised.

"Do I look stupid to you? Besides, your intentions are written all over your face."

"You want a ring, you want to make the marriage look real, you want me to wheel out the entire romantic nonsense... It's only fair that we have sex."

"It's not the same thing," I shoot back. "I was suggesting ways to provide evidence the relationship is real."

"What could be more real than us banging?"

I wince. "Your vocabulary really does need refining."

"And your romantic sentiments need pruning," he retorts.

"No sex." I scowl.

He looks at me like I just told him he could never masturbate again. "Yes, sex. Without it, they'll be able to tell right away that the marriage is a sham."

"How is that possible?" I throw up my hands. "No one can tell if we've been sleeping together except you and me."

"You don't know my brothers. Don't forget we're the Mafia. If they couldn't tell who's fucking whom, they'd never have been able to survive this far."

"You make them sound like gossiping busybodies," I scoff.

"They are observant." He raises a shoulder. "You have to be to avoid being killed."

Goosebumps pop on my skin. He talks about death so casually, like he faces it every day, which he probably does. How does one face the other side of life so frequently, and yet be so casual about it? Or maybe that's why he doesn't give it undue importance. Because he's so conversant with it, he understands, sooner or later, all of us have to meet our maker.

"What are you thinking?" He scrutinizes my features. "Is it because I spoke about being killed?"

"No. Yes." I shake my head. "It doesn't matter."

"Sure it matters. If we want to, as you say, put on a show that's genuine enough to convince my family, then we need to get to know each other."

"Somehow, I regret suggesting that now," I murmur under my breath.

"So, we're doing this, aren't we? Pretending to be married, including the entire 'romance'—" he air quotes the last word, "and of course, the sex that comes with it?"

"I never agreed to the sex," I protest.

"But you do agree that without fucking each other, this marriage will be a sham."

I raise my gaze heavenward. "I knew I shouldn't have brought that up."

"What do you have to lose? If nothing else, you'll get lots of orgasms out of this arrangement, that much I can promise."

"I don't just jump into bed with strangers."

"We've seen each other without clothes on, we're sharing a bed, hell, we're even having a reasonable conversation here. We're well past the 'being strangers' phase."

Sadly, he's right about that.

"I can't agree to the sex. It feels too cold and calculating. Too transactional," I declare.

"Sex with me is anything but cold, I promise."

My stomach flutters, and a slow beat flares to life between my legs. Tingles squeeze up my chest, and all of a sudden, my skin feels too tight for my body. "Doesn't change the fact that, technically, we'd only be sleeping with each other to bring veracity to our relationship," I manage to reply.

"So?"

"So, it's not natural or organic."

He draws in a breath and his massive shoulders flex. "Woman, you are driving me crazy."

"That has been known to happen. Never said being with me was going to be easy."

"No shit." He brings his fingertips together. "So let me get this right. The only reason you won't sleep with me is because we didn't meet in a more normal course of events."

"Something like that," I agree.

"So, what if we let things take their normal course and see where it goes?"

"You mean, we just—"

"Allow the chemistry between us to dictate what happens next."

13

Luca

"You'd do that?" She searches my features as if she doesn't quite believe what I said. For that matter, I can't believe I suggested it, either. Let things take their natural course? Allow our chemistry to dictate where this relationship goes? Is that me speaking? The man who thrives on exhibitionism, who fucks any woman he wants. But then, no woman has ever hesitated at the thought of sleeping with me, either.

"You're going to marry me, aren't you?"

She nods slowly.

"Let's take the rest as it comes. Just remember..." I narrow my gaze on her. "It's you who'll have to make the next move. It's you who'll beg me to fuck you, and I promise you will, and when you do, I won't stop until you've orgasmed ten times in a row."

"Ten times?" She scoffs. "If you can get me off once, it'll be a bonus."

"You doubt me?"

"Actually, it's myself I doubt."

"Wait, what?" I sit up. "Are you saying that you've never climaxed during sex?"

"That's not what I said."

"That's what you alluded to."

"Well, it's not true." She glances to the side, then at me again.

"Isn't it?" I scan her features. "There's no shame in admitting that you haven't climaxed while being fucked."

"Shh." She glances at the walls. "I don't exactly want that to be publicized."

"So, it's true then?"

Her features flush. She folds her arms about her waist, and her towel inches down. "You don't have to act so surprised. Not every woman climaxes during intercourse."

"Only those who've never been with the right man." I flex my fingers. "Don't forget, I made you orgasm in the shower, and that was just with my tongue. When I fuck you—and you will ask me to fuck you—I promise I'll bring you to fulfillment so often and for so long that you'll be punch drunk on endorphins. I'll give you so much pleasure that you'll forget your own name. I'll fuck you so hard and so thoroughly that you won't be able to feel your own body, you won't be able to walk, and if you do, it will be with the imprint of my cock inside your cunt. I'll make you come with so much intensity that you'll forget every other guy you've ever been with and not want to be with anyone else but me ever again."

Her shoulders rise and fall. Her lips are parted, and her cheeks so pink, if I touch them, I'm sure I'll be seared. If I graze my fingertips over her arm, we'll both combust. If I breathe in her direction, I'm likely to leap across the bed and tackle her into the mattress and push her legs apart and make a meal of the soft flesh between her legs, before I bury myself inside her beautiful, tight cunt.

All of which goes to show, my earlier suggestion was made in haste. I'm going to repent for it every single moment that we're together, and even when we're not, thoughts of her are going to crawl into my gut and urge me to throw her down and fuck her the next time I see her. Damn, why couldn't I simply seduce her and be done with it? *Because this is my chance to redeem myself in the eyes of my family.*

I've always been the one with the chip on his shoulder. The second oldest legal heir to my father, with no prospect of ever becoming the Don. I've always known Michael would take over from my father, that the most I'd ever rise within the *Cosa Nostra* was to become *Capo*. And even that had been taken from me because I'd helped Karma, Michael's wife, escape when he had first kidnapped her. Michael had been pissed off at me, and when he took over as Don, he gave the title of *Capo* to Seb. Luckily, Seb met Elsa and decided to look beyond the *Cosa Nostra* to pursue his dream of a media company, and that meant I could take over as *Capo*. A title I'm grateful to own.

I've caused too much angst for my family, and while I wouldn't get married just to fulfill Nonna's wish... I know by doing so, I'll show Michael I'm ready to make amends and step into my role within the *famiglia*. It's the only reason I'm not turning up my charm and seducing her, but instead, allowing her to come to me, when she's ready. And she will be. No one has withstood my magnetism for any length of time. It won't be long before she crawls back to me and asks me to fuck her, and then... I'll oblige her, of course, but not before she pays for making me wait.

"I'll take it as my personal challenge." I turn over on my side, fold my arms and close my eyes. Taking a deep breath, another. And count one, two, three—

"What are you playing at?" she bursts out. "You can't just say those words, then turn over and pretend to sleep."

"No pretending. I'm tired and want to sleep."

"Not after you threw those words at me, buster."

"Why? Did they turn you on?" I allow a smile to curl my lips. "Remember, all you have to do is say the word and—"

"No, thank you."

The mattress shifts as she lays back against her pillow. There's silence for a few seconds. How long can she go without talking, I wonder? The mattress moves again as she turns over and tugs on the cover, yanking it toward her. I grab it at my end and hold on. She tries to pull the duvet in her direction, fails, lets out a breath. I yank on the sheets and they slide my way.

She yelps, "Hey, you're hogging the covers."

"I'm a big man."

"I'm cold."

"Come closer and I'll warm you."

She makes a noise deep in her throat. I can't stop the chuckle that wells up. I swallow it down, wait... wait... She slides closer under the sheets and toward me. The scent of her body envelops me. I draw it deep within my lungs. My groin hardens, and a warm sensation coils in my chest. It sinks into my blood, envelops me, and arrows straight to my balls. My cock elongates further. I glance down to find the sheet tented. *Gesü Cristo*, how the fuck am I supposed to sleep while sporting a hard-on? My fingers itch and my palm tingles. *Surely, you're not thinking of that. You can't get yourself off; not with her sleeping next to you.*

She makes a soft, breathy sound, and fuck me, my entire body tenses. My shoulder muscles are wound so tightly, they hurt. Just a touch; it won't do any harm. It'll help me sleep. And I need to sleep so I'm alert tomorrow and can take us both back to Palermo.

I reach for the towel I discarded on my nightstand and slide it under the cover and over my fully erect cock. I slide my fingers down my chest until I encounter the object of my discomfort. Finally, fuck. I wrap my fingers around my cock and begin to massage myself.

Next to me, she wriggles around, trying to make herself more comfortable. I freeze again. *This is crazy. Am I really going to jerk myself off to thoughts of the woman who's sleeping next to me?* If I were looking in on this scene, I'd call myself a loser. Which I am not. I'm merely taking matters into my own hand, literally. I smirk. I promised her I'd let things take their natural course, so I can't exactly cover her body with mine and slide into that hot, wet, juicy pussy of hers—fuck me, why am I thinking of her pussy? Her swollen cunt. The moisture that would lace her inner walls as I thrust into her with long, hard strokes that would draw cries of pleasure, whimpers of appreciation, and screams of surprise as I fucked her toward her climax.

I begin to tug on my cock in earnest, trying to stay quiet. Flicks of my wrist as I squeeze, tug, pull and fuck my own hand.

Next to me, I hear her breath catch. But she doesn't move. She's so still, I'm sure she's asleep. She must be, right? I increase the pace of my movements. Up, down, up. The blood drains to my groin, and a shudder radiates out from where I'm fucking myself in earnest. My thighs harden and my balls tighten. I speed up even more, still under the covers, under the towel. A growl rises up my throat; I swallow it. My muscles coil; every part of my body hurts, and my cells feel like they're going to self-combust at any moment.

I picture her big golden eyes staring up at me, pupils dilated, lips parted. Her gorgeous breasts heave, those ripe nipples large and pink. I bend down, wrap my lips around one of them and tug. She groans, digs her fingernails into my shoulders with such force I feel the pain all the way down to the tip of my cock. I gaze into her eyes deeply as my shaft distends, bite down on my lower lip as I come. I keep coming and coming. I come so hard, I see stars. I swear, I almost black out. *Che cazzo!* That was the most spectacular orgasm of my life, and I'm not even inside her yet. I am so fucking screwed.

I hear a noise. Was that a moan? I manage to crack open my eyelids and peer sideways at her, but her back is to me and she's still. Was it my imagination? Probably.

Keeping an eye on her profile, I wipe myself with the towel, before pulling it out from under the sheet and throwing it to the floor. Even before I sink back into the pillow, I'm asleep.

When I snap my eyes open, it's dark. I turn on my back, reach for her side of the bed to find it's empty. *"Cazzo!"* I jump out of bed, pull on my pants and my boots, then race out of the room and down the flight of steps. I'd been so sure she wouldn't leave. How could I have trusted her so implicitly? Was I so taken in by her innocence, and my attraction to her, I was sure she wouldn't run when she got the first chance? And what if they find her before me? What if the men who kidnapped her track her down again? What if they hurt her? I'll never forgive myself. This is the last time I'll be taken in by a gorgeous face and a beautiful smile. This is the last time I decide to be patient. I should have fucked her into a coma and then tied her to my side. That way, she'd never have been able to leave me. I burst into the pub downstairs and come to a stop.

"What are you doing?"

14

Jeanne

"What does it look like?"

I bring the glass of wine to my lips and sip from it. The bartender opposite me jerks his head around to watch Luca's approach. His features grow wary.

Luca comes to a halt next to me. Anger vibrates off of him. I shoot him a sideways glance, then wish I hadn't. The man's not wearing a shirt, revealing the expanse of that sculpted six-, no, eight pack of his.

Once more, I take in the tattoo that covers one arm from wrist to elbow. Then, because I can't help myself, I reach over and touch the raised skin. The muscles under his skin undulate. A hot melting sensation coils in my belly. It's like touching a dangerous predator. And oh, god, it's the most erotic thing I've ever done. Almost as erotic as hearing the sounds of the alphahole jerking off next to me, no doubt, thinking of me.

I know he was thinking of me, for he groaned my name as he came. I could feel him come and come, his muscles coiled with so much tension, I could feel the release all the way down to my core. And the heat from his body... OMG, it was like someone opened the door to a sauna and I received a full blast. I squeezed my thighs together, locked my fingers under the sheet, and pushed my heel into my pussy. Not that it helped.

A bead of sweat slid down my throat, and for all that, I hadn't even physically exerted myself. I sensed the bed move, heard the whisper of fabric, and realized he'd thrown the towel onto the floor. The towel he'd jerked off to while thinking of me. While imagining my body. While visualizing what he would do to me. Dirty, filthy, racy thoughts, no doubt.

Moisture coated my core and slid down between my thighs. But I didn't move. I stayed that way, clenching that ball of arousal that had grown bigger and tauter and tighter in my lower belly. When I was finally sure he was asleep, I crept out of bed. I'm not ashamed to say I rubbed one out in the bathroom. It helped, but not by much.

Still dissatisfied, and with a gnawing emptiness crawling between my legs, I dressed, all the while, refusing to take in the massive figure sprawled under the covers. If I did, I'd probably jump him and beg him to fuck me, and no way was I going to lower myself to that level. I crept down to the bar, and found a sole bartender shutting things down. Luckily, he was happy enough to serve me. Thank god. At least the alcohol helped dim the sharpness of my need... Somewhat.

He jerks his chin at the bartender, who retreats to the other side of the bar and out of earshot.

"Did it hurt?" I point at the ink.

He raises a shoulder.

"Why get the tattoos?"

"Why did you become an actress?"

Touché. I lower my hand to my side. "It's easier to pretend to be someone else than to be myself."

He holds my gaze. "It's a reminder."

"Of what?"

"Something I'll never allow myself to forget. This—" He raises his arm. "It's part of my penance."

I'd caught a glimpse of the design when he'd been working out, of course, and later, when he was in the shower, but this—a full-frontal view of his body is next level gorgeous. It lends him a lethal air and brings home exactly what he is. A dangerous Mafioso who is nothing like the suave characters I've seen on screen. This man is untamed, unpredictable, and by the looks of it, very angry. His shoulders are bunched. His jaw is clenched so tightly, the veins of his throat pop in relief.

"What penance? What will you never allow yourself to forget?" I ask.

"What the fuck are you doing down here?" he growls back.

Answer a question with a question? Typical. "If you don't want to answer the question, you only have to say so. No need to get all huffy about it."

"Answer. The. Question." He lowers his voice to a hush, and my nerve-endings spark. Something inside me wants to do as he commands. Wants to please him and give him what he wants. It's only an answer to a question. It doesn't mean anything if I obey him on this. I firm my lips.

"I woke up and was thirsty. I came down to find Vincent, here, closing up the place. He offered me a glass of wine."

The tension pouring off his body multiplies by a factor of one hundred. When he speaks, his voice is tight with suppressed rage. "There's water in the room."

"I needed something stronger," I shoot back.

He glances at the glass of wine I have my fingers wrapped around, then reaches down and takes it from me. He drains it, then makes a face. "What the fuck was that?"

"A rosé." I bite the inside of my cheek to stop myself from curving my lips in a smile.

"Figures," He scrunches up his face and signals the bartender, who moves to stand in front of us.

"A pint of Peroni," he snaps.

"We only have Stella," the man replies.

"Figures, only the Brits would pass off that swill as beer." He leans forward and grabs the edge of the bar with his big hand. "Do you have Grappa?"

"We have tequila."

Luca cuts the air with the palm of his hand. "Whisky, neat. Jameson?"

The man nods, then turns to grab the brown colored bottle from the shelf behind him.

Luca wraps his fingers around the nape of my neck and thrusts his face into mine.

"If you leave my sight again, I'll turn you over my lap and spank you, *capiche?*"

I dart my gaze to the bartender, who's moved to the other end of the counter and is busy pouring the whiskey into a tumbler.

"I don't need your permission," I hiss.

"You do. We're going to be married, or have you forgotten?"

"Why do you think I'm at a bar at two a.m. chugging down alcohol? It's not because I am all agog with happiness, you lummox," I snarl.

"That another of your schoolgirl insults?" He smirks.

"I was taught to be polite, you ass-clown, unlike some gangsters I know."

"So, you decide to use words which are an insult to be called insults?"

"Oh, my god!" I whisper-yell. "You're getting on my nerves."

"Oh, I'm getting on your nerves? You're so innocent, you don't realize the danger you're in."

"I'm in more danger from you than anything else in the vicinity, you numbskull."

"Numbskull?" He blinks, then his lips twitch. "Did you call me a numbskull?"

"Yes, I did." Pathetic, I know. But I'm running through my limited repertoire of rude names at an alarming pace.

We stare at each other, then he chuckles. The sound is rich, warm, and so masculine, a burst of need sparks to life deep in my belly. I can't take my gaze off of the curve of his lips, the tiny lines that deepen at the corners of his eyes, the flash of pearly white teeth, the heavy darkness of his eyelashes, which are so thick that they should look feminine, but instead, they only add to the overwhelming feeling of heaviness, thickness, larger-than-lifeness that is this man. This mobster. This villain. This anti-hero. The kind of man I'd never thought I'd run into.

He leans in closer, until his eyes are poised in front of mine, until his nose almost brushes mine, until his mouth is so close to mine that his breath brushes my skin. A thousand goosebumps seem to pepper my skin all at once.

"Angel," he breathes.

"Luca," I murmur at the same time.

Something shimmers in the air between us, and the goosebumps seem to multiply until every inch of my body is ablaze with a strange writhing need to close the distance between us. To rub myself up against that hard chest. To brush my cheek against his and feel the roughness of his whiskers abrade my skin. To lick him from top to bottom, then bury my face in that delicious hollow between his chin and his chest.

The bartender clears his throat. "Your whiskey."

I jump, try to pull back, but Luca doesn't release the hold on the nape of my neck. I glance sideways at the bartender, who looks between us with a frown on his face.

"Leave," Luca snaps without taking his gaze from my face.

Vincent pales. He opens his mouth as if to say something, and Luca holds up his free hand.

"Out," he says in a voice that whips across the room.

Vincent swallows, but he doesn't move away. He glances at me with a worried expression on his face. I appreciate his concern, but if he stays here, jerkhole, here, is sure to beat him up, and I don't want him getting hurt for no fault of his own. I nod and half-smile at him, trying to convey that I am fine.

He hesitates, then finally nods and backs away. A door bangs shut somewhere near the back, indicating he's left the building. Then, that sound, too, fades away, and I realize I'm alone. With a very angry Mafia guy. In a bar in the middle of nowhere.

"There are other people in the rooms above the pub."

"Nope," he makes a popping sound with the last syllable of the word. "There's only one room taken—ours."

"Oh," I gulp.

"Why? Are you scared of being alone with me?"

"Oh, pfft," I raise a hand to brush the hair back from my forehead, and of course, my fingers tremble.

"I... I'm not scared of you. I was alone in the room earlier with you."

"That was different."

"How?"

"You hadn't disobeyed me then."

"You didn't tell me not to leave the room."

"It was understood." The lines radiating from the corners of his eyes deepen further.

"How? I'm not a mind reader."

"You knew if I woke up and found you gone, I'd think you escaped."

"Escaped? So now I'm your prisoner?" I prop my hands on my hips. "Where would I go, anyway? I couldn't sleep. Also, your snoring was driving me up the wall so—"

"I don't snore." His forehead furrows.

"Yes, you do."

"I must have been very tired," he murmurs. He rubs his thumb across my throat, and tendrils of heat emanate from his touch.

"What are you doing?" I clear my throat. "No hanky-panky stuff, okay?"

"Your vocabulary is very strange, Angel."

"Don't call me that."

"You haven't told me your name yet."

"And I don't intend to either." I jut out my lower lip and his gaze lowers to my mouth.

"Is that a challenge?"

"It's my intention."

"And what will you give me if I get you tell me your name in the next five minutes?"

"Nothing, because I'm not—"

He moves so quickly, I yelp. He releases his hold on my neck, only to grab my waist, lower my feet to the ground, then push me into the bar counter so I grip it to support myself. He grabs the waist-band of my yoga pants—which is what I was wearing when those idiots kidnapped me—and shoves it down my hips, along with my panties.

"What the—! What are you doing, you—?" His palm connects with my backside with enough force that I rock up to my toes. I yell. A blistering line of heat sizzles across my butt. "Stop that, why are you—?" I huff, as he spanks my other ass cheek with the same force. A tremor cuts straight to my core, my pussy clenches, my nipples stiffen, and my breasts seem to swell. He brings that wide palm down on my first cheek, then in rapid succession, spanks me on alternating cheeks. Slap-slap-slap. Each one reverberates up my spin, down around my breasts, then arrows to my core.

"Stop that." I try to wriggle away, but alphahole here, once again, wraps his fingers around the nape of my neck. He squeezes, and it's as if there's a direct line to my center, for my pussy clenches. I squeeze my thighs together and he clicks his tongue. "You know, I'm not going to let you come; not until you tell me your name."

"Go to hell," I spit out.

"You shouldn't have said that." He brings his palm down on the curve of my behind with such force that my entire body shudders. Pinpricks of pain sizzle up my spine, down my thighs, and pour into my lower belly. He massages the burning flesh of my backside. I gasp. He rubs the pain into my skin and my core contracts.

"Oh, god. Oh, my god." I dig my teeth into the wooden edge of the bar counter to stop myself from crying out.

"You going to tell me your name yet?"

I shake my head.

I sense him draw in a breath, and close my eyes and brace myself for the next slap, which never comes. Instead, he straightens. He moves around to stand behind me, and the heat from his body covers my back-side. The pain pulses out from where he's spanked my ass. I wait. Wait for him to make his next move, then groan when he bends over and licks the nape of my neck.

"You taste so fucking sweet and spicy at the same time. I can't wait to taste your cunt again."

He straightens again, then kicks my feet apart. I yelp, then gasp when he slides his tongue along my seam.

"You're fucking soaked," he growls. The vibrations from his words swirl along my inflamed clit, then sink into my center. A trembling begins from somewhere deep inside. I sense him smile against my pussy. "You will not come, Angel, not until I give you permission."

I'm not going to listen to that. I'm not going to obey this... this... sadist. There's no other way to describe him, and yes, I know that word, as I know other swear words. I just refuse to say them aloud.

"You going to tell me your name?"

I draw in a breath.

The silence stretches for a beat, then another.

"Very well then," he rumbles against my melting core. He swipes his tongue up my slit, and my entire body shudders. He licks my seam and curls his tongue around my clit. My stomach clenches. My breasts distend until they seem too heavy for my body. I dig my feet into the floor for purchase as he slurps at my cunt. He nibbles on my pussy lips and my eyes roll back in my head. The trembling at the base of my belly intensifies. Oh, god, oh, god, I'm going to c—

He pulls back.

I push my butt back, chasing his tongue for the feel of that warm wet lave across the most aching, swollen part of me.

The orgasm begins to fade and I snap my jaws together.

"You going to tell me your name?"

"No, I will not, you imbecile, you rascal, you—"

He pushes his face into my pussy and stabs his tongue inside my sopping wet channel.

"Oh, my god! Please, don't stop. Please, don't stop."

He slides his fingers around to play with my pussy lips, then grinds the heel of his palm into my clit. My head spins. What feels likes a fountain of sensation ripples over my skin. The swirling tension at the base of my spine tightens, folds into itself, gets tighter, tauter, knotting into a hard ball of desire that thrums and throbs and— "Please, let me come, please," I cry out. "Please, Luca."

"Your name?"

I hesitate.

He pinches my clit, and that ball of heat pulsates and grows and quivers and vibrates. He thrusts his tongue inside my channel and sweat breaks out at my hairline. A chill grips my skin, even as the heat in my lower belly begins to pulse in tandem with the beating of my heart. The blood pounds at my temples and I curve my back. Close, I'm so close.

"Your na—"

"Jeanne," I yell, "it's Jeanne. Now let me come already."

"Your wish is my command."

He begins to lick and suck and eat me out in earnest, as he circles my clit with his fingers and stimulates the swollen bud. He brings his other hand up to grasp my breast and squeeze. He tweaks my nipple at the same time he pinches my clit, and the vibrations zing out from my core.

He pulls his tongue out from my pussy, rises to his feet, and slaps my already sore backside. *Thwack-thwack-thwack.* The pain pours into my blood, the heat from the contact sizzles straight to my cunt, and the ball of desire explodes.

"Come," he orders, and I throw my head back and shatter.

15

Luca

After she came, I pulled up her pants, then hauled her into my arms and kissed her until she slumped. I carried her up to our room and put her to bed. Then, I sat in the chair near the bed, content to watch her as she sleeps.

Her cheeks are flushed, and she's so still I've leaned over a few times and placed my finger under her nose, just to make sure she's breathing. When was the last time I was so concerned about another person? I wasn't close to my mother. Even as a young child, I understood she was weak, that she couldn't withstand the abuse my father doled out. I wanted to help, but didn't know what to do about it.

My father was too distant, and I was wary of him. Michael? I suppose I adored my older brother, but when he left for university and didn't take me with him, I was angry with him. Then, my father turned the wrath of his anger on me and Seb, and all I could focus on was trying to survive the daily beatings. Nonna was around, but she did little to stop it. That's when I lost respect for her. Oh, I loved her; she was the only constant caregiver in my life. But she never stepped in to protect me, and that changed the dynamics of the relationship for me.

As I grew, so did my anger, and I channeled it into my hate for my father, envy for my oldest brother, and my need for power. Until I met her. She's strong, feisty, and can hold her own against me, yet there's a core of her that's so innocent, I want to protect her; so pure, I want to sully her; so... confident, it's a clarion call to break her down and put her back together in a way that assures I've put my mark on her.

The phone in my hand vibrates, I take in the message on the screen.

Downstairs.

I rise to my feet, pull the cover up under her chin, then let myself out of the room. After calling my brothers, I expected help to arrive. Just not this soon. I shut the door behind me softly. Then, buttoning my shirt, I walk down the stairs and into the pub. I glance at the counter, remembering how she fell apart under my fingers and my tongue just a few hours ago. Awareness buzzes under my skin, and I tear my gaze away from the bar and toward the woman who rises up from the chair at the far end of the pub.

I draw closer and she holds out a hand. "Luca? I am Karina Beauchamp."

I shake her hand. "You're Axel's friend?"

"We've collaborated on projects in the past. I run my own security agency, based out of LA and London. When Axel started his own security agency, he approached me for help. We've been in touch since. So, when one of his brothers needed help—"

"He asked you to swing by." I prop my palms on my hips.

"You can trust me." One side of her lips kicks up in a smile. "My brother is Nikolai Solonik."

I stiffen. "The head of the Bratva?"

"The very same. He's one of your allies now, I believe."

"I still wouldn't trust him, so if that was meant to be reassuring—"

She laughs. "It was meant to show that I understand what you're dealing with here."

She grabs a paper bag I hadn't noticed before and hands it over. "That has clothes for the two of you, as well as money, passports, and everything else you need to leave the country."

I peer into the bag and spot the passports. "That was quick."

"You're Axel's brother." She pulls out a phone and holds it out. "It's a burner; no one can trace you through it."

I accept it. "Thanks." Then a thought strikes me. "How did you get into the pub? Weren't the doors locked?"

She laughs. "I have my ways."

"Karina?" A man walks into the pub through the front door. "There you are." He walks over to her, wraps his arm around her, and pulls her close. The two kiss and keep kissing.

"We do have rooms upstairs," I point out.

Neither of the two heed me.

Gesù Cristo, all this loving in the air; it's nauseating.

"Thanks for your help." At least my disgust doesn't show in my tone; that's something.

I turn to leave when Karina calls out, "Sorry, Arpad and I haven't seen each other for nearly two hours." Her tone is self-deprecating. "Hence—"

I pause, then turn to face him. "You're Arpad Beauchamp, one of the Seven who own 7A Investments?"

"Have you invested with us?" He scans my features. "Have we met before?"

"I don't think so." I turn to Karina. "Appreciate your coming through for us."

"If there's anything else I can help with…"

I hesitate.

"You can tell us. Any friend of Karina's has my full support," Arpad chimes in.

Not sure he'd be saying that if he knew the identity of my father. I shove that thought aside.

"We need to return to Palermo as quickly as possible and without attracting any attention."

"So commercial flights are out?" Karina narrows her gaze on me. "Whoever is after you—"

"Why do you assume someone's after us?"

She glances around the pub. "You're in a room above a pub, just far enough from any town that it's a deterrent to tracking you down, there are blood specks on your shirt—" I glance down at my sleeve and spot the drops of red. She continues, "And your brother just asked me to issue you fake passports." She arches an eyebrow. "Also, the woman standing behind you doesn't seem too happy with you. Not that it's connected to your question, but thought you should be aware."

I pivot around as Jeanne approaches us. She draws abreast and levels a look filled with curiosity at the couple. "Everything okay?" she asks.

"Everything's fine." I put an arm around her and pull her close. To my surprise, she melts into my side.

"And you are—" Jeanne prompts.

"Karina, and this is my husband, Arpad." The couple shake hands with her.

"Karina is a friend of my brother, Axel. She runs a security agency in London and has given us everything we need to leave the country." I raise the paper bag.

She glances at it, then at my face. "So, we can return to Palermo?"

"We can have a private plane fueled and ready for take-off from an airfield an hour away," Arpad adds.

"Or, you could first come to our place and freshen up." Karina glances between us. "When Axel called me and explained you needed help, we were at Arpad's country house, which is a forty-five-minute drive away. You're welcome to return with us and get some rest before you leave."

"It sounds like an improvement over the room we're in, but I want to return to Palermo. The faster I can get back to my rehearsals, the more confident I'll be for the premiere of my musical."

"You're an actress?" Karina glances at her with interest.

"A jazz dancer, actually, but when this opportunity came up, I couldn't refuse."

"Which musical are you starring in?" Karina asks.

"*Beauty and the Beast*. Have you seen it?"

"On Broadway, a few years back. Will you be touring the West End?"

"Maybe. If the response from the audience is good enough." Jeanne smiles. "Thank you so much for your help, Karina." She grips Karina's hand. "I truly appreciate it."

"Let me know when you're in London next." Karina gestures to the phone in my hand. "My numbers are keyed-in."

True to their word, the Beauchamps drive us to the airfield, and we are on Arpad's private plane and airborne within the hour. Before we get on the flight, I destroy the phone and SIM card I'd purchased at the service station as a precaution.

Now, I lean back in the plush seat and stretch my arms above my head. Next to me, Jeanne glances out of the window. It's still dark outside, but a silvery hue lights up the horizon.

"You okay?" I ask.

"I'm tired." She leans back into the chair with a sigh. "You do realize, this is going to spoil me for flying economy now."

"You won't need to again. Once you're my wife, we can use the Sovranos' private jet whenever you have to travel."

She stills. "So, you still want to go ahead with the whole marriage thing?"

"Why would you think otherwise?"

"Now that we are safe and on our way back, I just thought—"

"That I'd forget about the deal we made?"

"Something like that." She smooths her palms over her jeans. "You could find so many other women who'd be interested in playing the role of your wife. Why does it have to be me?"

"Because you owe me."

She whips her head in my direction. "So that's what this is about? That's why you offered to find a way to bring me back in time for my premiere, so you could use it against me?"

"When you hold something over a person, you have power."

"And power is the most important thing to you?"

"Yes." I hold her gaze. "My entire life, all I've ever wanted is to be the person who holds power over everyone else in the room. I want to be the person who never has to bow my head in front of anyone."

"Yet, you didn't have a choice but to accept help from Karina and Arpad."

"And I owe them, and will make sure I return the favor when they need it most."

"So that's how you build your connections? By this constant give and take?" She scowls.

"That's my life."

"It's transactional," she huffs.

"It's black and white. Makes it simple. Ensures I never find myself again in situations where I am not in control."

"Again? You've been in situations where you are not in control before?" She searches my features.

"If you're asking whether I've been in love, then the answer is a no."

"But you *have* been in an emotionally messy situation?"

"That's none of your business," I retort.

Her face falls. She purses her lips and glances away. A hot sensation hooks into my chest. I know I've hurt her, but that's for the best. The last thing I want is to open up more to her or keep up the flirty banter, which I admit, came as a surprise. I'm not into emotions, and definitely not into romantic overtures. I've been acting out of character. It's probably the surprise of being kidnapped, then waking up in a cell and finding myself alone with her that's responsible for it. It's going to make the situation more complicated. It's best to keep this entire arrangement straightforward by not bringing feelings into it.

"You do realize, if we have to pretend to be getting married, then we have to show some level of intimacy with each other," she says in a low voice.

"That's why I gave you those orgasms at the bar. Now, we're both comfortable with each other physically. Enough that no one will suspect we only met a few days ago."

"That's no replacement for showing we have an emotional connection."

"Well, we don't and we never will."

16

Jeanne

What the—? Did he just say that? And just when I thought we were actually beginning to get along. There in that bar, when he pushed me over the counter and proceeded to make me orgasm, I wasn't even resentful that I told him my name. The way he played my body, like Elle Woods had played with Emmett Richmond's emotions. And I do need to stop with the Elle Woods jokes in my head. That's what happens when you grow up with a steady diet of Elle Woods trivia as told to you by your mom, not to mention, having to watch *Legally Blonde* every Christmas. While I may have absorbed a lot of it subconsciously, it begins to wear you down after a while, know what I mean?

Also, he carried me up to the room after that orgasmfest and put me to bed. I'd been half asleep, drunk on the Os, but not so far gone that I didn't notice he tucked me in, pulled the covers over me, and kissed me on my lips, by which time I'd fallen asleep. And I agreed to marry him, so why has he gone all grouchy on me now?

"What's your problem?" I shoot him a sideways glance.

"I have no idea what you mean," he replies without opening his eyes.

"Something is the matter, else, why are you acting like a bear with a sore head?"

"Your imagination must be working overtime, Jeanne," he drawls.

"You're giving me whiplash with this on-again, off-again attitude of yours."

"No idea what you're talking about."

"You were all chummy and ready to engage in conversation in the pub, but now that we are on our way home, you seem to be pissed off with me."

He doesn't reply.

"If this is how married life with you is going to be, I'm not sure I want to go ahead with the ceremony."

"You have no choice in the matter. I came through on my promise of getting you back in time for your premiere—"

"We aren't yet back at the premiere," I remind him.

"We're almost there. Now, you need to deliver on your side of the promise."

"If I'd known you have friends who could loan us their private jet, I may not have made the deal," I confess.

His lips kick up. "Too late, baby. You're bound to me now."

"Why do I get the feeling I'm going to regret having agreed to this scheme?"

Two hours later, the plane taxis down the runway in Italy. I rise to my feet and follow him to the open door, where the stewardess and the pilot who has come over to join us, bid us goodbye. Luca ducks under the open doorway. He steps onto the small platform at the top of the short flight of steps leading to the runway and stops so suddenly that I bump into him. I grip his shirt to steady myself. "What's wrong?"

I pop my head around him and freeze.

There, at the bottom of the steps, is an entire reception committee. I count six men. Four of them have their arms around women. The other two flank the happy couples, all of whom are in various stages of PDAs. One of the couples is kissing, the other has his woman tucked into his side, the third has her in front with his arms wrapped about her shoulder and waist. The fourth hold hands. All of the couples are beaming at us. One of the single guys, the tallest and the broadest in the group, comes forward. He pauses at the bottom of the stairs and beckons.

Luca turns to face the plane.

"Hey, what's wrong?" I tip my chin up and take in his pale features.

"I think I might get on that flight and return to London."

"Go right ahead. I, on the other hand, am going to try to make today's rehearsal." I brush past him, and he thrusts out his arm so I don't have a choice but to stop. "Now what?"

"You're not going anywhere without me," he grumbles.

"Like I said, your on-off emotions are giving me a headache."

"What's going to give you more of a headache is if I tell you who's waiting at the bottom of the stairs."

"That's your family, I'm guessing?"

He nods. "Which means, we already have to act like we're in love, and I need to break the news to them about our marriage."

I pale. "Oh, crap."

"Exactly."

He places his hand on my shoulder. "You ready for this?"

I swallow. "I think I'm going to join you on that flight back to London."

"I suppose it was inevitable we'd have to face them." He draws in a deep breath, as if trying to gather his courage. "Might as well get it over with. Rip the bandage off and all that."

"Can't this wait until after the rehearsal?" I hunch my shoulders. "You know, let me just get on that stage first..."

"So you can abandon me and run away after that? Not likely."

"I have to appear in the musical every night for the next two weeks, dummy. I'm not going anywhere."

"Damn right, you're not. It's time for you to deliver on your side of the bargain."

"Fine, fine, no need to get all antsy about it." I pat his chest. His rock-hard bruiser of a chest, on which I can feel the shape of his abs through the shirt he's wearing. I press my palm against the sculpted planes, and the heat of his skin sinks into my blood. A spiral of heat swirls in my belly. My heartbeat increases in intensity.

"You ready?" he murmurs.

"For what?" I frown. I look into his eyes and spot the resolve. "What are you—"

He sweeps me up bride-style in his arms; I yelp.

"What are you up to?" I whisper-scream.

He bares his lips in the resemblance of a smile. Then tips his chin down at me. "Better get your game face on, Angel."

He swivels around, then begins to walk down the steps.

17

Luca

This is not just ripping the bandage off; it's tearing off sutures before the wound has completely healed. It's breaking the cast and yanking off the plaster before the bone has had time to set. I keep the smile—at least, I think it's a smile—firmly pasted on my face as I reach the last step and place my foot on the ground. Massimo watches me approach, a look of complete astonishment on his face.

"The fuck you staring at, *stronzo*?" I growl.

He blinks rapidly, then lowers his gaze to the woman I'm carrying in my arms. A sensation of knives stabbing into my chest assails me. An unknown emotion twists my insides.

"Eyes up here, you *coglione*!"

"What?" He snaps his gaze up to my face. "I can't look at her? Is that what you're saying?"

"Yes," I say.

"I'm Jeanne, by the way," the woman I'm carrying pipes up at the same time.

"Pleased to meet you, Jeanne." He holds out his hand. I make a low noise in the back of my throat. *What is wrong with me?* Why are my guts twisting in on themselves. Is that jealousy? Possessiveness? A combination of all those emotions that I would have never associated with myself.

Jeanne holds out her hand, but Massimo has already lowered his by then.

"Apparently, my brother has forgotten his manners, but I'd rather not risk him losing his temper and deciding he wants to shoot me," he explains.

"That's Massimo, and you can forget you ever met him." I brush past him and toward the crowd of people who are watching my progress with great interest.

I come to a pause in front of them. All of them watch me expectantly. The silence stretches for a few beats.

"You going to introduce us?" Karma finally asks.

"I can introduce myself." Jeanne struggles in my arms.

I tighten my grasp around her. "This is, ah, my wife-to-be, Jeanne…" I draw a blank. Shit, did I ask her for her surname? "Jeanne…"

"Watson," she supplies in a smooth voice.

"Jeanne Watson. We're, ah, to be married," I declare.

There's silence. Complete and utter silence. Every one of them looks at me like I have just crash-landed from the moon. Which, honestly, having heard my own words… I don't blame them for reacting this way. The magnitude of the challenge I'm about to take on sinks in.

I'm going to marry her. It's a short-term affair; not going to last long— or only as long as it takes to convince my family that our union is for real. And why didn't I put an end-date to the relationship when I had the chance? I'm acting completely out of character, but since I met her, my equilibrium has been compromised. Clearly it has to do with the knock on the head I took when that *stronzo* Freddie ambushed me. Yes, that's it. That's the only reason I scooped her up in my arms and walked down the steps, and am now introducing her to the rest of my family. It's the only reason I haven't called this entire thing off and boarded that plane back to London.

"Jeanne." Aurora, Christian's wife comes forward. "It's lovely to meet you." She holds out her hand and Jeanne shakes it. Theresa, Axel's wife and Elsa, Seb's wife, close the distance to us.

"Umm, you going to put her down?" Theresa titters. "Not that it's not romantic, but I'd like to hug my future sister-in-law and it's difficult to do so when you're holding onto her like you're afraid she's going to vanish if you let her go."

"What?" I glance down to find Jeanne looking back at me with an expression of bewilderment. One I assume is mirrored on my face. So I set her on her feet and take a step to the side. Instantly, the women cluster around her. Theresa kisses Jeanne on her cheek, Elsa throws her arms about my fiancé—um, fiancé? I try the word out on my tongue. It feels strange, and yet also, not. I watch her—or what I can glimpse of her from over the shoulders of my brother's wives. She smiles at them, returns their hugs and kisses, and replies to their greetings. She seems so at home. She seems like one of us. Only she isn't. She's someone who happened to be at the wrong place at the wrong time. Or the right place, if I'm being honest. Which I'm not. She's simply the woman who was there when I needed someone to take on the role of my wife and get my family off my back. Why is it proving to be so difficult to remember that?

"Luca." My oldest brother Michael's voice cuts through the babble of excited voices. The tension in the air spikes. The women quieten as they sense the unspoken unease that crowds the space between us.

I walk past them to where Michael stands in the center of my brothers. Tension prickles up my spine. My pulse rate increases. I've done nothing wrong, and yet, it feels like I'm being called to heel. I don't need a shrink to tell me that I have a problem with authority. Probably due to the fact that I never trusted my father, and when Michael filled in the role of an authority figure in my life, I wanted so much to please him. Only he left me. He opted to go study in LA when he turned eighteen. He left me behind. Oh, he sent for us in six months, but by then, the damage was done.

I'd grown to hate my father, hate my family, had wanted to run away—had actually run away, until my Nonna had sent men to track me down and bring me back home. And I'd hated her for that. I hadn't wanted to go to LA, but luckily for me, Nonna would hear none of it. She'd bundled all of us boys and left Italy behind, and that had been the best thing she could have done.

New school, new friends... The change in environment had done me good. I had come out of the negative headspace I'd been in and found a new lease of life. Only, my bitterness for what Michael had done never really faded away. Instead, it grew over the years into something tangible. A chip on my shoulder I could never shake off. Didn't want to shake it off. And when I realized that, as the second born, I'd never have the chance to be Don, it metastasized into the resentment I now carry around.

"Capo." He holds out his right hand in the formal gesture he uses with ranking members of our clan.

"Don." I clasp his hand, then bend and kiss the signet ring on his little finger. The first time I have done so since I took over as *Capo*.

I straighten and he pulls me toward him and wraps his arm around my shoulders. "You're safe," his voice is normal, but when I step back and look into his eyes, I spot the worry there. Huh?

"Of course I am." I try to pull away but he doesn't release me.

"And you've acquired yourself a bride?"

"It would seem so."

He looks between my eyes, apparently searching for something. *Well, whatever it is, you're not going to find any trace of emotion there.* "You can skip the show of concern. I wasn't going to die that easily."

He holds my gaze a second longer, then jerks his chin. "I had no doubt you would return. You're the quickest to the draw, Luca, and also, the bravest among us. Whatever challenges you faced, I had no doubt you'd find a way to overcome them."

"Just like I did when you left me and our other brothers behind and went off to the States to make your life."

Michael winces. A flash of something crosses over his features, before he replaces it with the mask of aloof superiority again.

He releases me and I step back.

"That motherfucker Freddie needs to be taught a lesson. If he thinks he can get away with what he did, he doesn't know the might of the *Cosa Nostra* yet."

"Which is why I'm going after him on my own."

"You will not." Michael's tone hardens, "I will not risk the life of another of my brothers."

He's referring to the death of our youngest brother Xander, who was killed by a car bomb rigged by none other than our own father.

"He came after me and mine; I need to track him down and teach him a lesson so he knows he can't ever fuck with us again."

"Revenge is good. Revenge drives a man to his optimal performance. But foolhardiness is a trait that only the foolish mistake for courage."

Anger contorts my stomach. My face heats. "Are you calling me foolish?"

"I will not let you go after Freddie on your own."

I draw in a sharp breath. The anger that beats in my chest solidifies into something uglier. Something harder. Something that pushes me to thrust my head forward and growl, "I'm not going to pussyfoot around what needs to be done. I'm not going to waste time strategizing, or whatever bullshit line you're going to feed me. You're married, with a child on the way. It's understandable that you don't have the balls for confrontations anymore. I, on the other hand—"

"Luca?" I hear her soft voice a second before her fingers wrap about my wrist. A zing of electricity runs up my arm, down my spine, straight to my groin. My balls stiffen and my shoulders bunch. The gnawing feeling in my chest eases.

The sweet scent of roses teases my senses.

I shoot her a sideways glance, and her amber eyes hold mine. The zing of electricity thrums and intensifies to a crash of thunder that echoes through the corners of my mind. Droplets of rain plop on my nose. On her cheek. One slides down her eyelid and balances at the edge of her eyelash. The scent of ozone fills the air, and the hair on my forearms stands to attention. All other noises fade away, and it's just me and her, trapped in a bubble from which there is no escape.

"Luca?" Michael's voice cuts through the silence. The bubble bursts. The sound of footsteps receding reaches me. A car door slams. I blink.

Then, Massimo draws abreast.

"Why don't the two of you come with me?"

18

Jeanne

"What was that?" I glance at Luca, who's staring out of the window of the car that Massimo ushered us to. He slid into the driver's seat while Luca opened the door for me—and I was surprised. For all his alphahole ways, he's a gentleman... Sometimes. I thought Luca would ride shotgun with his brother, but he shut the door to my side, then walked around to the other side of the car and slid inside.

Now I scrutinize his profile. "Was that your oldest brother?" I lean forward in my seat. "What were you talking to him about? Why were you so tense?"

"Not even married, and you already sound like a nagging wife," he drawls.

I draw in a sharp breath. "You don't have to always live up to your persona of an alphahole, you know."

He doesn't reply.

"I overheard the two of you speaking, and I tend to agree with what he said. You can't be hunting down the idiots who kidnapped me and managed to knock you out and haul you into that room on your own."

"No one asked for your opinion," he drawls.

"I am your wife-to-be," I retort.

He lowers his voice, "*Fake* wife-to-be."

"What you did earlier didn't seem very fake to me." I lower my voice to match his, "What were you thinking, carrying me down the steps from the aircraft, anyway?"

"Trying to make an impression." He glances over to where Massimo is driving.

"You may have overdone it," I whisper. "Everyone's going to know you were overcompensating for the situation."

"You don't know us Sovranos. We're given to grand gestures," he mutters under his breath. "I needed to pull out all the stops so I could distract them enough that they would look beyond what was in front of their eyes."

"Don't overdo it, else it will be too obvious what we're up to," I reply in a low tone.

"If I didn't know better, I'd think you want this little charade to work." His lips twist and a pulse of heat flares to life low in my belly. Oh, my heart! That smirk of his is so wicked, it's surely going to push me to do something illegal. Like crawling into his lap and licking his lips so I can taste the meanness that seems to cling to his every word.

"Of course I want this charade to work. You brought me back to Palermo in time for my premiere, haven't you? It's time for me to keep up my end of the bargain." I cover my mouth with my hand and cough. "At least, for now."

"I heard that." His grin widens. "You like to live dangerously, don't you, Angel."

"I wish you wouldn't call me that. Also, I think we're going the wrong way." I lean over and tap Massimo on his shoulder. "My home is to the left. I think you need to double back."

Massimo glances at the mirror and meets Luca's eyes. Something passes between them.

"No mistake." Luca tilts his head. "You're coming to my place."

"What? Your place? But we aren't even married."

"Relax. I'm not going to jump you. But whoever took you is still out there. It's safer if you stay with me. I have round-the-clock protection."

I bite the inside of my cheek. "This isn't something you mentioned earlier. I'd prefer to stay at my place."

"Out of the question," he says in a casual tone, as if it's not my life he's talking about, but some business transaction he's negotiating.

"You can't tell me what to do."

"Think again, baby. You're marrying the *Capo* of the Sovrano family; from here on out, your life is mine."

"Is that so?" I tip up my chin. "I may have agreed to help you out. Doesn't mean I'm going to agree to everything you suggest."

"You're coming with me. End of discussion." He pulls out his phone, the one Karina handed him, and begins to type out something on it. What the — he's ignoring me? Well, I'll show him what happens when he snubs me.

I roll down my window, lean over, grab his phone and fling it out, then roll up the window again. I lean back, fold my hands in my lap.

There's not a peep from him. No movement, except the waves of anger that radiate in my direction from him. I stare straight ahead through the windshield. Massimo glances at us in the rearview mirror, then goes back to driving.

The tension between Luca and me spikes. His entire body is motionless, but there's no mistaking the tension trapped in those coiled muscles. It feels like the Hulk gathering himself, pulling on all his internal stress and agitation and anxiety before he explodes.

My mouth dries. Sweat gathers in the hollows of my underarms. I risk a sideways glance, and his blue gaze instantly latches onto mine. In the depths of his eyes, silver sparks blaze. It's like he's eating me up with his stare. The car goes over a speed bump and I slide closer to him. Without taking his gaze off of mine, he reaches over and clamps his fingers around the nape of my neck. "You shouldn't have done that."

His cold, hard voice scrapes over my sensitized nerve endings. His blue gaze intensifies, until it feels like they are chips of ice so dark they're almost black. His fingers are so long, they meet around my throat. He presses his thumb into the hollow of my neck, and I can feel my pulse jackhammer against his touch.

"You were ignoring me," I retort, and am pleased that my voice does not tremble. Or my chin, for that matter.

"Did that upset you? You wanted my attention to be solely focused on you?"

Yes.

Yes.

"No." I shake my head.

"Liar." He peels his lips back and his pearly white teeth suddenly seem too sharp. Too lethal. I wriggle in my seat, try to pull away, but his grasp is unshakeable.

"You sassed me; I have to teach you a lesson."

"You can go take a hike," I say in my best convent school, prissy voice impression, because remember, I went to one of those. A la *The Sound of Music*, the nuns who taught me wore habits and were very strict, and drilled into me the notion of 'sin,' something I will not be recovering from anytime soon. No wonder I've been in therapy since I turned eighteen. And no, the nuns did not sing on hilltops. I left with a repressed sexuality, and a desperation to lose my virginity, which I promptly did with the first man I could find, and let me tell you, it was a forgettable encounter. Neither traumatic nor earth shattering. It was nice, and left me with a vaguely dissatisfied sentiment when it came to the thought of sex; that is, until I met this brute, and now my ovaries seem to have gone into overdrive.

He makes a noise deep in his throat, and it's so manly, so feral, so... dare I say, erotic, that my pussy clenches. A pulse flares to life between my legs, and my now awake ovaries seem to blossom further. Jesus, Mary and Joseph— Yep, if I swear, I prefer to do it in familiar language, especially because the nuns told me not to use the lord's name in vain. Of course, I must do the exact opposite. My nipples distend, and oh, god, if he glances at my chest, he'll see just how turned on I am.

He chuckles darkly, and the grasp around the nape of my neck tightens. Then he leans into me until his nose almost bumps mine, until his lips almost brush mine, until that dark chocolate and coffee scent of his makes my mouth water. A nerve throbs at his temple. The heat from his body slams into my chest and I gasp. The pulse between my legs turns up in intensity, until it feels like my heart has dropped to between my thighs. I bring them together, trying to squeeze down to contain the emptiness that is suddenly so obvious.

"You were saying?" His voice rumbles up his chest, and wraps about my shoulders, and down the valley between my breasts. If I thought my nipples were hard earlier, now they seem to swell until they feel almost too weighted for my breasts. My toes curl, and my scalp feels like it's about to catch fire. I lock my fingers together and hold his gaze.

"I said, go take a—"

He moves so quickly that I yelp. The next second, he's unbuckled my seatbelt and pulled me toward him, and his mouth is on mine. He kisses me firmly, his lips assured. He drags his tongue across the seam of my lips, and when I part them, he plunges it inside my mouth. A growl of satisfaction rumbles up his chest. The vibrations feather over my skin, sink into my blood. I dig my fingers into the front of his shirt and drag him even closer. He wraps his arm around my waist, closes the distance between us so we're plastered chest-to-chest. My breasts crush against the hard planes as he tilts his head and deepens the kiss. My eyelids flutter down—all the better to savor the taste of him that is all swirling darkness like the creamy topping of a cupcake that melts in my mouth and twines about my senses and pulls me into the vortex that is Luca. Heat flushes my skin, my thighs quiver, the flesh between my legs is melting and yearning, and I must have made a noise at the back of my throat, for the next second, the world tilts. I crack my eyes open to find I am in his lap, straddling his hips, and the thick, hard, column at his crotch is stabbing into my center. A moan wells up my throat. I dig my fingertips into his shoulder and begin to raise and lower myself against the welcome length. I spread my legs wider, trying to notch the rigid head against my slit. His big palms grasp my hips and he squeezes down, holding me in place.

He tears his mouth away, pushes his forehead flush against mine, and glares into my eyes.

"If you move again, I won't have a choice but to fuck you right now, and I don't want to do that in the backseat of a car driven by my brother."

19

Luca

The moment the words are out, I regret them, for she freezes. She raises and lowers her eyelids slowly and her eyelashes brush over mine. A weird sensation coils in my chest and grows and expands until it seems to drag down my chest and sink to the pit of my belly, where it settles as if having found a new home. I swallow down the ball of emotion that has appeared in my throat from seemingly nowhere.

Her pupils are dilated, the black of them huge enough to bleed into her irises until there's only a circle of gold left. It's the sexiest, hottest thing I have seen in a long time. I see myself reflected in the sheen of darkness, and it feels like a precursor to what is to come.

Me. Her. Us. Me giving up my freedom for this inescapable connection that binds us. That I never agreed to...

Which is why I had proposed to her in the first place. A marriage of convenience for a short period of time, until my family was convinced I'd tried it and decided it wasn't for me. In one stroke, I'd have delivered on Nonna's last wish, and I'd have convinced my brothers that I'd given this entire marriage thing my best shot. Then, I'd go my own way and she'd go hers. I'd compensate her, of course, to make sure she wouldn't want for anything for the rest of her life. I'll be rid of her sassiness, her need to always have the last word, which drives me up the wall, her penchant for swearing without using any known four letter word which is so annoying, and also, so adorable.

Hold on. Did I use the word adorable in relation to her? Pets are adorable. She… a grown woman who agreed to be part of this business transaction that we came up with to benefit the both of us, is, on the other hand, simply vexing. I have to put distance between us while I figure out what to do with this arrangement I suggested. At the very least, I need to get control of my thoughts and slam my emotions back into the hole where I've buried them for all these years, until she came along, and with a snap of her fingers, opened that Pandora's box.

I'm not falling into the trap like my brothers did. All of them married and happy and shit. A status that is not for me. I will not allow myself to be vulnerable toward another person the way my mother did. She fell in love with my father, and look what happened to her. He broke her heart. He abused her until she finally dropped dead, in the prime of her life. I will not let myself develop feelings for another. Every time I've been emotionally dependent on another, it has only resulted in betrayal. In me being hurt. I've learned enough from my past. Enough that I will not walk into this trap set by her beauty, her innocence, her beguiling charm. I know better than that, surely.

"Fine." I lean back into the seat so the air in the car rushes between us. "I'll take you to your home."

"Eh?" She opens and shuts her mouth, "You mean, you'll—"

"Take you back to your place. That's what you wanted, right?"

"You don't want me to stay at yours?" she bursts out.

I raise a shoulder. "My feelings don't count in the matter."

"And you mentioned it would be dangerous for me. You said the people who kidnapped me are still out there somewhere."

"I'll make sure you're picked up and dropped home from your play. I'll also post men outside your house."

She stiffens. "You will not. The last thing I need is more attention drawn to where I live."

"Take it or leave it." I curl a strand of her gorgeous dark brown hair around my finger. "Also, you won't be able to see the men guarding your place because they'll be discreet."

She pulls away and the strand of hair falls to the side. She tries to slide off, but I grip her hips and hold her in place. "I didn't tell you that you could move away, did I?"

"What stupidity is this? Can I sit back in my corner of the seat, please?"

"You'll sit there when I let you and no earlier."

"What are you waiting for then?" She folds her arms across her chest and pouts at me.

So fucking cute. A-n-d, I've officially lost it. She's endearing in the way that bees are when you see them buzzing around their hive. But let them close to you and you risk the chance of being stung. I'm making the right choice by returning her back to her home. It's best to keep her at a distance, until the wedding, and after. Especially after. My life will be much calmer without this pesky little thing hovering about and getting in the way.

I lift her and put her to the side.

She instantly shuffles away, putting as much distance between us as the seat allows.

"Seatbelt," I jerk my chin toward it.

She tosses her hair over her shoulder, but obliges me right away.

I lean forward and tap Massimo on his shoulder. "I assume you brought my phone?"

Massimo nods. *Stronzo's* done his best to keep his eyes on the road and away from the rearview mirror. I suppose I should thank him for it. But he's my brother and a fellow member of the *Cosa Nostra.* I'd expect nothing less from him, and would have done him the same favor if the roles had been reversed.

He pulls out the device and hands it over. I shoot her a sideways glance to find her narrow her gaze on me. I chuckle. She huffs, turns her head to look out the window. I slide my fingers across the screen, texting.

"We're headed to her place," I tell Massimo.

"Is that wise?" He frowns at me in the rearview mirror. "Both of you were kidnapped. Surely, it's going to be safer if she stays with you?"

Next to me, she shifts in her seat.

"It's what I've decided. She's *my* fiancé, after all."

"The fiancé of the *Capo* of the *Cosa Nostra.* Word will spread that you're engaged to her, and that will only attract more eyes on her," he points out.

I squeeze the bridge of my nose. "I am the *Capo*, as you said. So do as I ask you to." My voice is sharp, and for a second, I regret it. But fuck that. I am the *Capo.* I've waited a long time to be able to command respect within the clan. Of course, respect can't be demanded, which is exactly what I did. I blow out a breath. *"Cazzo. Mi 'spiace,"* I apologize. "I didn't mean that, *fratello.* It's been a long day and I am tired. Also, it's what Nonna would have wanted."

I tack on the last because it is what Nonna would have insisted on, were she still alive. She'd ensured Christian and Aurora were apart until they'd been married, which had only made Christian more desperate to be with Aurora, though he'd fought the pull of the relationship until the bitter end. In fact, it's probably why Nonna made sure they were kept apart. I bet she knew exactly the kind of impact that would have on Christian. It's one of the reasons he moved up the date of their wedding, but I'm not going to do that. I'm going to try to push back the wedding as far as I can, and ideally, try to elope so I can avoid the kind of circus my brothers had to go through.

Massimo's lips firm. "She doesn't have the keys to her place," he reminds me.

"I've already messaged Adrian. By the time we get there, he'll have found a way to open the door."

"No one can hack the lock in such a short time," she pipes up.

I shoot her a sideways glance. "Wanna bet?"

20

Jeanne

Good thing I'm not a betting person because when we reach my apartment, Adrian is standing by the door with a locksmith, who proceeds to use a key to unlock my door in one try, then hands me a duplicate set of keys, before bowing—yes, he actually bows to me, then turns and leaves.

Adrian introduces himself and apologizes that his brother, aka Luca, hasn't done so already. He hands me a phone, and when I look at it in surprise, he explains Luca asked for it to be arranged. Luca, himself, stands by silently, as if he can't wait to get out of here. Adrian mentions that he'll be along in an hour to pick me up for my rehearsal, before he, too, leaves.

Then, a man carrying various bags of groceries appears at the top of the corridor. He walks over to us, takes one look at Luca and pales. His hands shake so much, he almost drops the bags. Luca takes them from him, but before I can ask him to wait so I can find some cash to tip him, he turns and runs. O-k-a-y.

Now I follow Luca, who shoulders his way into the apartment and walks over to the kitchen to place the bags of groceries on the counter.

Then, he proceeds to walk around the flat, making sure all of the windows are secured.

"What are you doing?"

He doesn't reply.

"I thought you didn't care I'm likely still in danger from whoever kidnapped me."

He completes his check on the windows in the living room, then heads into the bedroom.

"Hey!" I rush forward and grab at his sleeve. "What are you doing?"

He glances down at where I've hooked my fingers into his shirt, then back at my face. Those blue eyes of his flash, and it's like I can hear waves crashing on the shore.

I blink and release my hold on him. He straightens his sleeve, walks to the lone window in the bedroom, shuts the pane and locks it.

"Why did you do that?" I protest.

He draws the shades then turns on me. "This stays closed, as do the windows in the living room."

"Aren't you taking things too far?"

He glares at me, and a little shiver of anticipation squeezes down my spine. *No, no, I do not find his anger a turn on.* I lock my fingers behind my back, then watch as he takes a last look at the bedroom and stalks out and toward the front door. There, he pauses and glances over his shoulder. "Make sure you eat something before you go to the rehearsal. Also, don't forget to lock the door behind me."

"You're boring for a Mafia man, you know that?"

He merely jerks his chin at me, then heads out of the door and shuts it behind him.

I blow out a breath and turn toward the kitchen, when he pushes open the door and scowls at me. "Told you to lock it, didn't I?"

"All right, okay. Seriously, you're turning out to be a nag."

He merely stands there and smolders, and god help me, my core melts a little. Maybe I can ask him inside my bedroom so he can stand in the corner and glower at me all day. I wouldn't need the heating at night. He could warm my room with the heat that pours off of his body. He could drive away my chills with the sparks that seem to fly every time our eyes meet. He could—

"Angel!" he snaps.

I jump. "What?" I frown.

"Shut. The. Door. And. Bolt. It."

"Fine, gosh. Some people have no sense of humor." I walk to the door, shut it in his face. *There, happy!* Then I bolt it.

I stand there for a few more seconds and place my palm on the door. Is it my imagination, or can I feel the heat from his body through the wood? I flatten my cheek against the door and tremors spiral down my spine. He's definitely standing there. I close my eyes, and the touch of his fingers on my hips, on my skin, as he'd tugged on the strand of my hair earlier in the car, washes over me.

Then I hear the sound of his footsteps recede. I open my eyes and step back. *Snap out of it, woman. You're home in one piece, aren't you?* And in time for the final rehearsal before the premiere tomorrow.

I glance at my phone and realize I have enough time to shower, change my clothes, and get something to eat before Adrian returns to pick me up. I head to my room, and in just under an hour, I'm ready. I head to the kitchen and look inside the paper bags to find fresh fruits, vegetables, eggs, pasta, and ready-made pasta sauce. I whip up a quick pasta and eat it, then make sure the perishables are in the fridge. Finally, I get on the phone with my bank to cancel my credit cards and order new ones. I have extra cash that I keep in the house. I shove that into my back-up purse, then place my phone in it. Right on time, too, for there's a knock on the door. Adrian sure is punctual.

I walk to the door, throw it open and stare.

"You?" I blink. "What are you doing here?"

21

Luca

Good question. Exactly what I was asking myself. I had planned on Adrian coming over and driving her to her rehearsal, but the thought of anyone else going over to her place and accompanying her had been too much for me. My guts had twisted, a stone had taken residence in my stomach, and it felt like a heavy weight was squeezing down on my chest. I didn't dare put a name to those feelings. It was probably just my system reacting to having a decent meal at home after not having eaten properly for a few days. Yeah, that's all it was. Indigestion. I grabbed antacids and chewed on them before I showered and slid into my car and came over to her place.

Now, I grip the top of the doorframe and glare at her. "Aren't you ready to leave yet?"

"You're going to drive me to the rehearsal?" She glances past me. "Where's Adrian?"

A sensation like knives being stabbed into my chest grips me. "Why do you care?"

"Wasn't he supposed to drive me today?"

"I'm taking you to rehearsal," I snap back.

"Not with that kind of attitude, you're not."

"My attitude has nothing to do with my driving skills," I retort.

"Of course it does. If you keep glowering at me, you're likely to have a coronary before too long, and I don't want that happening when I'm in the car with you."

"Nothing's going to happen to you, I'll make sure of that." The words are out before I can stop them. She tips up her chin and meets my gaze. Something electric stretches between us, zings through the air and super-charges the space. Her pupils dilate, her chest rises and falls, and the pulse at the base of her throat beats faster. My fingers tingle, and it's all I can do to stop myself from pressing a thumb to that spot and feeling the nervous-ness, the agitation, the tension that seems to have her in thrall.

She flicks out her tongue to wet her bottom lip, and I feel the swipe all the way to the crown of my cock. How would it be to have those lips wrapped around my dick, to have her run that pink tongue up the bottom of my shaft, to have her squeeze my balls as I empty myself down her throat?

She must sense my thoughts, for her mouth opens in a silent 'O' of surprise. She clutches at her purse, and the knuckles of her fingers are white. She brings her other hand up to her chest and flattens her palm against her heart. Her shoulders rise and fall. The scent of crushed rose petals intensifies. That's when I realize I've leaned in close to her.

I glance between her blown pupils and the blood drains to my groin.

"Luca," she whispers. The sound of my name from her lips is like the magnetic pull toward my true north.

True north? What is wrong with me? Why did I think that? She's a front for the fake marriage I'm enacting for the benefit of my family. She's only my fake fiancé, an asset I need to guard until my family is convinced of the veracity of our relationship. The possessiveness I feel toward her is because of that. It has nothing to do with how fiery she is, how I'm drawn to her, how she's the epitome of everything that pulls at me, hooks its claws into my guts and yanks at me so I can't stop myself from seeking her out when we're in the same space, and especially when we're not together. How I can't stop myself from thinking of her. How I can't help but appre-ciate her courage in the face of the ordeal we went through. Her ability to bounce back and focus on her craft, the way I'm focused on building my reputation as the *Capo* of the *Cosa Nostra*. All I have to do is keep her at a distance, something I've already failed at, for here I am, unable to tear my gaze off her face.

"Jeanne..." I take a step back, then sweep my hand toward the corridor. "Are you ready to leave?"

She glances between my eyes for a second longer. Her forehead pinches together. A look of disappointment seeps into her features before she pulls herself together. "Of course."

I put more distance between us, giving her enough space so when she steps out and pulls the door shut after her, there's no chance of our bodies coming in contact.

She locks the door, drops the keys into her bag, then spins around and marches down the corridor. Head held high, shoulders erect, hips swinging like a peach ready to be devoured and savored and licked across the curves until it's shiny and glistening, and *cazzo*. Why can't I glance at her without wanting to yank her to me, slap my chest and declare to the world that she's mine? The heavy weight pressing down on my chest intensifies. A dense cloud of emotion chokes my throat. It feels like someone just plunged a hot knife into my chest and twisted it. *Stocazzo!* What is wrong with me?

She turns to glance at me over her shoulder. "You coming, Gangster?"

Her voice slices through the noise in my head. I force my feet to move, force myself to shove those thoughts deep inside that black hole which is my heart and slam the lid down on it. There is no place for emotions in my life. No place for any feelings except this razor-sharp focus on ensuring that I consolidate my place as the *Capo* of the *Cosa Nostra*.

I need to do better than my brothers, not that there's a competition. Except, in my mind, there is. I need to outperform them. Even if I'm never going to be the Don, I can still ensure that my fame and reputation outshines his. Besides, Michael is married and with a kid on the way. He's distracted, and I can take advantage of that by doubling down and ensuring I take on the most difficult assignments. If I prove myself now, I have a chance at surpassing him. Yes, this is what I need to concentrate on. Not on my upcoming 'fake' nuptials or the charms of my soon-to-be-bride. Both of which have no place in my life. I square my shoulders and stalk forward. Brushing past her, I head down the stairs and out the front door of the building. I hold it open for her, and once she's walked through it, I head to my car and hold the door open. When she's seated, I bend, reach for her seatbelt, and she flinches.

"I'm not going to hurt you," I snap.

"What you say versus how you look is like Lady Gaga singing *Just Dance* without make-up."

I stare at her.

"You have no idea what I'm talking about, do you?"

I scowl.

She blows out a breath. "Sorry, I forget my cultural references are probably two decades too forward for you."

"How old do you think I am?"

"Um," she pretends to count on her fingers, "forty-six?"

I purse my lips.

"Forty-two?"

I glower.

"Forty?"

My fingers tingle. What I wouldn't give to take her across my lap and have my palm connect with that gorgeous derriére.

"Thirty-nine?" She clears her throat.

"I'm thirty-six," I growl.

"Ah." She raises her shoulders. "I'm twenty-two."

"I thought you were eighteen."

She huffs out a laugh. "Nice try, but I'm still not going to sleep with you."

"We'll see." I close the door, then walk around and slide into the driver's seat. I ease the car out onto the road.

Twenty minutes later, we pull up in front of the theater. I shut off the engine, then turn to face her. "What?" I ask.

"How did you know where I was going to perform?"

I allow my lips to curve into a smile. "Do you really have to ask me that?"

"Is there anything about me you don't know?" she retorts.

"I don't know if you'd prefer me to take your ass first or your pussy."

Her gaze widens, her jaw slackens, and a telltale blush rises on her cheeks. She opens and shuts her mouth, then turns and shoves the door of the car open. I push my own open, walk around the front of the car, and follow her to the door of the employees' entrance of the theater.

She wrestles with the heavy door, and I close the distance between us to slap my hand down on the wooden barrier.

She whirls around to face me. "If you think, by being mean to me, you can worm your way into my pants, you are sadly mistaken."

"Admit that it turns you on when I talk dirty. And it's closer to a python."

"What the—" She opens her mouth again and gapes.

"Seems the only way to shut you up is to shock you, Angel."

"It's not the way to woo me, though."

"First, not trying to woo you. Second, you've forgotten that you already agreed to marry me—"

"—fake marry," she interjects.

"And third, I can do with you what I want. You're hardly in a position to refuse."

"But you won't."

It's my turn to stiffen.

"For all your dirty-talking, full-on-dominance persona, you won't push against me if I say no."

I dig my palm into the wood that's been burnished by age, much like the way she's worn me down into a shell of myself, without even trying. It's true. In the face of her needs, I'm a slave, someone who won't push past her request to stop. Doesn't mean I'm going to surrender to her wants without coercing her to see otherwise.

"You underestimate me, Angel." I bend my knees and peer into her eyes. "I can be very persuasive."

"And I can be very stubborn." She juts out her chin.

"And by the time I'm done with you, you'll be begging me to fuck you. And I won't oblige."

Her breathing grows shallow.

"You'll implore me to throw you down and rip into your pussy, but I won't do so."

Color races up her cheeks to her hairline.

"You'll plead with me to let you come, and—"

Her amber eyes lighten until they seem like sunshine bouncing off water.

"I will not give you permission. Not even if you writhe and moan and are on the brink of the most phenomenal orgasm of your life. You feel me, Angel?"

22

Jeanne

"He said what?" Penny, my friend and co-performer in the musical, spits out the water she was about to swallow.

"Y-e-p." I pat my forehead with the lower half of my sleeveless T-shirt. "Not exactly the most romantic gesture in the world," I scoff.

"Are you kidding me?" Penny scoffs. "That's a level of X-ratedness which should, surely, have melted your panties clean off your body."

I glance at her from under half-closed eyelids. "Next, you'll be saying I should tell him my 'no' actually means 'yes'."

"Doesn't it?"

"No." I stare at her in shock. "Of course not."

"That's good." Olivia, another friend, who's also my understudy, stretches her leg out on the barre. She bends over with a flexibility that I envy. Not because I can't do the kind of stretches that she's contorting her body into. It's just that I have the tightest hamstrings in the world, which means I have to warm up for twice the time that everyone else does to reach that level of stretchability.

She straightens, then pulls off the scarf she's wrapped around her thick curls, and mops up the sweat from her collarbone.

"Because I wouldn't trust a Mafia man. With their larger-than-life personalities, they can convince you to do what they want, and all along, you think it's your idea." Her lips firm.

I narrow my gaze. "You sound like you have experience with the Mafia."

She flushes. "Only what I've seen in movies and read in books."

Penny and I exchange a glance.

"You hiding something from us, Olivia?" Penny scowls.

"Moi? Why would I do that?" She flutters her eyelashes.

"She *is* hiding something from us," I say with conviction.

"Of course not." Olivia glances between us. "Seriously, guys, there's nothing to it."

"It's a man," Penny declares.

"A Mafia man, by the looks of it." I nod.

"Oh, please. I told you, I want nothing to do with them." She stabs a finger in my direction. "And neither should you, if you know what's good for you."

I prop my hands on my hips. "Are you saying I don't know what I'm doing?"

She pales. "That's not what I meant. I'm only looking out for you, Jeanne." She twists her scarf around her fingers. "I don't want him to hurt you."

"What if he already has?"

"Has he?" She peers into my features.

"No." I pull myself up to my full height. "Of course not."

"You don't sound convincing," Olivia says slowly.

"I believe you." Penny shoots Olivia a glance, then turns to me. "This man was locked up with you, and by all counts, he tried to protect you. He brought you back in time for the final rehearsal for the premiere, and in one piece, so—"

"He kissed me in front of his family. He, ah… may have also made me come… hard."

"So, you got a few orgasms out of it." Penny raises a shoulder. "It's good for your skin. No wonder you're glowing. In fact—" She looks me up and down. "For someone who was kidnapped and then had to go on the run with a scary mobster, you're remarkably chipper."

I purse my lips. She has a point. But the alternative was…? Have a nervous breakdown and miss the one thing I've been working toward for so long? No way am I going to lose the opportunity of taking centerstage as the lead of the musical. "Maybe it will hit me later?" I confess, "I was so focused on making it in time for the premiere, that everything else felt secondary."

"Even the thought of impaling yourself on that thick, fat, Mafioso cock?" Penny smirks. "Even the thought of riding that Italian Stallion until you can barely walk?"

"Penny, seriously." I ignore the fact that I'm blushing so hard, it feels like my face is about to go up in flames.

"Do you like him? Is that why you're putting up with him?" Olivia walks toward me. "Or if he's bothering you and you want us to face off with him—"

"With what? That canon in his pants is not the only weapon he has access to, you know?"

Penny chortles.

Olivia ignores her and peers into my eyes. "He's not pushing you to do something you don't want, right? Because these Mafioso types can be very persuasive."

"Hmm." I narrow my gaze. "Since when do you know so much about Mafia men?"

She blinks, then raises her arms and stretches again. "Movies. Books. Information I've gathered along the way." She tucks her elbows into her sides. "I just want to be sure you're okay. If you need to rest up—"

"So you can take on my role on opening night?"

She pales. "You know that's not what I meant."

I press the heels of my hands into my eyes. "I know you didn't. I'm sorry; I didn't mean for it to come out that way. Maybe I'm not taking this entire experience as well as you think."

Penny draws abreast. "Take it easy, babe. Olivia is only worried about you." She pats my shoulder. "As am I."

I open my eyes and meet her worried gaze.

"Is everything okay? Did anything else happen that you're not telling us about?" Penny asks.

About that... I haven't told them about the arrangement he proposed. I mean, it's not a big deal, right? It's just a fake marriage that'll last for a very short period of time, and then we'll go our separate ways. There's no need to tell them about it, is there?

"Nothing else happened," I say the lie with a straight face, with my Oscar-winning, wide-eyed-gaze performance of a face. "In fact, I've never been better." I force my lips to curve up. Not too much; just enough to put them off track.

"Hmph." Penny purses her lips. "If you say so."

"I do, I—"

The door of the practice room opens and the director walks in. William is tall and skinny, and looks more like a rumpled college professor. But the man is brilliant when it comes to directing, as his two Tony awards will certify.

The rest of the cast stops warming up and everyone comes to attention. He didn't even have to clap his hands to call for attention. That's the kind of respect and fear he commands. He's handpicked each one of us after a torturous casting call which involved no less than eight casting sessions. No joke. A ripple of nervous energy zips through the crowd. Penny, Olivia, and I turn to face him.

Penny nudges me. "Wonder what fresh hell Lily-Willy has in store for us?"

I can't stop a chuckle bubbling up at his nickname. Pen's a bit more relaxed about the whole becoming-an-actress thing than Olivia or me. It's probably why I'm drawn to her. She tends to defuse the entire competitive situation that Olivia and I often find ourselves caught in.

William's sharp gaze flicks in our direction and I instantly firm my lips. Not in time, apparently, because his features become rigid.

"Not sure what you're cackling about, Jeanne, considering your last rehearsal was less than inspiring. If you'd danced with any less energy, you would've been mistaken for a wilted duck drifting on the surface of stagnant water."

Next to me, Penny winces.

I school my features into an emotionless mask. I will not let him get me down. Will not let his words hurt me. Part of becoming a dancer is learning to shrug off criticism like water off a duck's back. No doubt, that's why he alluded to that animal in his insult.

"Also, you missed rehearsal the last three days," he murmurs.

"It wasn't compulsory to make it. You gave us a choice."

"A choice which I expected my lead dancer to have made wisely." His lips thin. "And you turn up today, having lost the edge I thought you added."

"Excuse me?" I draw myself up to my full height. "It takes me a little time to warm up. You know that."

"So you should have started stretching much earlier."

"I couldn't, I—"

He tilts his head, and I bite the inside of my cheek to stop myself from saying something I might regret later. Asshole needs to vent and get it off his chest. Fine. I'm not going to rise to his bait. As long as I get on that stage tomorrow and—

"It's why I've decided Olivia will be taking your place tomorrow for the premiere show."

"What?" The world seems to tilt. A buzzing sound fills my head and I push it aside. I grip my fingers together in front of me and meet his gaze. "I don't think I heard you correctly."

"Giving you the option of coming to the rehearsal was a test to see who was the most committed to the musical. A test which Olivia passed with flying colors, unlike you, Jeanne."

"Are you kidding me?" I burst out. "I couldn't have made it if I wanted. I—"

"You—?" He lowers his chin to his chest, waiting.

I swallow the words that are coiled like a snake in my throat, ready to hiss out at the first possible opportunity. Will it seem too farfetched if I reveal what actually happened? I'm definitely not going to share it in front of everyone, though. I glance around and find the gaze of everyone is riveted on me. I jerk my head in William's direction again. Asshole probably brought it up in this open forum to put me at a disadvantage.

I shake my head. "I can't reveal the details." I wince as I hear my words. It sounds so weird, like I have something to hide. Which I do and don't, really. I mean, I don't want the rest of the team to know that not only was I kidnapped, but in addition, it was a Mafioso who rescued me. And I'm definitely not sharing those details with Lily-Willy. So, I square my shoulders and meet his gaze. "You could have mentioned it was important to attend the rehearsals."

"Would you have, if I had?" he shoots back.

I glance away.

"That's what I thought." The triumph in his voice is like a wrecking ball to my aspirations. "The lead has to be a person who is 1000% committed to this role. Someone for whom a personal life doesn't exist. Someone who'd sacrifice everything and everyone to get to where she wants to be, with laser focus. Someone like…" He turns his gaze on Olivia.

"No." I clench my fingers together. This can't be happening. He can't take my role away and give it to someone else. The role I've spent months… Years… My entire lifetime, to this date, working toward.

"Olivia." He stretches out his arm.

Olivia glances in my direction. "I'm sorry," she whispers.

"Don't take the role." I glance at her sideways. It's wrong of me to ask this of her. Wrong of me to put her on the spot. But I'm desperate, and honestly, I don't care that I'm crossing a boundary here. That I might lose her as a friend… That I may have already lost her as a friend.

"Don't do this. Say you can't take the role," I hiss.

"Olivia?" William lowers his chin to his chest. "Step forward."

"Olivia don't," I whisper-scream. "Don't do this."

She glances at William, then at me again. "Sorry." She steps forward.

23

Jeanne

"I didn't have a choice. What did you expect me to do? Say that I wasn't going to take on the lead role?" Olivia shoves the clothes she was wearing during the rehearsal into her bag. "Do you know how rare it is for the understudy to open the premiere of a musical?"

"It's rare, but it's known to happen. Jeremy Kushnier went on as Judas in Jesus Christ Superstar when Josh Young was sick for a couple of weeks," Penny offers.

The three of us are in the changing room of the theatre. After Olivia accepted the role, Lily-Willy offered me the role of the understudy. What was I going to do? Turn him down? I'd been tempted to, make no mistake, but that would have meant passing up on an opportunity of a lifetime, and no way could I do that.

"How do you know that?" Both Olivia and I turn to stare at her.

"Just like to remember random things that serve me no good purpose." She raises a shoulder. "At least it stopped the two of you from squabbling."

"It's a good comparison though." I whirl back on Olivia. "You're acting like a Judas."

Olivia straightens. She places her backpack on the bench, then turns on me. "That's not fair. It's not my fault that you were replaced as the lead, and you knew that was a distinct possibility going into the role. If something went wrong—"

"Nothing should have gone wrong. And it wasn't my fault that it did."

"I know," she wrings her fingers, "but I couldn't say no. You know that. It's a big opportunity for me."

"It was a big opportunity for me, too." I hunch my shoulders. "You're right. This is my fault. I should have been more careful walking home from the bus. I should have chosen to spend money I didn't have because this gig doesn't pay enough to stay in a safer part of town. I probably should have been dressed differently, too, right? I was asking for it. If I actually cared about this part, I would have never allowed myself to be kidnapped!"

A pressure builds at the back of my eyeballs. *No, no, I am not going to cry.* A thick lump of regret lodges in my throat. I can't stop the tears that squeeze out of the corners of my eyes.

"Oh sweetie." Penny throws her arms around me. Her gentleness is the last straw. To my horror, I feel the emotions well up inside me. I try to swallow down the tears, but there's too much going on inside of me. The culmination of everything I've been through in the last few days crowds in. I squeeze my eyes shut and cling to Penny. Then, another pair of arms comes around me. Olivia hugs both of us. We stay there for a few seconds. The silent tears keep flowing down my cheeks as my shoulders shake. Penny sniffles. Olivia chokes a little.

"Sorry you guys. I didn't mean to break down like this."

"You're entitled, babe," says Penny. "You realize this isn't your fault, right?"

I nod stiffly. Penny, or maybe it's Olivia, runs soothing circles over my back. I soak in the love that pours from both of them. It's always been like this. Since we met at drama school in LA, we've been inseparable. We've always had each other's back until... Now?

I pull away and they both release me.

"Better?" Penny stares between my eyes.

I sniff again.

Olivia reaches into her bag and pulls out a tissue. "Here," she murmurs.

I take it from her without meeting her eyes and blow my nose. Then I ball the tissue and fling it in the direction of the overflowing basket in a corner of the room and miss. Just my luck. The tears threaten again, and I grab my bottle of water and drink from it. When I lower it, both women are still watching me.

"I'm fine," I declare.

"I'm really sorry," Olivia says in a soft voice. "I wish it weren't you that I'm replacing." For a hard-nosed actress, she has a caring side, which she reveals only on occasion. And normally, only with Penny and me.

"It sucks." I half smile. "But if anyone were to replace me, I'd rather it be you."

"I know you're upset—"

"I was. I mean, I still am. But I know you did the right thing. I'm glad you accepted the role."

"Are you saying that just to make me feel better? Because honestly, I know I did a bitchy thing by accepting the role—"

"You had no choice. It's the done thing. I couldn't very well have expected you to turn it down."

"I should have. There's still time. Maybe if we go explain what happened to you." Olivia glances at the doorway, then takes a step toward it.

I grab her arm. "No! Don't. Really. It's okay."

"But it's not." Olivia turns on me. "This was your big break. You embody Belle. Your lushness, your voice, the way you seem virginal, even as the eroticism drips from your every move... You *are* Belle in the show."

"Thanks, but you don't have to humor me."

"It's true." Olivia grips my arm. "If anyone deserves the break, it's you."

"And you know how it is, talent is to us actors what luck is to card players." I forget who said it, but it feels apt to say it right now, especially when neither luck nor talent is on my side.

"This is your chance." I twine my fingers through Olivia's. "I'm truly happy it's you on that stage."

"You mean it?" she asks cautiously.

I swallow down the ball of churning emotions which seems to have hooked itself into my throat, then nod. "You bet. In fact, I think we should go out to celebrate."

"You sure?" Penny peers into my face. "Don't you want to go home and rest up after everything you have been through?"

"It's because of what I've been through that I want to celebrate that I made it back. So what if I'm not on stage. You are." I hold Olivia's gaze. "It's one of the three musketeers in the lead, and" —I turn to Penny— "a second musketeer playing the enchantress. That's cause for celebration, isn't it? After all, we celebrated when I got the lead, too."

"If you're sure," Olivia says slowly.

"I'm sure." I pull away from them, then grab my bag with the sweat stained clothes I wore during the rehearsal. "Let's go get dinner."

I head for the stairs, taking them two at a time. My head is full of everything that happened. It's the only reason I stumble on the crack in the rickety step half-way down. It's not because my vision is blurry. I'd have fallen, too, except Olivia grabs my shoulder and pulls me upright. My bag slips from my shoulder and the strap lodges in the crook of my arm as it hits the floor.

My heart somersaults in my ribcage and my pulse skyrockets. I pause and Penny grabs my arm.

"You okay, babe?"

"Yeah." I blow out a breath. "Of course." I shake my head.

"You sure?" Olivia exchanges a glance with Penny.

"We don't have to go out. You could come to our place, and we can just hang out. I even have the bath bombs you love." The two of them share an apartment, one in a really nice part of town, with a bathroom and a big tub to die for. A tub that I don't have at my place.

They offered the third room in the suite to me, but the rent for that room was twice the amount of the apartment I found. They told me I didn't have to pay, but the last thing I wanted was to be dependent on my friends. I know from experience that nothing kills a friendship quicker than when money inserts itself into the relationship. I wanted to stay clear of that.

And my apartment isn't that bad. It's further away from the theatre, but I can always take the bus. And that's why I ended up being kidnapped in the first place. Also because I was at the wrong place, at the wrong time. Isn't that what that horrible man Freddie said? This incident wasn't about me. It's about him... That alphahole Luca. It's all thanks to him that I've landed in this predicament.

"I'm good, really," I reiterate to my friends. With a last glance at each other, they release me. I sling my bag over my shoulder again and take the steps more cautiously this time. I've barely made it out of the door when he steps in front of me.

24

Jeanne

I pretend I don't notice him. I try to brush past him, but he moves with me so I'm confronted by that larger-than-the-Great Wall-of-China chest of his.

I swerve to the right, then feint left, but does that faze him? Nope. The alphahole simply parks his bulk in my way so I have no choice but to stop and scowl up at him.

"Get out of my way."

"No."

"I'm not coming with you," I retort.

"You are."

"I'm going out with my friends," I say through gritted teeth.

"I'll take you where you want to go."

"No," I snap.

"Yes." His lips twitch.

He finds this entire conversation a hoot, does he? I raise my foot and smash my heel down on his more-expensive-than-my-entire-monthly-salary boot. He doesn't even flinch.

"Who's this?" Penny's voice sounds from my left as she draws abreast.

"Is this the big, bad mob guy who rescued you?" Olivia asks as she flanks me on the other side.

"Ladies." Smooth as you please, the alphahole tips an imaginary hat in both their directions.

Penny visibly simpers. Olivia stares at him like he's an alien from another planet. Or a god who's descended from Mt. Olympus. Or an actor stepped off a runway at Fashion Week.

I clear my throat and both women seem to snap out of their befuddled state. Something burns in my chest. Clearly, it's because I haven't eaten dinner yet. I must be so hungry that my stomach's juices are attacking the lining. Yep, that's all it is. I'm not jealous at all that my friends find him so attractive. Not at all.

"If you think I'm going to simply fall in line with your command, then you have another thing coming."

"Think," he drawls.

"Eh? What do you mean?"

"You have another think coming. It's think, not thing."

"No, it's not. Think?" I scoff. "That makes no sense at all." I try to brush past him, and this time, he grabs my arm.

"Have you been crying?" He peers into my face. "You *have* been crying." His voice hardens. "What happened?"

Damn him and his over-attentive gaze which never seems to miss a thing. And this time, it is thing. Not think. It couldn't have been think in that previous sentence, could it?

I try to pull my arm away, but he holds on. "Tell me, Angel. What made you cry?"

"Nothing," I snap.

"It's something."

"She was removed from the lead role," Penny pipes up.

I shoot my friend a murderous look. Penny raises her hands with a 'what-did-I-do-wrong' look on her face.

"They replaced her with me," Olivia says in a low voice. "I was her understudy. I never expected to go on, to be honest, but our director decided otherwise."

"Why?" He glances from them, back to my face. He must see something in my expression because his features go solid. His already pronounced cheekbones seem to hone to a razor-sharp edge that could, surely, cut diamonds.

"Because you were away the last three days. That's why you lost the lead role," he surmises.

I glance away.

His entire being seems to coil with tension. Anger thrums off of him with such intensity that my chest tightens. My pulse begins to beat so hard, I can feel it at my wrists, at the base of my throat. I jerk my face in his direction, and his gaze sears me. It's as if forest fires flare deep in those eyes, the way he surveys my features.

A pulse tics at his jaw and a nerve pops to life at his temple. He releases my arm and brushes past me and toward the door that leads into the theater.

I blink once, twice, trying to compute what he's up to.

Next to me, Penny and Olivia stare after him, then turn to me.

"Of course he has to stomp away in anger. Typical Mafia guy behavior," Olivia mutters.

I narrow my gaze on her. She really does know more about the Mafia way of life than she's letting on.

"Is he angry?" Penny giggles nervously.

Yes, he is. He's angry on my behalf. He's pissed off that I lost the lead role. In fact, he looks so enraged, he looks like he's going to tear the building apart with his bare hands. Or, more specifically, a man.

"Oh hell." Yep, I'm allowed to use hell when I swear, just not the F word. At least, not aloud. I can think it though. *Fuck, fuck, fuck.*

He reaches for the handle to the door and I leap forward. "Stop." I close the distance to him and grab hold of his outstretched arm. Not that I can stop him, for he grips the handle.

"Stop it. Don't do this."

He twists the handle.

"Luca. Stop," I yell.

He blinks.

"You can't hurt him. He had a point. As the lead actress of this musical, I should have been there for the rehearsals every day. And I wasn't."

"Because of me." He glares at the door as if he can shoot through it with laser eyesight. "You couldn't make it because of me."

"I didn't make it because I was kidnapped."

He swivels to face me. "That *bastardo* took you only because of some warped plan to get back at me and my family."

He's right and I don't know what to say to that. It could have been me, or it could have been someone else. But... "I'm glad it was me."

His gaze widens. His nostrils flare. "Care to repeat that again?" he asks in a low voice.

I release him. "You heard me." I wrap my arms around my waist. "I'm glad it was me, okay? I'm not happy I lost the lead role, but on the bright side, because of that, Olivia gets to be the lead. And if it's not me, then I'm glad it's her, so it's not all bad."

"And why is it that you're glad it was you?" His lips curl.

Jerk. He knows exactly why, but he's going to make me lay it all out for him. Typical.

"I'm not going to say whatever it is you are trying to get me to confess."

He releases the door and turns to face me. "And what am I trying to get you to say?" His eyes gleam. He puffs up his chest, and if his shoulders get any bigger, he's going to go into full happy Hulk mode. Is there such a thing as a 'happy' Hulk? No matter.

I tip up my chin and jut out my lower lip. "You know."

"No, I don't."

"You know and that's why I agreed to marry you."

A shriek splits my eardrum.

I don't need to turn my head to know that was Penny. "You're marrying the mobster?" she gasps.

Olivia doesn't say anything, but I sense the unspoken questions she's chucking in my direction.

I hold my hand, palm face up, in their direction, signaling I can't deal with their inevitable interrogation.

"You know why I'm marrying you," I say in a voice low enough only for him to hear. "Because you saved my life, and because it's a deal to help you with your family situation."

"You accepted the deal because you wanted to get back in time to make it on stage and now you won't."

I shuffle my feet. "It doesn't matter."

"It does to me." He, once more, reaches for the door handle.

I jump forward and plant myself between him and the door. "You will not hurt the director."

"What's his name?" He lowers his chin to his chest. His entire body, once more, seems to bristle. This is not the happy Hulk mode, but the other one. Where he's about to burst out of his skin and go apeshit. Or is that Hulkshit?

"I won't tell you."

"You think I can't find out who the director of the musical is, or where he's staying here, or where his family is?"

I stare at him in growing horror. "You will not hurt him or any of his family, or his extended family and friends circle, you hear me? This is not how things are done in my world."

"It's how they are in mine."

"And that's why whatever this… thing is between us can only remain a farce."

He glares at me. Those blue eyes of his darken until they seem like a sheet of night sky, the moonlight turning the dips in the clouds into sleepy hollows.

We stare at each other for what seems like a long time, but must be only seconds. I sense something shift between us, but can't put a name to it.

I lock my fingers together and search his face. "Promise me you won't do anything illegal."

25

Luca

"I can't do that."

I search her features. In the world I live in, the Mafia are a part of life. As omnipresent as air. As inevitable as taxes. As woven into the fabric of the country as corrupt politicians. We provide the checks and balances that allow this country to function in a stable fashion. Well, as stable as any western economy trying to manage the clash of the rich and the poor; the struggle between those who have power and the powerless.

I've stopped thinking of my actions as illegal. I don't question my conscience anymore. I was born into this life, and there was never a question of accepting what we do for a living. But it's more than that. We see it as our duty to provide protection to those who can't fend for themselves. To provide a livelihood for those who find it difficult to get a job. To share our wealth, our happiness, and our sorrows with those whose lives we've improved, and who are our extended family, in a sense. It means we often take from those who have more and give it to those who don't. You might call it a Robin-Hood-esque style of living. I've never questioned it, not for one second, not until this slip of a woman came into my life and forced me to examine the very foundations on which I've built my existence.

Her features pale. She searches my eyes as if she's looking for an excuse to redeem me. Sorry sweetheart, you're not getting that here. I lost my soul a long time ago. Lost it when I saw how my father abused my mother, with no consequences. Lost it when he whipped me and my brothers. Lost it when my mother stayed with my father because she loved him. Lost it when she finally dropped dead one day. That kind of a love is not what I want. That kind of relationship is not for me.

My brothers may have found their happy endings, but that's not something I aspire to find.

I can't trust myself not to turn out to be like my father.

The door is pushed open and I retreat back. So does she. A crowd of people walk out, separating us. Likely, other members of the cast, leaving. Some of them call out to Jeanne and her two friends. A couple of them pause to say how sorry they are she lost the role. Others congratulate Olivia, then they move on.

All through it, I hold her gaze. Across the stream of faces. Across a chasm that I may never be able to bridge. A gap I hadn't even thought of until she pointed it out to me.

I take another step back.

She firms her lips. By the time the crowd has separated, she's pulled herself back together. But she still looks shaken. Her eyes are shadowed, and the hollows under her cheekbones seem more pronounced. She looks exhausted and I am the cause of it.

I gesture toward the car. "Can I take you ladies out to dinner?"

"No," she gripes.

"That would be lovely, but we couldn't possibly intrude on your romantic evening together," her friend responds.

"We're not going to have a romantic evening," Jeanne says through gritted teeth.

"But you two are getting married, right?" Her friend looks between us. "I'm Penny, by the way."

"Luca. Luca Sovrano." I take her proffered hand and air kiss her knuckles.

Penny sighs. Jeanne makes a noise at the back of her throat. I suppress the smile that threatens to break out on my lips and turn to the other woman. "And you are?"

"Olivia, Jeanne's friend," she murmurs.

"Any friend of Jeanne's gets the protection of my clan." I take her hand between both of my much larger ones.

Olivia fixes me with a steady gaze. "What are your intentions toward Jeanne?"

Jeanne stares. Penny gasps. Olivia doesn't take her gaze off of my face. She's looking out for her friend, which is good. Jeanne needs loyal people around her.

"My intentions are to marry her and take care of her."

Penny's gaze widens. Olivia glances between me and Jeanne. "Is that right? Are you going to marry this guy?"

"No," she replies.

"Yes," I counter.

"So, you're not marrying him?" Penny blinks rapidly.

She shuffles her feet. "I—"

"Oh, she is. She's just waiting for me to get her a ring before she shares the happy news with everyone. In fact, that's why I'm here to pick her up. Dinner first, then we go and pick out the ring, don't we, Angel?"

She sears me with a look that could cut right through me if I were the kind of guy who could be easily scared. Which I'm not. The more she pushes me away, the more something within me pushes to make this arrangement as real as possible. At least, for the time we have together.

"Jeanne, are you sure you're going to be okay?" Olivia asks. She moves forward and takes Jeanne's hand between both of hers. "Do you want us to stay with you through dinner?"

"Yes, if you want company, we'll be happy to stay. But it seems to me, it might be better off if the two of you had time together to figure things out," Penny adds as she walks over to flank Jeanne on her other side. I was right. The two of them are ready to protect her and stay with her and run interference if she asks them to.

Angel glances between her friends' faces, then at me. I hold her gaze, not allowing any emotion to show on my features. This is her call. If she wants to come with me alone, or if she'd rather have her friends chaperone us, she has to decide.

She finally looks away and shakes her head. "I'll be fine."

"You sure?" Olivia grips her shoulder. "If you'd rather we stay, we wouldn't mind at all."

"Yep, just say the word." Penny leans in. "Of course, if I were you, I'd rather have that hunk of a man all to myself." She drops her tone even lower and I miss the rest of the words, but whatever she says causes Angel to snort. She glances at me again, a slight blush painting her cheeks. Can she get any more adorable?

I fold my arms across my chest as she bids the two of them goodbye.

Finally, Olivia and Penny turn to me.

"Take care of her," Olivia warns.

"If you hurt her, you'll have us to contend with," Penny says with a pleasant smile on her face.

I bow in their direction. "I swear on everything I hold dear, I'll take care of her, protect her, and ensure nothing ever makes her unhappy. If anyone dares to wipe that smile off her face—" *Like her bastard director did today.* "I'll make sure I wipe them off the face of this earth."

She scowls at me.

"Unless I promise her otherwise," I add smoothly.

The two friends glance at each other. Olivia nods at me, Penny waves, then they depart. They walk away and the two of us are left looking at each other. I give her her space for a few seconds, then prowl toward her. She stiffens, her big amber eyes widen.

When I reach her, I hold out my hand. "Shall we?"

26

Jeanne

"You didn't have to make those false promises to my friends."

I glance down at my glass of wine, which the waitress who hadn't been able to take her eyes off of Luca had brought us. A wine he had chosen without asking for my opinion. A wine which, unfortunately, turned out to be very delicious. Bastard had the gall to smirk as I grudgingly told him so when he asked me if I liked it. Douche-canoe.

"What promises are you talking about?" He swirls the wine around in his glass and proceeds to take a sip. I watch in fascination as the tendons of his beautiful throat flex as he swallows. The man is a walking, talking, pornographic image. Before I met him, I didn't think people as good-looking as him existed in real life. And now? Now I am sure they don't, for surely, he, too, is an illusion. All those good looks, that charisma, that larger-than-life persona, those gorgeous shoulders, those eyes of his which track me wherever I go... Even as, in their depths, I sense a feeling of loss, something discontented, a restlessness which reaches out to me each time I hold his gaze. A melting sensation crowds my chest. My heartbeat seems to grow erratic. I cough, then raise my glass of wine to my lips and drink from it again. The fragrant liquid slides down my throat and soothes the scratchy feeling that had begun to develop.

"You okay?" He places his glass back on the table and touches his fingertips together.

"I'm not, actually," I murmur, because I'm not sure if I can keep up this pretense of having a civil conversation any longer.

"What's wrong?" His gaze intensifies. Those blue eyes deepen again, until they resemble pools of dark, clear water. You know what I said about sensing that core of loss I sometimes spy in their depths? Forget that. Any hint of vulnerability that glimmered there is blinked out, replaced by that hard, unforgiving, beast of a man as I first met him.

"Tell me, Angel," his voice softens.

And that's my undoing. Because as long as he gives no quarter, as long as he's pushing me out of my comfort zone, I'm compelled to push back. I'm compelled to hold my stance, and match him word-for-word, action-for-action. I'm pressed to go toe-to-toe with him. But the moment he backs down, the moment he shows me a hint of tenderness, the minute he reveals any sentimentality... I'm mush.

Tears prick the backs of my eyes and I swipe them away.

"Are you crying because you've lost the role you've prepared for all this time?"

"How do you know I've prepared for it?"

"Because you seem like the kind of woman who's very passionate about what she does. Someone who'd give herself completely to the task at hand, someone who loves what she does for a living. Don't forget, I saw you dance in that room."

"Yeah, stupid method acting. I confess, I tend to wear the skin of the character I'm playing for a long time afterwards. I'm not the kind of actress who's able to shed the persona and move on." I sniffle, then reach for a napkin and dab at my cheeks. "I bet I look a sight."

"You always look like the most beautiful woman in the world to me."

I freeze. Those words, said in that tone of voice, with that steady gaze of his. A shiver swoops down my spine and my stomach flip-flops.

"You're only saying that to make me feel better."

"One thing you should know about me, Angel. I never lie."

"And yet, you'd try to pass off a fake marriage as real to your family?"

"That's different." He rolls his shoulders.

"How is it different?" I lean forward. "You say you don't lie, and yet, you're trying to convince your family that this relationship between us is real."

"I'm doing this for their happiness." He drums his fingers on the table. "I'm doing it because it's what Nonna would have wanted."

"So, it's okay to lie if it's to make someone else happy? I never met your Nonna, but I doubt she'd want you to be in a fake relationship for her benefit."

"More like, she'd be happy I'm, at least, in a fake relationship. She's probably up there looking down on us and trying her best to convert this fake relationship into a real one. Which, by the way, is never happening."

"You seem very confident about that."

"I am." He leans back in his seat and flattens his palm on the table. I take in the breadth of his hand, the long, thick fingers which he used with great effect when he held me in place as he ravished my lips, as he'd plunged them into my pussy and my ass and made me come so hard I saw stars. I shift around in my seat.

"I'm never going to fall in love," he declares.

I tip up my chin. "What do you mean?"

"I mean, I do not intend to allow myself to develop feelings for anyone."

"What about your brothers and your parents?"

"My father abused my mother so much, she dropped dead one day. Then, my brother killed my father."

I squeeze the stem of the wine glass. My guts churn. That's not what I expected him to bring up. I didn't think he'd share more of himself with me. And I don't want to feel this empathy that fills me up inside. I don't want to allow myself to feel more than what I already do for this man. Which is already a complex set of emotions, to be honest. I'm already attracted to him, and now he's trying to humanize himself in my eyes, so I begin to understand him better. Which is only going to make this entire situation even more dangerous.

I only agreed to fake marry him. And yeah, perhaps sneak in a few—okay, many orgasms, if I give in to this attraction between us again. And I admit, I'm tempted to ignore all of the reasons why I shouldn't ask him to fuck me. But if I do, I might want this arrangement of ours to turn into something permanent, and I don't think that's something he'd entertain. So, I really need to find a way to pull back from whatever the hell this thing is I'm beginning to feel for him.

And he already told me that one of his brothers died, also killed by his father. With so much violence in his past, it's a wonder he still seems so normal.

"I didn't say that to elicit sympathy." He picks up his wine glass and tosses back the rest of the contents. At once, the waitress appears at his elbow and picks up the bottle of wine.

"May I?" she murmurs.

He tilts his head. She leans over, making sure that her blouse dips a little as she tops up his glass. She straightens and flashes him a smoldering look. I expect her to offer the wine to me, but she places the bottle back on the table, then turns and walks away.

"What the—" I stare after her, then turn to him. "Did you see that? She didn't offer to pour the wine for me."

"That's because I own this restaurant; also—" He leans forward. "I left strict instructions that the only person taking care of you this evening is me."

27

Luca

Nice one. Did you actually say those pathetically possessive words to her? Can you get any sappier? You're beginning to sound like an eighties love song. Only it seems to have an effect on her, for her gaze widens. That telltale dilation of her pupils kicks in, and even across the table, I can make out the way her dark pupils take over the expanse of those large amber eyes of hers. As tawny as a lioness' gaze, as sparkling as dappled sunlight, as deep as the heart of a topaz.

This woman vexes me. What is it about her that I find so fascinating? What is it about her that tempts me, and awakens the chords inside of me that I thought were silenced so long ago?

I can't take my gaze off of her delicate features—that heart-shaped face, the thick eyelashes that flutter over her exquisite cheekbones, the beautiful bow of her upper lip, that upturned chin, the slim shoulders and dainty fingers she has wrapped around the stem of her wine glass. Her almost empty wine glass.

I snatch the bottle of wine, then lean over and fill it up.

"Thank you." She stares into the depths of her glass. "You don't have to put up a pretense when we're alone," she says in a low voice.

"It's not a pretense."

She raises her gaze to mine. "You confuse me. You're the one who proposed this arrangement, then you say that we should sleep together so it feels genuine. Only you retract that later by claiming you are happy for things to take their natural course, and now, you come across as all possessive. It makes my head spin. In fact, if I didn't know better, I'd say that—"

"That?"

"You're developing feelings for me."

Ridiculous. I kick out my legs and lean back in my seat. "You're mistaken. I do intend to sleep with you, and only so the relationship comes across as genuine to my brothers. It's the same reason I specified no one else fill your glass but me. I am Mafioso. It's expected that I'd be possessive about my intended. And I wanted things to take their natural course because I have no intention of forcing myself on you. Unless—" I lean forward. "Perhaps, you'd prefer that I did so."

Her breath catches.

"Is that what this is about? Do you prefer I take you without giving you a choice? Would you prefer I show you how it could be between us without asking for your consent?"

Her chest rises and falls. The pulse fluttering in the hollow of her throat speeds up.

"Is that what you want, Angel?"

Color flushes her cheeks. She gulps, then shakes her head. "Of course not."

"Are you sure? It's okay to tell me if that's what turns you on."

Her amber eyes turn to flint. She firms her lips. She jumps up and turns to leave, but I'm faster. I swoop over and grab her wrist.

"Sit down."

Her shoulders rise. Her entire being is so wound up, I worry her pulse rate is through the roof.

"Angel," I say softly, "you know I mean you no harm."

She watches me warily.

"I was merely saying I'm here to oblige your wishes. If you want me to fuck you, you only have to ask."

"You bastard. You know exactly how to get under my skin, don't you?"

"It's too easy," I admit. "Your instant reactions to my suggestions are a turn on. Your sensitivity to my nearness is an aphrodisiac nothing can ever equal. The way you stand up to me at every turn, how you don't hesitate to speak your mind without regard to the consequences, how you look me in the eye, and yet, are unable to give voice to your deepest desires, which are written into every curve of your body, is a contradiction which appeals to me, even as you confound me."

Every muscle in her body vibrates with an emotion I don't dare name. She's attracted to me; she wants me. Yet, she stops herself from reaching out to me. Oh, her body betrays her every time, but her eyes, that resolution in them as she grapples with the intensity of her passion, holds me in thrall. Everything about her holds me in thrall. The conflict bleeds from every cell in her body and draws me to her over and over again. It's why I'm here, instead of attending a meeting with my brothers. Something I suspect they'll never let me live down.

It'll be worth it, to get to spend this time with her. This time on which there's a sell-by date. For we can't stay together for too long. So why hadn't I given her an outer limit for the time we're to be together? Why hadn't I been able to tell her that, at the first instance possible, I intend to break things off and set her free? Is it because I already know I won't be able to let her go once I have her? Would it be better to sleep with her before we get married, and fuck it out of my system, so her nearness doesn't affect me so much anymore?

"One month." I tighten my grip on her arm. "Give me one month after we're married and I'll release you."

She searches my features. "So, one month after we're married, you'll divorce me?"

"There are no divorces in the *Cosa Nostra*," I point out.

She pales. "S-so what, then?"

"One month. We stay married for that time. Then, you're free to leave. Of course, all of your needs will be taken care of. As the wife of the *Capo*, you'll have a monthly deposit made into your account that will take care of everything. That'll continue, even if something happens to me." Her eyes widen, but I continue, "You won't need to work, unless you choose to."

She tugs on her arm, and this time, I release her.

She slips into her seat and toys with her glass of wine. "How much money are we talking about?"

A heavy sensation presses down on my chest. My stomach bottoms out. And I thought she was different from other women. That it wasn't my money she was attracted to. I know, already, it isn't my status.

Most women in this country look on the fact that I am *Cosa Nostra* with awe... Indeed, marrying into the Sovrano family is a social ranking they aspire to. But she's already made it clear it has the opposite effect on her. The Sovrano family name means nothing to her. As for being part of the

Cosa Nostra? She's against the very idea that my livelihood is based on often being on the wrong side of the law. I thought it extended to her view on money, that it held no meaning for her. But I was wrong, it seems. Like most females, wealth equals security for her, the attainment of which is a goal to aspire to reach. So why had I thought of her as being different?

"A hundred-thousand every month."

She laughs. "Is that all being the wife of a Mafia *Capo* is worth?"

I reach for my own wine glass and take a healthy swig. "Two hundred-thousand."

"Come now, *Capo*, you and I both know you could do better."

I tighten my fingers around the glass. The hostess comes by to top me up, and I snarl at her. She pales and skitters away. When I turn my gaze on my wife-to-be, she's watching me with a placid expression.

Anyone else would know it's not a good idea to dare me when I'm in this mood. But she doesn't have any sense of self-preservation. It's the only reason she's sitting here with a gleam in her eyes and an innocent look on her features as she taunts me.

That emptiness in the pit of my stomach grows until it seems to fill my entire body. My hands and feet feel numb. My chest feels too heavy for the rest of me, and every breath is a struggle. I shake my head to clear it.

What's wrong with me? Had I expected anything different from her? Had I hoped that she'd be someone who'd see through my bluster to the man I am underneath? Why should she when I've promised her nothing? When I've told her there's no way I could ever love her, when I've made it clear there's no chance of anything more long-term between us. I squeeze down on the stem of my wine glass and it snaps. The remnants of the blood-red liquid stain the white tablecloth.

She gasps, then turns her gaze up to my face.

I release the broken stem and allow my lips to curl. "A million dollars a month. On one condition."

28

Jeanne

He believed me when I said the money was not enough. He thought I would go through with this farce of a marriage, and then the separation, for the money. And when I asked him to up the figure he'd pay me monthly, he didn't hesitate.

I saw the certainty in his gaze and a kind of satisfaction that he was proven right. He was expecting me to pull this money-based negotiation on him all along. In fact, he's surprised I didn't bring this up with him earlier. Now, he has the gall to throw his money in my face and tag on a condition with it. I almost jump up and leave, but curiosity keeps me rooted. What could he possibly want? What does he think a million dollars a month could buy him?

"What is it?" I ask in a voice that sounds polite, and even a little distant, with just a hint of curiosity. Damn. Elle Woods has nothing on me when it comes to putting on a front.

"We get married tonight—"

"What?" I gasp.

"Then you'll beg me to take your pussy and your ass and your mouth all in one go on our wedding night."

The blood drains from my face. My stomach flip flops. The wine glass

I'm holding tips, and I place it back on the table. Jerk. Does he really think I can be bought? Does he think I'll give in to his demands so easily? Does he think I'm an idiot with a pretty face, who'll be so overcome by his money, I'll let him have me every way he wants?

A pulse thuds between my legs. My thighs quiver. My breasts feel too heavy for my body and my nipples tighten. How dare he take me for granted. How dare I find his filthy words a turn on. How dare my body betray me again where he's concerned.

"You know what?" I lean forward. "I have no choice but to…"

"To?" His smile widens.

"To refuse you, you smug, conceited, horrible man." I jump up to my feet, throw the remainder of my wine in his face, then grab my bag and pivot so fast, I knock my chair over. I race past the startled diners toward the exit. *There, almost there.* A breath of relief escapes me, then a heavy hand descends on my shoulder. I yelp as I'm turned around and slammed into his very hard chest. Tremors of heat ignite all over my skin. Lust pools low in my belly. I tip up my chin and his blue gaze is ablaze with the anger of a thousand exploding suns. I gasp. The hair on the back of my neck rises. I've never seen him this overcome by emotion. His features wear a confluence of surprise and relief and something else. Something smoldering, something so intense that it slices me to my core. My guts churn. My heart overturns in my chest. He twists my arm around me, notches his knuckle under my chin and glares into my eyes.

"Say that again," he growls.

"What?"

"Say you refuse my offer. Say you don't want my money."

"I don't want your money, you self-absorbed, egotistical, full-of-your-self, pompous—"

He closes his mouth over mine. He absorbs the rest of my words, and sucks on my lips, and kisses me with such fierceness that my heart seems to be pulled up into my throat. I forget to breathe. My knees turn to jelly. I slump against him, but he doesn't let go. He absorbs what little oxygen I have left in my lungs, and flickers of darkness spark behind my eyes. He tears his mouth away from mine, and I draw in a shuddering breath. My lungs inflate and my head spins. He bends, picks me up, and throws me over his shoulder.

"What the—"

My hair falls over my eyes so I can't see what's happening. There's a flurry of activity around us as if the diners have suddenly noticed us. I hear him rumble something, the vibrations shivering up my thighs and coiling in my belly. The heavy weight of his arm across the back of my thighs pulses a steady heat up my body. I shove the hair from out of my face and am presented with his perfectly-sculpted, superbly-tight ass. I bounce against his hard back as he stalks out of the door. There are more raised voices in Italian, his answering response, which I don't catch, then we are out of the restaurant. The cool air assails me and goosebumps pepper my skin. It cuts the jumble of thoughts in my head and I begin to struggle.

"Let me go."

"No," he snaps.

He prowls toward what I assume is the curb, and the screech of brakes being applied reaches me.

Oh, no. I am not getting into the car with him.

I wriggle in his grasp. "I'm not leaving with you."

"Yes, you are."

"No, I'm not." I dig my knee into his stomach. His very hard, unforgiving stomach. "Let me down," I snarl.

"Not a chance."

I join my fingers and bring my fists down into his back. His breathing doesn't even change. A sudden burn of heat flashes across my butt. I jump. *What the—?*

"Did you just spank me?"

"Just getting started, baby."

Another exchange of voices in Italian, then he lowers me into my seat. I instantly charge forward, but he shoves his head into mine and kisses me again. The kiss is hard and firm and has this sense of assurance threaded into it that indicates he knows what he's doing. It holds the promise he intends to not stop until he's had his way with me. It has an erotic need underlying it, a desperation, a vulnerability I've seen in his eyes before, which I only now taste. An unguarded sentimentality that makes me blink.

He leans back and holds my gaze and must read my confusion for he nods. "I won't hurt you..." His lips twist, and once more, he's the mean, dominant alphahole carrying me off to his lair. The confident, forceful *Capo* who always gets his way. "Not unless you want me to."

I swallow.

"Does the thought of what I could do to your body turn you on, Angel?"

Yes.

Yes.

I shake my head.

"Liar." He chuckles, then kisses me again. When he straightens, I realize the seatbelt has been drawn over my chest. He slams my door, walks around the car, and slides into the driver's seat. Before I can think of trying to undo my belt, he locks the doors, fastens his own seatbelt, and maneuvers the car onto the road.

"So, you're kidnapping me?" I burst out.

"Want me to stop the car and let you out?"

I open my mouth to agree, then hesitate.

"That's what I thought," he murmurs.

He steps on the accelerator, and the car speeds up. I should say something, should protest and rage and cry. And try to escape. Instead, I fold my hands in my lap and gaze through the windshield. My chest feels lighter. A load seems to have rolled off of my shoulders. He was right. Now that the decision has been taken out of my hands, I feel relieved. Is that what's been holding me back? That I've been fighting with my conscience and berating myself for what I feel for him? Am I so weak, I need a man to make the decision for me and put me in a situation where I have to fall in with his plan because there's no other way out?

"Stop thinking so hard. You're beginning to give me a headache," he drawls.

I shoot him a sideways glance and take in that gorgeous profile of his.

"You have to realize this is not normal for me. I've never allowed anyone to coerce me into a situation where I'm not in control, and now I've done it not once, but twice."

"Will it help if I tell you that I'm very persuasive?"

"Not really."

"What if I tell you you need to trust me?"

"Can I trust you?" I shoot back.

"Trust me to give you what you need." His lips kick up.

"Are you twisting around the words to suit your needs?"

"Maybe," he confesses, "but I also think you'll be much happier if you allow me to lead right now."

"I'm not sure I like the sound of that." We take a turn onto a road that curves away from the highway. "Where are we going?"

"You did say that you'd prefer to elope and get married."

"Umm, yeah?"

"In Italian, we have a word for it. It's called *fu'itina*, which means *little escape*."

"Why does it sound so much better in Italian?" I muse.

"Everything's better in Italy, and in spoken Italian, and with Italian men." He smirks.

"Good to know. Clearly, being humble is not one of the known attributes of Italian men."

"Humble? What's that?" His grin widens. "I'd have loved to take you to Vegas but—"

"Vegas," I screech. "I can't go to Vegas. I need to show up for rehearsal tomorrow, or I'll lose my role as understudy."

"Relax." The jerkface grins. "We're not going to Vegas; not exactly."

"What do you mean, 'not exactly'?" I cry.

"I'm taking you to the Vegas of Europe."

"Which is?"

"Malta."

"We're going to Malta?"

"It's a half an hour plane ride away."

"Why are we going to Malta?"

"It was easier for me to arrange for the paperwork related to the wedding there."

"Easier than your hometown?" I frown.

"If I'd reached out to my people here, the word would have spread to my brothers, who would've invited themselves to the wedding, along with their wives. I mean, you've met them already. Do you think any of them would have missed this opportunity to turn up for the ceremony?"

I shudder. "Guess not."

"That's why—" He gestures ahead to the small airstrip that comes into view. He halts at a gate that opens inward and drives the car through. We draw up to the small private jet, where a man is standing. He's tall, broad, and seems familiar. It's his brother Massimo.

"Thought you didn't want word getting back to your brothers?" I frown.

"Massimo's more discreet than the rest. If he sticks to his word, it'll buy us enough time to be out of here and married before anyone in *la famiglia* finds out."

He brings the car to a stop and I unbuckle my seatbelt. For a few seconds, we sit there staring at the plane.

"You sure about this?" I finally ask.

"No," he laughs, "but I like to live dangerously."

"That's not very reassuring." I clutch my fingers together in my lap. My heart begins to gallop so fast, I can feel it in my throat. My pulse rate booms, my stomach churns, and I'm sure I'm going to be sick. That's the last thing I need, puking all over his beautiful car. I swallow hard and squeeze my eyes shut. I try to take in a breath, but my lungs don't seem to function. *Oh, god, what am I doing?* Not only have I lost my role in the musical, the role that should have launched my career, but now I'm also going to marry a Mafia guy, one who says he can never love anyone. And I'm going to probably have to stay married to him forever, while he goes off and sees other women on the side. My lungs burn and my throat closes. I gasp as the world tilts.

"Easy, easy." A warm grasp over my hands draws my attention back to my body. I hear wheezing sounds and realize it's me. I try to take another breath, but bile clogs my throat. Then, I am pushed down so my face is between my knees.

His big palm rubs soothing circles over my back. "Breathe, baby, breathe."

Specks of darkness flicker at the edges of my vision. My hands and legs tremble. This is the second time I've come so close to fainting, and I've never fainted before in my entire life. I wheeze and pant and huddle into my seat, trying to draw oxygen into my starved lungs.

"Cazzo," I hear him swear, then he reaches over me, and my seatbelt loosens. He scoops me up like I weigh nothing and hauls me over the divider between the seats and onto his lap. He rocks me, and makes soothing noises that rumble up his chest and flow over me. The heat of his body cocoons me. He winds his arms about me; with one big palm, he pushes the hair back from my face and runs his fingers down the strands. With the other, he cups my cheek and presses my face into his chest.

I push my nose into the strip of skin that's bared between the lapels of his shirt. I draw in a breath, and the dark chocolate and coffee scent of his fills my lungs. It's like a signal to my brain to calm down. My pulse rate evens out. The burning in my lungs begins to subside. He continues to rock me and croon to me under his breath. I breathe in, drawing more of him into my body. Then, because I can't help myself, and because I want to see if he tastes as enticing as he smells, I flick out my tongue and lick him.

29

Luca

She drags her tongue down the demarcation between my pecs, and I feel the tug all the way down to the crown of my dick. My cock lengthens and the blood drains to my groin. I still, but don't draw away. She tugs on my nipple, and my entire body seems to come alive. I can feel my pulse in my throat, at my temples, even in my balls.

"Fuck. You're killing me, Angel."

She makes a sound at the back of her throat which is the most erotic thing I have heard in a long time. Then she cuddles in closer, as if she's trying to crawl into my body. A melting sensation squeezes my ribcage. I continue to caress her hair until her breathing is back to normal. She curls her fingers into the front of my shirt, then rubs her cheek against my chest. My pants feel too tight, and I know I need to get us out of here before my cock decides to poke its way through my zipper. I reach for my door handle, but she grips my bicep.

"Kiss me," she says in a low voice. "Kiss me, Luca."

"If I do, there's no guarantee we'll get out of this car anytime soon."

"Please." She wraps her fingers around the base of my neck and pulls my head down toward her. I gaze into those tawny eyes of hers and my heart stutters. We share breath for a second, then another. Then, she flicks out her tongue and licks my lips.

A groan rumbles up my chest. I twist her curls around my fingers and tug. Her head falls back. Her pupils dilate. Her breath hitches and I run my nose up her jawline. I inhale the scent of crushed roses, and every part of me seems to come alive. I press my lips to the corner of her lips, then nibble down on her lower lip. She tries to deepen the kiss, but I keep her in place with my hold on her hair. She scowls at me from under her heavy eyelids, and my already-shattered heart seems to splinter further. I brush my lips over hers, holding her gaze. She swallows, and the pulse at the base of her throat speeds up. She thrusts out her breasts, and I don't need to look down to know that her nipples are outlined against the fabric of her T-shirt.

She parts her lips and I sweep my tongue inside. I kiss her deeply, lose myself in her, and draw her closer, until she's pressed into my chest, and I can't tell where she begins and I end. Her hair flows over my arm, her breath sears my skin, and the curve of her hip under the palm of my hand quivers and draws me in, seducing me, coaxing me to grab at her butt and squeeze. A moan bleeds from her lips, and lust detonates in my gut. I slide my palm under her shirt and flatten my fingers against the soft swell of her stomach. Her skin is so soft, I might as well have dipped my fingers in silken cream. I tilt my head and deepen the kiss even more, when there's a rap on the window.

I tear my mouth from hers and swivel to face the window. The glass is dark, so our actions wouldn't have been very visible, although the outline of our figures would have made it clear what we were up to. I know it's Massimo outside. I pull my hand out from under her shirt and smooth it down. Then, I kiss her one last time. "Ready?"

"No," she breathes. "I don't think I can do this."

"You're stronger than you think, *tesoro mio*." I press a kiss to her forehead, tuck her hair behind her ear, and scan her face one last time to make sure she's okay. Then I unhook my belt, push the door open, and step out with her in my arms.

Massimo moves back to give us space.

"You all set?" He glances from my face to hers, then back at me.

I nod.

"The jet's fueled, the pilot's waiting, and I think I can hold off for at least six hours before Michael discovers the jet is not where it's supposed to be."

I wince.

"It's better than what happened at Seb's wedding, when everyone landed at the town hall for his supposedly secret wedding," Massimo points out.

"That's what happens when you try to sneak away and get married under the nose of the *famiglia*," I scoff.

"You're certainly setting the bar high." He rubs his chin. "Although, looking at the trouble you're going to, I'm glad I'm not going to be eloping."

"So, you're going in for the arranged marriage with the *Camorra* princess?"

"Not a chance." He scowls. "I won't be pushed into something unless I am a hundred-percent sure of it. And right now, marriage isn't on top of the agenda for me."

"But you did declare that you wouldn't be opposed to an arranged marriage."

"That was then." He glances between me and Jeanne again. "Watching the lot of you find true love—"

"We're not in love." Both Jeanne and I chorus together. Then we turn to look at each other, before turning to Massimo, who's watching us with a bemused look on his face.

"What?" I growl.

"Nothing." His smile widens.

Fucker watches us with a secret gleam in his eyes like he knows something I don't.

"Spit it out already," I grumble.

He chuckles. "Nothing the two of you don't know already."

"Not sure what you're trying to say here."

He grabs my shoulder with his massive paw and squeezes hard. Good thing we are equally matched in strength; a weaker guy might have keeled over with the pressure.

"Good luck, *fratello*." He grins. "If you want to beat the news of your elopement, which is probably on its way to our family as we speak, you might want to get on that jet, pronto."

Forty-five minutes later, we land at a private airstrip a few kilometers outside Valleta, the Maltese capital.

I turn to the woman who's sleeping in the seat next to me. I let her sleep as the engines of the plane wind down. Stillness creeps through the space as I take in the curve of her lips, the flush of her cheeks, the brush of her eyelashes, which flutter as she awakens and yawns.

She meets my gaze and smiles, then straightens.

"We're here?"

"We are."

I unsnap my seatbelt and rise to my feet then hold out my hand.
"Ready?"

30

Jeanne

I peer through the window of the limo which picked us up from the air strip. I wrap my arms about my waist. A frisson of restlessness sparks my nerve endings, and a thrill of excitement runs up my spine. It's always like this when I land in a new country. I feel energized and electrified and I can't wait to go out and explore the place, except... I won't be here that long. I have to be back tomorrow night, in less than ten hours, at the rehearsal. We'll barely have enough time to grab some sleep and get married and—my breath hitches. Jesus, Mary and Joseph. I'm getting married. I'm getting married to my Mafia guy. Not *my* Mafia guy; the Mafia guy.

When I woke up on the plane, it was to find Luca watching me with an expression on his face I couldn't quite decipher. Maybe the events of the night were catching up with him. More likely, he was wondering what other surprise he could spring on me. Before I could ask him any further questions, he rose to his feet and pulled me along and off the plane. We barely got into the car, and I switched my phone on, when the messages started pinging in the group chat I share with Olivia and Penny. I started to message them and stopped. Started, then stopped again. I finally gave up trying to tell them where I was and what was going to happen. Because really, what was I going to say? I'm in Malta and we're eloping? Isn't the point of eloping to keep things a secret until the deed is done? Not that I don't want to update them. It's just, maybe it's best to wait until I have a chance to catch my breath.

So, I put my phone away and turn to the window. Partly because I don't want to talk to Luca right now.

He held me in the car at the airstrip in Palermo when I fell apart. He soothed me and rocked me and then kissed me in such a way that I felt it all the way to the tips of my toes. I would have been happy to curl up in his lap and melt into him until our skin fused together. But Massimo knocked on the window, rousing me from my fantasy. Then, Luca carried me out of the car and onto the plane. He set me down in one of the plush seats by the window, strapped me in, asked for a blanket, and tucked it around me. He made sure I ate and drank on the flight, since we'd left the restaurant without eating, then coaxed me to get a quick nap. As a result, I'm now wide-eyed and wired. A feeling which is magnified because he's across the seat from me.

He hasn't spoken a word to me since we got off the plane. There was a convoy of black cars waiting for us. All of them had tinted windows. All except one of the cars were SUVs with men in black suits and grim faces standing next to them.

Luca didn't spare them a glance. He led me directly to the only non-SUV car, a limo. The driver held the door open. Luca made sure I was seated before walking around the car and sliding into the back seat next to me. The driver must know where we're headed; he raised the barrier between the front and the back seats, then drove off.

It's almost like he's afraid of getting on Luca's bad side. Which, I admit, I haven't seen so far. Even when we were in the cell, he was largely good-humored, as if the entire situation were a challenge he looked forward to overcoming. Come to think of it, he's more tense now than I've seen him in all the time I've known him.

The rest of the convoy fell in line in front and behind our car. Luca must be even more important than I thought if he managed to get so much security in place in such a short period of time. There's so much about this man I don't know. I place my palm on the seat between us. The bulk of his presence seems to take up so much room, and even though there's space between us, it feels like he's sitting very close to me. The heat vibrates off of him, pulsing, throbbing with unsaid emotions. His scent seems to intensify in the enclosed space until it's in my pores, in my skin, in my hair.

Until I've drawn his scent deep into my lungs, and my blood is saturated in his essence.

I hit the button to lower the glass on my window and the breeze rushes in. Incredible that just a few hours ago I was in Palermo, and now, I'm in Malta, a place I've heard of but never thought I'd actually visit.

I slide my hand out so the wind slides between my fingers. Some of the tension leaves my muscles and I relax my shoulders.

I withdraw my hand, lean back in my seat and close my eyes. The wind ruffles my hair and a strand blows across my face. I stay still, enjoying the play of the breeze over my features.

Then, the strand of hair across my face is pushed behind my ear. A tremor steals over my skin. I bite the inside of my cheek and refuse to open my eyes.

There's a feather touch as he skims his fingers… no, his knuckles, over my jawline.

My breath catches.

The touch continues down my chin, down the column of my throat, to my sternum. He hovers there for a second and my core clenches. My thighs quiver, and I have to stop myself from reaching up and grabbing his wrist to stop his progress.

A moan slips from my lips, and I sense his sharp inhale.

The heat of his body escalates, and I know he's moved closer. He continues to advance down the valley between my breasts, then to the side, where he pushes aside my jacket and circles a nipple, which instantly peaks. He draws another lazy circle and the space between my thighs grows moist. He moves his touch to my other breast and when he lightly flicks my nipple, my entire body jolts.

"Oh, god," I breathe. "Oh, Jesus."

"You called me, baby?" he retorts in a voice that has a thread of laughter running through it.

I snap open one eye and scowl at him.

"That was very corny," I grouse.

"It worked, though."

"That's what you think."

He cups my breast, and even through the clothes I'm wearing, the heat of his touch sears my skin. A pulse throbs to life in my pussy, a yearning deep inside that flamed to life when I first saw him in that cell. When he reached for me in his almost unconscious state and called me Angel. I don't know why it affected me so. Why seeing him vulnerable, with all his walls lowered, when I glimpsed his real self in his eyes, something inside me shifted and has continued to liquefy every time I've seen him since.

It's why I tear my gaze away from him, look toward the window, and swallow. I'm so close to falling for him, and I don't want that to happen. Don't want to fall for a person in a relationship that is doomed even before it starts.

"Luca, please." I bite down on my lower lip, and suddenly, he's there. He pulls my lips gently from between my teeth, then pinches my chin so I have to turn to him.

"What do you want?" His aquamarine eyes bore into mine. "Tell me what you need, Angel."

"You can't give me what I want."

"You haven't asked."

"What right do I have to ask?"

"You're my wife-to-be." His gaze narrows.

"Fake wife-to-be," I whisper.

"We're trying to keep it as real as we can for the sake of my family, aren't we?"

I nod.

"So, ask. Pretend for the remainder of this trip, at least, what we have is real. What would you ask me then?"

"I'd ask you to fuck me."

31

Luca

Her words echo in my ears and seem to find a direct route to my heart, then to my balls. I never would have thought the two are connected, but when it comes to her, nothing I thought was certain seems to be anymore. Not the way my body reacts to her presence, not the way the feelings I swore never to unearth seem to bubble to the surface when I look at her. Not the way thoughts of her crowd my mind when she's not around. How I obsess over her sweet scent, the quiver of her lips, the wobble of her chin, the way she scrunches up her forehead when she's trying very hard not to ask something; until her curiosity gets the better of her and she does. How she looks at me with that half-pleading, half-angry expression that hints at her inner turmoil. How the touch of her skin sends my heartbeat into a frenzy, and my pulse rate into overdrive, not to mention how the thought of making her mine feels so right. So right. So mine. *Mine. Mine. Mine.*

My breathing speeds up, and my chest rises and falls. I look between her eyes and see the confusion I feel mirrored in them.

"Luca," she whispers, and *cazzo*, the blood drains to my groin. My cock lengthens, the thumping of my heart a cadence matched by the *thump-thump-thump* of her.

I lean in closer, until I share breath with her. The glare from a streetlight shines through the window. I can make out every individual eyelash on her eyelids, the tiny beauty spot above her upper lip that's so enticing I want to suck on it.

"Luca," her voice cracks and I blink.

What am I doing? Why is it that I can never act as planned around her? Why is it that I lose my mind every time I touch her?

"Sorry." I glance outside my window. "Didn't mean to do that."

She stills.

I drum my fingers on my thigh. "It's not far to the safe house. You'll also find everything you need to get dressed for the ceremony, which is in a few hours."

"Luca," her voice is strident now. "Did you hear what I said?"

"I'll have you back in time for your seven p.m. dress rehearsal tonight."

"Luca," she says through gritted teeth, "are you turning me down?"

I turn and look her up and down. "You don't tell me what to do."

"So, you can paw me and it's okay, but if I ask you to finish what you started, you get upset?"

"Something like that."

"But you told me to tell you what I wanted," she growls.

"I didn't say I was going to give it to you."

She makes an angry sound at the back of her throat and my cock twitches. Goddamn, there's nothing she can do that wouldn't appeal to me, apparently.

"You are the most infuriating man I have ever met," she finally spits out.

"Goes both ways, baby."

"Don't you 'baby' me, you... you... dunderhead!"

I stare. "Is that supposed to be an insult?"

"Now it is."

"You sound frustrated." I try to stop my lips from twitching, but don't quite succeed.

"You would be, too, if your stupid fiancé, or whatever it is you are to me, decided to get all lovey-dovey, only to pull back when things begin to get serious. And this was *after* you told me we'd take things organically. In fact, wasn't it you who said that I'd need to ask you to fuck me before you did?"

"I told you when you beg me to fuck you, and you will, I won't do it. You'll plead with me to let you come, but I won't. Remember?"

Her mouth drops open, and I can see the gears turning in her head. Finally, her eyes gleam and she retorts, "Oh, I get it. You can't. That's why you've been teasing me since we met. You want me to believe you're some kind of fantastic lover, but when the time comes to act, you can't quite deliver the goods, you—"

I swoop across, grab her wrist, and pull her across my lap.

"What the—" She wriggles, and I place my arm on the small of her back to keep her in place.

"Let me go, you ass, or I'll scream."

"Go ahead; this space is soundproof."

"Is not." She peers up at me from under her eyelashes.

"Try it. In fact, I'll help you with it." I bring my hand down on her jeans clad butt and she squeals. I raise my hand again and slap her left ass cheek. She yells.

I spank her right ass cheek. She screams.

Thwack-thwack-thwack. I spank her alternate butt cheeks, and she cries out, then groans, until finally, a moan bleeds from her lips.

I massage the curve of her ass—which must be throbbing by now—through the seat of her jeans. She trembles, and fuck if I don't find that alluring. When she goes all soft and defenseless, she brings out that dark side of me that wants to possess her completely. Another shudder grips her, and I squeeze her ass. She groans, then pushes her butt out even more so it fills my hands.

"You like this, don't you, Angel?"

She shakes her head.

"Bet you can't wait until I take your ass."

She turns her head and scowls at me, her lips pursed up in a pout. So fucking adorable.

"Bet if I shoved my hand between your thighs, I'd find you wet."

Her scowl deepens.

I grip her shoulders and pull her up to a sitting position. She winces and my cock twitches in response. Bet it hurts to sit on her backside after how I spanked her. Why do I love that so much?

"You okay?"

She turns her head away and glances out of the window. I reach over and push a strand of hair behind her ear. She pulls away from me.

My lips quirk up. "Don't be like that."

"Don't talk to me," she spits out.

"You angry with me, baby?"

"What do you think?" she hisses back.

"I think you are mighty frustrated, is what."

"Can we get this over with so we can head back to Palermo?"

"Thought you wanted me to fuck you?" I retort.

"That was before—" She hesitates.

"Before?"

"Before I found out what a callous, cruel, brutal... fiend you are."

"I believe the word you are looking for is sadist." I smirk.

She whips her head around in my direction. "Thought you were an exhibitionist?"

"And a sadist," I clarify.

The color rises in her cheeks.

"Does that turn you on?"

She flips her hair over her shoulder. "Of course not."

I laugh. "Just remember one thing. When I decide to fuck you, no one can stop me, especially not you. When I decide to fuck you, it will be on my terms, on my schedule, and you'll throw yourself at me and beg me to show you no mercy."

32

Jeanne

I glance around the room he led me to before vanishing down the corridor. I'd expected him to bring me to a hotel, but instead, we've come to what he called a safe house. A gorgeous two-story building built in a Moorish architectural style, which I'm guessing must be typical for this region. From what I recall of my history lessons, Malta has Italian and Moorish influences.

He'd told me to freshen up and get dressed. *Dressed. Dressed in what?*

Before I could ask him the question, he turned and left.

Now, I cross the floor to the closet in the corner and throw it open. My breath whooshes out. Whoa! There's a full-length white dress on a hanger, complete with silver stilettos, and a hat box on the floor next to it. I reach for the hat box, lift it up, and open it to find a veil. I place the hat box on the bed, then take the hanger with the white dress, and walking over to the mirror, hold it up in front of me. It's a simple design. Sleeveless, then cut so it falls in a straight line to my toes. It seems shapeless, but the material is so light, it feels like I'm holding a cloud in my arms.

How did he have time to arrange all of this? Did he know we were coming here today? Did he plan all of this in advance? Was he so sure I'd leave with him? What if I'd said no? The questions swirling in my head almost cause me to hyperventilate again.

Instead, I lay the dress out on the bed and walk toward the bathroom. A quick shower later, I wrap the towel around myself and walk out. Then freeze. There on the bed, next to the dress, is a matching bra and panties set. It's brand-new, judging by the folds in the fabric, and clearly, my size. I glance around the room, then back at the lingerie. It feels as soft as butterfly wings. I shrug into the under clothes, then survey myself in the mirror.

The panties are simple white silk and cut high on the hips. The bra cups my breasts and lifts them, with the lace straps giving them a faintly S&M feel. What? Of course, I know about S&M. I've read about it. And I confess, I read *Fifty Shades of Grey*, in between the pages of my university text books. How else could you read it?

Did he choose this himself? Did he run his fingers over the undergarments before setting them down?

I step into the dress. It drapes over my shoulders, clings to my bust line, nips in at the waist, then flows to my feet. It's simple, elegant, and understated, except for the bodice, which has beads sewn into it. I turn this way and that, and the light from the spotlight in the ceiling bounces off the lattice work.

It's so beautiful; so perfect. How could he have guessed my style? More importantly, how did he guess my size? And have this stitched and delivered so quickly? I hold my hair away from my face, when there's a knock on the door. A woman pops her head around the door.

I blink. "Penny?" I yell. "Penny!" I pivot around, and in two strides, I meet her halfway across the floor. "What are you doing here?" I fling my arms open, but she holds her palms up, face forward.

"You look beautiful, and I don't want to spoil your wedding dress."

"You won't!" I throw my arms around her and hug her, and that tight sensation around my chest eases. How had he known I'd want to see a familiar face? I hadn't realized it myself until just now, seeing Penny.

"I'm not alone," she whispers.

"Wait, what?"

Another woman walks through the doorway.

"Olivia?" I stare wide-eyed as her features light up.

"Long time, no see, eh?" She grins and comes to a stop in front of us. Penny steps out of my embrace, and Olivia looks me up and down. Her chin trembles, and her eyes shine. Yeah, Olivia acts like she's the tough one, but inside, she's a softie. The one's who pretend to be hard-hearted always are.

"Wh-what are the two of you doing here?"

They look at each other. "We got a call from your Mafioso." Olivia half smiles. "He told us the two of you decided to elope, but he felt you'd prefer if the two of us were there as your bridesmaids—"

"He had Massimo pick us up and take us to this darling little boutique where we picked out our bridesmaid's dresses—" Penny gestures to the short blue dresses they're both wearing— "then Massimo took us to their private jet, and here we are."

He made sure my friends had bridesmaids dresses? The man thinks of everything. Speaking of... "We flew in a private jet," I say slowly, "then he sent you another private jet?"

"So, he has a lot of private jets?" Olivia raises a shoulder. "Also, your dress is gorgeous."

"He had this waiting for me."

"You mean, he had this all tailored and ready for you?" Penny asks.

"It would seem so."

"It fits you beautifully," Olivia murmurs.

"I'm so happy both of you are here." I glance between them, then throw my arms around both of them again.

"Your dress," Olivia protests.

"I don't care." I hold onto them.

"We care." Penny shrugs out of my embrace and I let them go.

"What are you doing to your hair?"

Half an hour later, I glance at myself in the mirror. Penny helped me put my hair up in a twist of some kind, and Olivia helped me with my make-up. The result is that I look radiant. Like a bride, I suppose. I am a bride... Even though it's all fake, it doesn't feel fake. That's the problem. It feels too real. It's happening; it's really happening. I squeeze my fingers together. I draw in a breath and my stomach protests. I taste bile on my tongue, and sweat breaks out on my hair line. "Oh, god, I'm going to be sick, I think."

"Don't you dare." Penny rubs my back. "Breathe, babe, breathe. Everything is going to be okay."

"You have no idea." I meet her gaze in the mirror. My face is almost as white as the dress. "Penny." I swallow. "I have something to tell you guys."

She and Olivia exchange worried glances. "What is it? You can tell us anything."

"It's... it's not what it seems." I twist my fingers together. I know I shouldn't tell anyone that all this is a farce, but it's killing me not to. "Luca and I, we—"

There's a knock on the door.

"Hold that thought—" Penny turns and flounces to the doorway and opens it. I peer in that direction in the mirror, but can't see who's on the other side. It has to be him, right? Who else could it be?

I hear the low rumble of his voice, though he's too far away for me to make out the words. Penny nods. Then she shuts the door and turns around with a gorgeous bouquet, filled with white and blue flowers, in her arms.

"What's that?" I ask.

She walks toward me, holding the bouquet in a reverential way. As she comes closer, the scent of jasmine drifts toward me. There are strands of star-shaped flowers on stalks and bluebells. Like the dress, it's simple, elegant, and utterly memorable.

"It's a bridal bouquet," Penny says in a hushed voice.

She holds it out to me. Tears gather in my eyes, and the bouquet fades in and out of my vision.

"Don't cry, babe, you'll spoil your make up," Olivia warns as she pats my shoulder.

I reach for the bouquet, and Olivia grabs a tissue and pats my cheek. "Are you ready?"

33

Luca

"What's taking them so long?" I tug on the sleeve of my shirt, then straighten the lapel of my jacket. Clearly, I hadn't thought this through. It was meant to be simple. We'd elope, get married, return, and that would be that. I'd expected us to fly from the airport to Malta, get married, then spend a few hours in our room consummating the wedding, and fly back. As easy as loading a gun and shooting.

I might have gotten away with it, too, if I hadn't involved Massimo in my plans. I'd gotten on the plane, and while she'd slept, I'd touched base with him.

I didn't have much choice. I couldn't arrange what I had in mind without his help. So, I broke the promise I made to myself not to let anyone in my family know that my marriage was an arrangement.

It was supposed to be an elopement, but watching her features relax, I realized the only other time I'd seen her this unworried was when she was with her friends. I knew, then, I had to invite them to the wedding.

Massimo helped get their phone numbers. Then, I spoke to both of them and told them Massimo would be coming by to pick them up. They were more than happy to join us. And Massimo accompanied them.

No, he didn't tell me that was his plan, either.

"Not sure what you're doing here." I scowl at him.

"Did you think I wouldn't turn up in person to witness your downfall?" He smirks.

"The fuck you talking about?"

His smile broadens.

"The fuck you laughing at, *stronzo?*"

"At you?" He rocks back on his heels. "Or should I say, at a man who's willingly knotting the noose around his neck?"

At the other end of the room, the official who waits to solemnize the wedding shuffles his feet. In the light from the overhead chandelier, his face seems bleached. Probably a combination of fear and greed. Which is what brought him here in the first place. Massimo suitably compensated him for his efforts, no doubt, but it wasn't until he arrived here and saw us, he must've realized who he was going to marry.

I scowl at him and he pales further. He takes a few steps back, until he's almost at the wall. Then, just for shits and giggles, I stab my forefinger and middle finger toward my eyes, then at him.

The man almost collapses before he shuffles toward a seat and sinks down into it.

"Stop playing with your food," Massimo says mildly.

"Fuck you very much, too." I run my finger around the collar of my shirt. Why is it that the tie seems to be getting tighter by the second? I slide my palm down the fabric of my tie. The silky smooth cloth rustles across my skin. As silken as the curve of her butt. As soft as her lips. As velvety as her cunt. Where she is concerned, I clearly have a one-track mind, which begins and ends with wanting to own her. And yet, when she asked me to fuck her, I backed away. Oh, I wanted to take her so badly, and I didn't care that our first time would be in the car, but a part of me wanted to have my ring on her finger before I finally bury myself inside her. Maybe I'm more old-fashioned than I realized. Or perhaps, it's simply that it satisfies some primal part of me to have my mark of ownership on her before I fuck her? *Stocazzo*, where are these thoughts coming from?

"Luca?" Massimo touches my shoulder and I start.

"What is it?" I growl.

"You've gone pale, *fratello*." He searches my features. "There's still time to call this off."

"Why would I do that?"

"Maybe you're deeper into this than you thought?"

"You're not making sense." I pull away from him and head to the window of the conservatory that's attached to the living room of the place. It might be a safe house, but it doesn't lack for luxury. After all, it's a piece of real estate purchased by the Sovranos, and we pride ourselves on owning the best. Like her. She's an asset. A commodity I acquired to help me get my family off my back. So why is my heart thumping so hard? Why is my pulse banging against my wrists? Why is my throat so dry, it feels like I swallowed sand.

"A drink?" I glance around the space, then spy the bar attached to the wall on the far end of the room.

I march over to the counter, grab a bottle of grappa—another dead giveaway that we're in a Sovrano space—and twist the cap off. I tilt the bottle to my lips and chug down a healthy portion. The honeyed liquid soothes the scratchiness in my throat and hits my stomach, where it imbues me with warmth. I lower the bottle to the counter and take a deep breath.

"Ever consider the possibility that you may have feelings for her?" Massimo's voice interrupts the stream of consciousness that I seem to be, of late, indulging in far too often.

"Feelings?" I cap the bottle and turn to him, feeling steadier. "I just met her."

"Yet you're marrying her?"

"She's the best candidate to fulfill Nonna's last wish," I retort.

"Like you couldn't have found anyone else? Any woman in the city would have offered herself up for the role, and you know it. Besides—" He looks me up and down. "Didn't think you took Nonna's last wish seriously?"

"Didn't you?" I glower at him. "Isn't that why you're considering the arranged marriage with the *Camorra* princess?"

"I haven't said yes, yet," he shoots back. "I may not agree to it."

"But you're thinking about it?"

He blows out a breath. "Hard not to, when Michael seems to thinks it's the only way to bring about peace between the *Camorra* and the *Cosa Nostra*."

"You'd think the old bat's hold on us would have declined once she died, but she's made sure, even in passing, she's forcing us to bend to her will," I say bitterly.

"Nonna only had our best interests at heart," Massimo protests.

"Doesn't seem that way from where I'm standing. I was happy in my single life, until she decided to put a ticking countdown timer on it."

"You could simply disregard what she asked of us," he argues.

"I've tried, I promise, but apparently, I'm sentimental enough to want to respect her wishes."

"By orchestrating a wedding you're not sure of?"

"Of course I'm sure of it," I scoff

"Are you?" He widens his stance. "It looks to me like you're in the process of trapping yourself the way our brothers did."

"Our brothers had feelings for their wives when they proposed to them."

"And you don't?"

"Of course not."

He laughs. The *pezzo di merda* throws back his head and guffaws.

I watch him, half-amused, half-angry. "I didn't say anything that funny."

"So you claim." He wipes the tears from his cheeks. "You forget, I witnessed our brothers bullshit themselves with similar arguments, then watched as they got pussy-whipped."

He has a point, but no way I'm falling for any woman. And certainly not for one as sassy, as opinionated, as gorgeous, and as breathtaking as her.

I set my jaw. "It's going to be different for me."

34

Jeanne

It's going to be different for me. It has to be different for me.

Going by the strike-out rate of the people I know, I'd say that more than 50% of marriages end in divorce. This isn't based on any scientific study, just what I see around me.

I'd always hoped things would be different for me. Call it my optimistic nature. Or rather, my romantic nature. Or perhaps, my blindly trusting nature. But my instinct has always said that when I get married, it'll be for keeps. I've always thought it would be different for me. That I'd marry the man I fell in love with and live with him happily ever after. Maybe it's my steady diet of smut novels that's nurtured that dream in me. It's why I can't help that thought echoing through my mind as I reach the doors that lead to the conservatory.

I come to a standstill. What am I doing? Am I going to bind myself to a man I barely know? A man I'm attracted to, all right, but not someone for whom I harbor those kinds of feelings.

And he certainly has no such tender emotions where I'm concerned. I'm merely an asset, a convenience... Someone who happened to be there; someone with whom he confesses he senses the chemistry that I do. Someone who'll help him get off the hook where his family is concerned.

That's all I am, a convenient prop in this game he's playing with his nearest and dearest.

So why does everything feel so real? Why does it feel like I'm wearing my wedding dress and about to say my vows to the man of my dreams? Can this monster be my savior? Can he be the man I've gravitated toward my entire life?

A touch on my shoulder shakes me out of my reverie. "Jeanne, you okay, babe?" Penny asks.

I nod.

"There's still time, honey." Olivia steps up and peers into my features. "I know these Mafioso men can be very persuasive. If you want to leave, we'll handle them in there. If you don't want to go through with this—"

"I do," I whisper, and oh, god, I mean it. My belly twists. My chest hurts. But something deep inside me tells me to proceed. "I know it seems crazy, but this feels right to me."

"Are you sure?"

I nod.

She peers into my features, then nods. "Okay then." She pushes the doors open and steps forward.

Rather than walk in front of me, I'd asked the girls to flank me on either side, mainly so I'd have moral support. We enter the room together.

I raise my gaze and see him. Luca. Clothed in a black suit, black shirt, and black tie—Luca. His hair is combed back from his face, except for that one unruly strand which flops down on his forehead. My fingers tingle. I want to reach out and push it back so I'll have an unobstructed view of that gorgeous face. Those piercing blue eyes, those thick eyelashes, the cheekbones which seem to be carved out of granite, that square jaw which I itch to place my palm against. The beautiful neck, those wide shoulders clad in a jacket which clings to him like it was stitched over his frame. The wide chest that stretches his shirt before narrowing down into that trim waist, those powerful thighs covered with pants that cling to every ripped muscle of his legs.

I gulp. My throat feels like I've swallowed a frog. My heartbeat cranks up until the blood pumps in my ears with such force, every sound in the room fades away. A bead of sweat runs down the valley between my breasts, and my skin feels too tight for the rest of me. I try to take in a breath, but my chest feels like it's being squeezed. My ribcage seems to have turned into an iron cage that compresses my lungs. My head spins and black spots speckle my vision. *No, no, no.* I am *not* going to faint, not now.

His eyes spark, his features harden, and every muscle in his body seems to grow rigid. Without breaking the connection of our eyes, he holds out his hand, and everything else in the room seems to fade. My vision tunnels. His gaze is a tractor beam that draws me in, slowly. Slowly. Only when I pause in front of him, do I realize I've covered the distance between us. I place my hand in his, and the warmth of his touch swoops up my arm, surrounds my chest, flows through my entire body. A breath I hadn't known I was holding rushes out of me. I guess that's why I couldn't inhale. With it, the sounds in the room filter in—the shuffle of feet behind me, from either Olivia or Penny, the clearing of the throat from the official who's standing on the other side of the table placed in front of us.

My knees have turned into jelly. I sway, and he tightens his grip on me. He holds my gaze until I feel steadier, then twines his fingers through mine and tugs me forward until the tips of my stilettos brush his shoes. From the corner of my eye, I notice Massimo hold up his phone to film the ceremony.

Luca jerks his chin in the direction of the official, indicating he should start. He turns to face me, and holds my gaze through the mercifully short ceremony.

I remember nodding and saying "I do," when it's my turn. Remember him staring deep into my eyes when he does the same. Then he releases his hold on me, long enough to slide something on my finger. I glance down at the platinum band with the citrine in the center and the tiny diamonds on either side. I hate to say it but the ring is gorgeous. It's not one of those ostentatious diamond wedding rings that are all money and no class. This one is discreet yet pretty, it's fragile and tasteful. It's beautiful and it suits me completely.

He holds both of my hands in his, raises my fingers to his mouth, and kisses the ring he placed on my finger. That's it. No ring for him. Of course not. Only the woman gets to wear a ring. So, he can stamp his brand of ownership on me for all to see, but apparently, I don't get to stamp my ownership on him. I glower at him. He ignores it, and kisses me on the forehead. A chaste kiss that could have been between friends. He pulls a pen from his pocket, leans forward, and signs on what I assume is the marriage certificate. He hands the pen to me, and when I'm done signing, he takes the pen from me, slides it back into his pocket, and wraps his arm around me.

We turn to face my friends and Massimo, whose attention is diverted.

His eyebrows are drawn down and he's staring at Olivia. Who's glowering right back at him. Huh? What did I miss?

Penny rushes forward and throws her arms around me. "Congratulations!" She kisses me on my cheek, then hugs Luca, who seems taken aback, then pleased.

"I know you'll make her happy. I know you love her. I see it in your eyes," she declares.

Seriously, this woman needs to take off her rose-tinted glasses and realize life is not all candy floss and white wedding gowns, and that even the most precious of rings, however beautiful they look, are not always symbolic of a love match.

The official behind us clears his throat again. "I need two witnesses to sign, as well."

"I'll do it." Olivia seems to tear her gaze off Massimo's with difficulty. She steps forward, then looks around for a pen.

"Here." Massimo pulls a pen from inside his coat pocket. He walks over and hands it to Olivia, who takes it with a muttered thanks. She finishes signing, then he does the same. The two of them stare at each other for a second longer, then as if by mutual agreement, they turn to face us.

"Everything okay?" I glance between them.

"Of course." Olivia pastes a big smile on her face. She steps forward and hugs me. "Congratulations. I hope you'll be happy."

"You still don't approve, do you?" I mutter under my breath.

"It doesn't matter what I think." She steps back and kisses my cheek. "If this is what you want, then who am I to disagree? Just remember, if you ever need help, I'll be there for you."

I hold her gaze. I want to stay angry with her for refusing to believe that the marriage between Luca and me won't last—which it isn't going to, of course, but she could, at least, feign happiness for me. I know she's only looking out for me, but still, why can't she just pretend to be thrilled for us? Probably because she's wiser than me.

She takes my hand in hers and squeezes it one last time, then steps back. "We're going to make our own way back to Palermo," she declares.

"But you won't make it back in time for the rehearsal this evening," I protest.

"I already checked the flights. I booked two tickets on the first flight out, which leaves in..." She looks at her watch. "In two hours. We'll be back in Palermo in plenty of time for the rehearsal."

"You're not taking a commercial flight," Massimo says in a hard voice.

"Newsflash: it's how we normal people do things. Which you are not."

She looks him up and down. "But I wouldn't expect you to understand, given your lifestyle. Also, I am not flying back in the same plane as you. I only agreed to come by private jet because I needed to get here in time to witness my best friend's wedding, which—" She turns to face me. "I have now done." She steps forward and kisses me again on my cheek. "See you back at rehearsal."

She walks past us and heads for the door, then stops and glances over her shoulder. "You coming, Penny?"

Penny looks at her pleadingly.

Olivia scowls back at her.

"You're leaving? So soon?" I cry.

Olivia bites her lips. Then she closes the distance between us and hugs me again. "I am so sorry. I know it's hurtful of me to take off like this. It's just... I can't stand your brother-in-law."

I glance from her to where Massimo is watching her closely.

"Huh? Is there something between the two of you? Something you haven't told us?"

She hesitates, then leans in even closer. "I can neither confirm nor deny that statement," she mutters.

"Oh my god. So, you two have definitely met before? Have you slept with him?" I whisper-yell.

"Shh!" She peers at Massimo from the corner of her eyes. "Don't worry about it. Anyway, today is not about me; it's about you. I truly hope that you'll be happy."

She kisses my cheek. "Please don't be angry with me for leaving, okay?"

I take in her flushed features, the widened eyes. She's spooked all right.

"Fine." I blow out a breath. "Go on, get out of here. But you owe me an explanation."

"Thanks Jeanne." She squeezes my arm. "I'll see you in time for the rehearsal, okay?" She steps back.

Penny rushes over and hugs me again. "See you in a few, babe. Remember what I said about riding the stallion?"

Before I can ask her to shut up, she squeezes my arm, then follows Olivia out. The door shuts behind them.

"Your friend doesn't like me very much," Massimo muses.

"Oh, she's like that with everyone. She takes a little time to warm up to people. Just give her time; she'll come around."

He scratches his jaw as if her entire reaction confused him.

"Uh, I should be leaving, too." The official hands an envelope to Massimo, then skitters away.

Massimo hands the envelope to Luca, who slips it into his coat pocket. Then, Massimo steps back and holds up his phone again.

"He needs another photo to share with *la famiglia*." Luca puts his arm around me and pulls me close. I try to smile, but my lips are frozen in a rictus. The heat of his body snaps around me and holds me in place as effectively as a noose. I draw in a breath, and the scent of him goes straight to my head. Oh, my god, there's no escaping him. He's all around me, in me, and now I'm married to him.

He turns and dips his head until his breath raises the hair on my forehead. "Relax, I'm not going to hurt you."

You already have. You just don't know it.

He tips my chin up and peers into my eyes. "Trust me, Angel. Everything's going to be fine."

I hold onto those sparks in the depths of his blue eyes like an ant clings to a leaf on the surface of a roaring river. He searches my features, hesitates, then as if unable to stop himself, lowers his head and presses his lips to mine. The softness of his kiss is a surprise. He holds his lips against mine as if content to savor the taste. His breath mingles with mine. The touch of his fingers is as if branded into my skin. The sensation of his mouth on mine is so tender. How can such a hard man feel so adoring? A shiver sluices through me. I tremble, and his grip on my chin tightens.

"That's a great picture, you guys." Massimo's voice cuts through the noise in my head.

Luca pulls back and so do I. His chest rises and falls. On his features is an expression of shock, which must mirror the confusion I'm feeling.

"I'll see you back home."

Luca nods without breaking our connection.

Massimo's footsteps recede, the door snicks shut behind him, but still, Luca doesn't glance away.

Tendrils of heat bubble under my skin. A yawning sensation opens in my belly. I shuffle my feet, then squeeze my thighs together. "I..." I clear my throat. "I think I should return to my room."

I turn away from him and take a step forward, when my wrist is caught, and I'm hauled back against him.

"I didn't give you permission to move," he rumbles.

"I don't need your permission for anything." I try to pull away from him, but his grip tightens.

"Do you know what it does to me when you struggle like that, Angel?"

I risk a glance at his face, then shiver when I see his eyes hooded with desire.

"Is that another kink of yours, forcing yourself on women who don't want you?"

His expression tightens. A nerve pops at his temple, then he releases me so suddenly, I stumble and would fall, except he rights me, then pulls his hand back again.

I want to say I'm sorry for what I said, but my stupid pride stops me.

He glares at me, then jerks his chin toward the door. "Go then, I won't stop you."

I hesitate.

He firms his lips. "For fuck's sake, leave, or I won't be responsible for what happens here next."

His big shoulders bunch. His biceps flex. The buttons on his jacket strain, as if there's a storm barely contained under his skin. He folds his fingers into fists at his sides, and the skin over his knuckles stretches white. There's so much nervous tension pouring off of him that my throat goes dry.

"Luca?" I swallow. "Please."

His glare intensifies.

"Luca. I… I… " I squeeze my fingers together, and my new ring digs into the flesh of my palm. Pinpricks of pain steal up my arm, and my nipples tighten. "Luca." I glance away. "I—"

"What do you want?" He lowers his voice to a hush and every nerve-ending in my body seems to catch fire. "Tell me, wife, what do you want from me?"

Wife. He called me wife. A longing bursts to life somewhere deep inside of me. It bleeds into my veins, and spreads to my extremities until it feels like I'm a mass of melting need. "I want you to take my ass, and my pussy, and my mouth, all at the same time."

35

Luca

Her words slice through the last of my defenses. I've been trying to hold back since placing my ring on her finger. Hell, I even managed not to kiss her, knowing once I started, I wouldn't be able to back down from consummating the marriage, and some still functioning part of my brain insisted that was the right thing to do.

Give her some space, let her come to grips with what's happened. All of my best intentions had gone out the window the moment we were alone. I wanted to grab her and throw her down and bury myself inside her right away. Wanted to savor the feel of her skin, the scent of her, the taste of her, how it felt to have her trembling in my arms as she tried to curtail her need.

Then, she said the very words I told her she'd ask of me, and the last of my restraint shattered. My groin hardens, my thighs tighten, and that melting sensation in my chest spreads until it feels like I'm drowning in a sea of craving. An ache. A hunger. A burning that won't be quenched until I've had her.

I bend and scoop her up in my arms. She winds her arms about my neck, then rises up and digs her teeth into my chin.

Cazzo! I feel the tug all the way to the tip of my cock.

"You don't know what you're doing," I growl.

"Don't I?" She licks the skin she's bitten and a tremor of heat shoots up my spine.

She buries her nose in the hollow of my throat. She inhales deeply, and a quivering grips me. My knees seem to tremble—they fucking tremble—and my bicep muscles tense. A fierce need sweeps through me until I feel I'm going to spontaneously combust. Whatever this madness is, I need to get it out of my system before it consumes me. I speed up, head for the door, and once out in the corridor, I turn and head for the main doorway and out of the house.

"Where are we going?" She glances up. "I thought you were taking me up the stairs?"

So had I. But I'm more possessive than I realized, for the thought of having her for the first time in any place other than my own bed is untenable.

"Luca?" She places her fingers against my cheek. "Where are we going?"

"Home."

When I reach the car, the same man who drove us here is already there and holding the door open.

I place her inside. When I straighten, she grabs my arm and tugs. I turn and bend my knees until I'm eye level with her. I press a hard kiss to her mouth. She throws her arms around me and holds on. She parts her lips and I sweep my tongue inside, chasing hers. The taste of hers sinks into my palate and goes straight to my head. My cock all but stabs a hole through my pants. *Cazzo.* I tear my mouth from hers. "Scoot inside."

She slides over. I follow her in and slam the door shut.

"Get us to the airport." I tap on the barrier between the front and the back seats and he raises it. Even before he's eased the car forward, she throws her leg over my lap and straddles me.

"Fucking hell." I grab her hips and hold her in place over my throbbing arousal. She digs her fingers into my shoulders, grinds down on my hard column, and goddamn, the sight of her with her head thrown back, riding me like she can't get enough of me, is enough to send me out of my body.

I curve my palm around the nape of her neck and squeeze. She draws in a breath, then gazes into my eyes. Her golden pupils resemble dark lava, her cheeks are flushed, and her hair is a cloud around her shoulders. Her neck is so slender, my fingers meet in the front.

I drag my other palm down the fabric of her dress, bunch it up around her knees, then slide it under the hem and up her thigh. She trembles. I slip my finger under her panties and brush her pussy lips. Her entire body jolts. A moan bleeds from her lips. Why didn't I take her straight to the bedroom when I had the chance? Now I'll have to wait another few hours before I bury myself inside her. I press down on the swollen nub of her clit, and she pushes out her chest so her breasts are right in my face. Damn. I bend my head and close my lips around her nipple over the fabric of her wedding dress. She wriggles around restlessly, parts her legs wider as she tries to invite my finger inside her melting pussy. I release her nipple, only to turn my attention to her other breast, then breach her channel with my thumb.

"Jesus. What are you doing to me?" I growl.

She brings up her knees, lowers her forehead to mine and pants. "Luca, please, please…" A tear squeezes out of the side of her eye and I lick it. I gaze into her eyes as I brush my lips over hers, and she flutters around my finger. A burning sensation ignites in my chest. My thighs harden, and my balls tighten. I can't let myself come, not yet. Not until I'm inside her. Not until I have her in my bed. Doesn't mean I can't shoot her high on pleasure, though. In one sweeping move, I turn and throw her down on the seat—thank fuck we're in a limo.

She yelps, stares up at me. "What are you doing?"

"You don't get to question me."

Her cheeks redden. "You're such a neanderthal."

"And you" —I warn her as I shove her dress up so it's around her chest — "are at my mercy." I grab her panties, pull them down her legs, then before she can react, I dive down between her thighs.

"Luca—" Her yell cuts out when I thrust my tongue inside her channel.

I notch my arms under her knees and lift them so they're pushed up on either side of her chest, then I swipe my tongue up her slit. She moans. I lick her again and again, then curl my tongue around the swollen nub of her clit.

She digs her fingers into my hair and tugs, I feel the pull all the way down to my cock. Goddamn. I need to get her to come before I spill in my pants. I suck on her clit, and a whine bleeds from her lips. Her entire body goes rigid, and I know she's close. I begin to eat her out in earnest. I slurp on her pussy lips, tug on them, then ram my tongue inside her channel again and again. I mimic exactly what it is I want to do with her when I finally have my cock buried inside her. I drag my whiskered chin across her soft flesh and she explodes. Her spine curves, and she throws her head back and cries out as her entire body jolts. Moisture bathes my tongue and I lap it up. I keep on licking up the sweet evidence of her climax, and she finally slumps. I raise my head, release my grip, and crawl up to plant my elbows on either side of her. Then I lower my head and lick up the tears on her cheek before I place my mouth on hers.

36

Jeanne

I can taste myself on his lips. And I can taste him. The joined taste is an aphrodisiac that causes my pussy to clench. Is this a sign of things to come? Where he's always able to silence me with an orgasm, or a look, or a kiss? And I'll never be able to think for myself again? Is his dominance so powerful that I'll always be forced to bend to his will?

"Stop. If you're still thinking, it means I haven't done my job well." He searches my features.

"Is that what I am to you? A job?"

"And what if I say you're more?"

"I'm not sure if I'll believe you."

He pushes back a strand of hair that's fallen over my forehead. The touch is so tender, so gentle. How is it that this big brute of a man always surprises me when I least expect it? Once more, tears prick the backs of my eyes. Damn, I must be close to my period. No wonder my mood is all over the place. I push at his shoulders but it's as effective as trying to move a brick wall.

"Luca." I swallow. "Let me up."

"Not until you tell me what's bothering you."

"Why does that concern you?"

"Because you're my wife?"

"Only for the time it takes to convince your family that we're married," I retort.

He narrows his gaze. "Exactly. The key word here being 'convince.' If we want to put on a good show, it's important that we understand each other. And that starts with my finding out what is bothering you."

"Do you always have to get your own way?" I grouse.

He laughs. "Do I have to answer that question?"

"It's so easy for you, eh? You snap your fingers and expect people to fall into line. Well, I have news for you, I'm not such a pushover."

"Which is what I love about you." His voice is perplexed, as if he's trying to figure out the meaning of his words. He looks between my eyes again. "Tell me why, after coming as hard as you did, you're resisting the aftereffects of your orgasm, and instead, seem to be upset?"

I want to protest that I didn't come that hard, but sadly, the evidence of it is all over his mouth and on his still-glistening chin. Also, if I said that, he'd simply try to prove me wrong, and probably coax me into another orgasm, and then I really won't be able to think at all. Instead, I settle for saying, "Let me up first."

He clicks his tongue. "You can't make demands of me, Angel. That's not how this works."

"See? That's what drives me up the wall, this... this... domineering way you have of commanding me."

"It's what turns you on."

"No, it doesn't."

"Sure it does." His smile widens. "When I order you to obey me, your heart beat increases. When I demand you give in to me, your pupils dilate." He leans in so close that his lips are almost on mine again. "And when I dominate you in bed, it drives you so crazy, your pussy contracts, searching for the only thing that's going to put you out of your misery. My cock."

Little flames of desire flare to life under my skin. My core clenches as if in response to the erotic picture he paints. Damn, he's a dirty talker, in addition to being the most potently masculine man I've ever met. I never did stand a chance against him, did I?

I'm going to lose myself in him, and when this short duration of whatever it is we're sharing is over, I'm going to have to let him go with my heart firmly in his grasp. I'll have fallen for him, and then, even though our marriage will be in name only, I'll never be able to look at another man again. All I'll have left is my passion for my career, which has been enough so far. It'll have to be again.

So why is it that the thought of not having him in my life feels so much worse than losing the lead in the musical? My heart crashes into my ribcage with such force that I feel the vibrations in my throat. The blood chatters in my veins. *No, no, no. It's not possible.* I can't be falling for this heartless, brutal mobster. He's on the wrong side of the law. He's a criminal, for heaven's sake. One doesn't go around falling in love with a man who commits grave transgressions for a living... Or agreeing to fake a marriage with one, for that matter. I never should have agreed to this scheme of his, but what choice did I have? Since I was kidnapped—which was also his fault—my entire, orderly life has been turned upside down.

"Luca, please let me go," I say in a low voice.

"No," he snaps.

"I don't want to be with you, okay?" I cry out.

Anger spools off of him and slams into my chest. His entire body seems to tense. His features change until that tenderness I glimpsed earlier disappears, to be replaced by a cunning look.

"And you didn't think of this when you agreed to my proposal?"

"It was a fake proposal, an arrangement, and I didn't think it would become this intense between us. Also, if you recall, you didn't give me a choice. The only way I could have returned in time for the premiere of my musical was if I agreed to your stupid scheme. I didn't except things to get so heated. Didn't think I'd be attracted to you. I can't do this, Luca, not with a criminal."

His chest rises and falls, and color smears his cheeks. His muscles grow rock hard. His shoulders seem to swell. Oh no, he's doing that Hulk thing again, where I'm sure he's going to explode out of his clothes and roar with anger.

"L-Luca?" I gulp. "Are you okay?"

He releases me and sits up. Cool air rushes over my body, and I realize how exposed I am. I manage to push myself up to a sitting position. I straighten my clothes, shoot him a sideways glance, then wish I hadn't.

He stares straight ahead, his fingers clenched into fists. With his massive thighs spread, and the muscles of his shoulders bunched, he seems to take up almost all of the space in the back of the car, and it's not a small area, I'll tell you that. A pulse beats at his temple. The tendons of his throat flex. Anger pours off him in waves. I squeeze further against my door, trying to put distance between us.

"So, if I weren't a criminal, you would feel differently?"

I twist my fingers together. The unfamiliar weight of the ring weighs them down. I stare at the gorgeous golden-brown stone. My birthstone. He'd had to have known it. How had he guessed it? That had been thoughtful on his part. He may be someone who shoots people, but damn, he has fine taste.

"Don't keep me waiting," he says in a hard voice.

I wince. "That's speculating. I don't want to think about ifs and buts... It is what it is. You're a gangster and I'm a jazz dancer and an actress, and never the twain shall meet."

37

Luca

The jet glides into the hangar, and the engines switch off. Throughout the journey, we didn't speak a word to each other. There's nothing left to say. This disaster of a marriage is over before it even started. Even before it was consummated, apparently.

A criminal. She sees me as the bad guy; someone on the wrong side of the law. Someone she doesn't want to be with. How had I not sensed that? Perhaps subconsciously, I did. But I thought I could overcome her objections.

Every time she was in my arms, I was sure she was attracted to me. Every time she looked into my eyes, I felt the connection between us.

Of course, I'm the Mafia. I'm not the kind of person she encounters on a daily basis. She's a normal person. Someone with dreams of becoming an actress. We live very different lives, hang out in very different circles. But the chemistry between us overrode all of the differences, or so I'd thought.

I'd been sure I could change the dynamic between us over the next few weeks. That I'd finally be able to get her to trust me enough so I could tell her more about myself and why I'm not in favor of Michael's plans to legalize the *Cosa Nostra* businesses.

But in one fell swoop, she shattered all of my dreams. She burnt down my hopes and exposed them to be illusions. The cravings of a lunatic who allowed himself to be so overcome by a sweet smile, a soft touch, a giggle that lodged in my heart and broke through the defenses of a lifetime... I should have known it was too good to be true.

I thought she was the most innocent woman I ever met. I should have known she used me for her own needs. Mainly, to ensure she wouldn't miss the opening night of her musical.

And I can't blame her. It's not like I gave her a choice. Besides, I only asked her to marry me to fulfill my promise to Nonna. Only, I began to see something more for her... For us. Too bad she doesn't see it.

She can't deny the chemistry between us. She knows I'm attracted to her, and I know she feels the same attraction to me. I thought I could make that work, that I could charm her.

But she was never going to let this go anywhere, despite agreeing to allow things to follow their natural course. She had no intention of ever allowing this to be anything more than a fake marriage. Because she disapproves of my lifestyle. I pushed her into something she didn't want, and used my resources—resources that only served to confirm said lifestyle—to coerce her. And I have only myself to blame.

Either way, there's no future for us. As soon as I'm sure my family is convinced of the veracity of our marriage, I'll ensure we separate. My heart spasms in my chest. That soft melting feeling I've been carrying solidifies. Good. I never should have allowed my walls to disintegrate. Never should have allowed myself to care for her. It's not too late. If I shut myself off now, I'll limit the damage caused by opening myself to her. All I have to do is get through the next few weeks, then we'll go our separate ways, bound only in the eyes of the law, but for all other purposes we'll have different lives. Strange, for someone who has never cared about the law. It's a legal technicality that will bind me to this woman until my death. I rise to my feet, head for the already open door, then turn to find her following me.

Her face is pale, features composed. She still wears the wedding dress I bought her. Her hair is brushed back from her face and flows down her back. In her hand, she carries the bag she took with her to the rehearsal yesterday.

"Leave it. One of the staff will make sure it gets to the car."

She hesitates, then drops the bag on the nearest chair. She walks toward me, and the image of how she'd glided in my direction when we'd gotten married a few hours ago crashes over me. Seeing her dressed in white, with her gaze locked on mine, the rest of the room receded, and I was sure there was a reason she came into my life. Now, I know it was to teach me a lesson. To confirm what I already knew.

I'll never fall in love with another person. Never allow myself to feel vulnerable again.

When she reaches me, I jerk my chin through the open door. She peeks through the window, then pales.

"They know?" Her voice is laced with horror.

"Apparently even Massimo couldn't persuade them to stay away from forming a reception committee."

I had peeked out earlier and confirmed that, yes, the family had gathered already to greet us. I had counted all of my brothers, except for Seb and Michael. Seb is forgiven for not coming to greet me, considering he recently got married. I assume he wants to spend time with his wife, and I'll catch up with him soon, I'm sure. But why isn't Michael here? When this entire charade is more for his benefit than anyone else.

Once more, she glances at the gathering of people, then back at me.

"I'm scared." Her chin trembles.

I raise a shoulder. "Soon they'll have bought into our story, and then you'll be free to do as you please... within limits of course."

"Of course," she says wryly.

If I were a gentleman, I'd hold her hand and lead her down the steps so I could shield her against the questions from my family that are sure to come our way. But considering she hasn't behaved very ladylike, by keeping that little secret from me, I don't see why I should protect her from what's to come.

"After you." I nod in the direction of the crowd.

"Luca," one of my brothers—Christian maybe?— yells. "You guys coming down, or should we come up there to congratulate you?"

I thrust my hand out and show him the finger, then straighten out my fingers.

"Shall we?"

She tips up her chin, brushes past me and her scent—*Gesù Cristo* that crushed rose-petals scent of hers invades my senses. I draw in a deep breath and allow it to permeate my cells, motherfucker. I should be shot for being weak. I stalk forward and follow her down the stairs. Before we reach the bottom, Karma, Theresa, and Aurora swarm around Jeanne. Karma hugs her. Theresa pats her back. Aurora beams at her, then glances at me. She must notice something in my expression, for her smile fades a little.

Christian closes the distance to me and slaps me on my back so hard that I stumble. "Congratulations, motherfucker. You did the deed eh?"

"It would seem so," I say dryly. I glance toward where Massimo leans a hip against my Maserati. I glower at him.

He raises his hands, palms face up. "I tried," he mouths to me.

"Well, you should have tried harder," I mouth back.

Axel draws abreast. "You decided to join the rest of us, eh?" he drawls in his English accent. Fucker always sounds like he's just had tea with the Queen. With his unshaven jaw and his penchant for casual dressing, he shouldn't fit in with the *Cosa Nostra*, but strangely, he has, from the very first day he decided to give up his role as an undercover cop.

And me... Would the transition be as difficult for me? Honestly, I don't know. If he could pull it off, no reason I can't, right?

Adrian stands next to Massimo. He rocks back on his feet, surveying us. He's the only one of my brothers who looks disgruntled. Massimo holds out his palm, and Adrian slaps a bill into it. *Che cazzo?* Did the two of them have a bet running at my expense?

Then Karma closes the distance to me and throws her arms about me. "Congratulations, I knew you were going to honor Nonna's word. The Don is going to be so happy."

"Where is Michael? Couldn't tear himself away from the business for one day to greet his own brother who's returning from his wedding?"

Karma's eyes dim, but there's no break in the wattage of her smile. Smart woman. Considering she doesn't come from a Mafia background, she's learned how to face the challenges of this life quickly.

"He had something urgent come up, but he's waiting at home to personally greet you and your wife." She takes my hand in hers. "You did good, Luca. I know you and Jeanne will be very happy."

You know what I said earlier about Karma being smart? Strike that. Apparently, not even she can see through the charade that is my marriage.

"I'm sure." I bare my lips in what I hope is the semblance of a smile. "I can't wait to start my life as a married man."

What utter nonsense am I spewing? But if it convinces my family about the authenticity of my relationship with Jeanne, it'll be worth it. I close the distance to Jeanne and wrap my arm around her. Her body is stiff, but I ignore it and pull her into my side. I rub my fingers in circles over her bare forearm and notice the goosebumps on her skin.

"You're cold?" I shrug out of my jacket and place it about her shoulders, much to the oohs and ahs of my three sisters-in-law. Women, it's so easy to convince them that a lie is anything but. All I have to do is play the part of adoring husband in front of them. Once more, I wrap my arm about Jeanne. I haul her close and kiss her forehead. That earns me another round of nods from the men, and more smiles from the women. I have so gotten this shit sewn-up. I can't stop the smirk from curling my lips.

That's when Jeanne turns to me. She stands up on tiptoe, wraps her arm around my neck, urges me to lower my head, and kisses me.

38

Jeanne

The alphahole decides he's going to make the most of this opportunity to convince his family our marriage is real. Well, two can play this game. If he wants to get all cozy, I'm more than happy to oblige. Yes, I know, I'm the one who got all flustered when I saw how my body responded to him earlier. And of course, isn't it better if his family buys into our little farce? The faster they're convinced, the quicker I can get the hell away from him. But I can't stand the thought of him winning this round.

The jerk pretends to be all polite by placing his jacket about my shoulders. But I know better. His every action is calculated to persuade his family we're the real deal. Which is understandable. He pulls me closer and kisses my forehead, and I don't protest. But then he smirks, and something inside me snaps.

If he wants to touch me, I can do the same to him, right? Why should I make it easy on him? Why should I be the only one who's suffering from this closeness? Somehow, I need to make him feel as uncomfortable as I am now.

So, I decide to do the one thing sure to get under his skin. I capitalize on the attraction he still feels toward me, on my terms. Does he really think he's the only one who can direct how and when we get intimate?

And surely, there's nothing he can do to me in front of his entire family, right? That thought gives me the courage to rise up on tiptoe, pull his head down and kiss him.

Now, his lips stay frozen, and I take advantage of his surprise to dart my tongue inside his mouth. I pull him even closer and deepen the kiss. A shiver runs over his skin.

A feeling of power unfurls in my chest. He's affected by me. This big, bad Mafia guy wants me, and I was the one to turn him down—albeit, with the help of a white lie. I told him I have a problem with him being in the Mafia, and initially, that was the truth, but the more time I spend with him, the more I realize that beneath that Mafioso exterior is a man who's thoughtful and sensitive and caring and sexy. I'm not a shallow person, but his personality, his charisma, his ability to own a room when he walks into it, to own me... weakens me at the knees. His strong, dominant nature appeals to the core of me. He doesn't take kindly to following orders. Yet, here he is, following my lead.

I thread my fingers through the thick hair at the base of his neck. My fingers brush his skin, and a low growl rumbles up his throat. The next second, he wraps his arm around my waist, lifts me in his arms so my feet are suspended off the floor, tilts his head, and proceeds to eat my mouth. There's no other way of describing it. The kiss seems to go on and on. The blood drains to my core and my nipples stiffen. I dig my fingernails into his shoulders and hold on as he ravishes my mouth. Then, just as suddenly, it's over.

I blink as the sound of clapping washes over me. He lowers me to the ground, but my knees seem to give way from under me. I have to grip the front of his shirt for support. My breathing is heightened. My cheeks must be flushed. But this guy? There's no change of expression on his face. If anything, his features are even more shuttered than before. He holds my shoulder until I've found my footing, then he slips his fingers through mine.

"That was some kiss." Karma fans her face.

"Seems the two of you are really in love." Theresa glances between us, a look of wonder on her face.

Only Aurora surveys my features, then Luca's, but doesn't say anything.

There's a buzzing sound, and Christian pulls out his phone. "Michael wants us home, let's get going."

· · ·

Forty-five minutes later, I hold a glass of champagne in my hand, in the front room of Michael and Karma's place. The view from the adjoining terrace is spectacular. Miles of sand and the blue-green waters of the Mediterranean stretch out in front. Theresa mentioned to me that all the brothers own independent homes next to each other on this private beach. There are guards outside the perimeter of each house and around the belt of land that borders all of their homes. Luca's home is a few buildings over, after Christian's, Axel's, Seb's and Massimo's. Adrian's is the outermost one. Seems he likes to keep to himself a lot more than the rest, that one.

The brothers and their wives toasted our wedding, then the men disappeared inside. Presumably for their whiskey and cigars, or whatever it is that Mafia men do when they get together.

"Doesn't it bother you?" I turn to Elsa, the newest member to marry into the Sovrano family. She and her husband Seb had joined us in time for the toast. Then, Seb had kissed his wife, as had all the other married Sovranos, before swaggering off. All that testosterone in one place was, frankly, overpowering. Luca, on his own, is larger-than-life and quite intimidating. Put him under the same roof as his brothers, and they seemed to reflect the machoness off each other until my skin prickled with awareness. Now I know how an antelope feels when faced with a pride of lions.

"Doesn't what bother me?" Elsa looks up from where she's put her daughter Avery to sleep on the large settee. The little girl is surrounded by pillows and her cheeks are flushed in slumber.

"All this posturing that the men indulge in. Not to mention, how they treat the women like second-class citizens."

Silence envelopes the crowd. *Oops.* I glance about the faces of the other women to find them staring at me. "Um, I didn't mean to offend—"

Theresa bursts out laughing, then Karma and all the other women follow.

"Second-class citizens?" Elsa chortles.

"She has no idea, does she?" Theresa wipes the tears from her cheeks.

"Oh, my god, I can imagine what it feels like looking in, especially when the guys decide to steal away for their 'business meeting'." Karma makes air quotes with her fingers. "Guess she doesn't know who holds the reins in this clan."

"No, she doesn't." Elsa says between bursts of laughter.

"Your face. Oh, my god, you should see your face in the mirror." Theresa stabs her finger in my direction, and that sets all of them off again.

Even Aurora, who so far, has contented herself with a smile, ends up grinning.

"Is this an inside joke or something?" I raise the glass of champagne to my mouth, then put it down on the table. I still need to get to rehearsal, so I can't really drink. Already, my sleepless night is telling on me. I stifle a yawn, then narrow my gaze on the women.

"Is someone going to enlighten me or what?" I say crossly.

Aurora moves toward me. "It's very simple, my dear. Things aren't always what they seem."

"What do you mean?"

"You think because the men left us here and disappeared inside to catch up, that means they're acting like chauvinists."

"Aren't they?"

She taps a finger to her cheek. "Mind you, I am not saying they're not chauvinists."

"Or sexist," Elsa interjects.

"Or way too possessive," Theresa adds.

"Don't forget, autocratic," Karma says with a smile.

"And all of us came up against it when we first met our men. Karma, here, was kidnapped by Michael before they fell in love. Christian first proposed a fake marriage to Aurora. Axel married Theresa with the intention of spying on the Sovranos—"

"Hold on, Axel intended to spy on the Sovranos?" I blink.

"Then he gave up his career as an undercover agent to start his own security company," Theresa murmurs.

"Brought to heel by the love of an honest woman." Elsa runs her fingers through their daughter's hair. "As was Seb, who proposed to me because he wanted to get married to keep his word to his Nonna. If I agreed, he'd help me get custody of Avery from my ex." The brightness in her eyes dims a little.

"So, he did help you get custody of Avery from your ex?"

She glances up at me. "I shot my ex, actually. Cass, Michael's housekeeper sourced the gun for me."

"Where is Cass?" Theresa asks. "I haven't seen her these past few days."

"Oh, didn't I mention, she's taking a sabbatical." Karma jerks her chin in Elsa's direction. "I think helping you find the courage to take down your ex, gave her the courage to face her past."

"I'm glad." Elsa says softly.

"Hold on—" I point a finger at her. "You shot your ex?" I take a few

steps back. The backs of my knees hit a chair and I sink into it. "Did you...
did you..."

"I killed him." She firms her lips. "He'd already hurt Seb, and he abused
me all through our marriage. He kept Avery from me, used her to make
my life a living hell. He used my own needs against me. He deserved to
die."

O-k-a-y, this wasn't what I expected to hear. It's bad enough that Luca
is a *Capo* of the *Cosa Nostra*. And his brothers are Mafia men. I'd expected
their wives, however, to be free of any criminal activities. Isn't that how
Mafia families work? The men protect their women and prefer the females
to stay away from any of their business dealings? Apparently, not with the
Sovranos.

"I've shocked you." She searches my features. "A few months ago, if
you'd told me I'd be married to a Mafia man and shoot my abusive ex—
who totally deserved it, by the way—I'd have the same reaction."

"So, what changed?" I wring my hands. "From what you say, your ex
was a bad man, but don't we have the law to deal with such things?
Shouldn't we let the police and the criminal justice system bring the
wrongdoers to heel?"

"My ex was the commissioner of police. He had the cops and the judges
in his pocket. If I hadn't done what I did, when I did it, he'd have made
sure I never got to see Avery again." She scoops up the still sleeping Avery
and holds her closer.

"But did you have to kill him?"

"It was either him or Seb. Either him or losing my child. Either him or
losing my own life. When it comes to my daughter and Seb, I'll do
anything to protect them."

Oh, wow. I don't agree with what she did, but I understand the sentiments behind it... I think? Would I do the same if I were in a similar situation? Would my emotions overrule all logic, too? Is this how people react
in fight or flight situations? My head spins.

Karma comes over to sit down in the chair next to me. She takes my
hand in hers. "I can see we've given you a lot to think about. But you
should know that the Sovranos will do anything for their women. Far from
treating us as second-class citizens, they make their decisions based on us.
They'd protect us and our children with their lives. While each of the
brothers, so far, started out on the path to love with the wrong intentions,
they ended up in the right place. They fell in love with their women, grov-
eled for their forgiveness, and turned out to be the most exemplary of

husbands. In fact, Michael is converting the Sovrano businesses into legal entities. It's only a matter of time before they turn legit."

I start. "You mean the dreaded *Cosa Nostra* is moving away from criminal activities?"

She nods. "I never asked him to. But he decided he has too much to lose now, so he's committed to selling off or handing over the illegal activities to other clans."

"Somehow, I can't see Luca agreeing to this." I hunch my shoulders. "The man has the *Cosa Nostra* philosophy running through his veins."

"And now he has you."

39

Luca

"You want to do what?" I scowl at Michael. He lounges deeper into his chair behind the massive desk in his study. My oldest brother is every inch the Don of the *Cosa Nostra* as he places his elbows on the table and touches the tips of his fingers together.

"This shouldn't come as a shock to you, Luca. After all, we have been talking about legitimizing our businesses for some time now," he replies.

"So, we become like the pigs and the politicians who pretend to be on the right side of the law but take bribes on the side and grant contracts only to those who'll offer them kickbacks. At least, in our line of work, we make no bones about where we stand."

"I understand your anger." Michael fixes me with a steady gaze. "Of all of us, you are the most committed to the *Cosa Nostra*'s way of life. It's in your blood—"

"And yours." I cross my arms across my chest. "You were groomed to become Don of the *Cosa Nostra*. This is what you always wanted. And now, when you have it, you're ready to leave it all behind? Have you thought about what your identity is going to be once you legalize the businesses? Once you are no longer known for the power and influence you wield...

Once you become a member of the normal populace, all you will be is a man—"

"And a husband and a father." His gaze softens. "Now that you're married, I'm sure you understand that my family comes first. I will not endanger their lives by becoming the target of our rivals. I will not risk painting a target on my back when I know they need me. I want to see my children grow up. I want to grow old with Karma. Surely, you understand that?"

"All I understand is that you're a coward. You're ready to give up the legacy that you were born into, that all of us strove for so long to nurture. You're ready to leave behind everything that we've built this far. You'll never be happy when you give up your title and your power, Don."

"Are you talking about me or you? Are you worried about what your identity is going to be when you are no longer the *Capo*? Or maybe it's something else entirely?" He tilts his head. "Maybe you're frustrated about your decision to get married. Maybe you decided to rush your wedding and are regretting it already. Maybe—"

I close the distance between us and slam my fist on his desk with so much force that the wood cracks. Pens and papers roll off. A glass of water crashes to the floor and shatters.

Silence blankets the room. Behind me, I sense my other brothers stiffen. The tension in the suddenly tiny space ratchets up.

"You've been through a lot in the last few days, so I'll forgive you this indiscretion." Michael's voice is nonchalant. "Nothing you say or do is going to change my mind in this regard. We *will* legitimize our businesses. I *will* move from being the Don to the Chairman of our new group of companies. *You* will learn to be CEO instead of *Capo*. As will your brothers."

I straighten, then spin around and glare at my brothers. "So that's it? All of you are on board with Michael's plan? None of you want to even discuss an alternative to this?"

Christian narrows his gaze. "I've been wanting to go legit since Xander's death. His dying could have been avoided if we'd been in a legitimate corporate business instead of the *Cosa Nostra*."

"If you think our father would have held back from rigging that bomb if we'd been in the business world, you're delusional," I say through gritted teeth. "He would have simply transferred his murderous instincts to the corporate arena."

Christian winces. "You're right. And you're only confirming what

Michael said. There's not much difference between the world of organized crime and that of any cut-throat business. Guess we'll do well there, too."

I dig my fingers into my hair and tug. Goddamn it, this is a losing fight. It's me against all of my brothers. None of them seem the least bit upset about leaving the world of the *Cosa Nostra* behind. None of them realize we're shedding our heritage, our history, a way of life propagated by our ancestors. I've never seen myself as a traditionalist. But I spent my entire life training to be in a position of power within the *Cosa Nostra*. And now, when I'm *Capo*, Michael decides to pull the rug out from under me?

"What about you, Massimo?" I scowl at the one man whom I can depend on to give an impartial response. He and Adrian are the most level-headed among us. They're the ones I turn to for back up. The ones who I can expect to have my back, no matter what kind of battle I go into guns blazing, a particular tendency of mine. I shoot first, ask questions later. And with Massimo and Adrian behind me, I can always count on them to smooth over any problems that arise from my hotheadedness. I'm never going to change what I am at my core, but I'm sensible enough to put checks and balances in place to stop me from going overboard; and those checks and balances take the shape of Massimo and Adrian.

"Massimo?" I widen my stance. "What's your take?"

Massimo straightens from where he's leaning against the door frame. He flicks his gaze to Michael, then back at me. "You're putting me on the spot, *fratello*," he chides me.

"But you'll speak your mind, as always," I state with confidence.

He rubs his jaw. "Michael has a point here. While we're the *Cosa Nostra*, well known and feared around the world, our influence has been dipping in recent times. Thanks, largely, to our asshole father."

The rest of my brothers nod. I don't disagree with him, either, so far.

"Michael's idea of reinventing ourselves by moving our assets into the corporate world and legitimizing our businesses is solid."

I open my mouth to speak, but he holds up his hand. "Let me finish. The talents we have honed being Mafioso will come in handy when we swim with corporate sharks. After all, board games are no less than games we play in the battlefield. As Sun Tzu said, to subdue the enemy without fighting is the acme of skill. And skill is what we have in boatloads. I specialize in finance. Christian is a lawyer. Axel's background as a cop means he knows how to navigate bureaucracy and red tape."

Axel winces. "Thanks, ol' chap."

"You're impulsive and lead with your gut, and normally, your instincts are right. So, you'll make a great CEO—able to take risks when no one else can. Adrian comes across as quiet, but put him in a room full of opponents, and he'll defeat them at their own game. As for Michael?" He jerks his chin in the direction of the Don. "His strength is being able to command respect. He's proved himself to be a visionary over and over again, exactly what a chairman's role is. To watch out for the long game and be strategic in how we get to it."

"So, you're with Michael on this plan?"

He pushes away from the door and walks toward me. "Think about it, brother." He pauses in front of me and grips my shoulder. "It's one way to ensure the longevity of our lives. We've taken a lot of risks and managed to survive this far. But Xander's death was a wakeup call. None of us want to go before our time. By legitimizing, we're moving into less murky waters. The corporate world is not dissimilar to the field we play in. Once we learn the rules, we'll beat them at their own game. And we increase our chances of going back to our families in the evening."

"Not even married, and you talk as if your balls have been chopped off and placed in your hands."

His features tighten. "This is the right thing. When you cool off and think about the situation with a rational mind, I'm sure you'll agree."

"What else can I expect from a man who doesn't have the balls to consider an arranged marriage with the *Camorra* princess for the sake of the family?"

"The two are completely different," he growls.

"How is that? Michael wants me to agree to a plan that benefits all of us. Yet when he asks the same of you, you're resistant."

"That's personal," he snaps.

"So is this. Very personal," I retort.

The two of us glare at each other. Then Massimo takes a step forward until his chest brushes mine. "You have something else to say, *fratello*?"

I hold his gaze. Take in his flushed face, the pulse beating at his temple. Then I raise a shoulder. "Nah, I think I'm done here."

I brush past him, making sure to slam into his shoulder as I pass him. A growl rumbles up his throat. He turns, but doesn't follow me as I walk to the door.

"It's been intense, and unexpected, and not wholly pleasant. I need to figure things out. Meanwhile, I'll be spending time getting to know my new bride better."

I reach the door when… "Luca," Michael calls out. "One more thing."

I pause, then glance at him over my shoulder. "Haven't we said everything already?"

His features soften. "Congratulations. I know it couldn't have been easy for you, but I'm glad you respected Nonna's wishes by getting married."

"I didn't marry out of respect for Nonna, but because I wanted to, and unlike the rest of you married folk, I don't plan to be pussy-whipped anytime soon." Whoa, didn't expect for that to come out like that. That first part is a lie, but somehow, it doesn't feel that way, which is strange. Time to figure this out later.

As I turn to leave, I hear Seb snicker. "Poor man, he has no idea, does he?"

40

Jeanne

I stand in the wings and watch Olivia go through the dance routine. The routine I rehearsed over and over again until I got it right. The people in the audience are friends and families of the cast and crew. As is tradition, we start the run in a new place with a soft launch day, with onlookers who are sympathetic toward us.

I should feel betrayed that she's out there on stage instead of me, but all I feel is pride. Not sure when my emotions toward the situation turned —probably when she and Penny flew out at a moment's notice to be there at my wedding. Probably because she was genuinely concerned about my marrying a Mafioso. She was looking out for me and was the only person to ask me if I was sure about what I was doing. She knows the circumstances in which I met Luca, and while she doesn't know the real reason I agreed to marry him, she suspected I wasn't revealing the full picture, and she didn't judge me for it. She's being a true friend, and for that, I'm grateful.

I step back from the wings and begin to go through the steps. I close my eyes, give myself up to the music, and allow my muscle memory to take over. I have rehearsed so often that, without conscious thought, my arms and legs move in tandem to the music.

As I dance, I allow myself to relive the last few hours... Luca stalked into the living room where I was chatting with the other women. With only a curt apology, he grabbed my arm, pulled me to my feet, and hauled me toward the exit. I wanted to protest, but the look on his face, the set of his jaw, and the coiled muscles of his body all warned me not to. So, I waved at the others, then allowed him to lead me to the car. He drove me to his home a few minutes down the road and informed me that all of my possessions had been moved in my absence. When I protested half-heartedly, he said that I'm his wife now. I stay in his house. End of discussion. Then he told me to get some rest and he'd drop me off at the theater for my final practice session.

I found my things in his room. He expects us to share a room? Of course he does. If we stayed in different rooms, the servants would speak, and word would get back to his brothers. And then our entire plan would be in jeopardy. At least he disappeared and didn't show his face again until after I'd showered, napped and pulled on my yoga pants and T-shirt. When I headed downstairs, I found him waiting for me. He drove me to the rehearsal, told me he'd be back to pick me up, and then he left.

I'm both grateful not to have needed to make conversation with him, and nervous for the night... Which will be our wedding night. Will he expect this to be the night we consummate, as well? He didn't mention anything or give me any sign that indicates so. But considering I committed to making this a real marriage in all possible ways, it's realistic to think he expects to fuck me tonight.

My breathing grows shallow, and a sliver of heat slides down my spine. Will he be rough? He *will* be rough. Everything I've learned about Luca points to the fact that he'll be dominating in bed. He'll position my body exactly the way he wants, he'll touch me, squeeze me, bite me... lick me, eat me out, spank me... I swallow. He'll take what he wants and ensure I love every second of it, too. That's assuming he wants to fuck me after I told him that I could never be with him since he's a criminal. But having gotten to know him better, those objections are quickly fading. Things aren't as black and white anymore. He may be a villain but... That only makes him so much hotter.

He may be a gangster, but he's my gangster. *Mine.*

And I can't allow myself to sleep with him.

If I do, I'll lose my heart to him, I have no doubt about it. And then I'll never be able to walk away from him. I'll be stuck in a marriage, in name only, unable to move on, while he'll be bedding every woman who crosses his path. I assume.

No, no, I'm not going to think about that.

Focus on the music, on the movement of my steps. Focus on flowing into the rhythm my body knows so well. Focus on—

There's a bang like a gunshot, and I lose my footing and hit the floor. I jump up at once. What was that? Where did it come from? The stage? I leap toward the wings, peek around the curtain, and find Olivia collapsed on the floor. She's surrounded by the rest of the cast, who are looking on, stunned. I race onto the stage, push through the cast members, and reaching her, I feel for the pulse at her neck.

Half an hour later, I sink down into a seat in the waiting area of the hospital. Olivia was shot, but she was alive when they rushed her to the hospital. Penny and I accompanied her in the ambulance, then she'd been whisked away. Penny went off to get us some coffee and I was directed to this waiting area. I glance about the space. The walls are a dull yellow color. There's a water fountain in the corner. A poster of a countryside on the wall. The seats are a faded blue and the tiles on the floor are silver with age.

I suppose I should call someone… But who? William messaged me to say he'd inform Olivia's family, so that's something. Something niggles at my thoughts; something of importance. I try to pin it down, but it disappears. Who could have shot Olivia? Why was she shot? Did it have something to do with the Mafia?

I place my hands in my lap, and line my feet parallel to each other. If I could just stay here quietly, maybe I could forget everything that happened. My fingers begin to shake and I squeeze them together. The golden-brown stone on the ring winks back at me. I stare at it. *He couldn't have done it, could he?* Why would he? No, that doesn't make sense. Tears prick at the backs of my eyes. Goosebumps pop on my skin. I hunch my shoulders, trying to stay warm. Heavy footsteps sound, then Luca bursts through the door. He lunges across the floor, and sinks to his knees in front of me. He stares at my face as if he can't believe I'm here.

"Angel," his voice cracks. "Angel." His chest rises and falls. His face is so pale, the circles under his eyes stand out. His shoulders are coiled, his chest planes so rigid, I'm sure he's going to crack open to reveal the Hulk I've always known he's hiding inside. A bead of sweat runs down his throat and into the demarcation between his pecs. He continues to breathe hard as his gaze eats up my features.

"Angel," he rasps. He drags his gaze down my throat to my chest. The color leaches from his face. He sways a little.

"Luca?" I frown. "Are you okay?"

"Am I okay?" His voice shakes. "Are *you* okay?"

"Of course I am. What do you mean? I—" I glance down at myself and spot the blood that stains the front of my shirt. I had changed into the dress my character in the musical wears. Standard protocol for understudies.

"That's not my blood. It's… it's Olivia's, she…" The words stick in my throat. "She was—" To my horror, I begin to tremble. My teeth chatter, and I slide my hands between my thighs in a bid to stop my shaking. "I-I am so sorry, I—"

Luca wraps his arms around me and hauls me against his chest. My arms are trapped between us, and my breasts are trapped against my biceps. The tears I'd been holding at bay slide down my cheeks. I bury my face in his shoulder and allow them to flow.

41

Luca

She's safe. She's safe. I rub my cheek against her hair and draw in gulps of Angel-scented air. She's not hurt. She wasn't hit. When I heard the news from one of my men, they weren't able to confirm who had been hit. All they told me was one of the cast of *Beauty and the Beast* playing at Palermo Theatre had been shot.

My heart stuttered. Every organ in my body seemed to stop, then start again. My pulse rate shot through the roof as I raced out of Venom, the night club owned by me and my brothers, where I had returned to wrap up unfinished business after dropping her off at the theater. I broke all of the speed limits—not that the cops would dare to arrest me, anyway—getting to the hospital. I charged in here to find her sitting in the waiting room with a vacant look on her face. Then I saw the blood on her clothes and all thought drained out of me. My lungs burned, my throat closed, and I wasn't able to breathe. Then, when she assured me it wasn't her blood, the fear had drained out of me to be replaced with something so profound. Something so intense... I dare not name it. I pulled her into my arms.

Now, I rock her as she cries silently. Her body shudders and her shoulders are hunched. She tries to burrow into me, as if she wants to crawl under my skin and live there. Doesn't she know? She already has.

I rise to my feet, taking her with me, then sit down with her in my lap. I rock her as she continues to cry. I kiss her hair, her forehead, the corners of her eyes. Her lips. I close my mouth over hers and try to draw out her anxiety, her worry, the after-effects of what she went through.

How shaken she must be; I can only imagine. "You're okay," I whisper against her mouth in between kisses. "You're okay." I lick the tears off her cheeks and she snorts.

"What are you doing?" She half chuckles, half cries.

"Trying to make you feel better."

She twists her fingers into the front of my shirt and her ring catches on the cloth. I unhook the threads, then raise her hand to my mouth and kiss her ring.

"Luca," she breathes.

"When I thought you'd been hit..." I shake my head. "It was horrible. I painted all kinds of scenarios in my head getting to you. If something had happened to you..." I press my forehead to hers. "I wouldn't have been able to live."

"I'm sorry for scaring you." She hiccups. "Someone shot at Olivia. Someone shot at her while she was on stage, someone who—"

"Thought she was you," I say in a hard voice.

She glances at me, then away. "I thought... I thought." She bites down on her lower lip. Instantly, a flurry of heat zings down to my groin. My cock throbs. I try not to move, for fear she'll realize exactly what her actions are doing to me.

"What did you think?" I ask.

"I thought you had someone shoot at her," she finally admits.

"Why would I do that?" I frown.

"Because you knew how disappointed I was about losing the lead role."

"Do you think I'm that heartless, that I'd get someone to shoot your friend?"

"I—" She refuses to meet my gaze. "I wasn't sure. I didn't want to believe it, but you have to admit, considering you're a Mafia guy and this is your town..." She raises her shoulder.

"You thought I'd have your friend shot so you could take her place?"

"You didn't, did you?"

"Look at me, Angel."

She doesn't move.

"Look. At. Me." I infuse enough command into my tone that she turns her head. She raises her gaze to mine.

"I would never hurt you or anyone who's close to you. I'd never do anything to cause you grief. I'd kill myself before I'd do that. And if anyone dares to come after you or anyone you care about, I—"

"You'll kill that person?" Her gaze hardens.

I blow out a breath. "You're putting words in my mouth, but yes, I'd kill that person, okay?"

"So, you'd answer violence with violence? How long can you keep doing this without it coming back to haunt you? Don't you realize your way of life is going to backfire on you? Every time you use a gun, it's another bullet with your name on it that's being fired. Can't you see how you're hurting yourself by living by violence?"

"It's all I know."

"It doesn't need to be. You can find a way to put this behind you, and—"

"Live like a normal man? Work a nine-to-five job? Go to the office and return to a house in the suburbs with two-point-five kids?"

"Would that be so bad?"

Not if you were there waiting for me. I almost say the words aloud, then stop myself. What am I thinking? When did everything change? When did Angel become so important to me that I'd consider changing my way of living for her? Something not even Michael has been able to convince me of; but the thought of losing her, of someone harming her...? I can never let that happen. I really would put myself in the path of the bullet and take that hit if it meant she were safe.

I pull her close and tuck her head under my chin.

Penny walks into the room and comes over to us. She holds two paper cups filled with coffee. She offers one to Angel, who refuses. I take the cup instead, and Penny sits down in the chair next to mine.

"Any word while I was gone?" she asks.

Jeanne shakes her head.

We settle down to wait. I take a few sips of the coffee—which isn't too bad, considering it's from a vending machine—then make sure Angel sips from it, too. I place it aside, then wrap my arms around her.

I lean back against the wall, taking her with me. I must doze a little because the next thing I know, there's a doctor standing in front of us.

"Are you Olivia Johansen's family?" he asks.

"Her family lives out of the country. We're her friends," Jeanne replies. She pushes off my lap and stands up. "How is she?

The doctor takes in Penny's, then Jeanne's faces, before settling his gaze on me. A flicker of recognition dawns in his eyes. He probably recognizes me as one of the Sovranos, which is useful when it comes to situations like this. Nothing like the threat of being offed to make anyone perform at peak capacity.

"Doctor," Jeanne prompts him, "is she going to be okay?"

The doctor nods. He flicks his gaze between the two girls. "The bullet grazed her side. So, it's not life threatening."

"So, she's going to be okay?" Jeanne asks.

The doctor hesitates.

"When she fell, she hit the edge of a prop. It cut into her cheek, and while the wound is not lethal by any stretch of the imagination, it's going to leave a scar."

"She's an actress. Her face... her face is the key to more roles," Jeanne whispers. "Can we see her?" She appears steady on her feet, but that doesn't stop me from holding her hand. She tightens her fingers around mine. "Is she awake?"

"She's sleeping. Likely, she won't wake up until the morning. I suggest you all go home and get some rest. Come back tomorrow."

Jeanne nods. The doctor turns to leave.

"Poor Olivia. She's going to get a shock when she wakes up." Penny draws in a breath. "But the doctor's right, we should go home now."

Just then, Jeanne's phone vibrates.

42

Jeanne

I pull the phone out of the pocket of my jeans and glance down at the message. The blood drains from my face. The world tilts. It's a good thing Luca's holding my hand; otherwise, I might have fallen.

"Angel!" He jumps up and wraps his arm about my shoulder, steadying me. "What is it?"

I swallow, open my mouth, but the words refuse to come. Instead, I hold up my phone so he can read the message.

Penny, too, is on her feet and walks over to peer at my screen.

"Oh, my god, he wants you to play the lead?" She gasps.

"The premiere is tomorrow, and now Olivia can't play the lead, so..." my voice trails off. I glance up at Luca. "I feel terrible about this. I should refuse. This is my fault."

"Why is it your fault?" Penny asks.

"We... we think whoever shot at her thought it was me. Not that we look the same, but likely, they were told to fire at the lead actress, and instead of me, she was hurt."

A furrow appears between Penny's eyebrows. "You think it's the same people who kidnapped you, who shot at you?"

"It's possible." Luca pulls me closer. "And while I'm sorry Olivia was hurt, I'm glad it wasn't you on that stage."

A shiver spirals up my spine, and I melt into his side.

"It's not right. It should be her on the stage tomorrow."

"It was supposed to be you." Penny props an arm on her hip. "And William decided he wanted Olivia to play the part. Now, it's back to you. Maybe it's fate and you're the one who should be on that stage tomorrow." She raises a shoulder.

Just like it's fate for me to be with him?

"What do you think?" I turn to Luca. "Should I go on that stage tomorrow?"

He cups my cheek. "I'd be lying if I said I wouldn't be worried if you did. Whoever shot at you is still out there. I've already put my men on trying to find out who did it, but the perpetrator is likely long gone. Even if we do find him, it may not be within the next twenty-four hours."

"What are you saying?"

"That you should fulfill your heart's desire and star in the premiere tomorrow. And I'll make sure that the security around the theater is so strong that nothing and no one can get in or out without my knowing."

"Thank you, Luca." I sway closer to him when footsteps sound behind me.

Luca glances past me and frowns. "Massimo?"

I turn in time to see Massimo barreling into the room. "Is what I heard true?" He scans Luca's features. "Is she hurt?"

"It was a flesh wound. The bullet didn't hit anything vital," Luca responds.

"*Grazie a dio!*" Massimo exclaims.

"She hurt her face, though. The doctor fears it may scar, but he can't be sure."

"She's alive, though? That's the most important thing." Massimo rolls his shoulders. "Can I see her?"

"The doctor said she's resting, and we can see her tomorrow," Penny replies.

Massimo walks over to a chair and lowers his bulk into it. "I'll wait."

I exchange glances with Luca.

"Are you sure? You can come back in the morning," Luca murmurs.

Massimo kicks out his feet and pulls out his phone. "I'll wait. I can work from here as well as I can anywhere else. And I'll feel better if I'm here, in case something comes up. Why don't you all go on home?"

I hesitate.

"I'll call you if anything comes up. Also..." He glances between me and Luca. "Isn't this your first night as a married couple? You don't want to spend it in a hospital waiting room."

Half an hour later, we draw into the driveway of Luca's home. My eyes are drooping, and when he comes around to open the door on my side and scoops me up in his arms, I don't protest. He carries me inside, then up the stairs and to his room. He walks into the bathroom, sets me down on the edge of the bath tub, and runs a bath. Then he pulls me up to my feet and grips the bottom of my blouse. I raise my arms and he pulls it off of me and tosses it aside. I notice the blood on the fabric. Her blood. Olivia's blood has been on my clothes all this time. I had noticed it, but it hadn't quite registered.

"It could have been me who was shot." My knees tremble. "Me who could have collapsed on the prop and hurt my face and—"

"But it didn't happen." He unhooks my bra, tosses it aside, then helps me out of my skirt. He pulls my panties down my hips. I step out of them. He doesn't spare a glance at my breasts or the flesh between my legs. Should I be relieved or disappointed? Maybe he's not going to fuck me tonight, after all.

Then he shrugs off his jacket, begins to unbutton his shirt, and all thoughts drain from my mind. He undoes the last button, pulls off his shirt, and drapes it over a chair.

I take in his chiseled chest and the words, **Non Dimenticare Mai,** tattooed onto his forearm.

"You never did tell me what that means," I point out.

"Never forget," he retorts.

"Never forget... what?" I tilt my head.

He hesitates. "Never forget how my father abused my mother until she dropped dead from a heart attack. Never forget how he abused me and my brothers. Never forget how he broke the trust of those he supposedly loved."

He shucks off his boots and socks, then unbuckles his belt and shoves down his pants along with his boxers and adds them to his growing pile of clothes. When he straightens, the breath rushes out of me. I take in the heavily muscled shoulders, the sculpted biceps, the hewn planes of his chest, which narrow down to his trim waist. Those corded thighs, and his monster cock, which stands up against his lower belly and has a vein running up the bottom.

My mouth waters. My nipples throb. The flesh between my legs contracts. A piercing ache flares to life deep inside. Moisture squeezes out from between my pussy lips, and a shiver slinks under my skin. Jesus, Mary and Joseph. Is this what sin looks like? Is this how the devil appeared to Eve? Is that why she ate the apple when he coaxed her to? As I'm going to do?

As if he's aware of the direction my thoughts have taken, his nostrils flare. His eyes flash, and a nerve throbs at his temple. His gaze grows heated. The heat in the bathroom seems to shoot up. A bead of sweat slides down my throat and his gaze darts there. His blue eyes deepen in color until they seem almost black. He glances past me, then in one smooth move, swoops around me. He bends over, shuts off the water, and straightens.

But not before I notice the tattoos on his back. Of course, I saw when we were imprisoned together, but now that he's my husband, it elicits something poignant, something painful and strident, deep inside of me. The combination of the ink with the puckered slivers of skin looks both heathen and holy. Both barbaric and sacred. It's as if his back was torn to pieces and put back together in a form meant to give expression to whatever pain he's carrying deep inside. The colors are brilliant, almost too bright for my eyes, but that's not the only reason my vision wavers. I blink away my tears, then reach out to trace the curved lines.

The muscles under his skin jump. It's like having a writhing beast under my fingertips, one that's standing still only for my perusal. A thrill squeezes my chest. I drag my fingertips across the shape of the face, the soulful, yet piercing eyes, the serpents that spring from the head and entwine with three sheafs of wheat painted the most brilliant yellow, and the three legs bent at the knee, which radiate out from the head. The design is haunting, macabre, primal and somehow, very Luca.

"It's a *trinacria*, also known as *triskelion*. Meaning three-legged. It recalls the shape of Sicily, which resembles a triangle. *Trinacria* is actually the earliest known name of the island of Sicily," he rumbles.

"Is that Medusa?" I touch the cheek below the haunted eyes of the woman's face in the center of the tattoo.

He nods. "It's for protection. In the past, it was customary to place a *trinacria* behind the main door as a symbol of protection for the house."

"And the three legs?"

"They symbolize the three ends of the island. The wheat sheafs represent the history of Sicily as a major wheat provider of the Roman empire; they also symbolize the fertility and prosperity of the region."

"Now I recall where I've seen the symbol. On the flag of Sicily."

One side of his lips kicks up.

"You decided to carve it into your skin? Why?"

"Why do you think?" He turns to face me.

"Because… the land is in your blood? Because you are a proud Sicilian? Because..." I search his features. "Because the *Cosa Nostra* is your religion?"

"And you are my salvation."

43

Luca

As soon as the words are out of my mouth, I regret them. Where did that come from? Am I comparing what I feel for her to the love I have for my calling? Which I've always thought was to take the *Cosa Nostra* forward... So far, I've committed my life to it, have never questioned my search for power, have never thought what I reached for was wrong. Not until she came into my life. She shook my focus. Distracted my singular intention. Displaced my attention, until I'm not sure what's important to me anymore. That is, aside from her.

"When I thought you'd been shot, everything changed." I cup her cheek. "When I thought I'd lost you, I knew my life would never be the same again. I believe in God, but it's the first time I prayed to him from my heart, on the way to you. I told him if you were unhurt, if by some miracle, you were alive and not wounded, then I'd never take what we have for granted. I promised him that I'd do anything to keep you safe. Even if it means leaving you."

"Luca," her voice emerges shaken. "I'm not sure what you're saying."

"You made it clear to me that as long as I am part of the *Cosa Nostra*, our future together is apart. I wish I could leave what I am behind... but it's a part of me. I wish I could walk away from the *Cosa Nostra*, that I could fall in line with Michael's plans to legitimize our businesses. But I'm not as optimistic as he is. You can't just leave this life of crime behind."

"You can try."

"You don't get to separate yourself from the past."

"You can make amends," she insists.

"This... The lifestyle of the *Cosa Nostra* is not something that you can shake off overnight."

"So, it'll take time; that's okay. You can work through it. *We* can work through it."

"I... I can't." I rub the back of my neck. "This isn't me, Angel. This... putting on a suit and going to an office and sitting in a conference room to discuss quarterly revenue numbers is not the life I saw for myself."

"I didn't see someone like you for myself, either. I never thought I'd be fake-married to a Mafioso and in a relationship that twists my insides in knots every time I see him, but here we are." Her chest heaves. "Also, what you just described doesn't sound much different from what you're already doing. You wear a suit now and sit in a closed room talking business with your brothers. How's the picture you described any different?"

"Because it is." I dig my fingers in my hair and tug.

"I call bullshit on this," she snaps.

I stare. "Did you just use a four-letter word?'

"It's an eight-letter word, and I'm done being polite, especially when the most colorful insults don't do justice to describing your pig-headedness."

"And now you compare me to a filthy beast?" I can't stop my lips from quirking. I can't help it. She's so cute when she's all fired up, with her golden eyes spitting sparks, her thick curly hair flowing around her like Medusa's snakes. My first impression of her had been right. She enticed me, and now she's going to turn me to stone; then she's going to shatter me, and every piece of my body will sing one name. Hers.

Cazzo! I am completely losing it. I need to find a way to walk away from her. For her safety. For my sanity.

I lower my hand to my side, then jerk my chin toward the almost full tub. "You need to get in."

"And you need to get your head out of your ass."

"My, didn't realize you were hiding such a gutter mouth, Angel."

"And I didn't know you were hiding behind the excuse of the *Cosa Nostra*."

"What do you mean?"

"You covered the marks on your back put there by your abusive father with the symbol of the very land he comes from. Clearly, you're trying to make up for what he did by trying to do better, while staying in the same life that he introduced you to."

"My allegiance to the *Cosa Nostra* has nothing to do with my father," I growl.

"Doesn't it?" She narrows her gaze. "Isn't that why you have a chip on your shoulder about Michael being the Don? Isn't that why you wanted to be the Don? So you could control the *Cosa Nostra*, and hence, control your future. The very future that your father screwed up by being abusive toward you."

Anger thrums at my temples. My guts twist. I squeeze my fingers into fists at my sides. "You have no idea what you're talking about."

"Oh, please! I don't have to be a shrink to read the signs loud and clear." She leans forward on the balls of her feet. "You hate your father. Technically, you should hate the lifestyle he introduced you to. Instead, you're panicking at the thought of walking away from the *Cosa Nostra* lifestyle. You embraced his way of life, hoping to undo the wrongs he did to you and to your brothers—indeed, to the entire community. You may pretend to be a hot-headed, out-of-control *Capo*. But really, you're an altruist."

Sweat drips down my chest. My head spins. It must be the heat which has built to sauna-like proportions in this space. Yes, that's the only reason I'm feeling lightheaded. It's nothing to do with this little spitfire who's seen through me in a few days, when my own brothers haven't understood my motivations—hell, when I haven't understood my impulses—most of my life. "You're confusing me with someone else."

She sets her jaw. "No, I am not. I see you, Luca. You're worried about losing the control you have. You're frightened that, without the power that comes with being *Capo*, you'll be nothing. You're scared, Luca, scared."

A hot burst of anger flares in my chest. My blood pounds through my veins. The pulse thuds at my temples, and I bend my knees, then glare into her face.

"You're calling me a coward?" I snap.

"Yes."

"You think you can say that to my face and get away with it?"

"Maybe not, but at least I tried. Which is more than I can say of you. You're willing to let go of what we have. Willing to shove aside what you feel for me—"

I scowl.

"Yeah, yeah, I know you want to deny it, but I saw how you burst into that waiting room in the hospital. I saw how pale you were when you saw the blood on my shirt, then the relief when you found out it wasn't mine. I saw how your arms shook when you carried me from the car. You're still not over having discovered you have feelings for me, and given a chance, you'll spend your life denying it."

"You think I am pushing you away because I don't have feelings for you?"

She nods.

I laugh bitterly.

"I'm pushing you away because it's the only way I can keep you safe."

"What's that supposed to mean?" She lowers her eyebrows toward the bridge of her nose.

"Exactly what I said. You think I can't acknowledge my feelings for you, when it's the exact opposite. I feel too much. *Maledizioni.* Can't you see, you're driving me crazy? Every time we're in the same room, I can't look away from you. And when we're not together, it's even worse. Then, I walk around like some bumbling idiot with a strange smile on my face. It's why I can't be with you. You wreck me, Angel. And I will not be the cause of something far worse happening to you. And let's face it, the chances are far worse when we're together."

"And if we're not together, will that change anything?"

"At least I can guard you without my emotions being involved."

She stares. "So, you won't be with me, but you still plan on stalking me?"

"On looking out for you, yes."

"So you can prevent your enemies from hurting me?"

"Precisely," I snap.

"Even though doing this will hurt me more?"

"At least you'll be safe," I mutter.

"Argh!" She blows out a breath. "Can't you see how flawed your logic is? It'd be much safer, for all concerned, if you made peace with your rivals, put the illegal activities of the *Cosa Nostra* behind you, and became the CEO of a legitimate enterprise."

She plants her hands on her hips and the action pushes out her breasts. Not that I haven't been aware she's naked, but after that initial survey of her body, I've managed to keep my eyes on her face. Kudos to me. Not that my body isn't reacting to her nearness. Not that my dick isn't throbbing and lengthening with every whiff of her scent that I draw into my lungs. Her breasts seem to swell under my gaze and her nipples extend. I'm not the only one caught between the conflicting signals of our body versus whatever discussion it is we're having. What are we talking about, anyway?

"Hey!" She snaps her fingers. "My face is up here."

"But the rest of you is naked and gorgeous, and the parts of you down there are especially luscious."

"A-n-d there he is, alphahole extraordinaire. Mister Filthy McDirty himself."

"Who?" I whip my gaze to her face. "You're talking about another man when you're with me?"

She laughs. "And you think you can walk away from me? You idiot. You can't even stand it when you think I'm speaking about another man. You really can't be so full of yourself that you can't see what's standing right in front of you."

"Oh, I see all right. Question is, what am I going to do about it?"

"You mean what are *we* going to do about it, right?"

We stare at each other for a second; then, as one, we move.

44

Jeanne

Maybe I throw myself at him, or maybe he moves toward me first. Either way, I find myself in his arms, with my legs around his waist. His palms are under my butt holding me up. His lips on mine, his tongue in my mouth, he kisses me like he can't get enough. Like he wants to steal my breath. Like he's starving for me. I dig my fingers into his hair and tug, strain against him, and push my breasts into his chest as I plaster myself to him. I sense him move forward, but don't take my eyes off of him. He holds my gaze as he strides out of the bathroom and toward the bed, all the while, still kissing me.

"Wait, what about the bathtub?" I ask.

"What about it?"

"It's filled with water."

"Fuck that."

He lowers me to the bed, bends over me, and resumes kissing me. I sigh as his weight pushes me into the mattress. As his thick hardness rubs into my core. As the sculpted planes of his body dig into my curves. Where he's hard, I'm soft; where I'm small, he's big. Where my body dips, his pushes forward boldly. The contrast when his body covers mine, when his heat wraps around me and his limbs are entwined around mine, is mind-boggling and so damn erotic. Goosebumps pepper my skin. My toes curl, my scalp tingles, and I can barely keep my eyelids propped open. I want so much to close my eyes and lose myself in him.

He raises his head and stares at me as if looking at me for the first time. His blue eyes are, once again, that midnight blue which I now know means he's aroused. Not that there is any mistaking that column between his legs that prods at my entrance asking to be let in.

I slide my palm between us, down to his cock, and fold my fingers around it.

His entire body jolts.

"Fuck." His chest heaves. "Are you sure? Because if you're not—"

I tilt my hips up and he slips in.

I groan. He growls. He plants his elbows on either side of me, then lunges forward and fills me and stretches me completely. I gasp, unable to move. Jesus, he's big. So big. I'm immobilized by his monster dick. He has me pinned to the bed. He's so deep inside me, I'm sure I can feel him in my throat.

"Oh, god," I moan. "Oh, my god."

"It's Luca. Say my name, Angel."

"Luca."

His shaft throbs inside me.

"Again," he snarls.

"Luca."

He seems to grow even bigger and harder inside me. Pinpricks of pain skitter up my spine. I whine and try to pull away, but he leans a little more of his weight on me, and that's it. I can't even struggle. I'm locked in place, spiked to the bed with his monster shaft. A chuckle wells up from somewhere deep inside of me.

"Are you laughing?" He scowls.

"No. Yes. No." A gale of laughter sweeps out of me.

"I'll show you what happens when you poke fun at me, you little hellion." He pulls out of me so slowly that I can feel every individual ridge of his cock, then he thrusts forward with such force that the entire bed jolts. I move up the bed, and he plants his knees on the mattress and hauls me up so I'm balanced on his giant thighs. At this angle, he's skewering me. Oh, god. Tomorrow's headlines are going to read:

Actress screwed to death by giant cock.

. . .

Another peal of laughter bubbles up. He must sense it, for he closes his mouth over mine, draws in the sounds, then digging his fingers into my hips, he lowers me back to the bed and rams into me, over and over and over again. Each time he buries himself in me, he hits that spot deep inside that I had despaired of ever discovering. Not even my trusty Hitachi managed to nail it.

What? So I went to a convent and try not to use four-letter words when I swear, but I'm allowed a vibrator, right? Only, nothing can equal the sensations that pour through me as Luca thrusts into me with such force that his balls hit the delicate skin of my butt. As he grinds his pelvis against my clit, he stares into my eyes, then releases my hip, only to slide his finger down the valley between my butt cheeks and into that forbidden puckered hole.

"Oh," I gasp, or at least, I think I do, for he's swallowed that, too. A shudder sweeps out from where he's planted in me and my spine curves.

He releases my mouth and whispers, "Come for me, Angel. Fly with me." And I shatter. The climax powers over me, overwhelms me, entombs me or sets me free, or both. I'm really not sure. I see flashing lights at the corners of my vision, see his big body bend with me as he roars and pours himself inside of me.

When I come to, I'm sprawled over his chest, and he's still inside me. And still hard. I know because I can sense him between my legs. He draws lazy circles over my shoulder and my back as I press my cheek into his chest. My arms and legs feel weightless. I definitely saw God, I think. I'll never tell the nuns that— Not that I plan on ever meeting them, but if I did, I'd be sure not to hint about the new form of worship I've discovered. No wonder some poets compare an orgasm to a holy experience. That, what happened, is nothing short of a miracle. For me.

I rest my chin on the demarcation between his pecs and peer up… to find him watching me with a very satisfied smirk.

"You don't have to seem so pleased with yourself."

"You're right, you've only had one orgasm."

"That's not what I meant."

"That's what I mean." He flips me over on my back once more, without losing the position of his cock in my pussy—how does he do that?—and brushes his lips over mine.

"That was incredible," he says softly. "I haven't come that hard since…" He pretends to think. "Since never."

"Right answer." It's my turn to smirk.

"I've had good sex, but this is different." He frowns as if trying to make sense of his words.

"Thanks, I think?" I twist my lips.

"That didn't come out right." He pushes a lock of hair behind my ear. "It's different because of what you said earlier."

"What did I say earlier?"

"That feelings thing that you hinted at. Clearly, it makes a difference."

"Is that an admission?" I smirk.

"Maybe. It doesn't change anything though."

"I know." I reach up and cup his cheek. "Maybe this will, though."

He tilts his head. "What do you mean?"

"We didn't use a condom."

45

Luca

We didn't use a condom. *Didn't use a condom. Cazzo!* Of course we didn't use a condom. The thought hadn't even crossed my mind. I had been consumed by her. Had found myself drowning in her. Had fallen into her and hadn't been able to think, let alone have cognizance that I hadn't protected myself.

"You didn't stop me, either."

"I didn't," she replies.

"So, the thought did cross your mind?"

She hesitates, then shakes her head. "In all honesty, no. I got, ah, a bit carried away," she murmurs.

"And you're not on the pill."

She shakes her head.

"Fuck." I withdraw from her and she winces. I pause. "Are you sore?"

She nods. "In a good way."

A rush of heat swirls through me. She should be sore. She should wear my mark inside her and on her. It should be clear to the world that she belongs to me. She's mine. *Mine. Mine. Mine.*

A-n-d there's that part of me that cannot shut up since I laid eyes on her. That feral, possessive part of me that's determined to get me into trouble. The one that leads me by the dick. And my heart, and my mind, and my soul—whoa, stop that. I rein in that train of thought, then push away from her and to my feet. "Stay there." I stab a finger in her direction before I pivot and stalk to the bathroom. I pull out the plug in the bathtub to let the water drain out, then grab a washcloth and wet it before I prowl back to the bed. I'm about to press the cloth between her legs, then stop. I reach down, rub the remnants of my cum into her pussy, then frown.

"Are you sure I didn't hurt you?"

"I am, why do you ask?"

"Because you're bleeding." I hold my fingers up to show her the droplets of red clinging to my fingertips.

Her gaze flicks to my digits, and she blinks rapidly. "Oh, no, I got my period. I knew it was coming, but I'd hoped it wasn't for a couple more days."

"Is that why you didn't stop me to get a condom?"

She raises her shoulder. "Maybe. I mean, subconsciously, I knew I was going to get my period any day, but in all honestly, I wanted you to come inside me."

"And what if you had become pregnant?"

"I'd have had it." She smiles a secret little smile. "And you'd have helped me bring up the baby."

"Woman, didn't you hear what I said earlier? It's not safe for you when you're with me."

"And it's not safe away from you, either. So, I'd rather be with you than not." She reaches out her hand, palm facing up.

"What?" I glare at it with suspicion.

"Give me your hand, Gangster."

"First, you try to convince me to leave the *Cosa Nostra*; then, you call me Gangster. You're driving me crazy, you know that?"

"So you've mentioned. Now, give me your hand."

Holding her gaze, I lick my fingers one by one, deliberately swallowing down her period blood.

Her pupils dilate.

Then, I place my palm over her much smaller one—reluctantly, it should be noted—and she brings it to her mouth and kisses it. Angel kisses each of my knuckles, then turns my palm over and presses her lips right in the center. "There. Now you have my kisses in your blood." She smiles hugely.

I have you in my blood, in my veins, in the thing that's beating so fast in my chest, I'm sure I'm going into cardiac arrest. I grip her wrist, pull her up to sitting, then toss the towel aside and rise to my feet with her in my arms.

She snuggles into me as I carry her back to the bathroom. I place her on the rim of the tub and replace the plug. The water has reached the half-way mark, so I toss in a tennis ball-shaped thing called a bath bomb, or something equally inane, before I fill the tub with hot water.

Bubbles begin to form almost at once, and the scent of roses fills the air.

"Bath bombs?" She sits up straight. "You have bath bombs?" She shoots me a look. "Did you buy them for me?"

My neck heats. "Don't attach too much importance to it. I bought it by mistake."

"And coincidentally, they turned out to be rose-scented—my favorite scent, by the way... Mistake, too?"

"Exactly."

She smiles so widely, she almost cracks her face.

"Don't look so pleased," I mutter.

"For a big, bad Mafia *Capo*, you're such a softie." Her smile grows bigger, if that's possible.

"What's wrong with your face?" I growl.

"It's the endorphins." She smiles goofily. "Thanks to your magic dick, I had the best orgasm ever, which is good. It means I won't kill you."

"What?" I blink. "What does that mean?"

"It's an Elle Woods quote."

"First Plath, now Elle Woods; you are a study in contradiction, baby. I suppose I should be grateful you're not throwing some random actor's name at me."

"I wouldn't dare, as possessive as you are, *baby*."

I wince. "I changed my mind. I prefer you call me Gangster."

"How about Gangster Baby?"

"What? No. No fucking way, woman. And don't you ever stop talking?" I rise to my feet, then grab her hips and lower her into the tub. She sighs as she sinks into the water.

"Scoot forward."

She does, and I climb in after her. I plant my legs on either side of her, then pull her back into my arms and onto my chest. I adjust her so my dick settles happily in the cleavage between her butt cheeks. I reach around and shut off the tap. I lean back, and for a few seconds, there's only the sound of the water lapping against the sides of the tub.

"This is a big tub," she finally ventures.

"I'm a big man."

"I noticed." She wriggles her behind against my cock, which instantly extends to full-length. Just like that.

"*Gesù Cristo.* You're pushing it, woman.*"

"Run out of steam already, old man?" She snickers.

"Who are you calling 'old man'?"

"You, of course. I—" she yelps as I raise her, then position her exactly over my throbbing cock.

"Open your legs, Angel."

She does, and I lower her inch-by-inch onto my shaft

"Oh, god. That feels so good," she moans as my dick disappears slowly inside her.

When I'm buried inside her, up to the hilt again, a tremor runs up my spine. That melting sensation is back in my chest, in full force. I push it aside, focus on thrusting up and into her—long, deep strokes that flow one into the other, without stopping. In, out, in. I continue to propel up and into her until her body trembles, then stiffens. Her back arches, and I know she's near. I grip her hips, and raise her off of my cock.

She whines.

Before she can complain, and I know she's going to, I flip her around and position her entrance over my cock again. Then, I push her down, all the way down my shaft, until I'm, once more, up to my hilt in her hot, wet channel.

"Oh." Her mouth forms the sound, and her gaze widens.

"*Che culo,* that shut you up. Though, I admit, I had much more pleasurable ways in mind, if that didn't work."

"Luca I—" she begins, and I tug her forward so I can cover her mouth with mine.

I kiss her and pull back. "Less talking, more fucking. Got it?"

"But—"

"No more words. I only want to hear the sound of you coming around my cock again, you feel me, Angel?"

Before she can nod, I pump up and into her, doubling my speed and hammering into her over and over again. Each time I drive into her, her breasts jiggle. Her nipples are dark and enlarged, and I can't stop myself from leaning forward and taking a mouthful.

She cries out, then grabs hold of my hair and tugs. She pushes her chest forward, filling my mouth even more. I suck on her nipples, and my balls tighten. To see her breasts full and overflowing with milk as my child suckles on them... F-u-c-k, I almost come right then. I release her nipple, worship her other breast in the same way and she whines, "Luca, more, please, more."

I glance up to find her curls awry, her hair a halo around her head. She's a goddess. My Medusa. My angel. My wife. She's mine. I rise to my feet. The water flows off of me, and she pops her eyelids open. "What... Where—"

"Shh." I press a hard kiss to her lips. "Told you, no more words."

I step out of the tub, walk over to the counter with the sink, and place her on her feet. I turn her around, plant my hand on the small of her back, and push down. She bends, places her palms on the counter and leans forward. Her ass juts out. Her breasts hang heavy from her chest. I grip her hips, hold her gaze in the mirror. "Look at yourself in the mirror as I fuck you, Angel."

Her pupils dilate and color flushes her skin. Her chest rises and falls, and I notch the crown of my cock into her squelching, wet pussy. I tighten my hold on her, then I plunge forward.

46

Jeanne

In one smooth move, he plants his monster dick inside of me, to the root. One second, I'm empty; the next, he's inside me, stretching me, filling me. He nails me with such force that my entire body jolts. He's so big, so massive, it feels like he's skewered me around his cock. I open my mouth, but no sound comes out. Try to draw in a breath, but my lungs burn. As do his eyes. His iridescent blue eyes glow back at me as he holds my gaze. I'm so full of him, so packed with his thickness, his presence, his dominance—which holds me in thrall—that I can't move. I dig my fingers into the counter and watch his nostrils flare. His shoulders flex, his biceps—each of which are about the size of my thigh—knot as he pulls out of me. He stays balanced, with his cock at the entrance to my slit, then inch-by-inch, he buries his cock inside me. So slowly that I can feel every single ridge, every pulse, every silken centimeter of that beautiful shaft as he impales me.

A groan slips from my lips. Flares of sensation zing up my spine. A melting sensation opens up deep inside of me, and my knees threaten to give out from under me. His hold on my hips tightens. His jaw hardens. He grits his teeth as he holds himself immobile and lets me sense each throb, each pulsating beat, each vibrating reverberation that grips his cock. His jaw tics, and a pulse hammers at his temple. He looks every bit the avenging, confident *Capo* that he is.

"Hold onto the counter," he growls.

"Wha-what?" I swallow.

"I'm going to fuck you now." Then he does just that. He pulls out, then lunges forward again and again. He sets a tempo that's so fast, so strong, so assured that it feels like we're locked in a dance. Each time he thrusts into me, my breasts jiggle. Each time he pulls out, I try to brace myself, but nothing prepares me for the onslaught of his girth. Each time he buries himself inside of me, I feel complete. When he retreats, my pussy clamps down on emptiness. My breasts swell and my nipples are so tight that pain radiates out from them. The tension in me builds and extends out, a shimmering sense of something building, snowballing, and multiplying, until it seems to encompass my entire body.

"Luca," I whine. "Please, please, please, Luca."

The heat from his body pours over me, cocoons me, and tightens around me until it feels like I'm wrapped up in his essence.

"Luca, please," I moan, not sure exactly what I'm asking for, only knowing he's the only one who can give me what I need. What I want right now, in this moment. Something that will take me over the edge and catapult me into a space where I don't have this knot of hunger tightening, heightening until I can't bear to be in this skin.

"Fuck." In the mirror, his shoulders seem to swell. The tendons of his throat are so rigid, they might snap at any time. "Your pussy is so tight, so hot, so wet. The way you milk my cock drives me out of my head."

I part my lips as he drills into me again. A squelching sound fills the space as his balls slap against my flesh.

"Hear that, baby? Hear how wet you are for me?" He releases my hip, only to slide his hand around to place it at the point where we're connected.

"Oh, god," I moan. "That... that's so hot."

He circles his fingers around his shaft as he fucks me. A shudder rips through me. My entire body jolts. He picks up his pace even more as he rams into me over and over again. Shards of pleasure perforate my blood and my pores pop. Every cell in my body expands, drunk with the rapture that lurches through me each time he crams that monster cock of his inside of me.

"I can't take this anymore. I can't." My eyelids flutter down as all of my senses hone in on that spot where we're connected, where he's pumping into me right now.

"Open your eyes." He lowers his voice to a hush and my nerve endings pop. *Damnit, he's using the voice. THAT voice.* The one that brooks no argument. Not that I'm going to even try.

I am gone. Mush. Liquefied into a puddle of lust and horny desire and unspeakable needs and the kinds of dreams that will probably never come true, because that's what this guy does to me.

I force my eyelids open, and his brilliant gaze instantly captures mine. He holds the connection, then he pulls out of me, before he drives forward into me again. He bends over, pushing his massive chest into my back, and his big body overwhelms me. The sweat that drips down his temple plops onto my shoulder.

I take in the contrast between our bodies. How his larger-than-life size dwarfs me, making me look like a doll... like his fuck doll. A toy with holes that he loves to use whenever he wants.

He lowers his cheek to mine, then growls, "Come."

I bend my spine, throw my head back, and the climax rips through me. I see stars at the edges of my vision. My knees buckle from under me, and I'm sure I'd collapse, except his grip on my hips tightens. He holds me and continues to fuck me through the aftershocks. In-out-in, until I sense his muscles grow rigid and his dick lengthen inside me, and with a muted roar, he pours himself inside of me and follows me over the edge.

When I come to, I'm in his arms and he's carrying me to his bed. He places me down, draws the covers over me, and slides in next to me. He turns me over, my back to his front, and curves me against him, with his large arm across my middle.

"You do remember I'm not on birth control, right?" I murmur.

He stills, then flattens his palm against my stomach.

"If you keep fucking me like this, it's going to lead to one inevitable conclusion," I warn him.

He stays quiet for a few seconds, then a puff of air raises the hair on the nape of my neck. "Good," he declares.

A hot thrill rolls under my skin. *Whoa, whoa, hold on.* I'm not really thinking about children and a picket fence and a future with this guy, am I? He's the *Capo*, a Mafia guy. He'll never settle for something that ordinary. And I need to stop where we're headed with this.

"We never spoke about the possibility of kids," I point out.

"What's there to speak about? When you get pregnant, we'll raise them together," he says in a light voice.

"You mean, while we're still in a fake relationship?" I scoff.

"Don't know about you, but from where I am, it seems we've consum-mated this marriage pretty well." He thrusts his already hard dick into the groove between my ass cheeks. I try to pull away, but he holds me in place. "Aww, come on, Angel, don't be upset about that. The tension between us was building; it was inevitable."

"Speak for yourself. That was a mistake."

"Was it?"

I nod. "I'm not going to let you fuck me again."

"You don't *let* me do anything."

"Oh?" His voice takes on that hard edge that sends a shiver of delight racing up my spine. My god, what is it about this man, that when he puts on his mean face, it turns me on?

"You mean to say, you're going to fuck me even if I say no?" I shoot him a sideways glance.

"Are you saying no?"

"I am..." I try to say the words but they seem stuck in my throat. "I am..." I bite the inside of my cheek. "I am not saying no," I finally whisper.

He searches my features then nods. "Turn on your front."

"What?"

"Turn on your front, baby." His voice is still hard but there's a note of something—tenderness, maybe?— laced through it.

He lifts his arm and I comply. I push my cheek into the pillow as he shoves the cover off of us. Cool air assails my skin. I shiver. I hunch my shoulders together; he places his palm on the small of my back. "Relax."

"But I need to get a tampon before I bleed all over your bed," I shoot back.

"I'll get it."

The bed dips and I hear him move away.

I turn my head and watch as he heads for the bathroom and returns with one.

"You bought tampons, for me?" I gape.

He raises a shoulder. "Thought it best to be prepared."

I reach for the tampon, but he holds it out of reach. "Not yet."

"But I need it, I can already feel the blood trickling out."

"I'll take care of it." He places the tampon on the nightstand, then grabs his phone. He plants one knee between my legs, urging me to part them, before he leans between my thighs.

"Wh-what's the phone for?"

"You'll see." He swipes the screen, presses a button, then places it on the nightstand, angling it so I can see the screen.

The sound of a woman's groan, then that familiar squelching sound of wet flesh meeting flesh fills the air. A second later, my face fills the screen.

47

Jeanne

"What the actual fuck?" I gape as I watch myself stare at the screen. My eyelids are heavy, my cheeks flushed. My hair is in tangles around my shoulders. Behind me, Luca's swarthy features fill the space. His blue eyes have darkened to a midnight blue, a color I'm well acquainted with by now. The contrast between his wide shoulders that frame my pale face, the way my breasts jostle as he pushes into me from behind, the whine that emerges from my lips, and the answering snarl that rips from his throat is carnal and sensual, lewd and erotic, coarse, and also, a turn on. Moisture pools between my legs. My nipples harden until they stab into the sheets below me. Is that flushed, horny, sexual creature in the frame me? It must be.

"You... filmed us?"

"Told you, I perform even better when I'm being watched."

On screen, he rams into me again, and my entire body jolts. My vision wavers. A burst of liquid heat gushes through my veins. Warmth flushes my face. I turn, swoop out my hand, but he catches my wrist before my palm can make contact with his face.

"Have I told you it turns me on when you are angry."

"Angry? I am livid!" I toss my hair out of my eyes. "You filmed us without telling me. You have a camera in the mirror."

"I did. And now we can view ourselves come as I make you come again, in real time."

"Fuck you, Luca. This is not okay."

"Are you telling me no?" He arches an eyebrow.

Guess I was enamored by the tattoo on his back. His love for the *Cosa Nostra*, for Sicily, for the only way of life he's known and which he's now being forced to leave behind. I saw the man behind the gangster and thought I was glimpsing the emotions behind the facade he shows the world. I was wrong. He's always going to be the mobster. The made-man. The villain with the wounded past. And all he has to do is be mean and sarcastic and growl at me, and I fall apart at his feet.

I try to rise, but in one swoop, he throws me back on the bed on my front and plants his big hand on my back so I'm held in place.

"Let me go," I snarl.

On screen, I groan. The sound is so hot, so thick with lust, that I can't stop my gaze from veering toward it.

I writhe under his hold, trying to get free.

On screen, he pounds into me, and I throw my head back and moan.

My thighs tremble, my pussy clenches, and a shudder vibrates along my lower belly. No, no, no, I'm bleeding. I'm sure my period blood is gushing out of me. I turn to tell him that, but he's gripped my thighs under my butt and lifted me onto my knees. I try to squeeze my legs together, but of course, he pries them apart. Cool air flows over my exposed pussy.

"Luca," the screen me groans.

"Luca, what are you doing?" I cry, then gasp for he's buried his face between my legs. He licks my clit, then dives down between my legs and begins to eat me out in earnest. He shoves his tongue inside my channel and licks and sucks and curls his tongue inside me.

"Oh, my god," I cry out.

"Oh, god. That's so hot," on-screen Jeanne cries out.

He pulls out his tongue, only to spank my butt. The slice of pain cuts through the chattering in my head, and everything grows quiet. My entire focus is drawn to the shimmering patch of flesh on my behind where he slapped me. I open my mouth to yell, when he brings his heavy palm down on my ass cheek again, and on the other side, alternating until my entire butt is aflame. The fire sinks into my blood, warms my core, and sizzles up toward my breasts. My entire body feels too heavy. My arms and legs feel like they are weighed down.

On-screen Jeanne moans, "I can't take it anymore. I can't."

I can't take my gaze off her dilated pupils, her features, which are contorted into an expression of sexual desire so potent that it feels wrong to be watching the video, even though it's me and him, and we just enacted that scene not half an hour ago.

"Watch yourself come, Angel," his voice rumbles against my pussy.

"Come," on-screen Luca commands.

A second later, he thrusts his tongue inside my channel again. This time, he sweeps his tongue, once again, across my pussy lips, over my slit, then drags his finger around the forbidden knot of nerves between my ass cheeks. Everything he's doing is more than filthy, and unheard of, and... Oh, god, it's so arousing, so explicit and vulgar, and so earthy. It's so very Luca. And if he does it again, I won't be able to stop myself from enjoying it.

"No," I gasp.

"Yes," he rumbles. He curls his tongue inside my pussy, then sinks his finger inside by back channel. He adds a second finger, and oh, my god, the combination is too much. The climax detonates deep inside of me. He swipes his tongue in and out of me, then pinches my clit as he curves his fingers inside my back channel, and the orgasm crashes over me. I see stars. My chest hurts. My throat protests. That's when I realize I must have been screaming. He pulls his mouth from my pussy, and his fingers from my ass, only to replace it with something much bigger.

The image on the phone grows dark. In the silence that follows, I tremble.

"Luca," my voice comes out too thin, too scared.

"Shh." He slides his fingers around and plays with my already-sensitized clit. I whimper, or at least I think I do, because I'm too relaxed, still floating in my post-orgasmic state. He notches the crown of his dick against my back hole, and a tremor ladders up my spine. My stomach flip flops, and my thighs tremble.

"Luca please."

"Trust me, baby."

"You're too big," I whine.

"You can take it." He scoops up my cum from my slit and smears it around my puckered hole. "You're so wet, so moist, so heartbreakingly perfect."

He nudges up against my back hole and I stiffen. "It'll hurt."

"I'm counting on it."

"Wh-a-t?" I manage to crack open my eyelids and stare at him over my shoulder.

The skin around his lips is tainted pink. With blood. With my blood. My period blood. Jesus Christ. Why is that so forbidden? And so primal? So erotic?

He chuckles. The jerk actually chuckles. The vibrations rumble up his chest and seem to light up my veins. Even when he's being mean, he's so gorgeous.

"I hate you," I whisper.

"No, you don't." His lips curl and he leans down to place his mouth over mine. He breathes in my air, then nips on my lower lip, and I'm a goner. I open my mouth, and he swoops in. He curls his tongue over mine, and I can taste the metallic tang of my blood on him. Heat flushes my chest. I should find it gross, but somehow, it feels intimate. It feels like I'm baring myself to him. The fact that my being on my period did not stop him from taking me is so freeing.

He tilts his mouth and kisses me so deeply, I can feel it in my extremities. He fingers my pussy and circles my clit, and flames leap to life in my belly. He pushes his cock inside me, and pain shivers over my nerve-endings. He slides his finger inside my wet channel, then adds a second, and a third. He curves his fingers in a way that ignites a trail of lust under my skin. He pulls his fingers out, then thrusts all three of them inside me and I gasp. My thighs tremble. The scent of my arousal is so strong that my entire body seems to turn to jelly.

"Let me in." He licks my lips, and I can't deny him. I push my butt back and he slides in past the tight ring of muscle.

"Oh, god," I whimper. "Oh, my god."

He fits his lips on mine again and plunges his tongue inside my mouth. At the same time, he weaves his fingers in and out of me, then brings up his other hand to pinch my nipple. My scalp tingles, my toes curl, and my entire body seems to go up in flames. That's when he slips all the way inside. Too much, too full. He stretches me and holds me pinned around his cock, as I moan into his mouth. The heat of his body swirls over me, and the scent of him envelops me. His fingers, his tongue, his shaft... He's consuming me, holding me captive by filling each one of my holes with him. He tweaks my nipple harder, and I clamp down on his cock.

"*Gesù Cristo*," he growls into my mouth. "You're so fucking tight. So hot, so incredibly responsive, Angel. You're strangling my dick, and it's the most incredible sensation ever." He pulls out of me, then plunges into me with enough force for his balls to slap against my skin. My breasts jiggle, and my body jolts. He kisses me hard, then clamps his big palm around the nape of my neck and urges me back down. I push my cheek into the pillow, and dig my fingers into the sheets. He tightens his grip on my hip, then begins to fuck me in earnest. Each time he buries himself inside me, he seems to fill me further. Each time he pulls out, my body hungers for more. I didn't know it could be like this. I always treated anal with a healthy respect, but always thought it wasn't for me. I didn't realize just how erotic it could be with the right person. With Luca. With this crazy *Capo* who continues to restrain me with his fingers around the nape of my neck as he continues to bury himself in my ass. He pulls out, yet again, and this time, when he lunges forward, he bottoms out inside me. He releases his hold on my hip, drives his fingers inside my pussy and scissors them. That's enough. My entire body jolts. The ball of desire in my belly snaps. He leans forward, covers my back with his chest, and presses his mouth to my ear. "Come for me, Angel. Come right now." I climax instantly.

48

Luca

I weave my fingers through the strands of her curly hair. So silken, so smooth. I bring them up to my nose and sniff. Rose petals. If anyone had told me I'd be addicted to the scent of roses, I'd have laughed at them. Yet here I am, drawing in lungfuls of her scent, and my dick instantly twitches. Clearly there's a direct connection between her fragrance and my cock. I draw my hand back. She moans and turns in my direction, as if reaching for me. I freeze, waiting until her breathing grows more regular. Her dark lashes fan her cheekbones. Her pink lips are turned up slightly at the sides as if she's smiling in her sleep. I put that look of satisfaction on her face.

After I took her ass, she slumped into sleep. I pulled out of her carefully, then walked over to the bathroom, got a warm, wet towel and cleaned her up. Then turned her over, unwrapped the tampon, and slid it into her. I had just enough time to pull the sheets over us before I spooned her and fell asleep.

When I woke up—with a hard-on—we were facing each other. I allowed myself to survey her features for a few more minutes. Lingered long enough to risk waking her up. The morning light slants through the gaps in the curtains. Soon, she'll be awake, and I'll have to take her to the opening night show. She'll insist on going; I know that. And it's not going to be safe.

Whoever attempted to kill her last night will, no doubt, try again. I'm going to have to try to protect her, but how? It's not a job I can do on my own. I can't be everywhere all the time. Much as I hate to admit it, although I'm the *Capo* of the *Cosa Nostra*, I'll still need to ask for the Don's help. It'll help even the odds somewhat... I hope.

I head for the bathroom, have a quick shower, then pull on my clothes. I move toward the bed, pull the cover up, and make sure she's tucked in. Then, I kiss my wife carefully, making sure not to wake her before I turn and head down the stairs.

A coffee first, before I leave. I know I'm delaying, but *cazzo*, it's not every day one must swallow one's ego and ask one's bigger brother for help. I walk into the kitchen, then stop.

"The fuck you doing here?"

Massimo glances over his shoulder from his position in front of the doors that lead onto the deck. In front of him, the waves of the Tyrrhenian Sea stretch out. The morning light highlights the dark circles under his eyes. His cheekbones stand out in relief. His hair is mussed, his jaw unshaven. He's not wearing a jacket—a first for Massimo—his tie is loosened, and his shirt is rumpled.

"You look like shit," I drawl.

His face doesn't change expression. "Needed a cup of coffee."

As if to mark his words, the *bialetti* on the stove begins to bubble, and the scent of espresso fills the space.

I walk over to the stove and switch off the flame. Then grab two espresso cups and pour the coffee in them. I walk over to Massimo, hand him a cup, then slide the doors open and step onto the deck.

With the first sip of the espresso, my head clears. With the second sip, my blood begins to pump, and by the third, I'm almost ready for this upcoming conversation with Michael. Almost.

"You didn't come to my place to get a cup of coffee, did you? What's on your mind?" I ask.

He drains his coffee then places it down on the railing with a snap, before he glances away. "She's in love with someone else."

"What?" I blink. "Who are you talking about?"

"Olivia." His fingers tighten around the cup. "She's in love with someone else."

"Ah, so you stayed back in the hospital until she woke up?"

He glances into the distance. "I was with her when she came to. I asked her to marry me."

"What? You just met her."

"You just met Jeanne, and yet, here you are, married to her," he points out.

"I only did it because I had to find a way to get Michael off my back."

He glares at me.

"It's true. You know what a stickler for tradition he is. He wants us all to be married within the month."

"And she was the only one you could find?"

"I woke up in that cell where that bastard Freddie had thrown me, and there she was. It was like a sign from above."

"So, it had nothing to do with the fact that you love her?"

I glower at him. "*Stocazzo*, the fuck you talking about?"

His lips kick up. "Keep denying it. You were always good at deluding yourself."

"I've figured out my shit, man. I have my marriage of convenience in place. None of that messy falling in love shit for me. And I've still delivered on the promise made to Nonna."

"She turned me down." Massimo stares into his still full espresso cup. "Because she is in love with someone else."

"She just woke up from an injury, which is quite likely going to change her future... And you spring a proposal on her? Even I know it's not great timing."

He shakes his head. "How could I have not known she had someone else in her life? I could have sworn she felt something for me. I thought—" His throat moves as he swallows. "I thought she was the one."

"But she isn't." I reach over and grip his shoulder. "At least she told you now. It would have been far worse if you'd married her, only to find out she had someone else on her mind."

"If I'd married her, I'd have made sure she thought of no one else but me," he says in a hard voice.

I peer into his features. "*Che cazzo*, you have feelings for her."

"Of course I do, you *coglione*. Why else would I ask her to marry me? Unlike you and the rest of my dumb ass brothers, I know when I'm falling for someone, and I'm man enough to own up to the truth."

"Are you questioning my manhood?" I growl.

"You said it; not me." He wrenches his shoulder out of my grasp, then tosses back his espresso. "I could have sworn she had feelings for me." He shakes his head. "My instinct is never wrong."

"You're talking like the two of you have known each other longer."

His gaze narrows.

"So, you two knew each other from earlier? No wonder the two of you were eye fucking each other at my wedding."

"We weren't eye fucking each other." He raises both his shoulders. "Okay, maybe we were."

"No wonder when I asked you to accompany the two of them over to Malta for my wedding, you agreed so quickly."

His features don't change expression, but something in his eyes gives him away.

"I assume you made full use of the plane journey?"

He merely presses his lips together.

"Put it down to good pussy, and now you can move on, you—"

He tosses the espresso cup aside and grabs my collar. "Don't fucking talk about her like that."

"My bad, *fratello*." I raise my free palm. "I was merely saying that this clears the way for you to consider the arranged marriage with the *Camorra* princess."

He hesitates.

"Think about it. You took your chances, and it didn't pan out. Now, you can do the one thing that will help resolve this feud between the *Cosa Nostra* and the *Camorra*. Another thing that Nonna wanted. You marry the princess, and peace reigns between the families. It makes life safer for all of us, not to mention, it opens up a host of business possibilities."

"You do realize, it's because Michael wants to legalize the *Cosa Nostra* businesses that he wants this union to go ahead. This way, he's assured that they won't take advantage of our moving away from organized crime and endanger our lives."

I stiffen. Of course I'm aware of it. I've tried hard not to think about it. It's the done thing, after all. Thieves want to go straight. Criminals want to reform. Offenders want to make up for their transgressions. Me, though? I'm a villain. The one with a black heart. The one who's never dreamed of anything but being the head of the *Cosa Nostra*. Take that away from me, and what do I have?

Her, you have her.

And she married you because she needed to find a way back to the premiere of her musical, which is this evening.

I lower my hand to my side. "Or don't marry her. I mean, it will solve quite a few problems if you do, but if you don't, I'm sure we'll find some other way to work out our differences with our fiercest rival."

He glares at me, then rips the half-undone tie from around his neck. "Fuck! Fucking f-u-c-k."

49

Luca

"Fuck no." Michael glares between me and Massimo. "It's too dangerous. I'm not letting you do this."

"I'm not asking you for permission. I merely came to inform you, something I didn't have to do, by the way," I remind him.

His gaze narrows. Anger vibrates off of my older brother. He's in full Don mode. The fucker may be methodical in his approach, and he may be looking to break away from the business of our forefathers by looking to legalize the *Cosa Nostra,* but he still holds onto his power and authority, I'll give him that much.

"What about you, Massimo?" Michael turns to him. "What do you think about Luca's proposal?"

After our little heart to heart at my place, Massimo agreed to accompany me to Michael's place. Not that I need the extra support—okay fuck it, I totally do need the additional boost that Massimo offers by being here. If nothing else, he'll distract Michael enough that I'll be able to get him to agree to my plan… Or so I thought.

"Speaking of Massimo..." I lean forward on the balls of my feet. "Has he told you about his decision yet?"

Massimo tenses behind me.

"Decision?" Michael scowls.

"Regarding your earlier proposal to him?"

Michael straightens. "About the *Camorra* princess?" He tilts his head. "This *is* about the *Camorra* princess, I assume?"

Massimo lowers his eyebrows. "The fuck you up to, *stronzo*?" he growls.

"Asshole, here, is vacillating a little. You know how it is when it comes to your own wedding, it can be a little difficult to speak your mind? He wants me to inform you—"

"Luca." Massimo takes a step forward.

"—that he's ready to marry the *Camorra* princess."

"*Bastardo!*" Massimo closes the distance to us. He plants his heavy hand on my shoulder, then raises his other fist and pulls it back.

I hold his gaze. Massimo's taller than me, and slightly broader. While I'm strong, Massimo has a good few pounds on me. Whenever we've sparred in the past, it's always been a standoff. Of course, all those times I defended myself. This time, though, I refuse to raise a hand. With his fist almost in my face, he stops. Anger vibrates off of him. The pulse drums at his temple, and the tendons on his throat pop.

He glares at me for a second, then another.

"Is he right? Are you ready to marry the *Camorra* princess, Massimo?" Michael's voice cuts through the space between us.

Massimo glowers at me a second longer. Then, he lowers his arm and steps away. He straightens the cuffs of his shirt, rolls his shoulders, and widens his stance. "Yes," he says in a toneless voice, "I am ready."

Michael surveys his features, then nods. "Now that you're done distracting me..." He turns his gaze on me. "Are you sure you intend to go through with this plan?"

I nod.

"You realize, you could forfeit your life if something goes wrong."

If it means I'm able to guard hers, it'll be worth it.

"If you and your men stick to the plan, nothing will go wrong."

Michael's jaw tics. "Are you doubting my capability?"

"I never said that."

"And yet, you referred to them as my men. They are your men as much as mine, *Capo*. You've always wanted to take over the *Cosa Nostra*, but you've never seen the clan as yours. You've always carried a chip on your shoulder for not being first born. You've focused on trying to catch up with me, even helping my bride to escape, knowing it would make me lose face. I still forgave you. I took you back."

"You didn't take me back. I proved myself as being invaluable enough that you knew I would strengthen your stance if I were on your side. You didn't want me splitting the loyalties of the men. That's the only reason you accepted me back into the *Cosa Nostra*. You still didn't give me the title of *Capo* when you took over as Don. Despite the fact that I was on your side when you killed our father."

"Good riddance," Massimo sneers.

"The one thing we can all agree on." I crack my neck. "Still doesn't negate the fact that I only became *Capo* when Seb decided he wanted to move away from the *Cosa Nostra* and start his media company."

"And you did it on your own steam." Michael widens his stance. "It wasn't me deciding that you would become *Capo* simply because you're second born. You proved yourself to the clan. It was clear you were best placed to succeed Seb."

"And now you're looking to legalize the *Cosa Nostra* itself. The same *Cosa Nostra* which has been around since the early nineteenth century," I snap.

"Which you knew when you became *Capo*. Plus, we'll still be around; only instead of running guns and planning routes for illegal activities, we'll be planning corporate mergers and takeovers," Michael retorts.

"You mean, driven by the stock market and shareholders—"

"Instead of being driven by gun fights and clashes with our rivals," Michael cuts in.

"We'll be slaves to a nine-to-five routine." I roll my shoulders.

"And come back to our wives alive."

Michael and I glare at each other. My brother has all of the arguments down pat. I hate to admit it, but he also makes sense. I'd definitely like to start a day without having to worry about whether I'll be able to see my Angel again. I shake my head. *Cazzo!*

This is exactly what I was afraid of: You get married, have fantastic sex, know for a fact your woman is warming your bed, and just like that, you've lost your balls. You've already misplaced the edge that keeps you alive when you're out there facing down your enemies. That keenness that helps you survive when all else fails. That alertness, when all of your senses are firing and you feel completely in your body and one-hundred-percent alive... How I feel when I'm with her.

An electric shock runs up my spine. I straighten. *Fuck, fuck, fuck.* It can't be. I can't have fallen for her, can I? I've always known it was a possibility, but I thought I guarded myself against it. Apparently not. She was meant to be a means to fulfilling my Nonna's last wish, but I feel more for her than I've ever felt for anyone else in my life, Nonna included.

"Luca?" Michael's voice cuts through the noise in my head. "You okay, *fratello*?"

I shake my head.

"Luca?" Massimo touches my shoulder. "You seem like you've seen a ghost."

"Nonna's ghost having the last laugh, apparently," I say bitterly.

Michael and Massimo look at each other, then Michael turns to me. "You've been through a lot this past week. Getting ambushed—"

"—A moment of losing focus, that's all," I grouse.

"Getting married."

"A moment of what I thought was clarity, but which was, in reality, me walking into that old bat's trap," I grumble as I rub the back of my neck.

Michael's lips twitch.

"You laughing at me?" I scowl.

Massimo chuckles, then turns it into a cough when I turn my glare on him.

"What's so funny?"

"I think it best come from you, Don." Massimo raises his hands. *Coward.*

"Afraid you've walked into the same trap the rest of us did. The one that Massimo has avoided... So far," he adds under his breath.

It's Massimo's turn to knit his eyebrows. Good. He's so smug, watching each of us fall and acting as if he's above such things. He deserves to experience what I'm going through—the confusion, the turmoil, this bottomed-out feeling in my stomach that tells me something has shifted, even as the rest of me tries to ignore it. *Maledizione!*

I dig my fingers in my hair and tug. How could I have been such a fool? Why had I thought I'd be smarter than my brothers? Which, to be clear, I am. Except when it came to dodging the bullet of marriage, and feelings, and all of the emo shit that goes with it. Worst of all, it's not half as bad as I thought it'd be. I'm trapped, no doubt about it, but it's not something I don't want. I'm no longer as cut off from my emotions and guess what? It's not terrible. It's painful, it's eye-opening, gut-clenching, hair-raising, as adrenaline rushing as being in the crosshairs of my enemy's target... Only this time, I'm a willing victim. This time, at the end of the gunshot fire, there's only one inevitable conclusion. Life. Living. Loving. Fucking like my heart depends on it. Caring like my own future is not the only one at stake. Protecting—the one thing I was born to do. Cherishing, ensuring she comes to no harm. What this plan is about.

I square my shoulders, lower my chin, and narrow my gaze on Michael. "So, you with me on this?"

His jaw tightens. "I can't talk you out of this, can I?"

I shake my head.

"I understand why you're doing it. I'd do the same if I were in your place and it was my wife's life at stake. Doesn't mean I can't warn you to be careful."

"Oh, I will be. I have no desire to die. I have too much to live for," I say in a hard voice.

The tension in Michael's stance fades somewhat. He closes the distance between us and grips my shoulder. "We've had our differences, but when it comes down to the wire, I know I can count on you."

50

Jeanne

I come awake with a start. The sunshine streaming in through the gap in the curtain fills the space with a golden glow. I yawn, stretch. My core protests in that deliciously-used-by-a-hard-dick way. The other forbidden hole… throbs. A slight pain thuds up my tailbone and serves as a reminder to never underestimate that part of my body again. Who knew it could bring me such pleasure? Such forbidden, dirty, erotic pleasure. I rotate my shoulders and my scalp tingles. My bones are so mellow, I'm surprised I didn't melt into the bed while I slept. I lengthen my spine, rib by rib, then reach out with my toes. A sense of wellbeing fills me. So, this is what it feels like to be fucked to within an inch of my life by my husband. I still.

My husband. He is my *husband*. And he didn't panic when I asked what he'd do if I got pregnant. Luca surprised me again. He's not the mean, grumpy, alphahole he projects himself to be. There's more to him than meets the eye. The way he fucked me… It was more than sex. He put his entire body and soul and emotions into it. He told me how he felt about me with his actions. He didn't use the words 'I love you,' but he did tell me how he feels. It was surprisingly honest and raw and so very real. It touched my soul. I wish it were enough, that I didn't need to hear him also say those three words, but I do.

I sense a presence behind me, turn and gasp. "You..." I draw in a breath. "How long have you been watching me?"

Luca sits in a chair near the nightstand. His legs are kicked out in front, and he stares at me from under those thick eyelashes. Those stunning blue eyes of his glitter in the sunlight. They seem almost colorless this morning. Fascinating. His eyes definitely do change with his mood. More than Elle Woods's choice of footwear all through *Legally Blonde 2*.

"Her middle name was Jeanne."

"Eh?" A crease demarcates his forehead.

"Reese Witherspoon, she played Elle Woods in *Legally Blonde*, and her middle name was Jeanne. My mother named me after her."

"Did she?" He tilts his head.

"I suppose I should be grateful that she didn't call me Elle. I am so not an Elle. Can you see me as an Elle?" I pull the cover all the way up under my chin. I'm deflecting and vacillating... and delaying getting out of bed. Why am I suddenly shy about my body? That's not like me. But hey, it's not every morning you wake up from consummating your marriage to find your hotter-than-Lucifer husband watching you with something like intent in his eyes.

"Get up," he says in a hard voice and my pussy clenches. Jesus, Mary and Joseph. *Help*. Don't do this. Don't make me melt into a splatter of goo, or should I say, cum—my cum—all over again.

How can he look so dashing, so hot, so everything in that black suit he's wearing? He's wearing a black silk shirt, and his tattoo peeks out from the open collar. That black-on-black combination should be overkill, or look pretentious, but really, on Luca it only adds an air of menace that ripples in the air between us and curls around me.

"Don't ignore my order," he growls. That voice. Oh, god, that mean edge to his tone promises all kinds of evil punishments for not doing as he says. I should move before I make it worse for myself. I try to move, but my arms and legs refuse to obey my brain's commands. I'm trapped in the tractor beam that is his gaze.

His eyes gleam.

"On your feet," he drawls.

I shake my head.

"You can't hide forever."

"Wh-when did you wake up?" I swallow.

"A while ago."

"Were you watching me all this time?"

The skin around his eyes tightens. "I had a meeting with the Don."

"With Michael?" Yes, of course, the Don is Michael. If I didn't give away my delaying tactics before, then that question definitely revealed just how much I'm trying to postpone the inevitable.

"You called him Don. So, was this on uh, mob business?"

His jaw tightens. "It was work, yes."

"And did it go well?"

"As well as can be expected." He places the tips of his fingers together. "We can play this game all day; or rather, I can. Because you—" he pulls back the cuff of his sleeve to reveal that expensive watch of his "—have exactly four hours to get ready and show up for your rehearsal."

"What?" I always need to show up in advance of the others so I can stretch and warm up. I glance around the room, searching for a clock. I spot my phone on the nightstand, reach for it, but he snatches it up before me.

"Hey, gimme that."

He tosses it from hand to hand. "Come and get it."

I scowl, then sit up and shove my feet over the edge of the bed—all the while, making sure the sheet covers my front. I stand up, wrap them around me, then move toward him. I stick out my arm for the phone, but he holds it up and out of my reach.

"Give that back," I demand. As if I can demand he do anything.

"Take it back yourself." He smirks. Then, goon that he is, he actually chuckles, as if he's sure I'll never be able to get to it.

"Don't think I won't." I plant my feet on the chair in the space between his thighs and rise up. I grab for the phone, only in doing so, of course, I loosen my grip on the sheet, which slowly slides down my body. I snatch the phone out of his hand, and he takes the opportunity to yank on the sheet, which promptly falls to my feet.

"Oh no," I cry.

"Oh yes." He places his big paws on either side of my hips, and his touch instantly arrows to my core. I'm still standing between his legs and my pussy is on the same level as his eyes. My bare pussy. My naked pussy, which he stares at with intent written all over his face.

"No, no, no." I try to pull away, but does he let me go? Of course not. Instead, he pulls me even closer. Closer. Closer. Close enough for his breath to heat my core. The blood rushes to my clit and my inner walls throb. My thighs clench, and I resist the urge to squeeze them together. He continues to stare at my center with unabashed desire. His big shoulders are so broad, they block out the sight of everything else but him. His biceps are solid muscle and the width of my thighs. Positioned there between his legs, with his face an inch from my pussy, a shiver squeezes up my spine. My heartbeat is so loud, it fills the space between my ears. My pulse thuds between my legs and is echoed by the one at my wrists and at my temples.

"You have the most gorgeous cunt ever, Angel. Pink, juicy, and waiting to be devoured."

"No," my breath hitches, "I can't."

"You can, and you will." He presses his nose in between my pussy lips and draws in a deep breath.

"Oh, Jesus." My knees buckle. Not that he'll let me fall. He digs those thick fingers into either side of my hips and holds me immobile.

"You're filthy. An animal. A monster who—"

"Is going to eat you out, and you're going to love every second of it." He glances up at me from under hooded eyelids. The sight of him looking up at me from between my legs? There's nothing servile about it. I feel like I'm some kind of pagan offering, and he's the beast who's going to devour me in the most erotic fashion possible. Heat sluices through my veins. My skin feels too tight for my body. I glance down to find the tell-tale string of the tampon between my legs.

"Hold on, I don't remember wearing a tampon before I went to bed last night."

"You didn't."

"What do you mean, you—" I open and shut my mouth. "You...?"

He nods.

"You slid that tampon inside of me?"

"And I'm going to pull it out."

"Luca, don't you dare—"

He drops his chin, grabs hold of the string between his teeth and tugs. The tampon slides out. He tosses it aside, then dives down into my pussy.

"Wait, the blood from the tampon, it's un—"

He swipes his tongue up my pussy and my back curves. My body bucks. My already-sensitive flesh trembles.

"You were saying?" His voice is muffled.

"I was... I... I..." I sway a little, not able to string my thoughts together. "I..."

"You—?" I swear I can hear the laughter under his words. He slides his big palms over my butt cheeks, grabs big chunks of my ass and squeezes.

"Oh, god," I gasp. That shouldn't be erotic, or so stimulating, but heat zaps out from his touch and sinks into my blood. All of the pores on my skin pop.

He hauls me even closer, cups my butt, and tilts my pelvis up so I'm perfectly positioned for him to dart his tongue inside my sopping wet channel. Which is exactly what he does a second later. He weaves his tongue in and out. He shifts his hold to the tops of my thighs and coaxes me to part my legs. Then he grabs my leg and hauls it over his shoulder, baring me to his gaze.

"Luca," I whine. "What are you—"

He lowers his head and swipes that evil tongue of his across my pussy lips again and again. Then he thrusts his tongue inside my channel and curls it.

I grab hold of his hair and tug. "I can't take it. I can't," I sob.

"You can," he murmurs against my clit. The vibrations swirl about my pussy lips, driving me out of my head. I lean my upper body back, even as I yank his head closer, wanting... needing that something which is over the horizon.

He growls against my pussy, then lifts me up. I wrap my legs around his neck, and he straightens. One step, another, then he reaches the bed, throws me onto the mattress, and follows me down. He thrusts his face into my pussy, devouring me, consuming me, wrapping his lips around my clit and tugging until the heat in my belly explodes in a flash of white heat that sweeps over me. I throw my head back and scream as tears run down my cheeks. He still doesn't stop.

The climax grips me, moisture squeezes out between my legs, and he laps it up. Then he crawls over me and kisses me. I taste myself—the sweetness of my cum, the metallic taste of... blood? My period blood. It's unhygienic. It has to be, right? He slides his tongue over mine and positions his cock at my entrance.

51

Luca

I lunge forward and inside her. Her pussy instantly clamps down on my dick. "F-u-c-k," I growl. Why does she feel so good, so incredibly arousing? Why does she feel so much like home? I hook my arms under her knees and push them against her shoulders, then I begin to fuck her in earnest. Each time I push her, the bed rocks. Each time I pull out of her, she whines. She lifts her hips, chasing the sensation of my cock, and a fierce sensation grips me. The next time I bury myself inside her, I lean my weight forward. The angle rubs my pelvic bone against her clit and she whines. I grip one of her arms and wrench it up until she wraps her fingers around the headboard. Then I do the same to the other. "Hold on."

Her gaze widens.

I peer deep into those caramel eyes of hers, those gorgeous eyes that are seared into my brain. I hold her gaze and push into her over and over again. I pinch her nipple and she gasps. Color smears her wet cheeks, wet from the tears of her release, from being pushed so far beyond her limits, from the intensity of her orgasm. And I'm going to wring another from her, and push her even further. I twist her nipple, then the other and her entire body shudders. I slide my hand between us, tweak her clit, and she clamps down on me.

"Oh, god, Luca. Oh, god." Another teardrop squeezes out of the corner of her eye; I lick it up. Then I pull back, tilt my hips, and this time when I thrust into her, I grind the heel of my palm into her swollen bud. Her body bows off the bed and her spine curves. She opens her mouth and a keening sound emerges as she shatters. Moisture bathes my cock as I continue to fuck her through her orgasm. Aftershocks rip through her as I plunge forward and empty myself into her. I watch her eyelids flutter, then bend down and kiss her lips, her cheeks, her nose, her still closed eyelids. She makes a sound of contentment, which hits me deep inside and travels down my spine to my shaft. Why is it that when she's happy, I feel so content?

I peer into her features as she opens her eyes. We stare at each other, and I know something has changed between us. Something I can't quite put my finger on. My chest feels full, and my stomach is tied up in knots. Every part of me is alive in a way it has never been before. My cock extends, wanting to be embedded even further inside of her. She's an addiction. A dangerous craving. A compulsion I can't live without. A habit-forming drug that, now that I've sampled it, I can't do without. She's my fixation. My obsession. My weakness. The one thing my enemies can use to get to me. One I need to protect with my life. If something were to happen to her, I'd never survive. I stiffen. That can never happen. I'll die before I allow that. "If anyone dares even look at you, I'll kill them."

She holds my gaze, then chuckles. "That's a bit difficult, considering I'm going to be on stage with the audience watching me."

"If anyone dares hurt a hair on your head, I'll shoot him."

"As long as you're there, nothing can happen to me. I know that." She sounds so certain.

"It makes you happy to be on that stage?" I push a strand of hair back from her forehead.

"More than anything." She peers between my eyes. "What is it? What is it you're not telling me?"

I open my mouth to do just that, then change my mind. I thrust into her, and the full length of my swollen dick rubs up against her inner walls. "Does it make you happy to be fucked by me?" I growl.

She swallows. Her pupils dilate. "More than anything."

"Right answer."

I pull out of her, then flip her over on her front. I draw her up so she's balanced on her hands and knees, then palm her gorgeous butt. She shivers. I squeeze both of her ass cheeks, then pull them apart and thrust my face between them.

She yells, "What are you doing? What—"

I tongue that knot of nerves between her butt cheeks and she shudders.

"Oh, god, Luca."

My dick throbs. When she says my name in that tone of voice, it's all I can do to stop myself from tearing into her and beating my chest and claiming she's mine.

I squeeze her ass cheeks again, then reach around and strum her pussy lips. I bring my other hand up to her breast and massage her flesh. She whines. Then pushes her butt back, chasing more of the sensations. Searching for something more. Something thicker, harder, stronger to fill the emptiness that gnaws inside her. I plunge my fingers, all four of them, inside her channel. She gasps. Her entire body trembles, and that's my undoing.

I piston my fingers in and out of her, in and out. A squelching sound fills the space. She's so wet, her cum drips down her inner thigh and my wrist. I scoop it up, then straighten and smear it around her puckered hole. I slide my finger inside her, then another. I scissor them in her back channel and she sinks down, pushing her cheek into the pillow. Her harsh breathing and mine fills the room. I pull my fingers out and replace them with the crown of my cock. Then I push in. She gasps. Her entire body freezes. I'm already so wet from her cum that I slide in easily.

"Oh, god, Luca. You're so huge. So large. You're filling me up."

I grip her hips and grit my teeth to hold myself in place, allowing her to adjust to my size.

She draws in a breath, then glances at me over her shoulder. "Don't stop, not now."

This woman! She's going to be the death of me.

"Touch yourself," I snap.

She hesitates.

"Do it, Angel." I lower my voice to a hush and she shivers. "Now," I order.

She shoves her hand down between her legs and begins to strum her pussy lips.

"Slide your fingers inside your cunt," I command.

She does that, too. That's when I pump my hips and slide forward.

"Oh, god." Her eyelids flutter shut.

"Eyes on me."

She cracks open her heavy eyelids, and I hold her gaze as I begin to fuck her ass. She slips her fingers in and out of herself as I seat myself inside her fully. Then I pull her back so she arches into my chest, with my cock still sheathed in her tight little asshole. I place my fingers over hers, sliding them inside of her. Her spine curves. She thrusts her hips back, breasts thrust forward. With my other hand still on her hip, I keep her pinned in place as I thrust into her over and over again. I bottom out inside her, and she shudders. Her shoulders snap back.

That's when I gaze deep into her eyes and growl, "Come."

52

Jeanne

He told me to come and I shattered. I wanted to shut my eyes and give in to the flickers of darkness that threatened to overwhelm me, but he held my gaze. He continued to fuck me, with his fingers in my pussy and his dick in my ass, and in that moment, I knew... My life has changed forever. No matter that our marriage may have started out fake—it doesn't feel fake. It feels intense and raw and completely overwhelming.

I watch his blue eyes turn midnight dark as he continues to fuck me through the tremors that race up my spine in the aftermath of my orgasm. He picks up the pace and crams that dick into me over and over again. Each time he bottoms out inside me, he continues to hit that melting heart of me. The one I never knew I had. The one I discovered only after he thrust himself inside me. Sparks of silver flare in his eyes and I know he is close. He curls his fingers and mine inside me, and despite the fact that I'd just orgasmed, a traitorous heat ignites low in my belly.

"I can't," I wail.

"You can and you will," he growls. He releases his hold on my hip, only to grind his heel on my already-tender clit, and electric shocks had zipped under my skin. He slid into me again, once more hitting that secret spot deep inside of me, and the orgasm detonated out from the point of contact.

He bared his teeth, the sweat glistening on his temples, eyes flashing with triumph as he snarled, "Come with me, Angel."

I was helpless as I took off, riding the current of the climax, and he followed me over the edge. I fell asleep again, and when I came to, I was alone in bed.

There was a note on his pillow saying he'd had to leave urgently for work and that Massimo would be waiting to drive me to the theater when I was ready. That bothered me, but it was already two p.m. by then. I had napped for well over an hour and was really late. I jumped into the shower, and when I walked out of the house, Massimo was waiting for me. I asked him how Olivia was, but he replied that I should check with her myself. Strange, considering he'd decided to wait at the hospital yesterday to try to see her.

Anyway, I'd already messaged Olivia directly.

I'd been so aware that it should be her, not me, on the stage today. She'd messaged back with an, 'I'm fine and a best of luck,' which had only made me feel worse. I'd asked if I could come to see her, and she'd messaged back saying she needs some space and time to recover.

"I guess that's fair enough, right?" Penny asks me now as I stretch out in the small studio attached to the changing rooms in the theater.

"It's just, it feels wrong that I'm here dancing, and she's wounded and in the hospital."

Penny's eyebrows pinch together. "Should we show up unannounced?"

"That'd just make her angrier." I bend over, touch my toes, then float my arms up and weave them from side to side. "I'm not really sure what to do."

Between my guilt over Olivia and the fact that I haven't seen Luca for a few hours, my stomach is twisted up in knots. Today is my day. The day I've been working toward my entire career. So why is there a stone in my stomach, and an anchor seems to have attached itself to my chest? If I felt any heavier, I wouldn't be able to get up there on stage and dance.

"'Are you sure you're okay?" Penny asks again.

I pause, then reach for the towel around my neck and mop my brow. "Honestly, I don't know. I have mixed feelings about going out on stage."

"If Olivia were here, she wouldn't hesitate, despite the fact that this role was originally yours."

I roll my shoulders, then bend from my waist and begin to warm up again. What Penny's saying is right. I know Olivia wouldn't have thought twice before stepping on stage today.

"This is different." I straighten. "It's not only that I have her role, but she's hurt her face. She may never perform again."

"You know that's not true. There have been other actresses with injuries or scars who've made it."

"And they have outliers. It's hard enough to get roles, and now, with an injury to her face... It's going to take her a long time to recover her confidence."

"If anyone can do that, it's Olivia. She's tougher than both of us put together."

"I wish she'd at least agree to see us." Penny slides down into a split, which she makes look so easy. She's always had a more laid-back approach to her acting career. It's what I envy about her. I wish I weren't so focused on making it. I wish I was able to broaden my attention to include my personal life... Although, since meeting Luca, it has taken much more of the center stage, I admit. It's why I wish I could see him before the show.

"Did Massimo manage to see her? Did he tell you anything about how she is?" she asks.

"When I asked him how she was, he retorted I should check with her directly."

"Hmm." She kicks out both of her legs on the floor, then bends over and grips her toes. I slide down to the floor, mirror her actions, and almost manage to touch my toes, but with a lot more effort. My hamstrings really are tense today.

"Do you think there's something between the two of them? I was so surprised when he said he was going to stay back and wait to see her."

She's right. I hadn't given it much thought at the time, given how caught up I had been in my own drama with Luca, but come to think of it, it had been strange.

"Maybe he likes her." I raise a shoulder.

"And maybe your husband is waiting to see you." Penny glances past me, a small smile on her face.

I look over my shoulder and freeze. Luca stands just inside the door to the rehearsal room. He's wearing his black suit, black silk shirt, and black tie. It reminds me of the day I met him. When he had been pushed into my cell. That was only a week ago, but if feels like so much has happened since. I'd never have guessed that I'd end up being married to him.

As if he senses my thoughts, his gaze darts down to my left hand. A scowl mars his forehead. He closes the distance between us and snatches up my hand. "Where's your ring?" he growls.

Penny glances between us.

"Uh, just remembered I have to be somewhere else, I'll see you backstage Jeanne." She leaves the room and the door shuts behind her.

In the silence that follows, he continues to glare at me. That typical brand of Luca possessiveness is written all over his face, and why do I find that so hot?

"I'm going on stage soon. I had to take off the ring to fit in with my character."

His jaw hardens.

"I'll wear it right after the show is over, okay?" I say in a soothing voice.

He brings those flashing blue eyes to my features, and whatever he sees there seems to relax his shoulders. "I'm acting crazy, I'm sorry. It seems where you're concerned, I have a hard time holding back my caveman instincts."

"And I should find it annoying but—" I shake my head "—fact is, I love it." I place my palm against his cheek. "I revel in your ownership. In your near-psychopathic overprotectiveness. I bask in your dominating tendencies, your controlling actions, your nearly obsessive need to declare to the world that I belong to you."

"You do?" His eyes gleam.

"Don't let that go to your head. It's only because I'm about to go on stage in my first lead role that I'm feeling vulnerable. That's the only reason I confessed all of that to you."

He chuckles, then wraps his thick arm around my waist and yanks me up and close to him. "You're messing me up, playing havoc with my temperament and my good intentions. I thought I knew what I wanted, but then you came along, and nothing is what it was. The most important thing in the world is you, and if something happened to you, I'd never be able to survive it."

A band tightens around my chest. "You're worried someone will take another shot at me when I'm on stage."

"You have nothing to worry about. As long as I'm alive, I'll make sure nothing and no one hurts you."

Something in his tone makes me pause. I search his features. His eyes are as clear as ever, his lips curled in that familiar smirk. There's nothing on his face that indicates he's prevaricating, but I can't get rid of the cold sensation that's gripped my heart.

"What is it?" I wind my arms about his neck. "What's wrong?"

"Nothing," he assures me.

"You're stressed because of the upcoming performance?"

He hesitates. "I would be lying if I said otherwise. But you're an actress.

This is your passion. This is what you live for. It's only right you should perform today."

Something shadowed lurks in the recesses of his eyes, and I'd have missed it except for the fact that I'm watching him closely.

"Luca, you're scaring me."

"Don't be." He lowers his head so we share breath. He places his lips over mine, leaving a sliver of space between us. His gaze bores deeply into mine, and it's heady and arousing and confusing, all at the same time.

"What is it?" I ask again. "You're hiding something from me."

"I am." He grips me under my butt and lifts me. I lock my ankles around his waist. He leans into me and the unmistakable hard column in his crotch stabs me between my legs.

Flutters of lust spark at my nerve endings. "That's not what I'm talking about and you know it."

"That's what I meant." He brushes his lips over mine, his touch so sweet, so unlike any of our past kisses that my insides disintegrate.

"You're trying to distract me," I whisper.

"Not enough, if you're still talking." He pushes me into the wall and a sigh rises from somewhere deep inside of me. This—pinned against him, with nowhere to escape, with his presence holding me captive, his breath raising the hair on my temple, his scent teasing my senses, the heat from his body flowing around me, caressing me, pushing down on my shoulders and holding me in place... This... is where I have always wanted to be.

I raise my head at the same time that he lowers his. Our mouths fuse and our teeth clash, our tongues winding around each other, grappling with urgency. He shoves down my yoga pants, pushes aside my panties and pulls out my tampon. Before I can protest, he's tossed it aside and buried his fingers—four of them—inside me up to his knuckles. I gasp, feeling the wetness and hearing the squelch against his digits as he curls his fingers. The trembling instantly seizes me. I slide my hand between us, reaching for his waistband. I manage to undo the top button before he pulls his fingers out of me and shoves them in my mouth.

"Suck me clean. Taste yourself on me."

His gaze is fierce, his color high, as I follow his orders. I curl my tongue around his fingers, all the while grappling with his zipper. At last, I lower it, slide my fingers inside his boxers, and wrap my fingers around his big, thick length. My core clenches, and my chest hurts. Every part of me seems to be aflame with need. He pulls his fingers from my mouth and shoves my hand aside. Then he's there. The blunt tip of his cock teases my opening.

For a second, we stay there, my mouth open as I pant, his jaw hard, a nerve popping in his temple. Everything else in the room fades as I cling to him. He hauls me up so I'm balanced on his thighs. Then he's inside me.

53

Luca

I wanted to see her before she went on stage and tell her to break a leg. But then I saw she wasn't wearing my ring, and that animal part of me had rushed to the fore. Oh, I understood why she couldn't. Why she had to be in character when she went on. But goddamn, I wanted to stamp my mark on her, inside her, one last time. Wanted to ensure she smelled of me when she left this room, so everyone would know who she belongs to. Now, as I bury myself balls deep inside her, I wonder if I'm making a mistake.

I should tell her what I'm about to do... Only then, she'd stop me. And I don't want that, because this is the only way to keep her safe. They went after her to get to me, but if I make myself a target, I'll take the focus off of her. It's the only way to keep her safe. There's no way I could ask her not to go on stage today. This is her dream. She deserves to live it. As for me? I'll ensure no one harms her while she does it.

I plant my hand against the wall and my biceps tense. I balance her weight on my thighs while I grip her hip to hold her up. I lean more of my weight into her, and tilt my hips so my pelvic bone rubs up against her clit. Her body jolts and she rises up and off the wall. Her breasts thrust out and into my chest. Sensations burst to life under my skin, and the rest of my blood rushes to my groin. I pull back, then rock into her, and she moans.

She tightens her hold about my neck, and digs her heels into my back. I piston my hips forward, plunge into her, and feel every centimeter of her melting channel as I sink into her. One of her shoes falls off and hits the ground with a thump. It only adds to this craziness that burns in my chest. I pull back until my cock is balanced at the rim of her opening, then glare at her.

"Who do you belong to?" I ask.

"You," she replies.

"Damn right." I tilt my hips and sink into her, going impossibly deep inside her. She gasps. Her spine bends. Her pupils dilate. She opens her mouth and I lock mine over hers. I release my hold on her hip, only to wrap my fingers around the back of her neck. I suck on her, drink from her, and all the while, I fuck her. Then I release her mouth, stare into her eyes, and command, "Come."

Her pussy squeezes my dick, the orgasm crashing over her. She flutters around me as I impale her over and over again, until with a hoarse cry, I empty myself into her.

I push my forehead into hers. Sweat slides down my back as I memorize her features. Then I pull out of her. I lower her to the ground, my fingers still curled around her slender neck. I straighten her clothes with my free hand, not breaking the connection of our gazes.

"I love you," I whisper against her lips.

Her gaze widens. Before she can say anything, I pull another tampon from my pocket, slide it into her hand, then pivot. Yeah, I came prepared that way. I fix myself as I stalk out of the room.

The door swings shut behind me. I walk up the corridor, away from my love. My life.

Penny heads in my direction, a worried look on her face. "Is she okay?"

"She will be." I jerk my head in the direction of the door behind me. "She needs you."

"Did you hurt her?" Penny's expression grows fierce. "If you did, so help me, I'll kill you."

"You care about her?" I tilt my head. "That's good. She needs her friends around her."

Her forehead pinches. "What do you mean?"

I sidestep her. "Isn't it getting close to curtain call?"

"Oh, hell. Of course it is." She heads past me and into the room. "Jeanne, you ready, babe?"

54

Jeanne

Penny walks into the room. I stare past her at the door, wondering what just happened. He fucked me and walked out. He told me he loves me, and left me with his cum dripping down my thigh. I squeeze my legs together. At least he didn't tear off my panties, though I was sure he was going to do just that at one point. Perhaps because he knew I was going on stage very soon. Why had he seemed so somber? So serious. More growly than usual. He seemed like someone on a mission. Someone with a secret. Someone who fucked me as a goodbye... I stiffen, then push away from the wall.

"Jeanne?" Penny crosses the floor toward me. "It's almost time to go on stage."

"I know." I walk toward her. "I need to see Luca, one last time."

"I saw him come out of here. Didn't the two of you already say your fond farewells? You're going to see him after the show, after all."

I bypass her as I head for the door. "It's just..." I shake my head. "He seemed preoccupied, out of character."

"Probably already missing his wife. It's what? Only the second day that you're married."

"Our first day as husband and wife, actually. But it's not that; he just seemed... Not himself." I grab the door handle.

"You can't afford to be late, Jeanne," she says in a disapproving voice.

"I won't be but a moment, I just—" I wrench the door open and come face to face with William.

"There you are. I've been searching all over for you."

"Ah, I..." I hesitate. "I was just..."

"Heading for the stage," Penny cuts in smoothly.

"Good." He glances between the two of us. "Come on, I'll accompany you."

"That's not necessary," I retort.

"You're the lead actress. Of course it is." William holds the door open. "This way, please."

An hour later, I take the stage as Belle and mourn being away from my family. I admonish the Beast for keeping me against my will, but say I will stay to honor my papa's promise to him. I lament that I never dreamed a place this cold could be home, for home is where the heart is, and my home is with my father. My home is with him. *With Luca. He may be the Beast in my fairytale, but I've fallen in love with him.*

The realization comes to me as I sing, causing me to falter. I miss my cue, then pick up the lyrics again. I reach deep inside of myself as I sing, and the lyrics seem to echo what's happening in my life. It's as if the events on stage are being mirrored by those unfolding in real time. Which means, before this musical is over, my Beast will be shot.

The hair on the back of my neck prickles. A cold shiver runs down my spine. I continue to move through my paces on stage, glancing out of the corner of my eye at the audience. Of course, I can't see much because the lights are in my eyes. But I have to try.

Where is he? Where is Luca? Why did he say he loved me before he left me earlier? And the way he fucked me? It felt like he put his body and soul behind it. Well, Luca always does fuck with his entire being, but this time, there was an edge of desperation to his actions. It felt like he was memorizing my features, the feel of my body, the imprint of my pussy as it clamped down on his cock, the softness of my skin as it gave under his fingers. He absorbed me into himself and poured himself into me, filling me up as he came, and then he left me with his cum sliding down my thigh. He walked out of there as if it were the last time he was going to see me.

The music builds to a crescendo. I whirl around the stage as the mob descends on the Beast. I try to stop them and can't. I'm pushed aside on the stage as they move in on the Beast. Gaston approaches him. He raises his gun.

A figure darts out on the stage in front of me, and the sound of a shot rings out.

I scream.

The rest of the cast pauses. My heart pole-vaults into my throat. I try to draw in a breath, but my lungs burn. Sweat beads my forehead, drips down my back.

The lights come on. I glance down at his fallen body. I open my mouth, but no words emerge. I jump forward and drop to my knees in front of Luca's still form.

Blood. There's so much blood—pooling out from under him, staining the front of his shirt, smearing the wood of the stage under him. *Help, someone help him.* I may have spoken the words aloud; I'm not sure.

I need to stop the flow of blood. I glance down at my dress, reach for the skirt and tear off a piece of the cloth. Then, I press it to his chest. *Help, someone, please.* Moisture wets my cheeks and flows down my chin. I take in his ashen features, the dark hair that's fallen over his forehead, the curve of his eyelashes against his cheekbones... I already miss that piercing blue gaze. *No, no, no.* Nothing is going to happen to him. He's not going to die. "Luca, please, please open your eyes."

I bend over, brush my lips over his. "Luca, oh god Luca. I love you. I'm sorry I didn't tell you before. Luca, open your eyes and look at me."

A teardrop squeezes out the corner of my eye and plops on his cheek.

His eyelids flutter, and those blue eyes of his flash. He takes in my features and a fold creases his forehead. He raises his hand and wipes the moisture from my cheek. "Angel, don't cry." Then his eyelids close, his hand slides to the floor, and his body slumps.

55

Jeanne

"It's my fault." I wrap my arms about my waist. "My fault." A sharp pain hooks its claws into my chest. Pain slices through my guts, my lungs threaten to collapse, and I gasp for air.

"Jeanne." Penny's voice sounds from somewhere near me. "Breathe, Jeanne."

She pushes my head down between my legs.

"Breathe." She grips my shoulders. "Draw in a breath."

Air rushes into my lungs. The sudden onslaught of oxygen makes my head spin. I stay motionless, waiting for the weakness to pass, then push against her hold. She lets me up, and I lean back against the wall.

"It's. My. Fault." I swallow. "If I hadn't insisted on being on stage today, he wouldn't have risked his life. He wouldn't have put himself out there defending me. He wouldn't have been shot."

"He's going to make it." Penny takes my palm between her warmer ones. "He's strong; he'll be fine."

"And if he doesn't?" The rock on my chest seems to increase in weight, until I feel like I'm being crushed under a mountain. More tears squeeze out from my eyes. I haven't stopped crying since I took in Luca's fallen body. And even then, he reached out and comforted me. Me. The woman responsible for landing him in this life-threatening situation in the first place.

"I knew there was a chance they'd come after me." *I knew he would protect me.* It hadn't even occurred to me that he might get shot in the process. He always seemed so larger-than-life, so invincible, so able to withstand any threat and come out of it on top. To see him lying there, vulnerable and with his life force pouring out of him, had sliced me through my heart. A trembling grips me. I glance down at my dress. I'm still wearing the gown from the scene where the mob descends on the Beast and I'm unable to stop them from hurting him. The gown is soaked with blood. His blood. Only a day ago, I sat here with my clothes crusted with Olivia's blood. Is my career worth having if it means hurting two people in my life who are so important to me?

"If he... If he..." I pause, unable to say the words aloud. "I'll never forgive myself," I say in a low voice.

"He's going to be fine, Jeanne." Penny pats my shoulder.

I hear the sound of footsteps and glance up. Karma sweeps in, with Michael on her heels. She's wearing a bright red dress that's snug enough to show off her pregnant belly. She marches over to me, then sits down on my other side and opens her arms. I fall into them.

"Oh, god, what am I going to do? What if he..." I stop myself again. I will not say the words aloud.

"Hush, he's strong and pigheaded. Don't forget, he's a Sovrano. He's not going to submit to a bullet that easily."

"I shouldn't have stepped on that stage. I should have known it would endanger his life—"

"You still would've done it."

I pause, then glance into her features. "What do you mean?"

"If anyone understands what it means to be ambitious, it's me. Before I met Michael, I was focused on building my credentials as a fashion designer. I was all set to take over the world with my designs. Then, Michael kidnapped me and brought me to Palermo, and my life changed. I still fought him. I continued to create, in my own way. I stitched my wedding gown, then designed Aurora's gown when she got married. Given a choice, I'd have designed Elsa's and yours, as well, but you guys gave me the slip." She shakes her hair back from her face. "What I'm trying to say is, you don't need to sacrifice one for the sake of the other. If you hadn't taken the stage today, you'd have always regretted it."

"And if anything happens to him, I'll hate myself forever."

Within seconds of Luca being shot, as I held onto him and screamed for help, Christian and Massimo had appeared with Aurora in tow. They couldn't have been far away, I now realize. Aurora had proceeded to give him first-aid until the medics had arrived on the scene.

"He knew." I pull back from Karma's embrace. "He anticipated this happening. In fact, he was counting on it. It's why he was acting so strangely just before the performance started. That's why I couldn't see him in the audience. He was positioned by the stage. He knew I'd be targeted again and he was going to make sure he took the bullet for me. He knew there would be an attempt on my life, but rather than stopping me from going on stage, he decided to protect me with his life."

Karma doesn't reply, but I read the confirmation in her eyes.

"I'm right, aren't I?" I squeeze my fingers together. The pressure builds behind my eyes. "He put himself at risk for me."

Footsteps approach, and Massimo appears in front of me. "You shouldn't blame yourself. Once Luca makes up his mind, nothing can stop him."

"You could have told him his plan was stupid." I rise to my feet and brush past him. I take a few steps forward, then train my gaze on the men and women clustered on the other side of the room. "You should have urged him to stop me from taking the stage today. If all of you had pushed back on his plan, he wouldn't be lying in there injured."

Michael, the Don stays seated, no change of expression on his face. Christian and Aurora, who had been conferring in low voices, glance up at me. Adrian, who stands a little separated from the rest of them, folds his arms across his chest.

"I'm right, aren't I? If the lot of you had insisted, he'd have stopped me from taking part in the musical today and then he'd be safe and not fighting for his life."

"As I said, once Luca gets something in his mind, there's very little we can do to change it." Massimo moves closer and stands next to me. "He's the hot-headed one, the impulsive one, and the most stubborn of all of us. Also—" Massimo leans forward on the balls of his feet. "Do you think he'd have stopped you from fulfilling your dream? Do you think he'd have held you back from taking the stage when it means so much to you? He made it clear to us that he would never stop you from fulfilling your dream, but he'd make sure to watch out for you. He was determined to protect you and ensure no harm came to you. It was about your safety. His wife's safety. It wasn't our place to hold him back."

I whirl on him. "And now he's injured. Do you take responsibility for that? If something happens to him, can you live with it on your conscience?"

Massimo winces. "I understand you're hurting, but Luca would have done this, with or without our help."

I pivot, close the distance to Michael. "You're the Don. You could've ordered him to not go through with his plan. You could've stopped this from happening."

"He made it clear your life was of more importance to him," Michael replies.

"So, you stood by and watched him get shot?"

"We took precautions."

"Like what? Making sure the ambulance got there after he'd been shot? Getting to him after his blood had already stained the stage? What kind of a Don are you, if you can't protect your men? What kind of a brother are you, if you allow your own kin to risk his life unnecessarily?"

"Jeanne." Karma walks over and places her hand on my arm. "You have no idea what you're talking about."

"Don't I?" I pull away from her. "It's easy for the rest of you to try to justify your actions. But you knew what he was going to do, and you didn't stop him. If something happens to him, I'll never forgive any of you, I—"

"Mrs. Sovrano?"

I whip my head around. As do Karma and Aurora.

"Ah," the doctor's gaze bounces between the three of us, then settles on me. Guess the blood on my dress is a dead giveaway.

"Mrs. Luca Sovrano?"

I nod. A melting sensation grips my limbs. My heart feels like it's going to explode out of my chest. It's the first time someone has called me that. *Will it be the last?* No, I will not think that way. I will be positive. I take a step in his direction.

"Is he okay?" My voice trembles. My chin wobbles. Everything in the room fades away as the doctor shakes his head.

"I'm sorry."

56

Jeanne

It's been three days since that fateful moment. I know, because last night was the third time I've come off stage. Three days. One continuous, endless strand of white noise, punctuated by my stepping on that stage. The stage I now hate. The musical I now abhor. I'm revolted by what I have become—a widow who still goes up there to perform every day because I'm committed. The show must go on, after all. That's what William told me. He called me as I sat outside the room in the hospital where Luca was.

Penny held me as I collapsed in a heap after the doctor's proclamation. I was trying to work up the courage to go inside that room and see him. Stared at the door for what seemed like hours, until her phone rang.

She answered it, then glanced at me, telling me William insisted on speaking to me. I didn't want to take the call, but she said William insisted. The future of the musical was at stake. With the lead actress unreachable— Olivia had checked herself out of the hospital, and apparently, disappeared—that left me. The woman who lost everything on that stage... And he'd wanted me to go back and complete the run. The money from the ticket sales was riding on this, but if that weren't enough, so were the futures of the rest of the cast. It was the latter which gave me pause.

I know what it is to give up everything to focus on a creative career. One in which so much depends on being in the right place at the right time, one in which a musical like this could make or break a person. It broke me; doesn't mean it can't launch the future of the rest of the cast.

Ultimately, it's the fact that Luca, himself, encouraged me to go on stage... He'd have wanted me to keep performing; it's why he gave up his life, after all. That's what had convinced me to return to the musical the next day, and the day after, and the one after that.

Now, I glance at my reflection in the mirror in the dressing room adjoining the bedroom I shared with Luca. I barely slept the night, and my gaunt features stare back at me. There are black circles under my eyes. My cheekbones have grown more prominent. The light reflects off of my hair and I lean in close. I pluck at a strand at my temple. It's gray? That can't be right. Since when did I have gray hair? It's the first time I've noticed it. I definitely did not have gray hair before. Could it be...The strand slips from my grasp. The shock of what had happened—that's the only explanation.

There's a soft tap on the door before it opens and Karma walks in. Since that day at the hospital, she and Penny have been my constant companions. Karma had wanted me to move in with her and Michael but I refused.

I want to be alone with my grief and with my thoughts of Luca. I sleep in the bed where he fucked me, embrace the pillows which retain his scent, and I've taken to wearing one of his discarded button-downs around the house. I have to hold onto what I have of him—the image of him in my mind, the lingering warmth of his body, which I can almost imagine if I close my eyes and focus on his presence.

When I was on stage the first night after the incident and we reached the scene where the Beast—where Luca—was shot, I was sure I was going to collapse. That's when something had reached out to me. I imagined I heard him admonish me and order me to move on. I felt like he was there with me, urging me on. The hair on the nape of my neck rose, and it felt like he was there in the audience watching me. I flicked a glance at the darkened auditorium, not that I could see anything, then I had pushed myself to go through the well-rehearsed steps. I had channeled all the agony, the conflict, the torment I felt into the performance.

I must have said and done the right thing because, the next thing I knew, the audience was applauding and demanding encores, as they have been every night. The musical is running to packed houses—no doubt, also as a result of the notoriety from what happened on the first night—

and there's talk of extending it, even performing at London's West End. If only he were here to see it. He gave his life, and I have what I always strived for. A successful career as an actress.

"Jeanne?" Karma touches my shoulder. "How are you holding up?"

I raise my gaze to hers in the mirror. "I'm..." I shake my head, not sure what to say.

"I wish you'd move in with me and Michael. You need your family around you at this time."

What I need is Luca. His touch, the feel of his skin on mine, his voice rumbling under my cheek as I lay my head on his chest, his scent surrounding me as he wraps me in those big arms of his... His lips on mine, his gaze holding mine, a smirk on his lips as he orders me around in bed.

I reach for the moisturizer and begin to apply it on my face. "I'm fine." My voice sounds so cold, so dead. Good. How can you be expected to go on when everything that means anything to you is gone, and all that's left of you is a hollowed-out shell, a body that's going through the motions of living, but isn't actually there?

It should be easier to be on stage. You'd think I could pretend to be someone else; I could try to leave what happened behind. Except, each step on that stage, each piece of dialogue I mouth, each time I cross the spot where he fell, feels like I'm walking on knives. The space was wiped clean, but I'm sure I can see the outline of the blood that spurted from his body. Can smell the metallic tang of copper that leached into the air as he lay dying in my arms.

I place the bottle of moisturizer on the dresser, then rise. Karma watches as I walk over and pull the jacket from the peg on the wall. His jacket. Nothing else seems to keep out the cold. Even wearing the jacket, my bones feel like they've been dipped in ice. My blood feels like there are icicles embedded in the cells.

"You don't have to do this." She walks over and grips my arm. "You don't have to be there."

"I do." I tip up my chin. "He'd have wanted me to be there."

She peers into my features. "If I were in your position, I would've burned the place down, then likely thrown myself off a cliff. You've been too silent, Jeanne. You haven't even cried."

I frown at her words. I've been weeping inside. The kind of tears that leach into your skin and eat away at your insides. Acid rain which won't stop until every part of me has been consumed. I feel empty, floating, like I'm high up there, looking down on myself and the movements I'm going through, where I'm pretending to live. The daily performances stretch out in front of me. It's what forces me to get up in the mornings, what forces me out of the house. The musical that killed him is, ironically, the reason I'm pushing myself to live. At the same time, I feel trapped by my duty to the other cast members, to the profession that brought me this far.

A chill runs down my back and I pull the jacket closed around myself. "I'm ready," I say simply.

"Are you sure?" She rubs my chilled hands. "If you'd rather stay behind—"

"No." I pull my hands from her hold and slide them into the pockets of the too-big coat. "I... I'm ready to see him."

57

Jeanne

I'm not ready. I can't do this. I stand, frozen, at the entrance of the church. The aisle stretches out before me. The aisle I never did walk when we got married. This is the family church of the Sovranos, so Karma had told me on our way here. It's where she and Aurora got married. It's where they held the funerals for Luca's brother, Xander, and his Nonna. And now, it's his turn.

I try to take a step forward, but my feet seem stuck to the ground. I can't do this. I don't *want* to do this. I angle my body away from the sight of the open casket at the end of the aisle. That heavy sensation in my chest intensifies. My stomach churns. I'm going to be sick. I run my sweaty palms down the black dress I'm wearing. The one Karma had delivered to me yesterday. She grips my arm. On my other side Penny, too, turns to me.

"Jeanne? Do you want to sit down?" she asks.

I want to run out of here. I want to leave and pretend I never came to Palermo. That I never accepted a role in this musical. But then I'd have never met Luca. I'd have never known how it feels to want someone with your entire being. How it feels to subsume myself in another. To look at him and know my life has changed forever. To miss him with such gut-wrenching pain that every part of me knows I'll always hurt for him. I may move on from this, but I'll never know another man like him. Never feel this kind of overwhelming need to merge myself, my heart, my spirit, my life, my skin, my breath with another. Oh, god. A shudder grips me. My teeth chatter. I hunch further into Luca's jacket and squeeze my fingers together.

"Jeanne?" Karma peers into my face. "Do you want to leave?"

Yes.

Yes.

I shake my head. I can do this. I have to do this. For him. I need to be strong for him. Need to show the world that I have it together. Just need to get through the next hour, then I can collapse into a corner.

"You sure? If you want to leave, no one will find fault with it."

"I want to do this." I square my shoulders, and turn back to face the front of the church.

"Penny and I are with you." Karma links her hand with mine.

Penny does the same on the other side. I squeeze both of their palms, touched at their show of support. I haven't lost everything. I have his family and my friends, and my family back home. I may not be close to them, but they're still there for me. And I have my ability to perform on stage, though that's not my priority at the moment. Funny how quickly things change.

I move slowly up the aisle, flanked by Penny and Karma. The pews are filled with people I don't recognize.

"Townspeople," Karma leans in and whispers. "The Sovranos are the first family of this city. Their ancestors pretty much set up the groundwork for this community. Over the years, they've helped people, touched lives in a way the government never has. Everyone has come to pay their respects."

I knew the Sovranos were important, but just how far-reaching their influence is, only comes home now. There are men wearing suits, women in dresses, families with kids all dressed in black, all of them quiet and somber as we pass them, even the children.

A few rows from the front, the mix of people changes. Now, it's almost exclusively men, all wearing black suits, some holding their hats in their hands. They are of all ages, all shapes and sizes. What unifies them is the hardness of their features. Their narrowed gazes as they face forward.

"And these are the associates of the *Cosa Nostra*—members from other clans, including our closest rival, the *Camorra*. When it's a wedding or a funeral, everyone turns out, even enemies, to pay respects," Karma adds.

At the end of the aisle, the Sovrano brothers wait for us—Michael, followed by Massimo, Axel, Christian, Seb and Adrian. All dressed in black. All watching us approach with narrowed eyes. Hard jawlines, glowering gazes. They are so similar to Luca. *None of them is Luca.*

A cold sensation yawns in my chest. Why me? Why did this have to happen to me? I could have prevented it and I didn't. I know all the arguments against this line of thinking. Some of which I even believe… Yet nothing is a substitute for the man who is gone. Nothing I do will bring him back. I had one chance at finding true love. The kind that would last an entire lifetime. I had it and I lost it. And now nothing can replace it.

We pause a few feet away from the casket. Another shiver grips me. My shoulders quake. The coldness I've carried in my chest grows and spreads until my entire body is encased in ice. I don't realize I've stopped until Karma touches my shoulder again. "Jeanne, say the word and we'll leave. I swear, nobody will be upset with you."

I swallow around the rock that seems to have taken up residence in my throat, then shake my head.

I take another step, passing the row where Aurora and Elsa are seated. I reach the line of the Sovrano brothers, then tug at my hands.

Karma and Penny release them.

"You okay?" Penny whispers.

"We'll be right here on the front row, waiting for you." Karma squeezes my arm, then both of them step away. I straighten my spine. I can do this; I can.

Massimo moves toward me. Wordlessly, he holds out his arm. I accept it and allow him to lead me toward the open casket. Before I can reach it, I shut my eyes. *Oh, god, this is it. Oh, god.*

Massimo pats my arm. "I'll be right behind you." I hear him move away.

I hear someone cough in the church behind me, followed by the sound of a child crying, shushed by his mother. Footsteps shuffle, then everything fades away. Silence descends, a beat, another. I open my eyes, lower my gaze, and stare into the face of my dead husband.

58

Jeanne

He looks alive. He looks like he could get up from the casket, jump out, scoop me up in his arms, and walk out of here with me. He looks like he could take me home, bend me over the settee in the living room, and fuck all of my sadness out of me. He looks like... he's asleep. I draw in a breath and his scent of dark chocolate and coffee fills my lungs. How strange. Maybe it's my imagination playing tricks on me? His cheeks are slightly flushed, his hair combed back perfectly, except for an errant strand that's escaped over his temple. His jaw is shaved, so there's no trace of a beard. He's wearing a dark jacket, and underneath it, a pale blue shirt and a black tie.

That's not right; he'd never wear a blue shirt. He preferred black shirts. Someone should have remembered that. I wring my hands tighter, and my finger slips on my wedding ring. I wore it when I returned from the hospital, and haven't taken it off since, not even for the performances. I'm never going to take it off again. Not for anything or anyone. My fingers tingle. I want to touch his face. To kiss his forehead one last time. To brush back that errant strand, and cup his cheek, and tell him I'll always love him. I reach out my hand, when the sound of a car backfiring echoes around the space. It's followed by a woman's scream, quickly cut off, and I realize that wasn't a car. My heart begins to race. A shudder grips me.

Something solid crashes to the floor. I gasp and turn around to find Michael and Massimo have overturned one of the mobile pews. Axel and Christian do the same with another, and Seb and Adrian overturn a third. They line up all three pews, forming a solid barrier, behind which they position themselves with guns drawn.

Massimo glances over his shoulder. "Get down," he yells.

When I hesitate, he points to the floor and I follow his directions. I hear movement and look up to find Michael guiding Karma to join me. The other women follow her and we huddle behind the wall that is the Sovranos.

"What's happening? Was that a gunshot?" I ask.

"It would seem so," Karma replies. Her gaze is alert, but her manner is calm. The other women are tense, but no one seems alarmed. Except for Penny, who seems as confused as me, the rest of the women are remarkably calm.

"Is this normal? Gunshots and hiding from shooters. Is that why none of you is panicking?" I try to chuckle, but it comes out like a wheezing sound. "Why aren't any of you worried about what's happening? Is this like a day-in-the-life of the Mafia? Does this happen often?"

"Not that often," Karma murmurs.

The women glance at each other. Something passes between them.

"What?" I peer into the faces. "What is it?

No one answers. The hair on the back of my neck rises. My pulse begins to thud at my temples.

"What is it?" I glance between the women. "What are you not telling me?"

Elsa glances at Aurora, then back at me. She seems uncomfortable. "It's nothing that you won't know very soon." She closes the distance to me, reaches for my hand, but I pull away.

"I hate it when I'm the only one who doesn't know what's happening," I snap.

Beyond the wall of Sovranos, another gunshot rings out. One of the Sovrano brothers returns fire. It's difficult to know who's shooting, since all of them have pulled out guns. Clearly, the fact that we're in a place of worship is no deterrent for these men. No wonder in all of the gangster movies I've seen, guns and churches go hand-in-hand. It's clearly not a cliché, for here I am, witnessing what seems to be a full-on gunfight.

Karma moves toward me. "We need to leave."

"No." I glance at Luca's casket, then back at her. "I'm not leaving him."

"We need to leave, babe; it's not safe here." She reaches for me, but I move back.

"You can go. I'm staying with Luca."

She blows out a breath, then turns to the others. A look passes between her and Aurora. Then Aurora nods, turns, and heads for the back door of the church on one side of the pulpit.

Penny hesitates. Karma turns to her. "We need to go."

"Not without Jeanne."

"Jeanne will be safe, I promise." Karma grabs her hand. "We need to leave."

More gunshots ring out. More people scream. There's a clatter of foot-steps... Guess the rest of the people are leaving, too.

I turn to Penny. "Go!" I jerk my chin toward the exit door. "Please, go, Penny, I don't want any more of my friends hurt."

Penny nods. "Stay safe, Jeanne."

"I'll be with you very soon." I try to smile. "Now leave."

Karma moves toward the doorway, taking Penny with her. I turn to find Adrian and Seb breaking away from the Sovranos. The rest of the brothers move in to cover the gaps. Their movements are in synchrony, as if they've rehearsed it before. No doubt, they've been in similar situations together and have come out of it. So why is it that Luca had to die? If he decided to put himself at risk to save me, why didn't they protect him? Why weren't they better prepared?

Another shiver runs down my back. My throat is so tight, it feels like I've swallowed a bucket of mud. The heavy sensation in my chest intensi-fies. There's something at the edge of my consciousness that I can't quite grasp. A thought that almost materializes, only to be lost.

There's a disturbance beyond the wall of Sovranos. I peer in that direction to find Massimo in a scuffle with a stranger. He rams his fist into the man, who staggers back. Massimo levels his gun and shoots the guy point blank in the face. The shot reverberates around the room. Blood fountains out, one side of his head blown off as he crumples. My gut churns, bile boils up my throat. I swallow, close my eyes and take a deep breath. And another, until the sickness subsides. I should be shocked. I think I *am* shocked. I simply can't process what I'm feeling at the moment.

Three more men race toward us. Shots ring out. Was that Massimo who shot? Or maybe that was Adrian? Or Michael? More men run in from the side door. I gasp aloud. Are we going to be overpowered? To my relief, they join the Sovranos and shoot back at our opponents. All three of the strangers crumple.

More men join Freddie, more shots ring out. More bodies hit the floor. It's a constant pounding of footsteps, the muted hiss of shots, and the thwack of bodies hitting the floor.

My entire body is frozen. The heaviness in my chest drops to my stomach. It feels like I am encased in ice, inside and out.

I hear something hit the roof above before bits of plaster pour down on the heads of the Sovranos. Silence follows. Then the lights in the church cut out.

My breath catches in my throat. I need to get out of here. Need to leave before I'm hit, or hurt, or worse. I try to stand, but my limbs refuse to obey me. Try to say something, but the words are stuck in my throat. A snake has wrapped itself around my middle and is squeezing me slowly. My lungs burn, and my throat hurts. Fear licks up my spine, and for the first time since the shooting started, I feel terrified. Vulnerable. Exposed.

Is this how I'm going to die? Is it so bad if I do? The man I love is gone. I no longer feel the same kind of passion for the one thing that had brought meaning to my life—my ability to perform. What is there to live for?

Suddenly, the darkness is pierced by red beams of light that swing about the place before settling on each of the Sovranos' foreheads. What the— What are they? Laser targeting? Oh, no. There're snipers in the church. I glance up, as do the Sovrano brothers. Adrian curses under his breath.

"Put down your guns," a familiar voice rings out.

The men hesitate.

A red beam of light fixes onto the middle of my forehead. I gasp. My heart cannons in my chest with such force, I'm sure it's going to break through my ribcage.

"Put down your guns, or I'm going to shoot her."

That voice! I'd recognize it anywhere. It's Freddie. Luca died to protect me from him, but he found me anyway.

All of the men seem to turn to columns of rock. Then, Michael raises his arms. Slowly, he bends, places his gun on the floor, and slides it forward.

He straightens.

"Now the rest of you," the same voice says.

One by one, they lower their guns to the floor, then straighten.

The red beams of light continue to cut through the gloom. Then footsteps sound as a man walks out from behind a pillar. A short, compact man with a slight bulge around his center. His features are ruddy, his hair thinning.

Freddie levels his gun at Michael as he closes the distance to them. He skirts the fallen bodies, then walks over to Michael. He flips his gun, catches it by the barrel, then brings the butt down on Michael's temple. The sound of metal hitting flesh whomps through the space.

My guts knot. My belly churns. Bile sloshes up my throat, and I swallow it down.

In front of me, Michael doesn't flinch.

"Freddie," he says in a voice that is shorn of any intonation.

"Finally, fuck." The other man chuckles. "Took you long enough to acknowledge my existence."

"What do you want?" Michael asks in a bored tone.

"Everything you have." Freddie lowers his chin to his chest. "Your father took credit for my crime. It was a perfect crime. The kidnapping of seven young boys in London. Scions of the richest families in London. The notoriety alone should have ensured I was known to every lawbreaker in the underworld. The money from the ransoms would have set up, not just my children, but at least the next three generations.

"I planned it, I did the work and put in the hours, and your father? He took all of the credit. Not only that, you had to go and kill him, and remove any chance of my taking revenge for what he did." He leans forward on the balls of his feet. "Now, *you* need to pay the price."

"You want my life; take it," Michael replies, his stance relaxed.

"Oh, you don't get off that easily. You need to suffer the way I did. Stripped of my power, turned into a laughing stock. No one took me seriously for a long time. It took years for me to put together another team, to regain my position within the organized crime world. Aided, of course, by your brother." He tips his chin in Axel's direction. "Until he betrayed me and moved over to join you."

Axel's shoulders tense, but he stays quiet. As do the rest of the Sovranos. They seem to be waiting, watching, holding out for something to unfold. But what?

"You, Michael... You and your brothers are the cause of so much of what went wrong in my life." His lips twist. "And now, you're going to pay."

Michael must sense his intention, for he growls, "Don't you fucking dare—"

Freddie tosses his gun to his other hand, and brings the butt down on Michael's temple again. This time, Michael stumbles to the side. Massimo moves forward, but with an agility that he did not seem capable of, Freddie pulls out another gun from his waist and aims it at me.

I see the shot coming, feel the bullet splice the air as it rushes toward me, hear a thump next to me. Then, I'm pushed to the floor. A big body covers mine. A gun fires, and the reverberations travel through the muscles of the man who is bent over me, down my chest, to my toes.

There's another muted thump, as if a body hit the floor. I lay there with my cheek pushed into the floor... which is, at least, not dusty. I mean, it's fairly clean for a place which has seen a lot of footfall. My thoughts flicker. I try to breathe, then wheeze. That's when the weight disappears from my back. I'm turned over and promptly squeeze my eyes shut.

"You okay?" a voice growls.

His voice—like aged whiskey and sin and everything ever created to tempt a woman to the dark side. It can't be. It can't be.

"Open your eyes, Angel," he whispers. I shiver. My heart is racing so fast, I can feel the blood thump in my ears.

"Please," he murmurs.

A word he's never said before. Never asked me to comply in that tone of voice. A voice that is tender and fearful and so filled with anguish that I snap open my eyes.

I open my mouth to speak, but my words are trapped inside.

59

Luca

Her gaze widens. Those gorgeous, amber eyes of hers lighten until they resemble pools of silver. Her chin trembles. She opens her mouth, but all that comes out is a gasp. Her chest rises and falls.

"Angel, I'm so sorry," I whisper.

She shakes her head. "It can't be. You're dead." Her chest rises and falls.

"I'm alive."

"No," she whimpers, "no, no, no." She tries to wriggle out from under me. I grab her wrist, bring her hand to my chest, and place her palm over my heart. The thud-thud-thud of my heartbeat slides into her skin. She presses her hand into me as if she can't get enough.

"L-Luca?"

I nod.

"I saw you shot."

"I was wearing a bulletproof vest," I explain.

"I saw the blood." She swallows.

"You're an actress. You know how easy it is to fake a bleeding wound."

"I pressed down on it. I-I held you while your life bled out of you."

"It was all an act."

She blinks, then her features close. "You put on an act. You faked your own death?"

"I had to do it. It was the only way to draw out that *stronzo* Freddie. The only way to put an end to the danger he posed to us. None of us would ever be safe, as long as he was alive."

"You used me?" Her gaze narrows. "You pretended you were dead. You allowed me to believe that you were gone. That I'd never see you again. That I'd never hold you, or be close to you, or—"

"You realized that you love me."

Her amber eyes snap to life. She swipes out her hand, and her palm connects with my cheek. My head snaps back. I don't resist. She slaps me a second time, then a third. Pain cuts through my head. My ears ring. I deserve it. Deserve it all, and much more.

"Let me up." She begins to pound on my chest.

I hesitate.

She rams her fist in my shoulder. "Let me the hell up, Luca, or I swear, I'll hate you even more."

Goddamn. Going in, I knew there was a good chance she'd be pissed, that she might never forgive me for what I did. But to see the betrayal in her eyes... Nothing prepared me for that. I roll off of her, spring to my feet, and hold out my hand.

She ignores it. She pushes up, then dusts off her dress in slow precise motions.

"I'm sorry, Angel—"

"Don't call me that. I ceased to be your anything the moment you pulled this stunt on me. Do you have any idea what I've been through? How I've been blaming myself for what happened? How each time I go up on that stage to perform, I relive your death every night, Luca? Every night."

I wince. A hot knife stabs into my chest. My stomach hardens. I take a step toward her, but she holds up her hand.

"Don't come near me. I don't want anything to do with you."

"You don't mean it..."

"You lost the right to tell me what I can feel or do. I don't want to see you again."

She brushes past me, then stops when she takes in my brothers watching the unfolding drama.

"All of you knew?" She scans their faces. "Each of you knew he was alive, yet not one of you thought to let me in on it."

"It's not their fault." I draw abreast with her. "I gave them no choice in the matter. All of this was my plan."

"So you could see me hate myself for what I did to you? So you could see my pain, and relish the hell I was putting myself through?"

"No—" I close the distance between us. "It was the toughest thing I've ever done. I knew you would be upset when you thought I was dead, but I had no idea you would take it so badly. I didn't think that you—"

"Loved you? You thought I'd mourn your death for a day, and get on with my life, is that it?"

"I didn't think you'd get over it that quickly, no," I say slowly.

"So, you wanted to see me suffer, wanted me to weep over your body at the funeral, you—" Understanding dawns on her face. "That's what you wanted. You wanted me to come across as the grieving widow to the world, so it would lend an air of authenticity. You wanted everyone to see me mourn you, so they'd believe that you were really dead. You used my distress as a display to flush out your enemies."

I grimace, then square my shoulders. "It's true, I wanted the world to believe that I was dead. Another of the Sovrano brothers dying. This time, the *Capo* shot down by the gun of an assassin. I wanted Freddie to feel flushed with victory. To be confident enough to reveal himself and give me a chance to take him out. It was the only way to protect you. If I hadn't gotten him, he'd have tried to kill you again, and I couldn't allow that."

"So instead, you killed me while I was still alive. You turned me into the walking dead."

The band around my chest tightens until I am sure my ribcage is going to shatter. The heaviness in my stomach grows, until my entire body seems to be made of stone. I reach for her, but she pulls away.

"I had to do it." I swallow. "It was the only way. Protecting you while faking my death was the only way to draw Freddie out. He already tried to kill Axel and Theresa, and then Elsa and Seb. He almost succeeded in hurting you the last time. I couldn't allow that, Jeanne. I had to do everything possible to remove the danger that lurked around you. I had to ensure you could lead a free life."

"Mission accomplished. Now, I want to be free, too—free of you. I sever all relations with you, Luca. I hate you. I'll never forgive you for what you did to me. Never." She pulls off her ring and throws it at me. It hits my chest, bounces to the ground, and skitters away.

Every muscle in my body tenses. The band around my chest snaps, and a piercing pain cuts through me.

"Jeanne, wait." I leap toward her, but she raises her hand without turning around.

"If you have one iota of decency left in you, Luca, you'll let me go."

60

Luca

I let her go. I watch as she walks past the fallen bodies of the men my brothers and I shot down, past the crumpled figure of the man who attempted to take her life, twice. Her footsteps echo around the church as she heads down the aisle and away from me. She slips through the doorway of the church, and leaves without a backward glance.

The door clangs shut. The sound reverberates around the space, and echoes in my head. Somehow, it feels like the door to my coffin slamming shut. I spin around and kick the empty coffin I'd occupied just a few seconds ago. It's so heavy that it takes a second kick, and a third, to dislodge it. It slides to the ground and rolls over.

"Fuck, fuck. FUCK," I yell.

I raise my joined hands and bring them down toward the marble platform that the coffin rested upon. I'd have hurt myself, probably broken a few bones in my palm, too, if it weren't for Massimo grabbing my shoulder and pulling me back.

"Get yourself under control, *fratello*. Hurting yourself is not going to help anything."

"Oh, and you're an expert on relationships, are you?" I wrench my shoulder from his grasp and turn on him. "The *stronzo* who couldn't get the woman he fell for to marry him."

His shoulders bunch. The tendons of his throat pop. "Take that back, you *pezza di merda*."

"Or what?"

He bares his teeth. "Or I'll smash your face in."

I pull my fist back to do just that, when I'm caught from behind, and so is Massimo. We're pulled apart. Me by Adrian, and Massimo by Seb and Axel. The *testa di cazzo* is so fucking big, it takes two of them to restrain him.

We stare at each other, our breaths coming in puffs, chests heaving. Sweat beaded across our foreheads. Then Massimo shakes them off. He straightens his cuff and turns to Michael, who walks over to join us.

"The answer is yes."

"Eh?" Michael's forehead furrows.

"I'll marry the *Camorra* princess."

He steps over Freddie's body, then walks around the other fallen men. "I'll send people to clean this up."

He stalks up the aisle and out of the church, leaving the six of us alone.

"Fuck." I pull out of Adrian's grasp.

"I warned you," Michael says in a hard voice. "I told you this would hurt you."

"And if I hadn't done it, he would have hurt her." I glare at the fallen Freddie. "He's dead. We can all move on now. He's never coming back to hurt any of us or our families. And with Massimo ready to marry the *Camorra* princess, the feud with them will also be settled."

"You didn't have to take it on yourself to settle this single handedly. You are not responsible for all of our futures," Seb chides as he leans forward on the balls of his feet.

"I am the *Capo*." I bend and pick up my gun from where I let it drop after I shot Freddie. "It was up to me to ensure our safety."

"And I am the Don." Michael scans my features. "You've always tried so hard to prove yourself, Luca. You can rest assured that we owe you for this. What you did was difficult and gutsy. You put the welfare of the clan before your own happiness. You went above and beyond your calling." He grips my shoulders. "I'm proud of you, little brother." He pulls me into a hug.

My eyes burn. There is a ball of emotion stuck in my throat, where it has no business being. My chest hurts, and my limbs feel like they belong to someone else. I allow Michael to pat me on the back before he steps back.

"What are you waiting for?" he asks.

"Huh?" I shake my head. "What do you mean?"

"You need to go after her and woo her back," Michael says with a smile on his face.

"She's pissed at me." I rub the back of my neck.

"To be fair, the stunt you pulled was deplorable," Christian murmurs.

I shoot him a glance. "I had no choice."

The door to the back of the church opens and the women stream in. Karma breaks into a run, only for Michael to meet her half way. "I've told you not to exert yourself physically, haven't I?" he scolds her as he pulls her into his side.

Aurora walks over to Christian, and Elsa to Seb, while Axel crosses over to Theresa and kisses her.

I watch as the couples hug each other and speak in low tones, as if they've been separate for days instead of less than an hour.

"As you suggested, I told Penny everything and sent her after Jeanne to make sure she's okay," Karma calls out.

"Thanks." I jerk my chin. At least she won't be alone. That's something.

"What now?" Adrian, the only other single person in the group, turns to me. "You going after her, or what?"

"I don't know." I scuff the toe of my boot against the stone floor. "In case you didn't notice, she wasn't very happy with me. In fact, I distinctly remember her saying she hates me. And she'll never forgive me."

"Didn't take you for a coward." His lips kick up.

I scowl back. "I'm not a coward. I am just saying maybe, uh… I need to give her time to cool off."

"And allow her to stew over how you betrayed her trust?" Karma's voice rings out. "It was thoughtful of you to make sure Penny's with her, but it's not enough. You're aware of that, I assume?"

I wince, then turn to my sister-in-law. Over the past few months, I've seen her work her magic on Michael and come to grips with her role as the senior most female figure within the clan, after Nonna's passing. If there's one woman who knows what she's doing when it comes to affairs of the heart, it's her.

"What are you suggesting?"

"That you get over being a pussy and go after her and find a way to wriggle back into her good graces." Karma sniffs.

"And how do I do that?"

"Grovel." Michael chuckles. "You need to grovel."

"A lot," Christian adds.

"A whole bloody lot." Axel nods sagely.

Seb wraps his arm around Elsa and pulls her into his chest. "And some more." He rests his chin on top of her head. "And when you think it's enough, grovel some more."

61

Jeanne

I pace the floor of the rehearsal room at the theater. I hadn't wanted to go back to Luca's. Doubtless, that's where he'll go, and I have no intention of seeing that man ever again. I returned to my apartment and Penny arrived shortly after. She was worried about me. She made sure I changed out of my dress and into a pair of yoga pants and sleeveless T-shirt. Then she made me a cup of tea and put me to bed. I was too numb to protest and even managed to doze off. When I awoke, she was still there. I told her I was okay and asked her to go home and get some rest. She resisted but I insisted I'd be fine. She wasn't happy about it but I stood firm and she finally relented.

After she left, I wasn't able to go back to sleep, so I returned to the one place where I feel more comfortable than anywhere else. A place I've spent so much of my adult life. The place I was going to have to return to in a few hours anyway. The rehearsal room.

Now, I turn to survey my reflection in the mirror that covers an entire wall. My cheeks are flushed, and the makeup I wore earlier in the day has rubbed off, leaving my lips bare. My eyes are wide and feverish with... Anger? Hate? Lust? All of the above?

I should be so much angrier about what he did. I should be livid with rage at his having taken me for granted, enough that he actually pulled a fast one on me. He pretended to die in my arms. He allowed me to mourn him, to cry for him. To turn up at his funeral looking every inch the grief-stricken widow. I couldn't have played it better if I'd been acting. And maybe that's what bothers me the most. It's like he didn't believe my acting skills were good enough to let me in on his plan. Instead, he pulled my strings, arranging the set-up, so whoever was watching would buy the story... Enough to reveal himself. And Luca shot him.

I can go on stage again, and not worry for my life. Not that it had particularly concerned me the last few times. I'd been too focused on simply trying to make it through the performance each day. Maybe, subconsciously, I'd wondered if the person who shot at me would try again, but I couldn't bring myself to care.

This time, Luca wouldn't have been around to defend me... Except, he had been looking out for me all along.

He could have tried to stop me from going on stage, but he knew I wouldn't agree. In fact, he said he wouldn't dream of taking that opportunity away from me. Instead, he protected me with his body. Then, he used it to ensure we wouldn't always be looking over our shoulders.

He killed the man who was responsible for both attempts on my life. My shoulders slump. I had been so angry when I'd realized he was alive. So upset at what he'd done. Now? I don't know what to think. My head feels too heavy, my chest too painful. My shoulders are too tense and every part of me feels like it's been put through the wringer. I walk over to the system in the corner and choose a piece of music that has never failed to move me.

The strains of *Rehab* by Amy Winehouse fill the space. I swipe out my legs, then my arms, twirl, then dip, before I shimmy. People thought the lyrics were about Amy's fight with addictions, which it might well have been, but the tune and the arrangement of the music is far from depressing. Her defiant vocals turn it into something too irresistible. Too striking.

As far as personas go, she was the exact opposite of Elle Woods, but the two of them had something in common. They had a thirst for life. I often think Amy packed so much into that small frame of hers, singing her heart out when she was alive, burning brightly and too quickly, and then she was gone. It's as if she lived so in the moment, so hard, that she just combusted one day.

As for Elle... She was the light to Amy's darkness. The pink to Amy's purple. The silver lining to Amy's dark cloud. Maybe I have a bit of both of them in me, touched with that intensity that makes Plath's words irresistible. She was the ultimate feminist. And I am one, too... Except, when I'm in bed with him. Then, I want to be treated like a whore. I am a Jeanne, but I could well have been a Jade which is Amy Winehouse's middle name.

It doesn't escape me that two of my three idols committed suicide. And maybe that's why I'm so fond of Elle Woods. Her particular brand of sunshine balances out the darker thoughts that sometime cross my mind. Her... And the orgasms that Luca supplies in excess. Definitely, also the orgasms.

I perform a knee bend, then kick in the air, before bringing my legs together again on the ground, and again. I spin around the studio, move into a barrel turn, then kick my leg in a circular motion from in front of the other leg, up into the air at the full range of motion, over the head, and finally down in a resting position.

I strut forward, and again, cover the length of the floor, then leap forward arms up, knees bent, and land in front of the door, just as it's wrenched open.

I straighten, panting, and find myself face to face with him. I'm not surprised. I expected him. In fact, I planned it so we'd meet here in the studio, instead of in either of our homes. I'd have been too vulnerable there.

Also, I didn't want to make it too easy for him to find me. Which I knew he would. The music flows between us. Sweat slips down my temple.

I take a step forward until my breasts almost brush his chest. I tip up my chin, and draw in a deep breath, inhaling that dark chocolate and coffee scent of his. I raise my arms in tandem with the music, then shimmy down his body and up. I turn away, then lean back, and drape my outstretched arm over his shoulder. I slide down the length of his body, making sure my hips brush the thickness at his groin. I take a step back, then kick my leg up and hook my ankle around his neck.

He stares into my eyes. Those intense blue eyes of his blaze with regret, with heat, with lust, and with a plea deep in their depths that I resist.

I raise my arm, and slide my hand down his neck and his chest.

Without breaking my gaze, he bends, twists his arm under my hips, then straightens. He carries me across the floor to the center of the room, right in front of the mirror, where he lowers me to the floor. When he's certain I have my balance, he moves back one step, then another. He circles his fingers around my ankle.

A spark flares to life in my core.

He glances up at me, then brushes his lips across the inside of my knee.

That spark in my core bursts into flames. I'm soaked and I know he knows it. I expect him to smirk.

Instead, he weaves his fingers through mine, assuring I have my balance. I pull my leg back. He takes a step forward, closing the distance between us until we are standing chest to chest. The music fades away, leaving only the sound of breathing in the room. His and mine.

My breasts swell. My nipples poke through the sports bra and the sleeveless T-shirt. The flesh between my legs throbs.

The air between us thickens with unsaid words, with the emotions that seem to vibrate off of him. A bead of sweat trickles down my back. Still, he holds my gaze. The silence stretches. A beat. Another. Every time I draw in a breath it seems to fan the fire that's creeping through my veins.

Amy's gone. She'll never know what it is to grow old. Never get to experience life and love, in all its glory. Amy's gone, but he's here. He's not dead. *He's not dead.* He's alive and vital. The blood pumping through his veins. Oxygen circulating through his lungs. His big body, warm and hard and so completely real. He's here, with me. Everything he did was to protect me. Me. In the only way he knew.

"Jeanne," his voice comes out low, harsh. His throat moves as he swallows. "Jeanne." A pulse throbs at his temple. "I love you."

My palm connects with his cheek, and his head snaps back. His eyes flash, first with anger, which gives way to a searing need. His features grow fierce and then we both move.

Our mouths meet with such force, our teeth crash together. He thrusts his tongue inside my mouth and devours me. I wind my arms around his broad shoulders, pressing my breasts into his solid chest as I strain to get closer to him. He plants his big hands on my butt cheeks, taking big handfuls of my flesh. A moan spills from my lips and he swallows it. He lifts me up and I wind my legs around his waist. He turns, takes a few steps, and presses me into the mirror as he continues to kiss me. He grips the waistband of my yoga pants and shoves it down my legs, moving back enough to work it over my hips until it's caught around my thighs. Then he undoes his belt, lowers his zipper, and thrusts into me. He fills me so suddenly, so completely, that my vision blurs.

Sparks flare up my spine and behind my eyes. He pushes into me so his cock slides even deeper inside, then pinches my clit so what little rational thought is left in my head fades. My brain cells seem to combust, and my thighs burn as I cling to him. I lock my ankles around him as he lunges into me over and over again. He rubs on my clit, and the orgasm dazzles out from the point where he's connected to me. The ball of sensations at the base of my spine tightens, then folds in on itself. He pins me to the mirror with his cock, then winds his fingers around my throat. He presses down enough for my breath to catch. All the time, he's watching me with those sky-blue eyes of his. He pulls out just enough that his dick rims my opening. Just enough for my belly to flip, and my pussy to clench down on the nothingness. For my thighs to spasm as I dig my heels into his waist and try to draw him closer.

He chuckles then, the awful, awful man. Black spots at the edges of my vision flicker. He still holds back. His pressure around my throat increases. The last dregs of air filtering through to my lungs disappear. The darkness bleeds across my vision. My body twitches, my core weeps. It feels like I am having an out of body experience. A part of me seems to slip out of my skin to float up to the ceiling and look down on myself spread around his cock.

Then, he plunges into me. He impales me. Buries himself inside me with such force that his balls slap my flesh. He hits that place deep inside of me that only he can. My orgasm ignites out from that point of contact. It creeps up my spine. That's when he removes his fingers from around my throat. I gasp and my eyes widen. I try to draw in a breath as the climax booms through me, gathering speed and velocity and growing bigger, so much bigger. Until it consumes me. Spreads to every part of my body and crashes behind my eyes. He continues to fuck me through it. In-out-in, he rams his shaft into me. Each time he touches that point deep inside, my entire body jolts. My back bows off the mirror. He slides his palm behind my head, cushioning me. He feeds his cock to me one last time, then his muscles tense. I feel his body go solid, feel the planes of his chest contract. His dick pulses inside me, and with a hoarse cry, he pours himself inside me.

I assume I black out for a few seconds. I blink my eyes and find his hands are under my butt as he holds me close. His chest rises and falls. His jaw is hard, but his eyes are soft and worried.

"Are you okay?" he whispers.

"I hate you," I choke out, then I slap him again.

62

"No, you don't," I say with more confidence than I feel.

Of course, I deserve her slap. I deserve that, and a lot more, for everything I've put her through. But she's safe now. As safe as anyone can be in our line of work. For the time being, though, all known enemies have been squashed. For now, I can breathe easily. And once we legalize all of the of businesses of the *Cosa Nostra*, I hope the threats to her life will fade away completely. I still.

So, I'm going to do it then?

I'm going to walk away from the traditions of my ancestors. From the customs interwoven with that of this land in which I've grown up. The conventions that are in my blood, in my very cells, in every breath I take. I'm going to turn my back on all of it. For her. If I can keep her safe, if I can protect her and cherish her, it will be worth it. She is more important to me than my life, my past, the way of life that once meant everything to me. None of it matters if she isn't by my side. It's for her that I will shed the facade I once wore, the one that put me on a path endangering the lives of my near and dear. It's for her that I will become the kind of man she'd be proud of.

"You don't mean it." I hold her gaze. "You love me."

"I don't," she spits out. "You broke my heart."

"And I'll put it back together."

"It won't be the same," she snarls.

"It will be better."

"You don't know that."

"Don't I?" I squeeze her ass cheeks.

She draws in a breath. "Is that your answer to everything? Sex?"

"It's a start." I brush my lips over hers. "I love you. I can't live without you. I'm sorry for everything I put you through. But if I had to do it again, I wouldn't hesitate, because it was the only way to ensure that you would be safe."

Her forehead creases. "I know you meant well. I know you took a bullet for me. I know that, in your mind, it was the only way forward. But you can't deny that you used the situation to your advantage. You wanted to be the one to put Freddie out of commission."

"You mean, I wanted to be the one to kill him?"

This woman... She can't bring herself to talk about death, and I'm the man who deals with it day and night. *Not for much longer. Not if I go down the path of becoming the CEO of a company instead of a Capo.*

She tips up her chin. "Do you deny it? You wanted to take the credit for it. You wanted to show your brothers that you could do something that none of them have been able to do."

I peer into her features. So smart. This woman is so astute. So intelligent. "Fuck, when you get all incisive and perceptive, you turn me on even more, you know that?"

She scowls. "Answer the question."

I arch my eyebrows. "You don't get to order me around... but I'll allow it... This time."

"Well?" She huffs. "Am I right?"

"You are." I lift my shoulder. "I saw the opportunity and I took it. I knew there was a good chance Freddie would send someone after you. I also knew he was waiting to take us out. I figured I could not only protect you, but also use the chance to flush him out."

"By faking your death."

"But I didn't die," I point out.

"You allowed me to think you were gone."

"I'm still here." I blow out a breath. "What would you have me do instead?"

"You could have told me." She bursts out. "You could have shared your plan with me. Involved me. That's what husbands and wives do. That's what a marriage is about. You share your secrets with me, you allow me to weigh in with your opinion. Plus, I'm an actress, or did you forget that?"

"And would you have let me go through with this?"

She blinks, then glances away.

"That's what I thought." I pinch her chin so she has no choice but to look at me. "You're right, though. I should have been more transparent with you. I should have involved you from the beginning. I should have, at least, hinted at what was going to happen, given you something more to hold onto, given you a role. I'm sorry for the pain I caused you. What can I do to make it up to you?"

She tilts her head.

"You want to make it up to me?"

I nod. "I'll do anything you want."

"Anything?"

"Anything. So long as you forgive me."

"Hmm." She chews on her lower lip, and goddamn, I feel it all the way down to my cock. My dick lengthens inside her. I know by the widening of her eyes, she's noticed it. "Anything, eh?"

I have a feeling I'm going to regret this, but if it means I can earn her forgiveness, it will be worth it. "Anything."

"Can I tie you up?"

"Yes." I frown.

"And blindfold you?"

"As long as it means you fuck me at the end of it, yes."

"And you'll wear a wedding ring?"

I glower at her.

"Will you?"

I take in her flushed features, her parted lips, that thick, dark hair of hers that spirals about her shoulders. The creamy column of her neck, that delicate curve of her shoulders revealed by her tank top. If I died now, it would be with my dick inside of her, and that's all I could ask for.

"Fine." I nod.

"I didn't hear you?" She smirks. The little firecracker actually smirks. At *me*. Every part of me resists, but I push back that unwillingness inside of me. If I want to leave my mark on her, doesn't it make sense she'd want to mark me? She's my wife. If anyone can command me, it's her. She's the only one who can order me around, and I'll take it, willingly.

"I'll wear it," I growl.

"Oh, good." She bats her eyelids. "Will you let me down now?"

"Not until I've made you come again."

"First, I need to blindfold you."

"What if I close my eyes?"

"And tie you up."

"I need my arms to hold you up," I point out.

"Not if you're lying on the floor."

My gaze wars with hers, then I nod. I move away from the mirror to the center of the floor, then lower myself to the ground. All the while, I make sure I'm still inside of her.

She brings her knees up and straddles me. The action makes her sink deeper onto my already-engorged dick. I groan; so does she. Then, she pulls off her T-shirt, leans forward and places it over my eyes. "Raise your head," she murmurs.

I comply and she ties it around my eyes. It's effective enough that it cuts out the sight of her. My other senses come into focus at once. The way her thighs grip me, the feel of her cunt wrapped around my cock, her movements as she wriggles her ass across my thighs. I hear the slide of fabric against skin. Is she taking off her bra? My dick thickens further inside her. Then she leans forward, grips my wrist and forces one arm up, then the other.

She winds what feels like elastic around my wrists. I was right; she did take off her bra. Right now, her breasts must be free as she bends over me. Her flesh must jiggle as she unbuttons my shirt and pulls the lapels apart. She runs her palms down my pecs, and goosebumps scatter over my skin. She drags her fingers down to my stomach, to where we're connected. She wraps her fingers around where my cock is embedded inside hear and circles it. Every part of my body goes on alert. All of my attention is focused on where she drags her fingernails across the root of my shaft. Sweat pops on my forehead and I grit my teeth.

"*Cazzo!* What are you doing?"

"Getting to know my husband's body, of course." She slides down my thighs so I slip out of her, then pulls my pants down. I raise my hips, allowing her to shove them down to my knees. Then I sense her rise to her feet, the rustle of clothes over skin, the slight disturbance in the breeze, followed by the sound of clothes hitting the floor. She took off her clothes? She must be completely naked. My balls tighten. The blood rushes to my groin. My speculation is confirmed when she straddles my thighs again. Her bare skin brushes against the outside of my legs. Then, she leans forward and wraps her lips around my erect shaft.

63

Jeanne

His body bucks. A growl rumbles up his chest, and his dick throbs inside my mouth. He's so big that my fingers don't meet around his girth. His thickness stretches my lips. I slide my mouth down to take more of him inside.

"Fuck!" He bangs his head against the floor. "Fuck, fuck, fuck."

A hot sensation fills my chest. A thrum of power licks my blood. So, this is how it feels to be in control. No wonder he's addicted to it. No wonder I'm addicted to the taste of him, the scent of him, the feel of his velvet skin wrapped around the steel of his cock. I curl my tongue around his length, and he growls. I squeeze the root then swipe my fingers up and his thighs harden. I've never gone down willingly on a man before, but with Luca, the fact that I can reduce him to this needy, wanting mass of muscles is a high like I've never known. I lower my chin and take him all the way down my throat.

"So warm, so tight. *Cazzo*. You're killing me, Angel."

I glance up to find the veins on his throat stand out. His jaw is so hard, I know he's grinding his molars together. The planes of his chest stand out in relief, the valley between his pecs even more pronounced. His shoulders heave. Heat rolls off of him, and the tension is so thick in the air that it weighs me down, pushing down on my shoulders. Without taking my gaze off of him, I bring my other hand up to squeeze his balls.

"Fucking, fuck." He rams his joined hands down into the floor. The vibrations shudder across the surface, up my legs. My pussy spasms. Moisture bathes my insides. I begin to suck him off in earnest. I pull back until the crown of his cock is poised between my lips, then take him down my throat again. And again. The third time, I drag my teeth delicately across the sensitive slit at the top.

His back shoots off the ground.

"*Maledizione,*" he growls.

My mouth hurts from how long it's been stretched around his thickness, but I don't give up. I redouble my efforts as I slurp on him, bob my head, and hum around his length. Again and again and again.

"You take my cock so greedily, my Angel. You're gorgeous. Such a beautiful slut. Such a hungry whore you are, my wife."

Jesus, Mary and Joseph. That's filthy and dirty and so wrong. And every part of me responds to his sordid words. My breasts ache. My stomach bottoms out. My pussy hurts so fiercely, I almost give in to the need to sink down onto his thick length. Not yet. I need to make him come. Need him to give himself up to me the way he's made me surrender to him so many times now.

I slick up my finger with saliva, then slide it inside his forbidden hole and brush his prostrate.

His hips freeze, and the muscles under his skin coil so hard, I wonder if they're going to snap. His shaft grows impossibly big in my mouth, then with a roar, he pumps his pelvis up, and empties his load down my throat.

He keeps coming for so long, his cum fills my mouth, overflows my lips, and drips down my chin to plop onto his thighs. And still, he keeps coming. I swallow down the evidence of his arousal and continue to lick him off. When he finally collapses, his body is covered in sweat. The flesh between my legs is so sensitive now, I'd need only a touch to come, myself. I lick the cum from his dick, then crawl up his body and fit my mouth to his. Instantly, he closes his lips around mine and sucks on my tongue, and the taste of him, combined with the remnants of his cum, is so heady, so potent, that my head spins.

He tears his mouth from mine, and brings his still-bound arms down so he's imprisoned me inside of them. He holds me so close that my breasts are crushed into his chest, and he takes control of the kiss. He kisses me so deeply that all the breath seems to be sucked out of me. He kisses me with so much feeling that my heart feels like it's going to burst.

He kisses me with so much emotion that every cell in my body seems to fill up with what he's conveying to me. That he wants me, needs me, loves me, will never allow anything to happen to me again. That he's sorry for what he did, that he'll never let me go again. When we finally break apart, I'm panting. Unable to hold my head upright anymore. As if he senses it, he flips us over so he's poised over me.

"I guess blindfolding and tying you up isn't enough to stop you from taking control."

"I don't need to see you. I know my way around your body, Angel." He slides down between my legs until his mouth is poised over my pussy. He brings both of his big palms around my breasts and squeezes. Ripples of pleasure tear through me. My nerve endings spark. Then he buries his face between my legs and suckles on my clit.

The vibrations shriek up my spine. I bury my fingers in his thick hair and tug, and lock my thighs about his neck as he eats me out. I'm so turned on that, within seconds, my orgasm crashes over me. He licks up my cum, washes my slit with his tongue, before he pushes up to loom over me.

"I need to be inside you. I want to come in your pussy. Want to feel you flutter around my cock as you milk me," he growls against my mouth.

"Do it." I reach up to untie his restraint. He shrugs it off, and tears my T-shirt from around his eyes. That blue gaze of his snaps on me and I'm caught. He reaches between us, and positions his cock at my slit.

"I love you. I will love you until the day I die. I will never let anything happen to you, Angel. And I promise I'll never hurt you or cause you pain ever again. You are my life, my heart, my breath, my home. Without you, I am nothing. You are the only thing that makes my life worth living. I'll set the whole world on fire to protect you."

Oh, my god. I think I'm going to cry. I swallow back the tears that crowd behind my eyes.

"And you are hotter than Emmett Richmond. Not as hot as Bruiser Woods, but definitely hotter than Emmett." I clear my throat.

"Eh?" He blinks. "Who's that?"

"Emmet Richmond is Elle Woods' boyfriend who she ends up marrying in Legally Blonde 2, and Bruiser is Elle Woods' Chihuahua."

"You're comparing me to a Chihuahua?" His lips twitch.

"It's a compliment," I murmur.

"Hmm." His searches my features. "If you say so."

"I do. Also, thought you wanted to be inside me?"

He pushes the crown of his cock inside my pussy, and a groan spills from my lips.

"You were saying?" Inch-by-inch, he sinks inside me. I can feel every ridge of his shaft, every thick millimeter of his column, until he's finally embedded in me.

A breath whooshes out of him. He pushes his forehead into mine, gazes into my eyes, and whispers, "I'm home."

64

Jeanne

I bow deeply from the waist as the applause washes over me.

"Brava!"

"Bravisimma!"

"Well done!"

"Amazing"

The audience is on their feet, and their clapping doesn't show signs of stopping. I don't think I've ever been this amazed, this overwhelmed... Not counting the incredible orgasm Luca gave me last night, that is. More than one orgasm, actually, and every night since he fucked me in the rehearsal room two weeks ago. I'd managed to go on stage shortly after, and the endorphins floating in my system had gotten me through the rest of the performance. That and every performance since, to be honest. I don't think I've ever been this happy, this at peace.

I called up my mother back in LA and given her the news of my wedding. She was angry I hadn't given her enough time to make it down for the ceremony, but she was also relieved I'm settling down. She claimed she could sense the happiness in my voice, and that made her very happy. She plans to come down to visit the first chance she gets.

My fellow cast members join me, and holding hands, we take another bow. And another. The curtains finally come down and I throw my arms around my co-star.

"You were great!" he enthuses. "Every inch the Belle of the ball."

"And you were incredible, too." I hug him again, when a shiver runs up my spine. I break away, and even before I turn, I know he's there in the wings waiting for me.

I pivot, walk toward him, then leap over the last few feet and into his arms. Luca scoops me up like I weigh nothing and I lock my ankles around him.

He glances past me to level a glare at my co-star.

"You know it doesn't mean anything when I hug him, right?"

"I know, because you're mine. Only mine." He turns his devil blue eyes on me. "Doesn't mean I can't warn him to stay away from my girl."

I laugh. "You can take the mobster away from the mob, but can't stop him from acting like one, huh?"

"Isn't it enough that I'm wearing a suit and going into work at nine a.m., like an ass?"

"And you have a fine ass, Mr. Gangster, Sir." I dig my heels into those buns of steel that are his tush and his lips curl.

"I'm beginning to think you love being punished for your impudence, Angel."

"Promises, promises." I lean up and kiss his firm lips, which soften instantly. That's Luca. All prickly and growly and mean on the outside. You get past that rock-hard layer, and he's as soft as melted candy. And as gooey.

The cast comes off stage.

"Bye, Jeanne," my co-star calls out, avoiding Luca.

"Bye, Luca," one of the women calls out as they pass by us.

Yep, they're used to seeing Luca waiting for me in the wings each night when we finish. He's a Sovrano, so no one stops him from lurking in the wings where he watches my performance each night. The danger of Freddie being after the Sovranos may have passed, but Luca insists, he's more reassured if he continues to watch over me. He also still has bodyguards in place to accompany me when he's not around. I can't complain, though. It's not only the orgasms he keeps me replete with. He's tender, affectionate, attentive, everything I'd hoped to find in my soul mate. He carries me off stage and into my dressing room.

Normally, I'd share one with the other actresses, but Luca secured one for me and insisted I use it. Initially, I didn't want to, but he said it would be the best way to protect me against any future threats and I hadn't protested. I didn't like that he used his influence to provide me with amenities, but given the choice between that and putting his life at risk again? Yeah, I took the dressing room.

Once inside, he lowers me to my feet, then spins me around and presses me against the door. He runs his nose up the side of my face. "Mmm. I missed you," he says huskily.

"I was only gone for three hours." I laugh.

"Three hours too long." He brushes his lips over mine. "You taste so fucking sweet, Mrs. Sovrano."

I don't think I'll ever get used to being called that, either.

He brushes his knuckle across my cheek. "You're glowing."

"And you're… smiling." I trace the curve of his lips. "It's a good look on you."

He chuckles. "Turns out, being married to the right woman is good for me, too."

"Careful, Mr. Grumpy Pants, if you smile too much, you're in danger of losing that title to Massimo." I link my fingers with his. "Speaking of, is he actually going to go through with the engagement to that *Camorra* princess?"

"Seems that way." He brings my fingers to his lips and kisses them.

"We need to head to their engagement party."

He groans. "Do we?"

"Yes, we do." I rub my fingers over the dark, granite band he wears around the ring finger of his left hand—one I picked out for him, which has the words "Property of Jeanne" scrawled on it.

He hadn't refused. Turns out, my man is more than happy with my declaration of ownership. He's far more romantic than he gave himself credit for.

"Maybe we can skip it and no one will miss us?"

"Fat chance." I scoff. "Karma specifically told me to come by. Given you are the last Sovrano brother to get married, and their *Capo*, you need to be there."

"Given I am not going to be the *Capo* for much longer, and that the *Cosa Nostra* is well on its way to legalizing its last business, maybe we can cry off. Besides, Massimo is the main person. As long as he turns up, and Michael's there to solemnize things on behalf of the *Cosa Nostra,* everything should be fine."

"Do you mind the fact that it's Michael and not you who gets to formalize this arrangement?" I ask.

Luca curls a strand of my hair around his fingers as he thinks. "No," he finally says, sounding surprised. "No, I don't. For a long time, I wanted to be Don, then I met you and realized I had my priorities all wrong. I latched onto the notion of being Don because I thought it'd make me happy. I didn't realize having a title was empty unless I had the right woman beside me. And then, when I had the right woman with me, I realized everything else is secondary."

He cups my cheek.

"Are you sad about things changing within the *Cosa Nostra*?"

"No," he replies without hesitation. "Nothing can stay the same. And if one doesn't change, one dies. Besides, your safety is my priority. And this way, the risks to your life is greatly reduced. That's more important to me."

"So, you won't miss it then?"

He tilts his head. "I won't miss it because I carry the concept of what the *Cosa Nostra* is about inside of me." He brings our joined fingers to his heart. "Unity, family, loyalty to my brothers. Giving my life up for what I believe in, which is you. You are my belief, my religion, my faith, my hope, my future. All of my dreams rest in you."

Tears prick the backs of my eyes. "You're going to make me cry."

He bends his knees and presses his mouth to mine. He deepens the kiss until I'm panting for my breath, until my head is swimming, until all thoughts drain from my mind. "Better?" he whispers against my lips.

I nod, chest heaving.

"Good, then let's find my brothers."

An hour later, we walk into the living room of Karma and Michael's home. The door is opened by a grouchy older man who looks me up and down. Then, he turns to Luca and sniffs. "Took your time getting here. Everyone is expecting you." His scowl seems to deepen before he turns and leaves.

"Who's that?" I whisper.

"Gino. He was Nonna's companion-slash-chef-slash-housekeeper, combined. After she passed away, he decided to come work for Michael."

"You mean, Michael asked him to come work for them?"

Luca gives me a funny look. "Gino's an institution. He came with Nonna as part of her dowry. He accompanied her when the lot of us went to study in LA. He was her constant companion, and has a hand in bringing all of us up. With our parents and Nonna gone, he's the only link to that generation. So now, Gino is one person we don't tell what to do. He decided to come work for Michael and Karma, instead of retiring or staying on in Nonna's place, which she left to him in her will, by the way."

"Huh?" I scowl. "Why would he do that?"

"Probably because he wants to make all of our lives miserable." Luca shakes his head. "Come on, let's get this over with."

I move forward, when a ball of fur comes barreling down the hallway. It careens to a stop in front of me, and stares up at me with huge, limpid eyes.

"Aww, soo cute." I sink down to my knees and rub the kitty's stomach.

"Andy, where are you, boy?" Karma races down the corridor, only to come to a stop when she sees me. "Ah, I see you found Andy."

"More like he found me. I didn't know you had a cat."

"Michael gave him to me." Karma beams.

I scratch the cat behind his ears and he purrs loudly.

"Except for the fact that he thinks he's a dog, he's perfect. He keeps me company when I design in my atelier, loves to roll around my fabrics. He totally channels the creative spirit he's named after."

"Is that right?" I glance up at her.

"Andy Warhol," she explains.

"Right." The cat rolls back on his feet, then licks my fingers, before taking off in the opposite direction. Karma takes a step forward, then presses a hand to her back.

"Are you okay?" I close the distance to her.

Behind me, Luca stiffens. The tension rolls off of him.

"Karma?" I grip her shoulder. "Are you okay?"

"I'm fine." Her lips curve. "It's just that my back is taking the brunt of this pregnancy."

"Why don't you sit down?"

"Good idea. Let's go in and find our seats. Everyone is here already."

Luca walks over and kisses my forehead. "I'll head inside and find Michael." He moves past us and we follow at a more leisurely pace.

"Being married suits you." Karma smiles.

"Being pregnant suits you," I retort.

"Liar," she laughs. "I know I look exhausted. Not even the makeup I'm wearing can cover these black circles." She waves her fingers in the direction of her eyes.

"You look gorgeous," I reply sincerely.

She laughs and hooks her arm though mine. "I'm so glad you're part of the family. We need all the strong women we can get. Women who can hold their own against these alpha males and bring them down a notch."

"Don't know if I fit that bill, but yeah, I'm having to learn everyday how to push back so he never takes me for granted. Not that Luca would, to be honest. He's just so mushy inside. But it doesn't hurt to keep a few surprises in store that I can use to keep him on his toes, know what I mean?"

"You need to be open and share your secrets with your partner. But it also helps to keep something back, or else there's no mystery," she murmurs.

Something in her tone makes me glance in her direction. "What's your secret?"

She looks stricken for a second, then chuckles. "Guess it's been weighing on my mind, because I hadn't meant to be that transparent."

"So, you do have a secret?"

Her steps falter and she turns to me. "Elsa knows about it, and now, I guess you will, too."

"What is it?"

"I have a heart condition."

"A heart condition?"

"It's not something that would hurt me in day-to-day life. Not normally that is, except—"

"You're pregnant..." I hazard a guess.

She nods. "It could be life-threatening or not. The act of giving birth might trigger it... or not. It's all speculation. Nothing happens unless it really happens, you know what I mean? I can't spend my life being scared of my condition. And I really want this child. I want Michael to have an heir."

I open my mouth to speak, and she holds up her hand. "I know, how awfully parochial of me. Me, a woman who always speaks her mind, and then when it comes to something this personal, it seems I'm stupidly traditional. Who knew?"

"Your body is your business." I clap her hands between mine. "And it's natural for you to want a child. But I think you need to tell Michael about the risks involved. If he finds out later, or if something were to happen to you, imagine how distressed he would be?"

Her forehead furrows. "I know he's going to pissed off at me if I tell him. He'll prioritize me before the child. He'll want me to be safe, and probably tell me I'm enough for him and he'd rather do without kids. I don't want him to make that sacrifice. I want him to have kids. He deserves it."

"And he also deserves to know about your condition." I peer into her eyes. "Look, I'm not saying I know all of the intricacies of the situation you're in; only you know that. All I know is how I felt when Luca didn't share with me the risk he was taking. The one thing I do know is that this is something you don't want to keep from Michael. If he did the same to you, wouldn't you be upset?"

The color fades from her cheeks. She looks away. "You're right." Her chin quivers. "I've been so stupid. I should have shared this with him. I've wanted to tell him so many times, but I always stop myself. It never seems like the right time, you know?" She turns to me. "Thanks, Jeanne." She leans forward and kisses my cheek. "I owe you."

"Karma?" Michael calls out from the door to the conservatory. "I was looking all over for you."

"And here I am." She squeezes my hands. "Thanks again." She turns and walks over to Michael.

I follow them inside and gasp. The entire space is filled with flowers, shrubs, even a tree that grows from the ground on one side. The conservatory has been built around its girth to accommodate it. On either side of it are rows of flowering creepers and bushes. I draw in a breath, and the scent of roses, lilies, and jasmine surrounds me. Fairy lights have been strung up in various corners. The entire effect is like being in an enchanted space.

"So beautiful," I whisper.

"Not as beautiful as my wife." Luca wraps his arm around me and pulls me into his side.

"You sweet talker, you."

"No, sweetheart, just saying it like it is." He kisses the top of my forehead his touch so tender, so gentle, my heart skips a beat.

Ahead, I spot Seb and Elsa to one side, arms around each other. Next to them, Axel and Theresa hold hands. Ahead of them, Christian leans against a settee, his arm around Aurora's waist. Adrian stands in one corner with Massimo next to him. On the other side of the space, a group of people I don't recognize mill around. The men are dressed in black suits and ties. The women are overdressed in comparison to the Sovranos. Most of them wear formal dresses, with veiled hats, and high-heeled shoes. All of it, designer brands. Each of them is bedecked in jewelry. Pearls around their necks, diamond earrings, gold bracelets. At the front is a young girl. She has a slender frame and blonde hair that flows down her back. She's wearing a white gown that clings to her gentle curves. She stands with her head bent, every inch a shy bride-to-be.

"That's her?" I whisper to Luca. "She's the *Camorra* princess Massimo is going to marry?"

He nods.

"Does Massimo know what he's getting into?"

He winces. "Probably not, but from what he told me, he doesn't care. He wants to move on with his life."

I frown. "What does that mean?"

"He, apparently, proposed to your friend Olivia, but she turned him down."

"She did? I mean, he did? I mean—" I shake my head. "When did all of this happen?"

"During the last few weeks, when she was in the hospital. Somehow, I get the impression they knew each other from before."

"I knew it!" I bite the inside of my cheek. "I thought there was something between them, but I couldn't be sure."

"Anyway, that's in the past. This is Massimo's bid to move forward. With this arranged marriage, he also ensures peace between the two clans."

"Hmm..." I glance toward him, then back at the girl. "Why do I get the feeling this union is going to be anything but simple?"

Footsteps sound behind us.

Then a familiar voice sings out. "Hellooo, I'm not late for the engagement, I hope?"

I turn to find Olivia standing at the entrance to the conservatory. She's wearing a scarlet red dress that's cut low enough to reveal the tops of her breasts. The skirt has a slit up one side, all the way to the top of her thigh. She has one stocking clad leg thrust out through the gap. Her hair is dyed in streaks of purple, and flows around her shoulders. And on her face, she sports a scar that runs from the middle of her cheek to her temple. The scar doesn't deter from her beauty. If anything, it enhances it by lending her a mysterious, yet tragic look. It adds to her overall allure, bringing a mystique to her persona that hadn't been there before.

A murmur runs through the *Camorra* part of the gathering.

She smirks at them. "Not happy to see me, *famiglia*?" She pushes away from the door, takes a step forward, then promptly stumbles.

To FIND OUT WHAT HAPPENS NEXT READ OLIVIA AND MASSIMO'S STORY **HERE**

Read an excerpt

Olivia

Fuck them. Fuck all of them. Bet they're surprised that I crashed the gathering. And honestly, I wouldn't give a damn about being here or about any of them. Except it's Solene's engagement day, and my little sister means everything to me. She's the only part of my family I've kept in touch with.

Since the day she was born, Solene has had my heart. I remember when Ma placed her in my arms. A little bundle, wrapped up in baby clothes, with a shock of dark hair peeking over the top. She'd opened her blue eyes and looked at me, and my heart had stuttered. Something like love and a fierce need to protect had wound its way around my heart. I had rocked her to sleep that day, and sworn I'd never let anyone or anything harm her. And she's getting engaged today. She texted me the address and begged me to come. She'd told me she'd never met the man she was going to marry and she didn't really want to do this. She needed my support and no way was I going to let her down. I'd even face the ire of the rest of my family for her.

The scent of jasmine and roses surrounds me. I draw it into my lungs. Why is my heart beating so fast? They're only my family. So what if they hate me? I'm used to it by now, right? I take in the crowd in front of me. My brother and cousins are dressed in black suits and ties. So, what's new? At least none of them are wearing their sunglasses indoors which, I kid you not, they have been known to do. The women are turned out in designer dresses, shoes, and bags. All bearing the labels of the most expensive couture, no doubt. That's one thing we in the *Camorra* do well. Act as if every scene in our life is lifted from a Hollywood movie.

I plant my hand on my thrust out hip and strike a pose at the entrance. Sooner or later, someone is going to notice me, and I can't wait to see the looks on their faces.

One of my aunts turns in my direction. Her gaze passes over me, then swings back to rest on my face. Her features twist into an expression of dismay. It's comical, really. She nudges the woman next to her, my mother, who turns her head. When she sees me, her mouth opens and shuts before she firms her lips. She takes a step in my direction.

Shit, best to make my presence known before she marches over and tells me to leave. Not that I'm going to obey her. It's just, I prefer to be the one taking the lead. Nothing like going on the offensive where my family is concerned. I toss my hair back, shove my leg clad in sheer tights, with the nine-inch Louboutins on my feet, through the slit in my dress, then paste a big ass smile on my face. "Not happy to see me, *famiglia*?"

My mother takes another step in my direction. I step toward her. And promptly stumble. *Fuck, fuck, fuck.* It has to be the heels. It has nothing to do with the shot of tequila, okay, two... nay, three shots, I threw back to shore up my courage before I got here. I squeeze my eyes shut, shoot my hands out, and brace myself to hit the floor when my shoulders are gripped. I hit something hard—not the floor—something wide and tall, clothed in a soft cashmere jacket. I know it's cashmere because I dig my fingers into the lapels and hold on. Eyes still shut. My heart ricochets in my rib cage, and my pulse shoots through the roof. A trembling grips me, and my knees threaten to give out from under me again. I bury my nose in the wall... Not a wall. Something steely, ripped, and warm. So warm. Heat pours over me. Static electricity whips through my veins. The hair on my forearms stands on end. I drag in a deep breath, this one laced with darkness, dusk and testosterone. An unmistakably male scent. One that I know.

Hot breath, hard fingers that had gripped my hips, the friction of his beard as he'd dragged it across my core. Goosebumps sprinkle across my skin. My thighs clench. *No, no, no. It can't be. Not him. Please not him. Not here. Not now.*

"Open your eyes." His voice rumbles up his chest, sinks into my skin, and warms my blood. My nipples pebble. My scalp tingles and I shake my head.

"Open. Your. Eyes." He lowers his tone to a hush, and my nerve endings spark.

Only when his dark black eyes hold mine, do I realize I've raised my eyelids. I take in those elevated cheekbones, so sharp they could surely cut my skin, those hollows under them more pronounced than I've ever seen them before, the thin mean upper lip that hints at his sadistic streak, the one that had spoken to the darkness inside me. That pouty lower lip, which I had dug my teeth into and tasted blood. His jaw hardens. That square jaw, dusted with a five o'clock shadow that I'd teased him about, and which he'd confessed he made no effort to cultivate. That gorgeous neck, which I 'd fallen in love with even before I'd seen his features. Broad shoulders, so wide they block out the rest of the room, and for the moment, I'm grateful for that. I need a second, a few seconds, to digest what's happening here. His grip on my shoulders tightens, and I feel his touch all the way to my toes. My entire body is one mass of wanting, my stomach in knots, my chest so tight, I can barely draw in a breath.

Massimo. Oh, Massimo.

"Via?" He frowns, calling me by the name that only he uses.

"My name's Olivia, and don't call me Liv, I hate that."

"How about Via? Or I could call you O, for the orgasms I am going to bestow on you, one for every hour we spend together."

My heart aches for what he was to me. For what we once had. My guts twist, and my stomach churns. Darkness flickers around the corners of my vision and I taste bile on my tongue.

"Via?" He drags his fingers down my biceps to hold me above my elbows. His fingertips dig into my skin. Pain shivers up my nerve endings, cutting through the noise in my head.

"What are you doing here?" His scowl deepens.

"What am I doing here?" Anger flushes my veins. "What are *you* doing here?"

He tilts his head, and the skin around his eyes tightens. "This is my engagement party."

The world tilts. "Your engagement party?" I glance past him, to where my sister stands at the head of the crowd. She's wearing a simple white dress, so virginal, so pure. So everything I am not. A smile curves her lips, despite her obvious apprehension, and she glances from me to her would-be fiancé. The man who is my ex-lover.

The one who asked me to marry him before I turned my back on him. The man who betrayed me and broke my heart. The man who is now going to marry my sister.

A sense of inevitability grips me. Of course it had to be this way. Of course, the one man I had fallen for and then grown to hate more than anyone else in the world is the one my sister is promised to. My stomach chooses that moment to bottom out. The sickness boils up my gullet and my guts contract. I throw up all over his tailor-made jacket.

To FIND OUT WHAT HAPPENS NEXT READ OLIVIA AND MASSIMO'S STORY HERE

Read an excerpt from Mafia King, Michael & Karma's story

Karma

"Morn came and went—and came, and brought no day..."

Tears prick the backs of my eyes. Goddamn Byron. His words creep up on me when I am at my weakest. Not that I am a poetry addict, by any measure, but words are my jam. The one consolation I have is that, when everything else in the world is wrong, I can turn to them, and they'll be there, friendly, steady, waiting with open arms.

And this particular poem had laced my blood, crawled into my gut when I'd first read it. Darkness had folded within me like an insidious snake, that raises its head when I least expect it. Like now, when I look out on the still sleeping city of London, from the grassy slope of Waterlow Park.

Somewhere out there, the Mafia is hunting me, apparently. It's why my sister Summer and her new husband Sinclair Sterling had insisted that I have my own security detail. I had agreed...only to appease them...then given my bodyguard the slip this morning. I had decided to come running here because it's not a place I'd normally go... Not so early in the morning, anyway. They won't think to look for me here. At least, not for a while longer.

I purse my lips, close my eyes. Silence. The rustle of the wind between the leaves. The faint tinkle of the water from the nearby spring.

I could be the last person on this planet, alone, unsung, bound for the grave.

Ugh! Stop. Right there. I drag the back of my hand across my nose. Try it again, focus, get the words out, one after the other, like the steps of my sorry life.

"Morn came and went—and came, and... and..." My voice breaks. "Bloody asinine hell." I dig my fingers into the grass and grab a handful and fling it out. Again. From the top.

"Morn came and went—and came, and—"

"...brought no day."

A gravelly voice completes my sentence.

I whip my head around. His silhouette fills my line of sight. He's sitting on the same knoll as me, yet I have to crane my neck back to see his profile. The sun is at his back, so I can't make out his features. Can't see his eyes... Can only take in his dark hair, combed back by a ruthless hand that brooked no measure.

My throat dries.

Thick dark hair, shot through with grey at the temples. He wears his age like a badge. I don't know why, but I know his years have not been easy. That he's seen more, indulged in more, reveled in the consequences of his actions, however extreme they might have been. He's not a normal, everyday person, this man. Not a nine-to-fiver, not someone who lives an average life. Definitely not a man who returns home to his wife and home at the end of the day. He is...different, unique, evil... Monstrous. Yes, he is a beast, one who sports the face of a man but who harbors the kind of darkness inside that speaks to me. I gulp.

His face boasts a hooked nose, a thin upper lip, a fleshy lower lip. One that hints at hidden desires, Heat. Lust. The sensuous scrape of that whiskered jaw over my innermost places. Across my inner thigh, reaching toward that core of me that throbs, clenches, melts to feel the stab of his tongue, the thrust of his hardness as he impales me, takes me, makes me his. Goosebumps pop on my skin.

I drag my gaze away from his mouth down to the scar that slashes across his throat. A cold sensation coils in my chest. What or who had hurt him in such a cruel fashion?

"Of this their desolation; and all hearts
Were chill'd into a selfish prayer for light..."

He continues in that rasping guttural tone. Is it the wound that caused that scar that makes his voice so...gravelly... So deep...so...so, hot?

Sweat beads my palms and the hairs on my nape rise. "Who are you?"

He stares ahead as his lips move,

"Forests were set on fire—but hour by hour
They fell and faded—and the crackling trunks
Extinguish'd with a crash—and all was black."

I swallow, moisture gathers in my core. How can I be wet by the mere cadence of this stranger's voice?

I spring up to my feet.

"Sit down," he commands.

His voice is unhurried, lazy even, his spine erect. The cut of his black jacket stretches across the width of his massive shoulders. His hair... I was mistaken—there are threads of dark gold woven between the darkness that pours down to brush the nape of his neck. A strand of hair falls over his brow. As I watch, he raises his hand and brushes it away. Somehow, the gesture lends an air of vulnerability to him. Something so at odds with the rest of his persona that, surely, I am mistaken?

My scalp itches. I take in a breath and my lungs burn. This man... He's sucked up all the oxygen in this open space as if he owns it, the master of all he surveys. The master of me. My death. My life. A shiver ladders along my spine. *Get away, get away now, while you still can.*

I angle my body, ready to spring away from him.

"I won't ask again."

Ask. Command. Force me to do as he wants. He'll have me on my back, bent over, on my side, on my knees, over him, under him. He'll surround me, overwhelm me, pin me down with the force of his personality. His charisma, his larger-than-life essence will crush everything else out of me and I... I'll love it.

"No."

"Yes."

A fact. A statement of intent, spoken aloud. So true. So real. Too real. Too much. Too fast. All of my nightmares...my dreams come to life. Everything I've wanted is here in front of me. I'll die a thousand deaths before he'll be done with me... And then? Will I be reborn? For him. For me. For myself.

I live, first and foremost, to be the woman I was...am meant to be.

"You want to run?"

No.

No.

I nod my head.

He turns his, and all the breath leaves my lungs. Blue eyes—cerulean, dark like the morning skies, deep like the nighttime...hidden corners, secrets that I don't dare uncover. He'll destroy me, have my heart, and break it so casually.

My throat burns and a boiling sensation squeezes my chest.

"Go then, my beauty, fly. You have until I count to five. If I catch you, you are mine."

"If you don't?"

"Then I'll come after you, stalk your every living moment, possess your nightmares, and steal you away in the dead of night, and then..."

I draw in a shuddering breath as liquid heat drips from between my legs. "Then?" I whisper.

"Then, I'll ensure you'll never belong to anyone else, you'll never see the light of day again, for your every breath, your every waking second, your thoughts, your actions...and all your words, every single last one, will belong to me." He peels back his lips, and his teeth glint in the first rays of the morning light. "Only me." He straightens to his feet and rises, and rises.

This man... He is massive. A monster who always gets his way. My guts churn. My toes curl. Something primeval inside of me insists I hold my own. I cannot give in to him. Cannot let him win whatever this is. I need to stake my ground, in some form. *Say something. Anything. Show him you're not afraid of this.*

"Why?" I tilt my head back, all the way back. "Why are you doing this?"

He tilts his head, his ears almost canine in the way they are silhouetted against his profile.

"Is it because you can? Is it a...a," I blink, "a debt of some kind?"

He stills.

"My father, this is about how he betrayed the Mafia, right? You're one of them?"

"Lucky guess." His lips twist, "It is about your father, and how he promised you to me. He reneged on his promise, and now, I am here to collect."

"No." I swallow... *No, no, no.*

"Yes." His jaw hardens.

All expression is wiped clean of his face, and I know then, that he speaks the truth. It's always about the past. My sorry shambles of a past... Why does it always catch up with me? *You can run, but you can never hide.*

"Tick-tock, Beauty." He angles his body and his shoulders shut out the sight of the sun, the dawn skies, the horizon, the city in the distance, the rustle of the grass, the trees, the rustle of the leaves. All of it fades and leaves just me and him. Us. *Run.*

"Five." He jerks his chin, straightens the cuffs of his sleeves.

My knees wobble.

"Four."

My pulse rate spikes. I should go. Leave. But my feet are planted in this earth. This piece of land where we first met. What am I, but a speck in the larger scheme of things? To be hurt. To be forgotten. To be taken without an ounce of retribution. To be punished...by him.

"Three." He thrusts out his chest, widens his stance, every muscle in his body relaxed. "Two."

I swallow. The pulse beats at my temples. My blood thrums.

"One."

Michael

"Go."

She pivots and races down the slope. Her dark hair streams behind her. Her scent, sexy femininity and silver moonflowers, clings to my nose, then recedes. It's so familiar, that scent.

I had smelled it before, had reveled in it. Had drawn in it into my lungs as she had peeked up at me from under her thick eyelashes. Her green gaze had fixed on mine, her lips parted as she welcomed my kiss. As she had wound her arms about my neck, pushed up those sweet breasts and flattened them against my chest. As she had parted her legs when I had planted my thigh between them. I had seen her before...in my dreams. I stiffen. She can't be the same girl though, can she?

I reach forward, thrust out my chin and sniff the air, but there's only the damp scent of dawn, mixed with the foul tang of exhaust fumes, as she races away from me.

She stumbles and I jump forward, pause when she straightens. Wait. Wait. Give her a lead. Let her think she has almost escaped, that she's gotten the better of me... As if.

I clench my fists at my sides, force myself to relax. Wait. Wait. She reaches the bottom of the incline, turns. I surge forward. One foot in front of the other. My heels dig into the grassy surface and mud flies up, clings to the hem of my £4000 Italian pants. Like I care? Plenty more where that came from. An entire walk-in closet, full of clothes made to measure, to suit every occasion, with every possible accessory needed by a man in my position to impress...

Everything... Except the one thing that I had coveted from the moment I had laid eyes on her. Sitting there on the grassy slope, unshed tears in her eyes, and reciting... Byron? For hell's sake. Of all the poets in the world, she had to choose the Lord of Darkness.

I huff. All a ploy. Clearly, she knew I was sitting next to her... No, not possible. I had walked toward her and she hadn't stirred. Hadn't been aware. Yeah, I am that good. I've been known to slit a man's throat from ear-to-ear while he was awake and in his full senses. Alive one second, dead the next. That's how it is in my world. You want it, you take it. And I... I want her.

I increase my pace, eat up the distance between myself and the girl... That's all she is. A slip of a thing, a slim blur of motion. Beauty in hiding. A diamond, waiting for me to get my hands on her, polish her, show her what it means to be...

Dead. She is dead. That's why I am here.

A flash of skin, a creamy length of thigh. My groin hardens and my legs wobble. I lurch over a bump in the ground. The hell? I right myself, leap forward, inching closer, closer. She reaches a curve in the path, disappears out of sight.

My heart hammers in my chest. I will not lose her, will not. *Here, Beauty, come to Daddy.* The wind whistles past my ears. I pump my legs, lengthen my strides, turn the corner. There's no one there. Huh?

My heart hammers and the blood pounds at my wrists, my temples; adrenaline thrums in my veins. I slow down, come to a stop. Scan the clearing.

The hairs on my forearms prickle. She's here. Not far, but where? Where is she? I prowl across to the edge of the clearing, under the tree with its spreading branches.

When I get my hands on you, Beauty, I'll spread your legs like the pages of a poem. Dip into your honeyed sweetness, like a quill pen in ink. Drag my aching shaft across that melting, weeping entrance. My balls throb. My groin tightens. The crack of a branch above shivers across my stretched nerve endings. I swoop forward, hold out my arms, and close my grasp around the trembling, squirming mass of precious humanity. I cradle her close to my chest, heart beating thud-thud-thud, overwhelming any other thought.

Mine. All mine. The hell is wrong with me? She wriggles her little body, and her curves slide across my forearms. My shoulders bunch and my fingers tingle. She kicks out with her legs and arches her back, thrusting her breasts up so her nipples are outlined against the fabric of her sports bra. She dared to come out dressed like that? In that scrap of fabric that barely covers her luscious flesh?

"Let me go." She whips her head toward me and her hair flows around her shoulders, across her face. She blows it out of the way. "You monster, get away from me."

Anger drums at the backs of my eyes and desire tugs at my groin. The scent of her is sheer torture, something I had dreamed of in the wee hours of twilight when dusk turned into night.

She's not real. She's not the woman I think she is. She is my downfall. My sweet poison. The bitter medicine I must partake of to cure the ills that plague my company,

"Fine." I lower my arms and she tumbles to the grass, hits the ground butt first.

"How dare you." She huffs out a breath, her hair messily arranged across her face.

I shove my hands into the pockets of my fitted pants, knees slightly bent, legs apart. Tip my chin down and watch her as she sprawls at my feet.

"You...dropped me?" She makes a sound deep in her throat.

So damn adorable.

"Your wish is my command." I quirk my lips.

"You don't mean it."

"You're right." I lean my weight forward on the balls of my feet and she flinches.

"What...what do you want?"

"You."

She pales. "You want to...to rob me? I have nothing of consequence,

"Oh, but you do, Beauty."

I lean in and every muscle in her body tenses. Good. She's wary. She should be. She should have been alert enough to have run as soon as she sensed my presence. But she hadn't.

I should spare her because she's the woman from my dreams...but I won't. She's a debt I intend to collect. She owes me, and I've delayed what was meant to happen long enough.

I pull the gun from my holster, point it at her.

Her gaze widens and her breath hitches. I expect her to plead with me for her life, but she doesn't. She stares back at me with her huge dilated pupils. She licks her lips and the blood drains to my groin. *Che cazzo!* Why does her lack of fear turn me on so?

"Your phone," I murmur, "take out your phone."

She draws in a breath, then reaches into her pocket and pulls out her phone.

"Call your sister."

"What?"

"Dial your sister, Beauty. Tell her you are going away on a long trip to Sicily with your new male friend."

"What?"

"You heard me." I curl my lips, "Do it, now!'

She blinks, looks like she is about to protest, then her fingers fly over the phone.

Damn, and I had been looking forward to coaxing her into doing my bidding.

She holds her phone to her ear. I can hear the phone ring on the other side, before it goes to voicemail. She glances at me and I jerk my chin. She looks away, takes a deep breath, then speaks in a cheerful voice, "Hi Summer, it's me, Karma. I, ah, have to go away for a bit. This new...ah, friend of mine... He has an extra ticket and he has invited me to Sicily to spend some time with him. I...ah, I don't know when, exactly, I'll be back, but I'll message you and let you know. Take care. Love ya sis, I—"

I snatch the phone from her, disconnect the call, then hold the gun to her temple, "Goodbye, Beauty."

TO FIND OUT WHAT HAPPENS NEXT READ MAFIA KING HERE

Read an excerpt from The Billionaire's Fake Wife, Sinclair & Summer (Karma's sister)'s story

Summer

"Slap, slap, kiss, kiss."

"Huh?" I stare up at the bartender.

"Aka, there's a thin line between love and hate." He shakes out the crimson liquid into my glass.

"Nah." I snort. "Why would she allow him to control her, and after he insulted her?"

"It's the chemistry between them." He lowers his head, "You have to admit that when the man is arrogant and the woman resists, it's a challenge to both of them, to see who blinks first, huh?"

"Why?" I wave my hand in the air, "Because they hate each other?"

"Because," he chuckles, "the girl in school whose braids I pulled and teased mercilessly, is the one who I—"

"Proposed to?" I huff.

His face lights up. "You get it now?"

Yeah. No. A headache begins to pound at my temples. This crash course in pop psychology is not why I came to my favorite bar in Islington, to meet my best friend, who is—I glance at the face of my phone—thirty minutes late.

I inhale the drink, and his eyebrows rise.

"What?" I glower up at the bartender. "I can barely taste the alcohol. Besides, it's free drinks at happy hour for women, right?"

"Which ends in precisely" he holds up five fingers, "minutes."

"Oh! Yay!" I mock fist pump. "Time enough for one more, at least."

A hiccough swells my throat and I swallow it back, nod.

One has to do what one has to do... when everything else in the world is going to shit.

A hot sensation stabs behind my eyes; my chest tightens. Is this what people call growing up?

The bartender tips his mixing flask, strains out a fresh batch of the ruby red liquid onto the glass in front of me.

"Salut." I nod my thanks, then toss it back. It hits my stomach and tendrils of fire crawl up my spine, I cough.

My head spins. Warmth sears my chest, spreads to my extremities. I can't feel my fingers or toes. Good. Almost there. "Top me up."

"You sure?"

"Yes." I square my shoulders and reach for the drink.

"No. She's had enough."

"What the—?" I pivot on the bar stool.

Indigo eyes bore into me.

Fathomless. Black at the bottom, the intensity in their depths grips me. He swoops out his arm, grabs the glass and holds it up. Thick fingers dwarf the glass. Tapered at the edges. The nails short and buff. *All the better to grab you with.* I gulp.

"Like what you see?"

I flush, peer up into his face.

Hard cheekbones, hollows under them, and a tiny scar that slashes at his left eyebrow. *How did he get that?* Not that I care. My gaze slides to his mouth. Thin upper lip, a lower lip that is full and cushioned. Pouty with a hint of bad boy. *Oh!* My toes curl. My thighs clench.

The corner of his mouth kicks up. *Asshole.*

Bet he thinks life is one big smug-fest. I glower, reach for my glass, and he holds it up and out of my reach.

I scowl, "Gimme that."

He shakes his head.

"That's my drink."

"Not anymore." He shoves my glass at the bartender. "Water for her. Get me a whiskey, neat."

I splutter, then reach for my drink again. The barstool tips, in his direction. This is when I fall against him, and my breasts slam into his hard chest, sculpted planes with layers upon layers of muscle that ripple and writhe as he turns aside, flattens himself against the bar. The floor rises up to meet me.

What the actual hell?

I twist my torso at the last second and my butt connects with the surface. *Ow!*

The breath rushes out of me. My hair swirls around my face. I scrabble for purchase, and my knee connects with his leg.

"Watch it." He steps around, stands in front of me.

"You stepped aside?" I splutter. "You let me fall?"

"Hmph."

I tilt my chin back, all the way back, look up the expanse of muscled thigh that stretches the silken material of his suit. *What is he wearing? Could any suit fit a man with such precision?* Hand crafted on Saville Row, no doubt. I glance at the bulge that tents the fabric between his legs. *Oh!* I blink.

Look away, look away. I hold out my arm. He'll help me up at least, won't he?

He glances at my palm, then turns away. *No, he didn't do that, no way.*

A glass of amber liquid appears in front of him. He lifts the tumbler to his sculpted mouth.

His throat moves, strong tendons flexing. He tilts his head back, and the column of his neck moves as he swallows. Dark hair covers his chin— it's a discordant chord in that clean-cut profile, I shiver. He would scrape that rough skin down my core. He'd mark my inner thigh, lick my core, thrust his tongue inside my melting channel and drink from my pussy. *Oh! God*. Goosebumps rise on my skin.

No one has the right to look this beautiful, this achingly gorgeous. Too magnificent for his own good. Anger coils in my chest.

"Arrogant wanker."

"I'll take that under advisement."

"You're a jerk, you know that?"

He presses his lips together. The grooves on either side of his mouth deepen. Jesus, clearly the man has never laughed a single day in his life. Bet that stick up his arse is uncomfortable. I chuckle.

He runs his gaze down my features, my chest, down to my toes, then yawns.

The hell! I will not let him provoke me. Will not. "Like what you see?" I jut out my chin.

"Sorry, you're not my type." He slides a hand into the pocket of those perfectly cut pants, stretching it across that heavy bulge.

Heat curls low in my belly.

Not fair, that he could afford a wardrobe that clearly shouts his status and what amounts to the economy of a small third-world country. A hot feeling stabs in my chest.

He reeks of privilege, of taking his status in life for granted.

While I've had to fight every inch of the way. Hell, I am still battling to hold onto the last of my equilibrium.

"Last chance—" I wiggle my fingers, from where I am sprawled out on the floor at his feet, "—to redeem yourself…"

"You have me there." He places the glass on the counter, then bends and holds out his hand. The hint of discolored steel at his wrist catches my attention. Huh?

He wears a cheap-ass watch?

That's got to bring down the net worth of his presence by more than 1000% percent. Weird.

I reach up and he straightens.

I lurch back.

"Oops, I changed my mind." His lips curl.

A hot burning sensation claws at my stomach. I am not a violent person, honestly. But Smirky Pants here, he needs to be taught a lesson.

I swipe out my legs, kicking his out from under him.

Sinclair

My knees give way, and I hurtle toward the ground.

What the—? I twist around, thrust out my arms. My palms hit the floor. The impact jostles up my elbows. I firm my biceps and come to a halt planked above her.

A huffing sound fills my ear.

I turn to find my whippet, Max, panting with his mouth open. I scowl and he flattens his ears.

All of my businesses are dog-friendly. Before you draw conclusions about me being the caring sort or some such shit—it attracts footfall.

Max scrutinizes the girl, then glances at me. *Huh?* He hates women, but not her, apparently.

I straighten and my nose grazes hers.

My arms are on either side of her head. Her chest heaves. The fabric of her dress stretches across her gorgeous breasts. My fingers tingle; my palms ache to cup those tits, squeeze those hard nipples outlined against the—hold on, what is she wearing? A tunic shirt in a sparkly pink... and are those shoulder pads she has on?

I glance up, and a squeak escapes her lips.

Pink hair surrounds her face. *Pink? Who dyes their hair that color past the age of eighteen?*

I stare at her face. *How old is she?* Un-furrowed forehead, dark eyelashes that flutter against pale cheeks. Tiny nose, and that mouth—luscious, tempting. A whiff of her scent, cherries and caramel, assails my senses. My mouth waters. *What the hell?*

She opens her eyes and our eyelashes brush. Her gaze widens. Green, like the leaves of the evergreens, flickers of gold sparkling in their depths. "What?" She glowers. "You're demonstrating the plank position?"

"Actually," I lower my weight onto her, the ridge of my hardness thrusting into the softness between her legs, "I was thinking of something else, altogether."

She gulps and her pupils dilate. *Ah, so she feels it, too?*

I drop my head toward her, closer, closer.

Color floods the creamy expanse of her neck. Her eyelids flutter down. She tilts her chin up.

I push up and off of her.

"That... Sweetheart, is an emphatic 'no thank you' to whatever you are offering."

Her eyelids spring open and pink stains her cheeks. Adorable. Such a range of emotions across those gorgeous features in a few seconds? What else is hidden under that exquisite exterior of hers?

She scrambles up, eyes blazing.

Ah! The little bird is trying to spread her wings? My dick twitches. My groin hardens, *Why does her anger turn me on so, huh?*

She steps forward, thrusts a finger in my chest.

My heart begins to thud.

She peers up from under those hooded eyelashes. "Wake up and taste the wasabi, asshole."

"What does that even mean?"

She makes a sound deep in her throat. My dick twitches. My pulse speeds up.

She pivots, grabs a half-full beer mug sitting on the bar counter.

I growl, "Oh, no, you don't."

She turns, swings it at me. The smell of hops envelops the space.

I stare down at the beer-splattered shirt, the lapels of my camel colored jacket deepening to a dull brown. Anger squeezes my guts.

I fist my fingers at my side, broaden my stance.

She snickers.

I tip my chin up. "You're going to regret that."

The smile fades from her face. "Umm." She places the now empty mug on the bar.

I take a step forward and she skitters back. "It's only clothes." She gulps, "They'll wash."

I glare at her and she swallows, wiggles her fingers in the air, "I should have known that you wouldn't have a sense of humor."

I thrust out my jaw, "That's a ten-thousand-pound suit you destroyed."

She blanches, then straightens her shoulders, "Must have been some hot date you were trying to impress, huh?"

"Actually," I flick some of the offending liquid from my lapels, "it's you I was after."

"Me?" She frowns.

"We need to speak."

She glances toward the bartender who's on the other side of the bar. "I don't know you." She chews on her lower lip, biting off some of the hot pink. How would she look, with that pouty mouth fastened on my cock?

The blood rushes to my groin so quickly that my head spins. My pulse rate ratchets up. Focus, focus on the task you came here for.

"This will take only a few seconds." I take a step forward.

She moves aside.

I frown, "You want to hear this, I promise."

"Go to hell." She pivots and darts forward.

I let her go, a step, another, because... I can? Besides it's fun to create the illusion of freedom first; makes the hunt so much more entertaining, huh?

I swoop forward, loop an arm around her waist, and yank her toward me.

She yelps. "Release me."

Good thing the bar is not yet full. It's too early for the usual officegoers to stop by. And the staff...? Well they are well aware of who cuts their paychecks.

I spin her around and against the bar, then release her. "You will listen to me."

She swallows; she glances left to right.

Not letting you go yet, little Bird. I move into her space, crowd her.

She tips her chin up. "Whatever you're selling, I'm not interested."

I allow my lips to curl, "You don't fool me."

A flush steals up her throat, sears her cheeks. So tiny, so innocent. Such a good little liar. I narrow my gaze, "Every action has its consequences."

"Are you daft?" She blinks.

"This pretense of yours?" I thrust my face into hers, "It's not working."

She blinks, then color suffuses her cheeks, "You're certifiably mad—"

"Getting tired of your insults."

"It's true, everything I said." She scrapes back the hair from her face.

Her fingernails are painted... You guessed it, pink.

"And here's something else. You are a selfish, egotistical jackass."

I smirk. "You're beginning to repeat your insults and I haven't even kissed you yet."

"Don't you dare." She gulps.

I tilt my head, "Is that a challenge?"

"It's a..." she scans the crowded space, then turns to me. Her lips firm, "... a warning. You're delusional, you jackass." She inhales a deep breath, "Your ego is bigger than the size of a black hole." She snickers, "Bet it's to compensate for your lack of balls."

A-n-d, that's it. I've had enough of her mouth that threatens to never stop spewing words. How many insults can one tiny woman hurl my way? Answer: too many to count.

"You—"

I lower my chin, touch my lips to hers.

Heat, sweetness, the honey of her essence explodes on my palate. My dick twitches. I tilt my head, deepen the kiss, reaching for that something more... more... of whatever scent she's wearing on her skin, infused with that breath of hers that crowds my senses, rushes down my spine. My

groin hardens; my cock lengthens. I thrust my tongue between those infuriating lips.

She makes a sound deep in her throat and my heart begins to pound.

So innocent, yet so crafty. Beautiful and feisty. The kind of complication
I don't need in my life.

I prefer the straight and narrow. Gray and black, that's how I choose to
define my world. She, with her flashes of color—pink hair and lips that
threaten to drive me to the edge of distraction—is exactly what I hate.

Give me a female who has her priorities set in life. To pleasure me, get
me off, then walk away before her emotions engage. Yeah. That's what I
prefer.

Not this... this bundle of craziness who flings her arms around my
shoulders, thrusts her breasts up and into my chest, tips up her chin, opens
her mouth, and invites me to take and take.

Does she have no self-preservation? Does she think I am going to fall
for her wide-eyed appeal? She has another thing coming.

I tear my mouth away and she protests.

She twines her leg with mine, pushes up her hips, so that melting softness between her thighs cradles my aching hardness.

I glare into her face and she holds my gaze.

Trains her green eyes on me. Her cheeks flush a bright red. Her lips fall
open and a moan bleeds into the air. The blood rushes to my dick, which
instantly thickens. *Fuck.*

Time to put distance between myself and the situation.

It's how I prefer to manage things. Stay in control, always. Cut out
anything that threatens to impinge on my equilibrium. Shut it down or
buy them off. Reduce it to a transaction. That I understand.

The power of money, to be able to buy and sell—numbers, logic. That's
what's worked for me so far.

"How much?"

Her forehead furrows.

"Whatever it is, I can afford it."

Her jaw slackens. "You think... you—"

"A million?"

"What?"

"Pounds, dollars... You name the currency, and it will be in your
account."

Her jaw slackens, "You're offering me money?"

"For your time, and for you to fall in line with my plan."

She reddens, "You think I am for sale?"

"Everyone is."

"Not me."

Here we go again. "Is that a challenge?"

Color fades from her face, "Get away from me."

"Are you shy, is that what this is?" I frown. "You can write your price down on a piece of paper if you prefer," I glance up, notice the bartender watching us. I jerk my chin toward the napkins. He grabs one, then offers it to her.

She glowers at him, "Did you buy him too?"

"What do you think?"

She glances around, "I think everyone here is ignoring us."

"It's what I'd expect."

"Why is that?"

I wave the tissue in front of her face, "Why do you think?"

"You own the place?"

"As I am going to own you."

She sets her jaw, "Let me leave and you won't regret this."

A chuckle bubbles up. I swallow it away. This is no laughing matter. I never smile during a transaction. Especially not when I am negotiating a new acquisition. And that's all she is. The final piece in the puzzle I am building.

"No one threatens me."

"You're right."

"Huh?"

"I'd rather act on my instinct."

Her lips twist, her gaze narrows. All of my senses scream a warning.

No, she wouldn't, no way—pain slices through my middle and sparks explode behind my eyes.

To find out what happens next read Sinclair & Summer's story in The Billionaire's Fake Wife HERE

Read an excerpt from Karina & Arpad's story in The Billionaire's Baby

Karina

"Gah, you're a frustrating man, Wolfgang." The radio announcer groans. "You know that?"

"Exactly why you like me." Wolfgang chuckles. "And Ivy?" There's a pause when, I swear, I can imagine him leaning in closer to her. "The name's Wolfe."

"Errm," Ivy clears her throat over the airwaves, "so that's our favorite

TV trope, brought to life by Wolfe and me...which sounds like something out of Red Riding Wood."

"Hood." Wolfe chuckles.

"That's what I said." Ivy huffs. "Red Riding Hood. So, as I was saying, that's our favorite TV trope. Can you guess what it is? This is Ivy—"

"—And Wolfe," the male announcer interjects.

"And we are so very pleased to be guest hosting the Evening Show on your fave, Smile London FM. Email us, call us...and let us know—"

I lean forward and shut off the car radio. What a couple of twerps those two are. Firstly, the attraction between them is off the charts. Secondly, they have no idea about it and are clearly dancing around it, all but punching each other in the face with the force of the tension building between them. Thirdly...well...if they don't sort it out, they are going to blow up on the show in front of everyone. No doubt, smack each other in the face before smacking each other on the lips. Ha! I snort aloud. Good to know my sense of humor is somewhat alive... Especially considering I have to spend the evening evaluating and repairing security on the boat of Mr. Full-of-Himself-Douchecanoe, aka Arpad f'ing Beauchamp.

A man whose demeanor is every bit as pompous as his name. Yeah, he comes from old money, la-dee-dah. Like I care. But to see him stomp around with that giant stick up his ass, you'd think he's conscious of his status every single second of his life. Which, he probably is. Which is why he'd ordered me to get to his boat and fix the security camera on it that he claims has stopped working before he sets off to whichever island it is he is sailing off to next.

A camera, which had been set up by someone else before I came on board as his security consultant.

Some of us have to spend the evening working; others party till dawn, then sail off into the sunrise. Of course. Admittedly, he and the rest of the Seven pay me a lot... Like a l-o-t; enough for me to leave my life in LA and move to London to ensure that their security detail is top notch.

The Seven had been kidnapped as pre-teens by the Mafia. They had been rescued, but not before it had left them with a burning need to get even with the perpetrators of the incident. It also means that the men are ever vigilant about the Mafia attacking them or their loved ones. That's why they had asked me to increase the security on them and their families. Add to that, the fact that most of the Seven had recently met and married the women of their dreams... And it means I have a shitload of people to protect, from a security standpoint.

Which means... Yeah, I have never been busier. From finding the right talent to add to my team, to constantly upgrading the security details for the ceremonies when any of them decide to get married—the latest being Damian, the rock star who married his almost-nanny and produced a single that knocked the socks off of every single critic and countdown chart.

So, I can't complain. My bank account is happy...which means I should be happy. Only I am not.

I am not one to rest on my laurels, not one to bask in my success... I know what I want next—a family of my own. Good news is, I am already working on it.

In fact, I have a date tomorrow night to fire the first salvo in that direction. No pun intended. I snort aloud. I just have to get through this last chore on my list and then I can get some rest—and god knows, I need it—and be ready to get started on this latest project.

I ease the car into the parking lot of St. Katherine Docks, then grab my bag—which, while being stylish enough to take to a party, is also spacious enough to hold my emergency tools—and head down the line of gleaming vessels. Trust London's wealthiest to bag a spot in the center of London to park their toys. I search for one yacht in particular... What had he called it?

Heartbeat. A weirdly sentimental name for someone who is known as Killer... Not because he kills in real life, but for the killing he makes as an Angel Investor in Silicon Valley. Yep, that's how Arpad f'ing Beauchamp makes his money.

Investing in those who have the ideas but not the financial wherewithal to bring them to fruition. He has a knack for spotting talent, I'll give him that.... And that's all I'll ever concede, and definitely not to his face.

The man has a mean streak a mile wide, if any of our brief interactions are any indication. Rumor has it, he doesn't even spare the women he dates... But then, the kind of women he prefers are known for their taste in men who take charge in the bedroom... And push things beyond the point of comfort. Good thing I am not one of them.

I prefer my men amenable and my food spicy. See, the thing with food? It never lets you down. Finding the best restaurants in town and eating out is a particular fancy of mine. Table for one, please. Oh yeah, nothing like the silence of my own company to unwind in the evenings. I am not lonely, just alone. And there is a difference between those two words, right?

I reach *Heartbeat* and clamber overboard, then walk over to the cabin and key in the password. Letting myself in, I glance around and press what I think is the light switch. Bingo. The door clicks shut behind me as I glance around the space. Whoa, this is a yacht? More like a floating mansion. It had seemed reasonably sized from the outside, but in here... Wow! I walk down the steps to the sunken living room. Plush leather seats span one entire side, with a coffee table in the center, and a flat screen on the opposite wall. I walk through to a galley that has an island table, but only one chair. Huh? That's weird. Doesn't he entertain on the boat? Bet he does, so what's with the lone chair?

On the other hand, the gleaming kitchen equipment is more what I expected. It's top-of-the-line and would rival any five-star hotel, I am sure. Not that Mr. Alphahole, here, would ever deign to step into a kitchen. He probably travels with an entire crew to fetch and carry for him. Bet he spends his time jerking off to porno that he watches on that screen as he shoves his hand down his pants and... Please... Argh! Don't go there.

I walk past the kitchen and push the sliding doors apart to find—OMG! A complete, fully-furnished, massive bedroom. Complete with a super king-size bed that takes up almost all of the center of the room. On the far end is a door that, I assume, leads to the bathroom. There's a set of mirrored doors beside it that must lead to a walk-in closet? Clearly, he's spared no expense in doing up this space. Everything is gorgeously designed, if space efficient.

On the other side of the cabin is a narrow freestanding table, and on it, a neat coil of what looks like... A rope? How weird. I move closer, then reach out and brush my fingers across the cord. It's soft to the touch, almost sensual, the material reddish in color, with sparks of gold flecked through it. I bring it to my nose and sniff. An edgy, almost nutty scent tugs at my nostrils. My core clenches. Wow, what the hell does he use this for anyway?

I step back, glance around the room, take in the massive, sliding glass doors. Beyond them is the view of the now-darkening water, rays of sunlight from the setting sun painting the sky a smoldering red and orange.

I stare at the bed again... *Leave, turn and leave, right now.* Come on, surely, a sniff won't hurt? Besides, there are no cameras in the bedroom. At least, there were none indicated on the security detail for this boat I'd inherited from the previous agency... So he'll never find out, right?

I cross the floor, walk around the bed and run my hands across the pillow. Soft... Egyptian cotton, thread count innumerable, no doubt. Only the best for the asshole, after all. I lean over, bury my nose in the pillow... Don't judge.

Notes of bergamot and cloves, and something dark, musky, edgy—something dangerous—envelops me. I'm instantly wet. *What the hell?*

How can his scent turn me on so? And when I loathe the man? And his attitude, and the way he thinks he can boss me around, and expect me to drop everything and prioritize him above everything else. A shiver runs down my spine. Only my sense of hate getting the better of me, of course.

That's why my stomach flutters. That is the *only* reason my heart beats so fast in my chest. Shit, now I am turning myself on, and that will not do. Not when I have work to do. I pivot, then retrace my steps toward the cabin, and head for the captain's area. There, at the extreme right, I pull up the controls for the security cameras.

I get to work fixing the controls...and am done in fifteen minutes. There, that was easy. It took more time to drive here through the late evening traffic.

I stretch and yawn, suddenly overwhelmingly tired. It's been a long day, long week, long year, actually, setting up business in this city. But I am in a good place, confident my business is going to do well. I pack up my tools, head for the door, then hesitate.

Should I? Why not? It shouldn't matter. I pivot and head back toward the bedroom, then glance out the large window and admire the spectacle. So damn beautiful. If only I had someone to hold my hand while I enjoy it. Nah, doesn't matter. I have me...don't I? And my love for yoga. The only way I know how to unwind. I roll my shoulders, and my muscles protest. Shit, I am too tense.

I place my handbag on the bed stand, then raise my arms high above me. The skirt of my dress pulls tight against my thighs. This won't do. It's why I hate wearing dresses. Damn. I pull off the dress, drape it over the foot of the bed, then kick off my heels and walk over to the center of the room.

I face the window of the yacht, then raise my hands again, bring them down, flow down onto my hands and the tips of my feet, then push up into a downward facing dog. I hold the pose for a few seconds, until my hamstrings burn, my biceps stretch, give. I rock back and forth, then swoop up, back to downward facing dog, then jump forward, straighten. Take a breath in and out, then repeat the process.

By the time I'm done with my routine, my muscles are limber, sweat beads my forehead. I wipe it off, then stretch and yawn. A pleasant tiredness buzzes in my blood.

Yeah, I could rest for a little while, then get out of here.

Hold on, bad idea. *Honestly, are you actually thinking of staying on here for more time than is absolutely essential?*

I reach for my dress then stop, glance at the bed. It looks so comfortable. I yawn again. Coming down from a yoga routine always relaxes me so much. My limbs grow heavy, my eyelids seem to be weighted down, and I can barely keep them open. I could nap in the car, of course...but it's almost dark and that doesn't sound safe. And I know it's not safe to drive home without catching a few minutes of shut-eye.... I sneak a peek at the bed again; it looks so comfortable.

Just a short nap. That can't hurt... Can it? It'll rejuvenate me enough for the ride home which, again, I am in no condition to navigate when I am this exhausted.

I slip into the bed and draw the covers up to my chin. His dark scent wraps around me. Goosebumps flare on my skin. It's as if I am surrounded by him, as if he's cocooned me with his body, and he's all around me, with me, in this bed. Should I set an alarm on my phone to wake up? Nah, I'll be fine. It's only a quick nap, after all.

Besides Arpad a-hole isn't going to come back before the morning, and I'll be long gone by then...

A delicious warmth envelops me and I close my eyes.

A rumbling creeps into my consciousness and I push it away. I press my cheek into the soft pillow, draw in that scent of bergamot and cloves. His scent. Mmm. A languid heaviness tugs at my limbs. My muscles relax and I drift off again. Until a loud creak tears through the silence in my mind. I jackknife up to sitting position, my heart pounding in my chest. My pulse rate ratchets up. I strain to see through the darkness. Where the hell am I?

That's when the entire room seems to tilt. I scream and slide off the bed. I hit the ground on my ass, roll over to hit the glass wall of the cabin. I turn and press my nose into the transparent barrier and stare out. Darkness, broken only by the white-tipped foam that crashes against the side. I gasp, then scramble back until I hit the bed. The boat! I am on the boat, which is no longer harbored. It's at sea, with me on it.

The entire yacht creaks again, the walls seem to groan, the boat lurches up, and I hold onto the edge of the bed, anchor myself, as it seems to grunt and screech like it's possessed, then straightens. Silence, for a second. The hair on the back of my neck rises, I smell the ozone in the air, then the boat groans, and hurtles down.

The momentum carries me forward toward the wall of the cabin.

I throw out my hand, manage to grab the edge of the bed, hold on as the boat seems suspended in space, before it hits something—the water I presume?— with a crash. The sound echoes in my ears, reverberates down my spine. Then the vessel tilts in the opposite direction. I glance out the glass wall and scream again. Water. So much water, I am surrounded by a wall of water. What the hell is happening? How did the boat get here? I hit the ground on all fours, crawling my way up to the door. Grabbing the handle, I pull myself up, then twist the knob open. I lurch forward as the entire boat goes into another incline. Damn it. I race forward, throw myself onto the couch in the living room and hold on until the boat rightens again. Then cross the living room, up the steps toward the captain's cabin.

That's when I see the man silhouetted against the wheel. He's wearing shorts that cling to his tight ass. And what an ass it is. The fabric outlines the indentation on each side, only to stretch across the girth. The waistband shows off his inverted V figure and his back... I gulp. The planes of his back flex and buck as he grips the wheel of the boat, widens his stance, and leans into the next wave. The next wave... What the—? It's a huge, huge wave. A behemoth of a WAVE. I glance up and cry out, for he's driving the boat straight up the crest of a monster of a wall of water. There's a crash of thunder, then lightning flickers beyond the boat and I gasp again. An entire sea of darkness, capped by furious white tips, and in the foreground, his massive shoulders that bunch and knot as he grapples with the wheel, holds the boat on course.

Another clap of thunder in the distance, and the alphahole—for it is him, Arpad f'ing A'hole, the bloody owner of this boat, my crazy-ass employer, my frigging boss, who's driving this boat straight into the storm.

He throws back his head and laughs. What the hell? Is he crazy? Does he have a death wish or something? I stomp forward to ask him just that, when the boat groans and begins to slide back, taking me with it. My legs seem to go out from under me. I scream as I hit the decking and roll back. The boat pitches and I am thrown against the wall. Darkness envelops me.

When I open my eyes again, I am back in the bed, in the bedroom of the boat, the sheets pulled up to my chin. Huh? Was it all a dream? I sit up and pain slices through my forehead. I groan, fall back against the pillows.

"Take it easy." A low voice rumbles across the space. I glance over to meet familiar grey-blue eyes.

"You?" I cough. "What the hell are you doing here?"

"It's my boat?" He leans forward and my gaze takes in his bare chest, the sculpted six-...no, eight-pack? Nah...not possible. No one has an eight-pack, do they?

"Enjoying the view?"

I tip my chin up, meet his gaze.

"I've seen better," I lie.

He chuckles. "You must be feeling better. Though, I admit, I preferred it when you were flat on your back in my bed, naked."

I peek under the sheet. "What the hell?" I gasp, "Where are my underclothes?"

"Had to take them off, since you bled all over them from your head wound."

I touch my forehead, and the pain flashes behind my eyes. "Ow," I moan.

"Let me see that." He leans over me and his scent intensifies. His chest planes ripple and his biceps bunch as he reaches across.

I pull away. "It's fine," I grumble, "it's just a bump. It's not bleeding."

"I won't hurt you," he rumbles.

Why don't I believe you?

"Unless you want me to..." His lips twist, "Do you want me to, hurt you, my little stowaway?"

"What?" I scowl, "Of course, not."

"Then why are you here?"

To find out what happens next read Arpad and Karina's story **HERE**

Want to be the first to find out about L. Steele's new releases? Join her newsletter **HERE**

Want more of the Seven? Binge read the Big Bad Billionaire Series here

US

UK

Other countries

Binge read all the books in the Arranged marriage Mafia Series **HERE**

Claim your **FREE** contemporary romance boxset

Join my secret Facebook Reader Group

More books by L. STEELE

More Books by Laxmi

FREE BOOKS

CLAIM YOUR FREE CONTEMPORARY ROMANCE BOXSET

CLAIM YOUR FREE PARANORMAL ROMANCE

JOIN MY SECRET FACEBOOK READER GROUP

ABOUT THE AUTHOR

Hello, I'm L. Steele. I love to take down alphaholes. I write romance stories with douche canoes who meet their match in sassy, curvy, spitfire women :) I also write dark sexy paranormal romance as NY Times bestseller Laxmi Hariharan.

Married to a man who cooks as well as he talks :) I live in London.

CLAIM YOUR FREE BOOK => HTTPS://BOOKHIP.COM/ZMLZLG

FOLLOW ME ON BOOKBUB: HTTPS://WWW.BOOKBUB.COM/PROFILE/L-STEELE

FOLLOW ON GOODREADS: HTTPS://WWW.GOODREADS.COM/AUTHORLSTEELE

PPS: I AM DYING TO MEET YOU! JOIN MY SECRET FACEBOOK READER GROUP AND SAY HI => HTTP://SMARTURL.IT/TEAMLAXMI

ALL MY AUDIOBOOKS => HTTPS://WWW.SUBSCRIBEPAGE.COM/LAXMIAUDIOBOOKS

FOLLOW MY PINTEREST BOARDS => HTTPS://WWW.PINTEREST.CO.UK/AUTHORLSTEELE/BOARDS/

READ MY BOOKS=> HTTPS://READERLINKS.COM/MYBOOKS/950

facebook.com/AuthorLSteele

twitter.com/Author_L_Steele

instagram.com/authorl.steele

✸ Created with Vellum

Printed in Great Britain
by Amazon

14435483R00193